Praise for
THE ANIMALS

"[Kiefer] is a gifted stylist unafraid of writing on the edge of sentiment. . . . Beautifully written . . . . *The Animals* moves at a heart-quickening pace, and the counterpointed stories frequently intersect and gather a fierce momentum. . . . The book is not just a galloping great read; it's a violent, tender, terrifying, genuine work of art."   —*San Francisco Chronicle*

"Moving gracefully between different periods in Bill's life, author Christian Kiefer weaves a trenchant, profound literary novel . . . . *The Animals* is a novel of action and emotion, style and substance, and I am looking forward to whatever Kiefer produces next."   —Amazon.com

"Every once in a while, a book moves me to tears with the grace of its prose, the depth and humanity of its characters, and the ferocity of its singular vision. Christian Kiefer's *The Animals* is such a book: a startling and beautiful novel about friendship, grief, and the urge to start over, to be blameless. I loved it."   —Edan Lepucki, author of *California*

"Eloquent and shattering, this novel explores, in gritty detail, how penance sometimes does not lead to redemption, a modern take on the story of Eden. Kiefer is a master wordsmith, and his dense and beautiful language intensifies the pain and isolation of the main character. . . . Devastatingly beautiful. This novel embodies why we write and why we read."   —*Kirkus Reviews*, starred review

"The deep, dense prose Kiefer uses makes you slow down and take it all in. Word by word and sentence by sentence, Kiefer reels the reader into his world."   —*The Life Sentence*

"Outstanding. . . . The juxtaposition of Kiefer's portrayal of past with present, the lost with the found, and a life without love with one filled with it gives this novel great depth and feeling. And then there are the animals. Kiefer beautifully brings to life the German philosopher Arthur Schopenhauer's famous statement: 'Men are the devils of the earth, and the animals are its tormented souls.' If you love great fiction—and animals—the raw emotional power of this book will leave you devastated. . . . Exquisitely wrought prose combined with a contemporary noir thriller create a heartbreaking tale of one man's quest for redemption."   —*Shelf Awareness*

"This novel came at me like some creature of the wild, caught my breath and rushed my heart and filled me with awe and wonder and gratitude at having witnessed it. From prose that made me want to linger to a story that ripped me ever forward, *The Animals* is simply that good. With it, Christian Kiefer proves himself that rarest of writers, one who matches an artist's brave vision with a craftsman's sure hand. I was blown away—and am still haunted—by this beautiful, masterful book."   —Josh Weil, author of *The Great Glass Sea*

"Don't let *The Animals* get past you. . . . It's a haunting, darkly exquisite piece of rural noir that will chill you from its somewhat sedate beginning to its apocalyptic-like ending. . . . Kiefer builds and then entrenches your expectations before beginning the slow and uneasy task of deconstructing them. It's been quite a while since I've seen this done so well."   —Bookreporter.com

"In *The Animals*, Christian Kiefer has created an unusual and compelling amalgam of noir classic—a man's past comes back to haunt him—and the lyrical extended metaphor in the form of the North Idaho Animal Rescue, where his main character finds refuge and purpose. This tough-minded thriller weaves a hot red thread through an introspective, sensuous landscape, a meditation on instinct, memory and the nature of friendship between species and between men."

—Janet Fitch, author of *Paint It Black* and *White Oleander*

"Kiefer creates a wilderness for us in these pages with as sure a hand as any god. All of life's hardest questions are put to us with such confidence we do not see the hand at work. *The Animals* is beyond a pleasure to read."

—Tupelo Hassman, author of *Girlchild*

"Amid the wild backdrop of a blizzard-wracked Idaho winter, Kiefer weaves loyalty, self-destruction, and survival into a story that's equal doses of raging suspense and thought-provoking gray areas. A great choice for mystery and literary-fiction book groups."   —*Booklist*

THE ANIMALS

ALSO BY **CHRISTIAN KIEFER**

THE INFINITE TIDES

THE ANIMALS

A NOVEL

CHRISTIAN KIEFER

LIVERIGHT PUBLISHING CORPORATION

A DIVISION OF W. W. NORTON & COMPANY

INDEPENDENT PUBLISHERS SINCE 1923

NEW YORK • LONDON

James Dickey, "The Heaven of Animals" from *The Whole Motion: Collected Poems, 1945–1992*, © James Dickey 1992. Reprinted by permission of Wesleyan University Press.

For information about permission to reproduce selections from this book, write to Permissions, Liveright Publishing Corporation, a division of W. W. Norton & Company, Inc., 500 Fifth Avenue, New York, NY 10110

For information about special discounts for bulk purchases, please contact W. W. Norton Special Sales at specialsales@wwnorton.com or 800-233-4830

Manufacturing by RRD Harrisonburg
Book design by Fearn Cutler de Vicq
Production manager: Julia Druskin

Library of Congress Cataloging-in-Publication Data

Kiefer, Christian, 1971–
The animals : a novel / Christian Kiefer.—First edition.
pages ; cm
ISBN 978-0-87140-883-9 (hardcover)
1. Betrayal—Fiction. 2. Ex-convicts—Fiction. 3. Wildlife refuges—Fiction. I. Title.
PS3611.I443A85 2015
813'.6—dc23

2014038445

ISBN 978-1-63149-149-8 pbk.

Liveright Publishing Corporation, 500 Fifth Avenue, New York, N.Y. 10110
www.wwnorton.com

W. W. Norton & Company Ltd., Castle House, 75/76 Wells Street, London W1T 3QT

1 2 3 4 5 6 7 8 9 0

Macie

Here they are. The soft eyes open.

If they have lived in a wood

It is a wood.

If they have lived on plains

It is grass rolling

Under their feet forever.

—JAMES DICKEY, FROM "THE HEAVEN OF ANIMALS"

THE ANIMALS

PART I

ECOLOGY

1

1996

WHAT YOU HAVE COME FOR IS DEATH. YOU MIGHT TRY TO convince yourself otherwise but you know in your heart that to do so would be to set one falsehood upon another. In the end there is no denying what is true and what is only some thin wisp of hope that clings to you like hoarfrost on a strand of wire. At least you have learned that much, although you are loath to admit it just as you are loath to come down the mountain, down from the animals, to confirm what you already know you will find. All the while you can feel their shining eyes upon you, their noses pulling at your scent, their bodies pressed tight against the interlaced fencing of their enclosures. The world in its bubble and you holding fast to its slick interior as if to the blood-pumped safety of a womb. You and the animals. And yet after everything you have done, everything you have tried to do, everything you promised yourself, today you know you will have to put on the old clothes of the killer once again.

It was not his own voice, or rather he did not think of it as his own. After all the years and all the conversations he had shared with Majer, he had come to think of that voice, the voice of his own conscience, as coming not from him but from the bear, a sharp reckoning that now, as he descended the dirt path between the enclosures, seemed to drift down upon him like fresh snow. He could feel the animals watching but he did not return their collected gaze, focusing instead on the weight of the black case slung over his shoulder and then on the heavy thump of his boots as he continued toward the parking lot that hung below him beyond the fence wire. There, a jagged line of conifer shadows bifurcated a flat patch of colorless gravel at the edge of which was parked his pickup.

He managed to avoid the rest of the animals but he knew he could not avoid Majer. When he reached that enclosure the great bear cocked his head at an angle as if waiting for him to approach the front fence but Bill only kept walking, his steps taking him past the cage and toward the gravel parking lot below, toward the truck and the drive south to Ponderay. The other animals still watched him, he could feel their eyes upon him everywhere, but it was the bear's sightless gaze that cut him most of all and finally he stopped in the center of the path, near the door to the blocklike construction trailer he used as an office, and turned to face the rising ridgeline, the enclosures spread out in their circle, the animals all moving against their separate fences.

There stood the bear. He had risen onto his hind legs and towered now near the front of the cage, the clear surface of the little pool blocked by his bulk, the size and shape of him staggering, enormous, a creature of fur and claw and, in some universe not so far from this one, of killing, balancing there with a grace that seemed impossible and staring through the fence at Bill with eyes like small milky stones, the depths of which revealed only a surface of cataracts as pale and featureless as a frozen lake.

What? Bill said. He stood there for a long moment, as if waiting for the bear's response. Then he said, Don't. Don't you even start.

The bear seemed to shift momentarily from one foot to the other but he continued to stand, his face, peppered gray with age, watching Bill as he stood in the path. If there was judgment in those pale, sightless eyes it was without expression, the bear's gaze only holding within them the same acceptance that Bill had always seen there, as if nothing would be asked of him, not ever, as if the only thing Bill could ever do wrong was not return.

I gotta go, Bill said. I'll be back in an hour.

There was no response, no grunt or huff, no tilt of head, and yet as he turned toward the path again he could not help but feel that all their eyes, Majer's among them, held the foreknowledge of what he was likely going to do, of what he was likely moving toward.

When he reached the parking lot he locked the gate behind him and started the truck and turned out off the gravel, tipping down onto a road that tunneled through a verdant shadowland of bull pine and lodgepole and red cedar, and then on along the river, its surface, in the fading light, the color of dead fish, and at last lurched out onto the highway.

All the while he could feel their eyes upon him, even now, even as he downshifted, turning through a forest going slowly dark, the stand before him faintly blurred and drifting with low strips of tattered white clouds, like a forest out of some fairy tale where bears and men and wolves sometimes swapped bodies to fool women and children into trust and sometimes committed acts of murder, these images encircling him as they sometimes did on the birch path from the trailer to the big gate, even though he knew, of course, that such bleak thoughts would do nothing for him in the hours to come. Yet there was little to brighten them. Such calls as he had received over the years had most often ended in death. The doe he had called Ginny had been the first, if it had indeed been her in the road, broken-spined and crying. The image of her came to him as he drove, not of her in the agony of her final moments, but as a small frantic creature hanging nose-down from a fence, the day he and his uncle had rescued her. But the highway was an abattoir, and with an animal of this size—a full-grown moose—it was likely there would be nothing he or anyone else could do except what had to be done. He had brought the rifle in response to such odds but despite this, despite everything he knew, he still held out some hope that he would not have to use it, that somehow the animal would have suffered some superficial injury and he would not need to remove the rifle from where it lay with the dart gun in the zippered case beside him. When his voice spoke into the engine hum of the cab it was to this falsehood: You know there is no truth in it at all. Every scrap a lie.

And indeed when he pulled the truck to the side and stepped out onto the street at last, the scene was much as he knew it would be. The pickup that had struck the moose sat in the center of the road at the edge of a scant collection of battered businesses cut into the surrounding forestland, its hood crushed nearly to the windshield, the animal a few dozen yards before it, one rear leg clearly broken, swinging and dragging from its new hingepoint, its hip likely shattered as well, its faltering motion like that of a crab or an insect, or like some newborn of its own species, unsure of its footing, head swinging back and forth as if on a pendulum and chocolate brown eyes rolling in their sockets. And then its sound, the sound of an animal of blood and bone that seemed to call out to him and to him alone—*Come! Come to me!*—a call not unlike the honk of a goose or the weird blast of a tuneless horn, each note short and rising in volume and then cut off as the lungs were emptied, and each loud enough that Bill nearly brought his hands up to shield his ears.

The sheriff said his name and Bill glanced at him briefly and then returned his attention to the moose. A young male, a bull, not more than a year old. Bill walked sideways around it, toward its head, the sheriff following his motion. The moose's eyes rolled, brown and wet, watching him, watching them all. How long? he said.

I think they called you right after, the sheriff said. So half an hour maybe. What do you wanna do here?

As if in response, the animal started its terrible bleating honk again, mouth open, body once again lurching forward, slowly, as if possessed of some awful errand, down the street and toward the town. Bill moved as close to it as he could, squatting before it on the asphalt, voice calm even as his heart beat wild in his chest, his own blood pulling toward the animal all at once as if magnetized by the agony. Shhh, he said. It's gonna be all right. We're here to help. It's gonna be all right.

The moose quieted again and he stood slowly and stepped backward to the sheriff. Who ran into him?

Some mechanic from Sandpoint, the sheriff said.

He OK?

In the hospital. Broke his ribs up and slammed his face into the wheel. There anything you can do here? I'm supposed to call the new Fish and Game guy.

You haven't called them yet?

Not yet. You want me to?

Not very much.

Then it's slipped my mind.

Bill glanced back at the smashed truck and then to the moose again. A half hour ago it had come down from the mountains, perhaps following a line of fragrant moss in the trunks of trees that lined a muddy creek bottom, and now it stumbled along that scant black road among men and women and children gathered for no reason other than to watch it go to ground.

He breathed out, slowly. There was a tightness in his chest and a feeling that he was caught up in something of which he could not let go.

When he looked to the street beyond, he caught sight of her pickup as it trundled between the buildings and then came to a stop. She leaped down from the cab in her purple coat and came to the moose, kneeling directly before the animal much as he had a few moments before, her voice the same quiet hush as his own, the moose's head moving, the breath coming in bursts of hot steam.

He turned away now, returning to his pickup, opening the door to pull the canvas gun case toward him and unzipping its front pocket. Two or three loose shells spilled out onto the seat and he scooped them into his hand and then, from the pocket, extracted a small black box, inside of which rested a hypodermic needle and two vials of clear fluid, and a plastic tube containing a thin dart with a brilliant red tail. The shells he returned to the pocket, zipping it closed. Then he set to filling the dart, first sucking the fluid from one of the vials and then holding the syringe up to the light and squeezing a small quantity into the air before slipping the needle into the larger bore of the dart and pressing home the plunger.

When he looked up from his work, Grace was there, her eyes wide.

I was loading point eight carfentanil, he said. Is that what you want?

She sighed, her breath outspiraling into steam. He's got a broken hip.

You sure?

Well, yeah. Aren't you? When he did not respond, she put her hand on his shoulder. It would be better to just do it, she said. Get it over with.

Can we just check him first? Just to make sure there's nothing we can do?

Baby, he's not going to make it. He's in pain.

I know that, he said.

It's not humane.

I just need you to tell me that there's nothing we can do for him. I mean one hundred percent sure. Can you do that?

She stared at him. Shit. You really know how to put me over a barrel, you know that?

He said nothing, his hands hovering over the tranquilizer gun, hovering in the grim cold air.

Well, she said at last, you got anything else besides the carfentanil?

Ketamine, he said, but I don't think I have enough to put down a moose.

She exhaled. All right, so let's go a full milligram of the carfentanil and hope that knocks him out the first time.

He nodded and returned to the vial and then to the dart, the small bottle from which he had extracted the medication nearly empty now, and then unzipped the larger compartment on the case. He knew that she saw the rifle there but she did not comment and he shifted the firearm to the side and pulled the tranquilizer gun from the case, opened the bolt, and slid the dart into the breech.

The moose had started up its sound again, its sharp terrible bleating. Grace's forehead wrinkled as she glanced behind her and then returned to Bill. You want me to do it? she said.

No, I'll do it. He lifted the gun to his chest and pumped it, three times, four, five, and then wrapped the strap once around his forearm and stood by the door of the truck. You should ask Earl if he can get someone to bring a flatbed tow truck out here.

She nodded and left his side, moving in the direction of the sheriff as Bill walked to the moose, raised the gun, and in one quick, sure movement, fired the dart into the animal's shoulder.

He had used the dart gun many times. On a wolf and a coyote and an elk. In each instance the animal had hardly even registered the shot. The sound like a puff of air and the animal's response maybe only a brief twitch of furred hide. But this time the moose released a long bray of surprise and anger and anguish and staggered forward on its spindly legs, its massive head rocking from side to side, the broken leg cycling in a weird sickening orbit around the break, the hoof backward, ungulate points ticking against the asphalt as its front legs scraped forward a few more yards, the human bystanders jerking out of its path. Then it went down, the whole of the thing collapsing, hind end first, not from the medication but from its own broken body and from gravity itself, its pelvis hitting the asphalt, and then its chest, the front legs splayed out for a terrible moment and then the head rising again, the animal clattering up on its front hooves, legs stilted out, everything about it agony and the will to live, to survive.

Christ, Bill said. Go down. Please go down.

He did not look up at Grace but he heard her voice now. He will, she said. He will, honey. She put her hand on his own and he realized then that his hand was trembling where it gripped the dart gun.

How long's this gonna take to work?

The voice had come from the sheriff, and then Grace's voice in answer: Twenty minutes, she said. We might have to dart him again, though.

All right, the sheriff said. I called for a tow truck. Probably'll be here around the same time.

At these words, the moose let out another series of honking cries. Bill stood watching for a few moments and then stepped back to the car with the gun and opened the breech and returned it to the black zippered case. When he turned, he could see the sheriff moving toward the bystanders again.

And now we wait, Grace said.

He nodded. They stood side by side, watching the animal as it stumbled forward on its spindly front legs, panting in short, heavy breaths, the rear of its body sloped down toward the street and the dart's bright red tuft waving from its furred shoulder like an ornament.

Bill leaned against the truck.

I was just gonna call you, Grace said after a time.

Now you don't have to.

No, I do not, she said. She smiled at him briefly and he tried to smile in return. I was thinking I might come over for a visit.

You got a sitter?

Maybe. Why? You busy?

Well, I wasn't before.

Yeah, she said. Neither was I.

They fell silent then, the two of them in the cool dusk with their bodies just touching, hip and shoulder and ankle. Her hand came into his own and squeezed and then held there, her fingers interlacing with his. He looked out at the moose standing spraddle-legged in the road. Once upon a time, you told yourself that you would be no killer, that this was how you would live your life. And yet you learn and relearn that everything is the same. The animals will call you. And sometimes you will answer them with gunfire. Majer's voice again, or maybe it was only and always himself and himself alone.

When the moose began to go down, Bill stood in the street and spoke to it softly, in human words, telling it that it would be asleep soon and that it needed to lie down so that it could be taken care of, and then the moose did so, as if it had considered the intent of Bill's words and had determined to comply, first by setting its head upon the road in an attitude of rest, of relaxation, then lifting that great head once and then again and then setting it down and moving it no longer, its chocolate eyes closing slowly and the head falling sideways, a limp tilting like a wooden basin tipping onto its side.

Grace placed the silver disk of her stethoscope against its chest. Heartbeat sounds good, she said. She shifted to the animal's flank and ran her hands along its hip again and again, her hands pausing and squeezing and then lifting the moose's rear leg and examining the break. When she was done, she returned to him, the stethoscope dangling loose around her neck. That hip's pretty much shattered, she said. Even if it wasn't, that back leg would need to come off at the joint. It's just hanging by a tendon there.

Shit, Bill said.

I'm sorry, baby.

I don't know why I expected anything else. Moose versus pickup. There's only one way that story ends.

Sad but true.

You're not gonna say I told you so, are you?

How about I love you.

That's better, he said.

When the tow truck arrived, the hooked cable was wrapped around the animal's still-intact rear leg and those who remained helped guide the body up the ramp and onto the bed of the truck: Grace and the sheriff and a deputy and a couple of wool-shirted men from town. Bill held the moose's great head in his arms, the animal's breath blowing against his chest in a great flood of exhaling air, and he remained there at the edge of the bed even after he had laid its head down upon the cold steel, its deep brown flanks growing darker as the buildings and forestland around them drifted into their night colors.

Grace's hand was on his shoulder. You don't have to, you know. We can call IFG.

No way I'm doing that, he said.

OK, she said. Earl wants to take him up to Muletown Road.

He know someone to butcher it up there?

I don't know, Bill, she said. Probably. You want him to just lay out there?

No, he said. Maybe. Coyotes and bears could get a meal out of it.

So could some family. Of people.

He looked at her. Her dark eyes. Her brown hair in its loose curls, moving to shadow. Muletown, he said at last. All right.

THEY FORMED an unlikely caravan then: the sheriff, with his lights flashing, followed by the tow truck carrying the incapacitated moose, then Grace and Bill, the two of them side by side in Bill's truck, moving up the highway to the north and then onto Muletown Road and into the deep forest, following that path to a turnout where the sheriff exited his cruiser and waved the tow truck back until the metal platform of its bed extended off the shoulder and into the trees.

They parked and watched as the bed tilted and the winch unspooled and the moose slid from the metal to the dirt and grass, tilting at an odd angle and actually rolling over once, its three good legs flopping around the orbit-line of its body before coming to rest.

When the sheriff unholstered his pistol, Bill cleared his throat. I think I better do it, he said.

You sure about that? the sheriff said.

I'm sure.

The sheriff looked at Grace for a moment. Bill did not know if she gave some sign of her acquiescence to such a plan, but the sheriff's pistol went back into the holster on his belt. He nodded at Bill and then stood there, waiting.

The moose lay in the ferns and grass under the cedars, silent but for its breathing. Bill had removed the rifle from the case, the same Savage 99 he had owned since he was a teenager. His actions now were not unlike those he undertook when loading the dart gun with its tranquilizer. He pressed the cartridge into the breech and then stood with the lever down, the breech open.

He could feel Grace near him somewhere, her hand, or perhaps her quiet voice nearby. The sheriff. The tow truck driver. A deputy whose name he did not know.

You know where to hit it? the sheriff said.

Bill did not look at him and did not answer. He could feel, once again, the animals in their dens, their noses lifted to scent the air, watching him with their poised and myriad senses even from all these many miles away.

Above him, above them all, the sky had gone full dark and stars seemed all at once to rise from the tops of the trees, their pinpoints wheeling for a moment across that black expanse only to return once again to those needled shapes, as if each light had come up through the soil, through the epidermis of root hairs and into the cortex and the endodermis and up at last through open xylem, the sapwood, through the vessels and tracheids, rising in the end to the thin sharp needles and releasing, finally, a single dim point of light into the thin dark air only to pull one back from that same scattering of stars, the cambium pressing down the trunk, pressing back to black earth. Time circling in the soil and the silver-tipped needles. Time circling in the big sage and cheatgrass of everything to come before.

He pulled the lever back to the stock, the breech closing with a smooth almost silent whisper. I'm sorry, he said, not to the sheriff or to himself but to the moose before him in the underbrush. Then he lifted the rifle to his shoulder, leaned forward until the barrel was just a few inches from the hard curl of its skull, and squeezed the trigger.

2

1984

HE SHIVERED AND STARTED THE CAR AND SAT WITH THE heater vents blowing, cold at first but then increasingly warm, a procedure he had already repeated several times as he waited in the cramped confines of the Datsun, his eyes tracing the shape of the prison over and over again: the white guard tower and the blank plate of the door, the fence line topped with barbed wire that leaned inward toward a stone building so imposing and bleak that it looked like something out of a horror movie. It had been past noon when he first pulled into the parking lot and over the course of the subsequent hours the shadows of the tower and the door and the fence had shifted across the asphalt under a flat white sun that descended all day through a wash of pale clouds, its movement marked by the incongruous soundtrack of the Van Halen cassette that reversed again and again in the dashboard deck. Now Diamond Dave was singing, *Might as well jump!* for the tenth or eleventh time. *Go ahead and jump!* The melody spelled out by a synthesizer.

He had been thinking of that night in front of Grady's all day and he thought about it again now as he dozed, mumbling to himself softly as had long been his habit, his head lolling against the cracked vinyl of the seat. How lucky they had been at first. The Quik-Stop had been empty, the cashier out back smoking a cigarette. Rick simply tapped the square green key on the register and when the drawer rolled out he grabbed the cash and the two of them returned to the car and drove away. And then, later that same night, how quickly their luck had changed. The two policemen had looked crazed under the yellow streetlights. And their words. Faghetti, one had said, and the other had laughed. They already had Rick pinned to the hood of the car then, his eyes wide but his voice still defiant, calling the police cockholes. Their response had been to punch him hard in the kidneys and Rick's face had curled in upon itself like a fist. Nat had watched all of it with his back slipping against the brick front of the building, moving sideways, unable to turn away from the sight, slinking toward the barroom door like a coward. And what he was thinking in that moment was not that his best friend was being arrested but that the money they had gotten from the register at the Quik-Stop was in the inside pocket of Rick's jacket.

He could feel the rough surface of the wall and could hear the thump of the bass from the jukebox inside the bar, but then he was no longer on that dark street in Reno, was not in Reno at all but instead stood beside a different road in the failing light under huge shadowed pines. The feeling was the same—from Reno to wherever this was—his stomach churning and a tight feeling of despair rising in his chest. There you are. There you are.

It was from this image that he jolted awake. The cigarette had burned almost to his fingers, the ash falling upon his hand now and scattering across the seat. Dang, he said into the vacant interior of the Datsun.

He had just removed another cigarette from the glove box when the door in the fence opened, opened and then closed and at last swung wide. And there he stood. He looked, at a glance, just as he had that night in front of Grady's, as if no time had passed. Not thirteen months. Not a single day. Thin. Freshly shaven. Even wearing the same tight jeans and rust-colored leather jacket. The dark curls of his hair cut short but otherwise the same. Holding a cigarette with the tips of two fingers as if holding a straw. And what a flood of relief. In an instant all those empty days wiped clean. Alone in the apartment watching lions stalk antelope across the box of the television screen. Marlin Perkins in the Jeep with his binoculars, Jim Fowler at his side. Nothing but an endless strip of empty days, broken at last as the guard shook Rick's hand and Nat stepped out of the car into the drizzling rain. Hey hey, he said.

Rick said nothing at first, but his grin matched Nat's own. The door closed behind him and he shifted the small bag to his left hand as they embraced.

Welcome to the free world, Nat said.

It's free now, is it?

Nat shrugged as Rick threw the little bag onto the back seat and they both stepped into the car. Despite the chill, Rick rolled the window down immediately, the crank squeaking as Nat pulled back onto the highway.

Where's Susan? Rick yelled over the wind roar.

Don't know.

What's that mean?

Means I don't know. I haven't seen her in like a week.

Shit, Rick said. I thought she'd be with you.

Me too.

Well, shit. He sucked at the cigarette for a moment and then held it in his hand and pressed his face to the wind, squinting as the occasional raindrop spiked through the open window. Then he cranked the glass back up again, the same squeak marking each rotation. The car silent now but for the hum of the engine and the rush of an occasional oncoming car in the southbound lane.

Beyond the windshield ran fast food restaurants, a grocery store, a run of gas stations all in a row. Above them: the dim yellow sweep of the mountains to the west, their crests backlit under a gray sky the texture of curdled milk. All beyond already in shadow: the town disappearing into itself and the desert opening into scrubby underbrush. An onrushing darkness. Jackrabbit. Rattlesnake. Digger wasp. The owl preparing for its night hunt. The mouse slipping into its burrow.

To their right, outside Rick's window, Washoe Lake: a dark strip taking on the color of the night.

So what do you wanna do on your first day of freedom?

I don't know. Get a burger. Have a beer. I'd like to know where Susan is.

She'll show up. She always does.

Yeah, well, she should've shown up already, Rick said. She don't even answer her phone. It's not like I can keep calling all day until she's around, you know? He cracked the window enough to flick the butt of his cigarette through the gap and then rolled it closed again. What's new around town?

Not much.

Who's around?

I haven't been out much.

Why not?

Working.

You're not getting soft on me are you?

Let's find out, Nat said.

Rick laughed. Then he said, I'm gonna need a job too.

Yeah, I figured.

You think they'd hire me out at the dealership?

Maybe. You mean in the shop?

Anything, Rick said. He was silent for a long time then, the darkness in motion all around them. Then he said, My mom's gonna need another surgery.

Shit.

Yep.

What's that gonna cost?

Six or eight thousand probably. I ain't even worried about that. That's Medicaid's problem. What I'm worried about is getting her a nurse or someone to take care of her afterward. They said it'll be like three months before she's really up and around. State's not gonna cover any of that.

Nat did not respond. The yellow line seemed to run through black space and the empty geography of thin clear air. From the edges of the road, a few scraggled and flashpopped shadscale bushes wheeled their skeletal shapes against the headlamps.

Ah fuck it, Rick said then. I don't wanna deal with that shit right now. I just wanna get drunk and high. And laid, if I can find Susan.

Right on, Nat said.

And so they drove on into the increasing darkness in silence but for the quiet entanglement of guitars from the cassette deck, northward along the eastern slope of the Sierra, the temperature dropping so that the spattering rain turned to slush that thwacked against the windshield in uneven punctuations like diminutive gunfire. A grainy and disconsolate luminescence lining the scalloped and rolling clouds to the north. Soon the tower of the MGM Grand appeared in the distance, faintly glowing. Then, on the road before them, the Peppermill coffee shop with its modest casino room and motor lodge marking the edge of town. Beyond it came the towers and the lights, enormous clean rooms of clanging bells and tweedling sound effects. Everything a container for a possibility that would never actually materialize. That was why they had tried the Quik-Stop to begin with. Neither of them would speak such a thing—not then and not now—but Nat knew it was true. There was no getting ahead in this world. That much was true as well.

This the new Van Halen? Rick said. He had lifted the cassette case from where it lay near the gearshift and sat turning it slowly in his hands.

Yep.

Van fucking Halen, Rick said.

Van fucking Halen, Nat repeated. You wanna start at Grady's?

Sure, Rick said. Fucking Grady's.

Fucking Grady's, Nat said.

A quarter mile on, he pulled to the curb and switched off the car. The engine sputtered and died. On the sidewalk beyond Rick's window, a woman in a shiny dress moved up the street toward the bar. They both watched her progress in silence.

Goddamn it's good to be out, Rick said when she was gone from view. Shall we?

Hang on a minute, Nat said. He cleared his throat.

What?

So look, Nat said, I know that it, you know, could've been me.

Oh man you're not gonna get all sappy on me. Are you?

I just want you to know that I appreciate what you did.

I didn't do anything.

Yeah you did. I know you came out because they were hassling me.

I just came out to see where you were.

Well, I'm glad you did. I just wish I would've done something.

They were dicks, Rick said. Nothing you can do about a couple of dick-ass cops. Better me than you anyway.

Why's that?

Just because it is. Gotta take care of your people.

That's what I mean, Nat said. That's what I didn't do.

Rick exhaled sharply as if laughing or coughing. What's done is done, Natty, he said. Talking about it doesn't change anything. He sat there in silence for a moment. Then he smiled. Let's go get fucked up, he said.

Dang right, Nat said, and in the next moment they had both stepped out onto the curb.

* * *

WITHIN TWO hours Nat was so drunk and so high he could barely walk, the room hanging on an axis that seemed to shift each time he moved. Were it not for the cocaine Rick was offered again and again—and in which Nat was included each time—he likely would have passed out altogether. His face was numb from smiling and laughing.

Goddamn fucker didn't know what hit him, Rick said. He slapped the palm of his hand against the table. A kind of punctuation. All the glasses jumped.

Just boom, like that. Flat on his ass. Rick smiled and started laughing at his own anecdote, a prison story none of them had heard before. Like a sack of shit, he said. Then he was gone-laughing, hard and constant.

Sack of shit, Nat said between breaths.

The barlights swung in their orbits. The stools tipping.

Oh God, Nat said. If I don't stop laughing I'm gonna puke.

The people at the table with them kept changing into other people. Billy Carl was there but when Nat looked again he had become Sheila and later Dave Vollmer. All people he had not seen since Rick had been put away and now he found that he could not keep track of any of them. He had been telling Billy Carl a story and now Billy Carl had become someone else entirely but then he was too high and too drunk to remember the story and Rick was here and he was talking and they were laughing and it had been a long long time since he had laughed.

He had even forgotten to look for Susan, although when they first arrived at Grady's he had done so without cease, searching for her shape in the bar, for the dark sweep of her hair, but with the alcohol and the cross tops and cocaine and the laughter he had forgotten for a moment and so had also forgotten to hope and to fear that she would arrive. So when her arm came across Rick's chest and her hair fell across his shoulder it was as if she had materialized out of thin air, her body leaning into Rick's. A feather in her hair like an Indian princess out of *Peter Pan*. Where the hell have you been? Rick said, and in the next moment their open mouths were together.

Nat's smile was frozen on his face, stuck there for a long moment as the others around the table mumbled their oohs and ahs. When they broke apart at last, her eyes glanced over at him, just for a moment. It's not polite to stare, she said.

Oh, he said, a small involuntary sound that he hoped covered the guilt that flooded through him like a hot wave.

She leaned in to Rick and whispered something in his ear, or seemed to, and then slid onto his lap. I missed you so much, she said.

I missed you too, baby, Rick answered, but I'm still pissed.

How come?

You were supposed to be there to pick me up.

Didn't Nat pick you up?

Yeah, but that's not the point.

I'm here now, aren't I?

They kissed again, quickly this time, and then she took the beer from his hand and took a long drink.

Don't be mad, Susan said. She kissed him on the cheek this time and then settled back and looked across to where Nat slumped against the table, held his gaze for a long moment above that surface, over the scratched wood, the furrows running with spilled beer and the wet ash trails of burned cigarettes.

From the jukebox came a power ballad that had been everywhere on the radio, and Susan dragged Rick out onto the dance floor and draped herself upon him under a dim and rotating light that moved slowly from red to green and back to red again. At the table, Billy Carl was still Dave Vollmer but Nat thought Sheila had reappeared to become both Peter Mendy and some girlfriend of his or maybe the girlfriend was Sheila, he could not be sure, and he thought the other guy was named Danny something but he could not remember that either. But then he did not have to because they all began to scatter, slowly floating back to the bar or to other tables, their bodies like flotsam adrift in some current that could be felt but not seen.

The room shifted into some lower speed now, as if a record player had clicked from 33⅓ to 16 revolutions per minute, everything kicking down a full octave, even the beating of his heart, of all their hearts, Rick and Susan tilting on the dance floor under the colored lights and Nat alone at the table, the feeling of it not unlike the silence of those empty homes when they were teenagers in Battle Mountain, a silence that was not empty because it was filled with absence, like finding within that silence a clear tone like the sound of a tiny bell, its ringing flung out beyond the streets and buildings and into the bare sloping hills beyond.

When he looked up, he saw Grady staring back at him, his hands resting on the polished surface of the bar, stained rag over his shoulder.

Nat nodded and stood. The room tilted in all directions but he managed to cross it and to slump onto a stool.

Incarceration hasn't mellowed him any, has it? Grady said when he arrived.

Not by the looks of it.

You want another?

I think I'm pretty well tapped out, Nat said.

You're looking pretty cross-eyed anyway, champ, Grady said.

Naw. Barely started.

Grady smiled briefly beneath the drooping mustache. Then he tilted his head, his eyes meeting Nat's. Johnny's been in here looking for you, he said.

Even at the mention of the name Nat felt his stomach churn. What'd he say?

Just asked if you'd been around.

What'd you tell him?

That I haven't seen hide nor hair in—what's it been?—a year, I guess. Or damn close.

I appreciate it, Nat said.

Not like I had to make it up, Grady said.

Nat nodded, leaning into the bar. The sense of drifting immediately slowed into a dull soft wave that lifted and descended like the motion of a swing.

You got a job?

Still at the Ford dealership. I've been there two years.

Selling?

I wish, he said. I'm in the shop. Lube and oil.

Well, a man's gotta work.

So they say. Nat shrugged.

Grady set an ice-filled glass on the bar and filled it with vodka. This one's on me. Keep your head down and your pecker up.

Thanks for the advice, Nat said.

Someone down the bar called to Grady and he glanced in the man's direction and nodded but did not move from where he stood in front of Nat. You watch yourself with Johnny Aguirre, he said. That guy isn't messing around.

I'm taking care of it, Nat said. Even to himself, his voice sounded like a white blur.

I hope so, Grady said. I was a little surprised when he said your name.

Why's that?

Just don't seem like the type to get tangled up in all that.

Nat shrugged and after a moment Grady seemed to dissolve, reappearing farther down the bar. Nat sipped at the vodka and then forgot it was there and remembered and sipped again, huddling over his drink as wave upon wave of fatigue flowed through him. He wished that he had Dottie's number from the front office of the dealership and that she might be willing to sell him a couple black beauties to get him through the rest of the night but he possessed no cash and did not think he could successfully drive anywhere to meet her even if he did.

Natty man, Rick said.

He looked over to where Rick was settling onto the stool beside him, smiling. Beyond his friend, Susan leaned against the bar, a thin sheen of sweat across her face, her skin luminous in the neon glow of a beer sign. From the Land of Sky Blue Waters, the sign read. Nat lifted the vodka and smiled weakly.

Rick waved down the length of the bar. Grady stood at its far end, talking to a woman in a tight black T-shirt. Hey there, you horny old man, Rick called. Grady glanced up and nodded but did not yet move in their direction.

You look terrible, Rick said, his voice slurring the syllables into one long word.

It took Nat a moment to realize that Rick was now speaking to him. The light in the bar had begun to fade, as if the whole room had flooded and they now sat, all of them, underwater.

You do, Susan said to him. You look like a sad sack.

You need to get laid, Rick said. We need to get him laid.

Nat leaned on the bar, bleary-eyed, watching him fade into and out of focus.

My best friend here needs to get laid, Rick said.

A collection of screechy female voices hooted up from the darkness around them.

Jesus Christ, Nat said, laughing. You asshole.

Just helping my buddy, Rick said. No charge.

What's your name?

The voice came so quickly that it seemed as if the woman had materialized on Rick's command. And perhaps she had. She might have been forty, although she wore so much makeup it was difficult to tell, eyes wiped with turquoise as thick as paint and hair like a bundle of blond wires. She licked her lips. He had seen animals in nature documentaries perform similar actions while feeding on carcasses in the plains of Africa.

This is my pal, Marlin, Rick said. His voice slurred so profoundly now that he could hardly finish the words before bursting into laughter once more. Marlin Perkins. But he's not related to *that* Marlin Perkins.

She did not seem to catch the joke, or if she did she did not care. Perhaps she had never heard of Marlin Perkins. Nice to meet you, Marlin. I'm Vickie. She extended her hand. Nat took it.

The whole world had blurred into vowels. Nat tried to catch a word from that current but then Rick's hand shot into the air, pointing down toward the far end of the bar, where a small color television hung from a metal bracket. Fuck all, Rick said thickly. On the screen was a map of the United States with nearly every state colored in red. Across the screen fell white static as the station bled into and out of range.

What the hell you complaining about? Grady said. He had come back from the far side of the bar and stood with the rag over his shoulder once more, staring up at the television. You vote for Mondale?

Shit no, Rick said. I didn't vote for nobody.

You? Grady looked at Nat now.

I voted, he said thickly.

You voted? Rick said. What the hell for?

Mr. Mitchell. Civics.

I failed that class, Rick said.

Yes, you did.

Who'd you vote for?

I'm not telling you that, Nat said. The television on the wall disappeared into snow. Returned. Once again faded.

Why the fuck not?

He paused, looking for the words. Then he slurred out, It's private.

Says who?

Mr. Mitchell. Civics.

Fuck, Rick said. I fucking hate Mr. Mitchell. Civics.

He hated you too, Nat said. Probably still does.

The television on the wall showed nothing but static now. Grady stood beside the box and banged it with his fist and the image skipped and rolled like a blank space on a slot machine. No red 7s. No bunched trio of cherries. No map of Reagan's reelection. Then white static, the red map appearing for a moment and then covered once more like blood disappearing under new-fallen snow.

Wanna dance? the woman next to Nat said into his ear. He could not remember her name.

I don't know if I can stand up, he said.

Maybe we should go lie down.

Nat could only smile weakly in response.

Across from Rick, Susan flashed him a thumbs up. Her hair shining in darkness. Her smile radiant in the dim light of the bar.

And somewhere outside, in a nearly endless dry basin that once contained a vast inland sea, night creatures swarmed the sagebrush. Windscorpion and pocket mouse and kit fox skittering through Mormon tea and shiny hopsage, rustling the bottlebrush, the ricegrass, and rustling too the tilting neon room, the men and women within, all adrift under the surface of that impossible dead ocean.

3

THAT NIGHT THE MOOSE CAME TO HIM IN HIS DREAMS. HE was on the road but it was twelve years ago and he was coming up out of that last blasted winter in the desert. The eyes that stared back at him from the rearview mirror were young and red-ringed and crazed with panic, set against a receding darkness from which he expected, at any moment, the red and blue flashing lights of the highway patrol to appear. But there was only the fleeing and faintly luminous night road that led backward to Battle Mountain. Nothing more.

He had thought he would drive nonstop, through the night and into the next day, through Oregon and eastern Washington and dipping at last into the Idaho panhandle, chain-smoking all the while, the burning torment of what had happened, of what he had done, rolling through the shell of his body like a fire. But then he had grown so tired so quickly, sleep rushing in on him with a ferocity he had never before experienced, and he pulled the laboring car into the gravel beside the road and dropped his head back and was already asleep.

He slept in the dream and in the dream he woke to a quiet breeze and an ocean of grassland in all directions. Twelve years ago. He could not remember where he was or what he had done to come to such a place, but then the whole of it returned to him, every detail stark and absolute and irrefutable. His body sticky with sweat despite the chill and the interior of the car coated with a thin layer of colorless dust. What he had done. What he could never undo.

A few feet away began a low hill covered in golden grasses that shook and trembled and seemed to extend forever into a landscape endlessly rising and falling in all directions like an ocean of slowly undulating waves.

And then he saw the animal. It stood atop the hill, its thick horns and black eyes staring back at him with apparent disinterest, all of it so still that it seemed at times to waver back into the grasses from which it had come, an animal that appeared, even then, as if it had stepped directly off the cover of the field guide he had had as a child and which was now, at least in the moment of the dream, of the memory that was the dream, with him in the car, the book his uncle had given him so many years before and which he had read and studied, both out of interest and, later, out of sheer boredom. The animal on the cover was exactly this animal in exactly this location, as if the color image had become real and extant before him in the grasslands beside a road the numbered designation of which he could no longer recall, the only missing item the title that would have been emblazoned across the grass in thin white letters: *Wildlife of the Intermountain West*. He thought of reaching down into the floorspace behind him for that book, but he could not do so. It seemed impossible to move somehow, impossible in his past, impossible in the dream.

But then he looked again and saw that the animal was not the pronghorn antelope but the moose of the evening before, its head partially blown apart and its leg twisting behind it on that awful hinge-point of broken bone, his own heart sinking in his chest even as his skin blew into pinpoints and the landscape everywhere flew away into thin blue darkness.

When he woke his throat was dry and seemed coated with the same floury dust that had lain upon every surface of the car he had returned to in the dream. He sat up in the trailer on the stiff mattress and coughed and then rose and drank from the sink and stood there in his long underwear, alone in the dark, beer gut pressed to the edge of the counter, staring into the scant black rectangle of the window, into the reflection of his own wild eyes and scraggly beard. Beyond that visage lay a vacancy of empty space.

He returned to the mattress but his eyes would not close and he lay there, awake, watching, for what seemed like hours, as a blue square of moonlight slanted across the cracked vinyl paneling of the adjacent wall. After the clock had passed two in the morning, he rose to his feet once again, dressed and lit a cigarette before lacing up his boots and stepping outside. The night was cold, well below freezing, and the forest around him glowed under the blue light of stars and a sliver of waxing crescent moon. The birches faintly radiant, their bases pooled in black shadow, and the path he followed invisible in the darkness. And yet he followed it nonetheless, arriving at the gate and turning his key in the padlock and stepping through into the rescue.

He stood there for a time, puffing at the cigarette, a habit he had quit many times but could not master. Before him, the enclosures lay arrayed in their wide curving loop on the slope of the mountain. From the gate he could see nearly all of it: the cages shining with silver light, the jagged silhouettes of giant pines and furs rising everywhere against a night sky in which the Milky Way appeared as a clear bright spillage of clustering stars. Across from him stood the office trailer, inside which he had slept for many years before his uncle moved in with his girlfriend and left him the travel trailer, and uphill, on his right, he could just make out the edge of the big shed that housed the refrigerators and freezers, the tools, the snowmobile.

It was Majer he wanted to see most of all but the bear was asleep in his den at the center of that great loop of cages, as he knew he would be, and so he snuffed the cigarette and dropped the butt into his coat pocket and then walked a slow circuit among the other enclosures, pausing to look in on each animal as he passed: Napoleon and Foster, their quilled bodies trundling slowly across the expanse of their cage, noses sniffing the air at his approach; Baker in his den, napping, only the raked claws of one forepaw visible; the twin martens swirling along the branches that crisscrossed their enclosure. The remainder of the animals asleep or awake, depending on their species and activity level, but all safe and secure. The two bald eagles silent. The turkey vulture as well. Of the raptors, only Elsie was awake. She hooted from her enclosure, swiveling her head as he approached, her great round eyes examining him with some mixture of interest and boredom, waiting until he passed before starting up her call once more.

These he had saved, had brought back from whatever deprivations had been enacted upon them, most often, like the moose he had lost, the result of collision with the various blunt and sharpened instruments of the human world—vehicles, firearms, fences, traps, poisons—and whatever sense of unease he had carried back from Ponderay, back from Muletown Road and that single rifle shot, back from the dream, dissolved slowly in their presence, his feet moving along the fence lines and those animals nocturnal and active running their noses along the wire in investigation of his scent. He stood by each and spoke in low, quiet tones, telling himself what he already knew: that the promise he made was a false one. There are times when you must become the instrument, when you must deliver a living, breathing thing to whatever heaven exists for such a creature. To the heaven of the moose. And the fox and the badger and the bobcat all watching him with their eyes bright and shining under the shadows of the black trees, watching him without comprehension, but he did not ask for such a thing. He only needed them to be there, and there they were.

When he came to Zeke's enclosure, he stood at its edge, watching the darkness for a long time until the wolf appeared, drifting forth from the shadows of the trees like a silver ghost and pausing only to squat and urinate and then to sniff the sticks that lay strewn upon the ground, rocks and dry pine needles, after which the animal dissolved again into the shadows from which it had come, its three-legged motion like the flow of some hobbled ghost.

He spoke now into the absence that the wolf had left behind, telling him that he knew which side of the fence he was supposed to stay on and thanking him for the reminder. The palm of his hand against the chain link. He told him that they were still looking for a companion wolf, a female, but that they had been unable to find one suitable. Then he told him that he would not give up, that they would find a mate, a partner, that he would no longer be alone. Words into a vacancy, the wolf somewhere much deeper in the enclosure, perhaps watching him; perhaps not.

He did not know how long he stood there, but after a time he unzipped his jeans and urinated a long, steaming stripe a few inches from the outer edge of the fence. Then he turned and walked back up the path through the birches to the trailer and, at last, to sleep.

HE RETURNED to the rescue just past dawn. Majer had not been out of his den when Bill first walked the enclosures but the bear was awake now and stood upon the big rock over his swimming pool, staring down at the water as if a fish might materialize from its depths.

Hey there, Bill said. I came down to see you last night but you were snoozing.

The bear looked at him with its pale eyes and then walked heavily to the zookeeper door and lay its head against the small opening there.

Is that how it is? Bill said, but he walked to the door and put his hand through the opening and scratched the bear's rough fur, the skull underneath a hard uneven shape. How we doin', buddy? he said, repeating those words and words like them as he scratched, the bear shifting so that Bill's hand scratched the top of his head and then behind his ears and then the thick fur of his neck, Majer's breath coming short and loud with the pleasure of it.

Don't get too excited, Bill said, smiling. He patted the bear twice on the head and pulled his hand from the opening, stepping back from the door. You ready for breakfast?

Majer looked up at him, still panting, his lips curled in a wide grin.

Dang, you're a cheap date, Bill said. I'll go get it. We got salmon from BTC.

He walked to the barn and opened the big sliding door. Straw dust circling in beams of light. He went to the bank of refrigerators and freezers and opened one and extracted a whole salmon and two heads of lettuce and dropped them both into a bucket and then returned to Majer's enclosure and slid all of it into his metal feed box. Majer stood and watched him all the while, or seemed to, his blind eyes following as he moved, standing in his great silver-tipped bulk beyond the fence until Bill pulled the heavy counterweight so that the second gate slid up along its track. Breakfast time, Bill said, and the bear stepped through to eat, his bulk rocking slowly from side to side with the motion of his body.

The air's chill was deep and sharp. Winter was coming. In the mornings along the birch path: bubbles flowing under shells of November ice. They would need to pull the water into the heated sections of the enclosures soon, for already the first task of the morning was breaking loose the bright clear windows that encased each animal's drinking trough. How those sharp-edged shields glowed in the morning sunlight. Rime ice curling the office windows. Hoarfrost boxing the fence wires. By late morning the bunched needles would drip sunlight onto dark soggy earth, but there would be fewer such days now. He knew it. The animals knew it. All of them, in their ways, preparing for the snow. Bedding for the martens and for Zeke. The raptors scratching about in their nests, lining them with rags and tufts of cotton and dry leaves. Even Majer, despite his age, swelling in size, putting on the fat-weight that would get him through the four or five months of his hibernation. Soon he would disappear into the cave at the back of his enclosure. Months in the snow-dark, not moving, his heartbeat and body temperature slipping down and down until it was nearly indistinguishable from death, silent in that darkness of hibernation for the months of the heaviest snows.

The lesson is that we all go to ground. Some by slowing. Some by quickening. Some by consuming more and doing less. Some by curling into their own dark interior places. Dying into the winter's cold and clambering out of our dens when the snowstorms break and spring begins. Thin green seed leaves from black earth. Dwarf shoots. Spiral scales. The fascicles curl from the bud, and we clamber out of our dens sniffing the air for the scent of a meal.

Next month, he would close to the public for the winter and send the volunteers home, opening up again once the roads were clear enough for day-to-day movement from town. Grace would come up when the weather allowed it, sometimes in her truck, occasionally via snowmobile, but for long stretches he would be alone with the animals and the snow and no sound but that which they made, sometimes for many days. The martens streaking across white hills. The owl peering out at him from her perch. The mountain lion's silent flowing motion. The wolf's yellow eyes watching him through the black trunks of the big pines. A geography of snowed-over silence. Elk would come down through the trees on their way to the meadows in the south, their calls echoing up from those blank white plains. And moose on the river road.

For the first four years he had anticipated those months of isolation with a mixture of relief and dread. Now was the time he looked forward to most: the silence of it, the rhythm of those short days, waking at dawn and coming down the birch path, the big trees frosted over and so very quiet, his snowshoes crunching against the ice. Of the path itself, he had once told Grace that it was like something out of a fairy tale. He had thought of it that way when he was a child and had first visited his uncle David and when he returned so many years later the path from the trailer to the animals seemed even more so. My god that you could walk through such a landscape. My god that such a landscape existed anywhere but in your dreams. And yet here it was. Were a fox to step out from behind the trees and speak in human words, or a raven to descend wearing a suit coat and a top hat, you would not have been surprised. Worlds overlapping.

He unlocked the office and started the coffeepot and then unlocked the tiny gift shop down by the parking lot and then the medical room and finally stood in front of the wolf enclosure once more. He thought he had seen Zeke when he had turned up the path from the gift shop, the wolf's body a quick blur against the fence line, but there was no sign of him at all now. Though he waited there for the animal's appearance, the wolf did not come. Bill resigned himself to that fact and returned to the bare, box-like construction trailer that he used as an office, pouring himself a mug of coffee and then sitting for a time looking at invoices he knew he could not currently pay, a process he had hardly started before Bess arrived, knocking twice on the office door and then opening it. Morning, she said.

Morning.

She stood in the doorway, a woman perhaps ten years older than he was and whom he had hired soon after his uncle had died because he knew he would be unable to run the rescue on his own and because he had begun talking to the animals in earnest, talking and listening, a habit that sometimes made him doubt his sanity.

There's coffee, he said.

Sounds good.

His words were her cue to enter the office trailer and pour herself a cup and begin going over the day's schedule with him: the feedings, the turkey vulture's antibiotics, some planned maintenance on the lower fence, the building of a new raptor enclosure, which volunteers they would have that day and which they would not. But instead she stood there unmoving near the closed door. So . . . uh . . . what happened? she said.

With what?

Last night. You left in a hurry.

Moose, he said.

In town?

Down near Ponderay. Hit by a pickup.

He did not want to talk about it but there it was. He told her what had happened and when he was done she said nothing for a long time, standing there in the doorway in silence. He did not look at her, kept his eyes focused on the paperwork on the metal surface of the desk. At last she said, simply, Awful.

He nodded. Well, he said, let's do the schedule.

She moved forward into the trailer and they went over the day's routine just as they might have without the moose. She reminded him she was taking two of the eagles out to an elementary school in Sandpoint later that morning and he told her he would help her load the bird. Then she nodded and stepped out the door, the coffee cup steaming into the chill air.

He returned to the trailer in the late morning. The plastic thermometer that hung by its door read just under thirty degrees, but the sky was bright and clear and so there had been a few visitors when they opened the gate at ten: a family of three on vacation from somewhere farther west, and two women, perhaps mother and daughter, neither younger than sixty. What do you think, old man? he said to the bear when the women started up the path.

The bear looked at him, swinging its nose up the fence.

That's gonna be us one day. Old men stumbling around. You want a grape?

The bear's lips curled in a smile again. Bill removed a ziplock from his jacket pocket. Don't tell anyone I'm giving you treats for no good reason, he said. He slipped a grape through the fence. Majer took it carefully in his distended lips, one after another until the bag was empty. I'm serious about keeping this secret, Bill said. You know the rule: Don't feed the bears.

Majer sat looking at him, or at least looking in his direction, the bear's eyes filmed in milk and Bill returning that vacant stare. A blind bear in a cage. You can feel the tug of the heart in those gray pools. It is the pull of other worlds within this one, where time and memory and vision have meanings you cannot begin to understand.

All right, now, Bill said. Grace's coming this week to look at you, so you'd better not be cranky with her.

The bear's head rocked slowly from side to side, a thin stream of drool suspended in a silver strand from his lip.

I'm off to pay more bills. If you all would just stop eating, this whole thing would get a lot cheaper.

He slid off the stump. Below him, an olive-green SUV had appeared in the parking lot and a man in a similarly colored uniform had just stepped out onto the gravel. Shit, Bill said. He looked around quickly and when he saw Chuck coming down the path he said, Hey, go find Bess. The new Fish and Game guy's here.

Gotcha, Chuck said, turning on his heel and heading back in the direction from which he had come.

The officer had passed through the public gate below and Bill walked down to meet him, his jaws clenched. Morning, he said.

Morning. He was older than Bill, perhaps fifty, thin and fit with salt-and-pepper hair and a dark mustache. His official title, the title on the business card Bill had been handed a month earlier when the man first walked up the path, was District Conservation Officer, but Bill thought of him as a game warden. Around his torso was zipped a down vest that matched the rest of his uniform.

It's Steve, right?

Steve Colman, the warden said. He reached his hand out, and Bill took it gravely.

Right, Bill said. What can I do for you?

Just came by to talk about a couple things.

What things?

Well, that moose hit down by Ponderay for one. Sheriff says you dispatched it.

Bill looked at him. Their breathing was visible as white smoke upon the air. Yeah, he said.

Well, it creates a mess of paperwork when a citizen does it on their own. Better if you could just call me next time. I told the sheriff the same thing.

Bill stood staring at him, saying nothing. Having the warden there at all sent a thin shiver of nervousness through him. The badge. The sidearm. The authority he seemed to assume.

Anyway, let's say we just look the other way on that, this one time. This is assuming next time you'll call me if something like this comes up again.

It's not like I did it for fun, Bill said.

Why did you do it at all?

Someone had to.

I get that but why you?

He shrugged now, and when the warden spoke again it was into the long drift of silence that had risen between them.

All right, all right, he said, lifting his hands in a gesture of surrender. Behind him, Cinder, the rescue's resident mountain lion, watched them both, her one undamaged eye expressionless, outsize paws resting on the stone beneath her head. Look, that's not even the real reason I came out here, the warden said. I need to talk to you more about all that permitting stuff.

I was afraid you were gonna say that.

Like I told you before, that's the job. Part of it anyway.

Bill thought the warden might say something more but there was nothing and so Bill said, I guess we'd better head up to the office. He turned and walked back up the hill then, the warden behind him, Bess appearing at a distance, a look of concern upon her face. The animals were all at their fences now, pacing, watching them as they came up the trail between the enclosures: the mountain lion first and then the badgers and raccoons, the raptors hopping about on their perches. It's all right, Bill said to them. He expected the warden to comment but again there was nothing. Farther up the trail, Bill could see Majer's back as the bear moved toward the rear of the enclosure, a vast mountain sinking slowly from view.

You want a coffee or something? Bill said as they entered the office.

No coffee for me, thanks. The warden sat down immediately and Bill refilled his cup and then sat at the desk, the coffee curling steam.

Well, the warden said, let me just get to it then. We've got some real immediate concerns out here.

What kind?

I don't even know where to start. You're operating what's essentially an illegal facility.

How's that?

You've got to be licensed to run a zoo.

It's not a zoo. It's a wildlife rescue.

I think you might be missing my point, the warden said. His face looked pained and he did not seem willing to meet Bill's eyes.

No, I get it. You're talking about some kind of paperwork thing? Like a permit?

It's a bit more involved than that.

That's fine, Bill said. Let us know what you need us to fill out and we'll start working on it.

It's not really that simple, the warden said. I mean, look, you've got two federally protected species here. Grizzlies and wolves fall under US Fish and Wildlife.

So what does that mean?

Means Department of Interior.

So we're talking about more paperwork?

No, the warden said. And then, I don't know. The thing is, you can't— He took a breath. Look, it's my understanding that the grizzly wasn't born in captivity. Do I have that right?

My uncle bought him from a gas station.

Where?

Bill almost said, Montana, but caught himself. Just a few miles north of here. Orphaned, I think.

See, that's the problem. If that bear wasn't born in captivity what you have is a big game animal. And a wild one at that. That's going to be an issue at the federal level.

Bill smiled as if the warden was making a joke of some kind. Majer's about as wild as a poodle.

That may be, but the law's pretty clear on what can and can't be put in a cage in the state of Idaho. And that's even clearer if we're talking about a federally protected species like wolves and grizzlies.

Majer's lived in captivity all his life.

But he wasn't born in captivity. See? That's the distinction.

Bill sat looking at him, not speaking for a long time. Sure he was, he said at last. Yeah, I just forgot. That's what my uncle said. The gas station guys bred him or something.

We'd need some kind of proof of that but there are lots of other issues here.

Like?

Like I know the wolf just came in a couple of years ago. Same problem, really. Federally protected species.

Yeah, you keep saying that, Bill said. But what am I supposed to do with him?

Well, that's a good question. It's possible you could find a registered, licensed zoo to turn him over to. The other possibility is that we'd need to officially dispatch the animal.

Dispatch, Bill repeated.

I'm afraid so, the warden said. Look, Bill—can I call you Bill?—I'm an officer of the law. You can't have these kinds of animals without permits. Hell, I don't even think there are permits for what you're doing up here.

What I'm doing? What's that supposed to mean?

It's not supposed to mean anything. Except that you're breaking the law.

Why not just issue me a permit?

It's not that easy.

Zoos get permitted.

Zoos don't keep wild animals.

Come on, Bill said. We've been doing this for, like, twenty-five years.

I know you have. And the bear's been here the whole time, right?

Sure he has.

Look, the situation is this. My predecessor was a nice guy and all, but he left me more messes to clean up than I thought possible. And then there was that Ligertown stuff last year. Hell, Bill, I got the governor looking over my shoulder now to make sure that kind of thing doesn't happen again.

Bill shook his head. We're not like that place, he said.

I know you're not but that's what everybody else is going to think.

Just do your inspection and tell us if there's anything that needs changing and we'll do it.

It's not that simple. That's what I'm trying to tell you. I can't retroactively permit you for animals you already have. That's the situation.

The door opened in the awkward silence that followed and Bess stood in its lit rectangle. Do you need me? she said, tentative, quiet.

Yeah, Bill said.

The warden introduced himself to Bess and she shook his hand. We getting inspected? she asked him.

No, no, the warden said.

I don't understand what I'm supposed to do here, Bill said from the desk.

I'm just here to give you a heads-up on the situation.

But what you're talking about, Bill said, his voice coming in a kind of rush, what you're talking about is killing my animals.

The warden shook his head. Let's not . . . , he said. Then he started again. Let's not go there. Not yet.

But that's what you're saying, right?

I didn't mean to suggest that was what was going to happen. I'm just telling you what the regulations state.

What do the regulations state? Bess said.

That they want to kill the animals, Bill said.

Now, wait a minute. That's not what I said. No one *wants* to kill anything.

Bill did not speak now. From the black mouth of the coffee cup on the desk drifted a slanting column of white steam.

What do you need us to do? Bess said.

OK, now, that's good. That's positive thinking, right?

Bill did not speak. Not a word. There was a twisting inside him now, a twisting that was anger and frustration and also the thin sharp blade of panic.

To start with I'm gonna need to see a lot of paperwork, the warden said to Bess. You got a vet that comes around?

Nat could feel Bess looking to him for permission to answer the question but he did not move and after a moment she said, Grace Barlow. She stepped into the room now and closed the door behind her.

OK, the warden said. You have records of all that?

Sure, Bess said.

Look, bottom line, the warden said. You're breaking the law if you don't have the permits. And I don't think permits exist for what you're doing here. I'm not saying that what you're doing isn't a good thing but there are laws in place. You don't get to decide what you can put in a cage.

Who decides then?

The law, the warden said simply.

Bill sat looking at him, teeth tight in his jaw. The warden held his gaze for a moment and then looked away. When Bess spoke, Bill thought he could see a wave of relief pass through him.

Can you get us a list of the paperwork you'll want to see? she said.

The thing is, the warden said, the law's pretty clear on this.

I'm sure we can work together on this, Bess said. Right, Bill?

Bill did not look at her, instead continuing to stare at the warden.

I'm sure you're right, the warden said. He looked at Bill once more and when there was no response he stood. Well, I've gotta get moving, he said, extending his hand.

Bill looked at it. I'm not—*we're not* doing anything wrong, he said.

I know you're not but that's not really the issue.

We're taking care of animals up here, Bill said. Feeding them, taking them to schools, and . . . hell, it's not like we're getting rich doing this. You know? I spend every day and night here.

I understand that, the warden said. His hand had been floating before him in the air above the desk but he let it fall now. I don't make the laws. I just enforce them. That's my job.

Bill stood looking at him.

I'm not your enemy here, the warden said. He waited a moment for

Bill's response and then shrugged. All right, I've gotta head out, he said. You folks have a nice day. He stepped past Bess, who mumbled that she would walk him back to his truck, and then the door swung closed behind them and they were gone.

He sat behind the desk for what seemed like a long time. At some point Bess returned, the door opening just enough for her to poke her head inside. You OK? she said to him.

Yeah, I'm all right, he said.

We'll get the paperwork together. We've got records of everything.

He nodded. You need help getting the birds loaded?

The boys already did it.

Ah, he said, what school again?

Stidwell.

He nodded. She stood there, watching him. What? he said at last.

You sure you're OK?

I'm fine. Really.

He's just doing his job, Bess said.

He shrugged and sipped at his coffee.

Bess stood for a moment longer in the doorway and then said, I'll be back about one, and he nodded and then the door closed slowly and she was gone.

He sat for a long time behind the desk in the silence of that room, listening to the ticking of the heater, sipping at his coffee. Then he stood and descended the path toward the parking lot, crossing the gravel and standing at the edge of the forest where the ridge fell away and the big trees—firs and pines—stretched over the landscape in all directions. The pen where he kept orphaned fawns and elk and moose calves stood to his left and near the open gate were gathered four young deer, those he had bottle-fed through the summer and released six weeks ago and which returned every three or four days, as if holding to the hope that he would bottle-feed them once more.

What are you doing down there? he said.

They looked at him, querulous but not alarmed, and he moved

down the gravel to the railroad tie path that led to the pen, all the while the deer watching him come, only the one he had named Chet appearing skittish at all, the deer's hoofs worrying the black earth as if it might spring away into the thick shadows of the trees at any moment.

Don't get agitated, Bill said. It's the same old me it's always been.

The other male, Pancho, merely stared at him, and the two does, Jolene and Darlene, sniffed at the ground as if Bill was of little interest, raising their heads only when he stood directly before them and then moving forward, all four of them, into a tight semicircle like students awaiting an assignment. The starting antlers of the two bucks stood atop their heads like thick gray knobs, single rounded and velvet-covered pedicles that would, the following spring, begin growing into full antlers, first of a similar blunt and sensitive velvet-covered bone, and then into the full collected rack, eight or ten points. They would have long forgotten him by then, moving through the deeper forest, over the ridgetops and down into the misty draws between, fighting other bucks for territory and for the right to mate, their bodies shadowing through landscapes into which they had been born and into which they would return.

I got nothing for you, Bill said.

The deer stood watching him. After a moment, one of them, Pancho, leaned forward and nudged his arm gently with the side of its black nose.

I really don't, he said, smiling now. He tapped his pockets as if it was a gesture the animals might understand. You guys are supposed to be wild by now.

Their hooves shuffled against the dirt and crunched in the fallen needles, their eyes so darkly brown that they appeared black, watching him, then looking away, and then watching him again, as if in doing so they might catch him with a handful of dry corn or an apple.

Have fun out there, he said at last, still smiling. And don't play in the road.

He turned and came back up the path and when he looked down

toward the gate again the four of them were drifting about the small clearing in front of the enclosure, sniffing the ground, their ears twitching.

When he returned to the office he dialed Grace's number at the veterinary clinic, expecting to leave a message at the desk, but then she came on the line and he leaned back in his chair, a sense of relief flooding through him all at once.

Boy, it's good to hear your voice, he said.

That's nice to hear, she said.

I thought I'd have to leave a message.

You caught me in between, she said. How are you doing?

He told her about the fawns, about the small knobby antlers of the two bucks and that all four looked healthy and well. And then about his encounter with the wolf in the night, how the animal had marked its territory.

Wow, she said. Old Zeke's getting used to you after all.

At least at night.

It's a start.

Definitely, he said. It felt great to see him like that. I've been worried about him.

And he's gonna be fine, she said. They don't all have to come right up to the fence, you know.

Two years is a long time to be pissed off, Bill said.

You'd be pissed off too if you lost a limb.

True, he said. It's just nice to see him feeling comfortable. Or at least less skittish. It was silent on the line for a moment and then Bill said, Hey, that guy Steve Colman from Fish and Game came by today.

Crap, she said. He still barking about the permits?

That and the moose, he said.

He told her what the warden had said, both about the moose and about the permitting, his anger rising and falling as he recounted the details.

What a dick, Grace said.

He laughed then. Yeah, for sure, he said. I'm not gonna lie: I'm worried about it.

I'm sure he's just trying to get you to pay a fine or something.

Didn't sound like it. Sounded more like he wanted to shut us down.

No one would want that.

I don't know, he said.

Was Bess there?

Yeah.

What does she think?

Pretty much same as you.

See, she said, you're outnumbered. Reason and logic win.

He was pretty serious about it.

Then take it seriously, she said. Just don't obsess about it.

I'm not obsessing about anything.

Really?

Really, he said. When do I obsess?

All the time.

When? He had been running his finger along the edge of his coffee cup but he stopped now.

Seriously? Any time an animal's poop looks weird you talk about it for a month.

I learned that from you.

I'm sure, she said. You want me there tomorrow?

I want you here now.

Baby, I wish I could, she said.

Can't you tell everyone you got parvo or something?

They probably won't believe me.

Dang, he said. What if I have a sick dog?

You *are* a sick dog.

Exactly, he said, and I need a house call.

Tomorrow, unless you want to come over tonight.

I can probably come tonight.

Works for me. I'll let Jude know.

All right. How about I bring something to eat?

Perfect, she said. Oh, Jude has a thing next Monday night if you want to come with. It's a recital. Fall Festival or something like that.

Yeah, for sure I'll come.

It's at seven or something. I'll let you know tonight. I have a flyer somewhere.

All right.

Gotta get back to dogtown, she said.

He was smiling now, faintly, the thread of panic that the warden had brought upon him already unraveling. I love you, he said into the phone.

I love you too, she told him.

He hung up the phone and sat looking at the stacks of paper on the desk. Debts paid. Debts waiting to be paid. Delivery manifests. He wondered about Fish and Game, wondered what the end result of their interest would be, hoping that Grace was right, that they would lever some fine and that they would find a way to pay it and then the rescue would be left alone. But he knew the odds were not nearly that good.

When the phone rang again he thought it would be Grace once more, even though there was no reason for her to redial the number.

North Idaho Wildlife Rescue. This is Bill.

Bill? the voice said. The voice of a man.

Bill Reed. Can I help you?

The voice hissed, a kind of sharp exhale. Bill Reed? That's rich.

There was something now, something in the voice, a texture or timbre or quality that came back to him all at once. Can I help you with something? he said again.

Shit, the man said, you don't recognize my voice? He added, hissing: *Bill Reed.*

I don't know. Should I? But already he was lying. Of course he recognized it. Of course he did.

I didn't think you'd forget.

Rick, he said.

Bingo.

You're out?

Yeah, twelve years later.

He was standing now, although he did not recall rising to his feet. I'm glad to hear it, he said, his hand gripping the receiver, the room around him sharp and bright and small.

Are you?

Sure I am. Why wouldn't I be?

The voice on the other side of the phone hissed again, that sharp exhale of breath. I tell you what you should be, he said. You should be pissing your pants. That's what you should be.

Why's that?

You know why.

A sharp tingling was radiating through his chest. What do you want? he said softly.

What do I want? To start with, I want my share.

Your share of what?

What the fuck? Rick said. You think I'm stupid? I want my fucking share.

He glanced around the room, the vinyl-paneled walls, the box of light streaming in through the dirty window. All right, he said at last. Give me your address.

It was silent for a moment, the line clicking and popping and hissing as if aflame. Then Rick said, I got a better idea. I'll come get it.

It's a long way. I'll just mail it.

There was a long moment of silence on the phone. Then Rick said, Your brother's name, Nat? That's what you picked?

Bill could think of nothing to say. His throat felt dry and his teeth were clenched tight together.

You'd better have it when I get there, Rick said, and then the line clicked into silence.

Bill slumped back into the chair, holding the phone in his outstretched hand. The space heater hummed from across the room. After a time he set the receiver down, his eyes on the dust motes that spun in the air before him, their golden whorls like fingerprints suspended in the slashing light. His teeth ached from clenching them and his chest buzzed as if filled with insects.

When he stepped outside, Bess was walking toward him. I'm off to the school, she said.

He waved a hand in her direction, walking on past the grizzly enclosure, where Majer stood watching him, and the wolf enclosure, which appeared empty as always, and up to the perimeter fence and through the gate. The day had begun cold and the rising sun had hardly diminished its sharp edge, perhaps not quite freezing now but still frosting his breath upon the air. A hint of snow somewhere across the mountains. The path running from the gate to his trailer farther up the hill was cut through with the same slashed light as the office he had stepped out of, as if those shapes had come with him, trailing some filament of meaning he could not decipher even were he to try, a turning of worlds, a history of fingerprints and shadow and thin cold air.

The interior of the trailer a dark and curtained space. His worn sofa. The bed, covered in its tattered blue blanket. A few spy novels and some reference material from the office down the hill beyond the birch path.

It had rested on the floor of the closet for all these years, so long now that he had ceased thinking about it at all, even though he knew, of course he knew, that there was a chance it might one day be important again. Grace had asked him once what it was, why the squat black safe was in the trailer at all. She asked him what it held and he told her that it had been his uncle David's and that it was empty. He knelt before it now and pulled it forward, out of the tiny closet, tilting it over the vinyl lip on the floor and walking it, corner by corner, out into the room. Not quite so heavy as he remembered and yet still significant as he slid it into the kitchen, its base scratching furrows into the linoleum. More than anything he wished he had simply left it behind. That such a thing could hold fast to him, its voice a faint cry ever calling a name he knew now would be impossible for him to forget.

4

THE BUZZING WAS A FLY CAUGHT BETWEEN THE CURTAIN and the window glass. Nat listened to the *tap tap* of its body as it ricocheted over and over against that lit pane, his head's throbbing coming in concert with his pulse and with each pump of his heart his stomach seemed to flip with nausea. He reached for the curtain and waved it gently and the fly rattled against the glass once more and then found the opening in the slider and disappeared into the cold bright day.

The clock read two thirty. A little past. The cigarette burning down to a stub between his fingers. Through a gap in the curtain he could see a black sedan moving over the speed bump in the parking lot below, the slab of its hood rising and falling again. Farther down the row of parked cars, a bare-armed man in a flannel shirt with torn-off sleeves walked slowly away until he was out of sight.

He had been waiting for Rick and Susan to come out of his bedroom for more than an hour now but he knew they too would likely be hungover and he did not know if they would come out of the bedroom at all. He might leave for work without ever seeing them, a thought that brought a slow wave of disappointment. He had been waiting for thirteen months for Rick to emerge from one door and now he waited for Rick—and for Susan—to emerge from another.

The phone's ringing jolted him out of his thoughts and he rose and stumbled back to the Formica counter that separated the kitchen from the tiny living room. Hello, he croaked into the handset.

Nat?

He exhaled, already lamenting that he had answered. Hello, Mrs. Harris, he said.

Hi there, honey. How are you?

I'm fine.

Did Ricky get out?

He's out. I picked him up last night.

He didn't call me. He was supposed to call me.

We were out pretty late. You know how it is.

He still needs to call his mom.

I know.

Rick's mother began to cough, the sound sharp and hard through the plastic grill of the phone. How are you doing? he said when it was done.

Comes and goes. I have some new medicine. I don't know if it works or not. The doctor doesn't seem to know his ass from a hole in the ground. Her voice was weak and far away now. Can you put Ricky on the phone?

How about I have him call you as soon as he's up.

She coughed briefly. Then she said, simply, Don't forget.

I won't.

Promise?

I promise.

You're a good boy, Nathaniel. I'm glad you were the one Ricky became friends with.

Well, so am I, he said.

I remember when we first came into town. On that very first day.

Look . . . um . . . I was just . . . He fumbled for a reason, then said, I really have to get ready for work.

Oh, I'm sorry, honey. I'm just talking on and on.

I'll tell him you called.

She said good-bye in a voice utterly deflated of attention or enthusiasm and he set the phone back into its plastic cradle. His head still throbbed. He knew Rick's mother would call back repeatedly over the course of several days until she actually managed to get Rick on the phone but even this felt normal to him now, felt like a return to the way things had been.

Good morning.

He looked up to where Susan was just coming out of the hall. She wore one of his own T-shirts, her legs bare and long below its black hem.

Morning, he said. He had not pulled on his jeans but he did so now, and then the T-shirt from the night before, both from a crumpled pile next to the tattered and unraveling sofa.

When he rounded the counter she was bent over, staring into the open door of the refrigerator, pink panties fully visible. You guys need some OJ, she said.

For sure, he said.

She stood and closed the door.

His eyes snapped to her face. Rick still asleep?

Yeah. She looked at him now. You boys can't hold your liquor.

I don't think it was the liquor.

Same thing.

You look like you're feeling all right.

Like I said, you boys can't hold your liquor. She was opening cabinets now, one after another. Don't you have any coffee?

I don't think so. Percolator doesn't work anyway. Rick melted the cord.

No instant or anything?

Sorry.

She looked for a moment like she did not know what to do next, hand lingering on the faucet. Bum a smoke? she said at last.

He handed her the pack and she took one and he turned the burner on and she leaned in to light the cigarette, her head below him, hair a tangled nest where it had rested in sleep.

She came up drawing on the cigarette and then exhaled, the first puff swirling inside itself like a tiny whirlpool. Thanks, she said. She settled on one of the barstools at the Formica counter and sat staring around the room.

What do you do here all day? she said into the silence.

Me?

Who else?

He shrugged. Watch TV. Play Atari.

You got any weed?

I wish.

You need to go shopping. No OJ. No coffee. No weed. I'm going back to bed.

When she turned off the stool he said, Hey, where were you yesterday anyhow?

Yesterday when?

When we were gonna go pick up Rick. I waited for you but you didn't show up.

Just got busy. That's all. Probably just missed you.

He stood looking at her there, her eyes ringed with shadow, the cigarette in her hand. The T-shirt she wore had been purchased as a souvenir when he and Rick drove out to Reno from Battle Mountain for the Rush show at the Coliseum. A man leaning away from a five-pointed star. The band's name in rainbow colors above it. Rick had been obsessed with the band's then-new album, *Moving Pictures*, blasting it from a portable boom box that lay upon his lap as Nat drove them around Battle Mountain in the Datsun, often rewinding to play the cassette's first song, "Tom Sawyer," over and over again, the guitars and drums distorting from the tiny speakers. The show had been the first full-blown concert either of them had ever seen and it felt as if it had permanently altered something in both of them, not the music or the show but the whole of it: the drive to Reno, just the two of them, feeling as if they had burst through into some dream of the adult world that Nat, at least, had never even imagined could be real. With it came the understanding that there were places outside that ring of bare treeless hills so that when they returned from that first trip he could feel the constant tug of the long strip of highway that fled west through Winnemucca and on to the city. Even now every time he heard that song, a thin whip of anticipation cracked through him. Modern-day warrior. Mean mean pride.

Now here was the T-shirt on Susan, her nipples poking the fabric at the edges of the star.

All right, he said at last. Just wondered what happened.

She continued to stand there, not speaking, watching him.

What? he said.

That thing, she said. That's still just between us, right? I mean, you're not thinking of telling anyone about it.

I'm not. I wouldn't.

Good, she said. There was no humor or friendliness in her voice now, just a cold clarity, and before he could think of anything to say in response she turned and he was left to watch her recede down the hall, the shirt's black fabric pulling against her bare pale skin.

*   *   *

RICK FINALLY appeared two hours later, materializing from the bathroom with hair dark and wet from the shower, dressed in a T-shirt and black jeans, his eyes bruised with exhaustion. Susan was gone by then, had been gone for nearly an hour. She had said nothing to Nat as she passed through the room and out the door, did not even acknowledge that he was there at all.

Back from the dead, Nat said from the sofa.

I'm not sure about that yet.

Feelin' it?

Shit, I haven't even had a beer in thirteen months. You?

Like a truck ran me over.

You see Susan leave?

Yeah. Like an hour ago.

Shit, I must have really been asleep, Rick said. Hey, thanks for letting us use your bedroom.

No problem.

You're gonna have to wash the sheets.

Kinda figured.

Rick smiled briefly, an expression that became a yawn. What's for breakfast? he said, slumping onto the stool by the kitchen counter.

There's no food.

Why not?

Ran out.

Shit, Rick said. No cereal or anything?

Nope.

You got any cash? I've been dreaming of Landrum's for thirteen months.

Probably a little, Nat said. He had been watching a Channel 5 documentary on the lions of the Serengeti Plain. The big yellow cats had come down to a muddy watering hole in an increasingly bare and cracked desert wasteland. A small herd of water buffalo stood warily in the pool, their tails twitching like the tails of cattle, white birds riding on their smooth black backs. He turned the volume knob until it clicked and the animals became a bright white star and then were gone altogether.

Your mom called, he said.

How'd she sound?

Tired.

I need to call her, Rick said. Nat thought he might have a cigarette first but he settled onto a stool at the kitchen counter and lifted the handset and dialed the number. A moment later he said, Hey Mom. Yeah I'm out. Feels great. How are you doing? There was a softness in his voice now, a quiet care.

Nat stood and lit another cigarette on the stovetop and then opened the slider and exited into the low sunlight heralding the end of the day.

The patio was a simple railed platform that looked down on the farther reaches of the parking lot with its bare trees and dead strips of grass and the colorless stucco expanse of the building itself where rows of matching patios floated in the faintly humming air. He stood and smoked, leaning down over the parked cars. Through the slider came a few snatches of Rick's telephone conversation until he turned and slid the door closed and the sound was gone.

He had smoked his cigarette down to the nub when the sliding glass door opened behind him and Rick stepped out onto the patio, his own cigarette held between thumb and index finger as was his habit.

How is she? Nat said.

Fucked up. His voice was quiet and when Nat looked over at him he realized that Rick had been crying, his eyes dry now but red and ringed with dark circles.

She'll be all right, Nat said.

I don't know, man. She sounds tired out.

You wanna take a trip out there?

Yeah, I think so.

We could go this weekend, maybe.

I'd have to talk to my parole officer about it first.

Really?

Yeah. And I need a job. Like right now.

We can swing by the dealership. The guy who hires is in until five or six.

That would be good.

You should wear a tie.

Rick was silent for a moment and then he said, Maybe we should go tomorrow then.

That's all the parole guy needs you to do?

Yeah, and to make sure I'm not doing shit they don't want me to do.

Like what?

Like pretty much everything we did last night.

Can they tell?

How could they tell?

I don't know.

Fuck no, they can't tell. He puffed the cigarette. Like piss in a cup or something?

How would I know?

Shit, Rick said. I didn't think about that. Shit. Maybe they *can* test for it. That would be just my luck, wouldn't it? Out for one fucking day.

I don't think they'll do that.

Maybe I should drink like ten gallons of water to flush my system out.

Probably wouldn't hurt.

Shit, Rick said again. Shit shit shit.

Nothing you can worry about now, Nat said.

But I am anyway, Rick said. I sure as shit am. Goddamn this day just keeps getting better and better.

A few rooms away, an old woman in a pink bathrobe stood smoking and waved her cigarette at them. Rick nodded to her. New girlfriend? he said.

Something like that.

They stood in silence for a time, puffing smoke into the late afternoon. Below them a young couple exited a car, laughing, and then disappeared into one of the first-floor apartments. Rick stood leaning out over the rail, his hair shorter than Nat had ever seen it but all else the same. He kept circling that thought. That everything was the same. That everything would be the same once again.

Why are you staring at me, man? You're freaking me out.

Sorry, he said, looking away across the parking lot. I'm glad you're back.

Not as glad as I am, Rick said.

What was it like in there?

Just about like you'd imagine.

I'm not sure how I'd imagine it.

I tell you what, he said. You could take everyplace you ever go—

Grady's and the Zephyr and your work and the apartment and even Battle Mountain—and maybe those are the only places you ever *will* go, I mean in your whole life. But if someone put a fence around them all and made them the only places you *could* go, then the whole thing flips on you. He took a drag on the cigarette. It's the possibilities, man, he said, exhaling smoke. They take away your choices. That's what it comes down to. You just got no choices at all.

Nat nodded. He could think of nothing to say, in part because what Rick had said did not sound so different from how his own life had felt since Rick was gone, and perhaps since long before that.

So who moved into the old apartment? Rick said.

Don't know.

You want to try to get another double?

I got three months' lease on this one yet.

Three months?

Three months.

Shit. What's this one cost?

Two hundred.

Well, that's better at least. So I gotta come up with a hundred in, what, like three weeks?

You don't have to do that. I mean, not in three weeks.

Rick said nothing in response, his eyes casting out across the parking lot, the apartment building, the parking lot again. More cars trundled through as day-shift workers returned to their dingy apartments, others pulling out of the lot and onto Fourth Street to start their workday or to continue it or to clock in at a second job. Day shift at a restaurant. Night shift at a casino or hotel. Perhaps the other way around. Nat had held down his job at the dealership shop for more than a year now. It seemed hard to believe. He had thought of trying to get a second job when Rick went to prison if only to fill all the hours that remained but he never had and now that Rick was back he knew those hours would fill themselves.

You ready for eats?

Starving, Rick said. He flicked his cigarette out into the parking lot beyond and Nat did the same. The woman in the pink robe waved to them again.

That really is your girlfriend, isn't it?

Maybe, Nat said. You know how I love the toothless ones.

Rick giggled and they returned to the living room, Nat closing the slider behind them and locking it. The apartment had darkened, the sun's disappearance behind the mountains plunging the rooms into shadow. Their coats were both draped over the chair near the door where they had landed when the three of them stumbled back into the apartment from the bars. He could remember Grady's and the 715 Club and Bishop's. At some point he must have driven them back to the apartment in the Datsun but most of the night's events had fallen into a dull haze of static and the return itself was utterly blank.

It was exactly when they turned out of the apartment that Nat saw the man coming up the stairs from the parking lot. He was backlit by the low sun, his body a dark, heavy-shouldered mass, but Nat knew it was Mike, his leather loafers thumping up the stairs as the sun played on the flat surface of his buzz cut.

And there he is, Mike said, his voice upbeat, almost jubilant.

Hey, Nat said. I was just gonna call you.

Yeah? Mike said. Now you don't have to. He smiled, eyes squinting. Who's your friend?

He was just . . . uh . . . going out, Nat said.

What? Rick said. He looked from Nat to Mike and back again and then said, Who are you?

Name's Mike. Let's go back inside.

We're headed to get some grub, Rick said.

You can do that in a minute.

Nat stood there in the doorway, not speaking, not moving, his chest a tight blaze of heat.

What's this about? Rick was looking at Mike, but it was Nat who answered him.

Just some business, Nat said. There was a tremor in his voice.

Nathaniel and I need to have a talk, Mike said. Maybe you wanna wait outside?

I'm not waiting outside, Rick said.

I think you. Mike's voice was calm and clear and tinged with the faintest sense of ebullience, as if he was glad to be of service in this way, or in any way at all.

Nat? Rick said. What the fuck is this?

This is already taking too long, Mike said.

All right, Nat said. He stepped backward through the door and Mike followed him, Rick trailing behind, the three of them entering the apartment and then standing in a kind of shadowy tableau, Rick in the still-open doorway, Nat near the sofa, and Mike between them.

That an Atari there? Mike said.

Yeah, Nat said.

What do those cost?

I don't know, Nat said. We got it in a trade.

What kind of trade?

I don't know, Nat said.

You don't know?

I can't remember.

Mike stepped forward and in one quick, almost graceful movement slammed his fist into Nat's stomach and then turned to face Rick, who was already moving forward those few last feet across the room. Don't, Mike said. This is business.

What the fuck does that mean? he said, standing now just a few inches from Mike's face. Get the fuck out of here.

Rick, Nat said, doubled over, still trying to catch his breath. It's OK.

What the fuck it's OK? Rick said. And then, to Mike, again: Get the fuck out of here.

Don't do that, Mike said.

I'll do anything the fuck I want. Who the fuck are you?

I'm Mike. Maybe you need to wait out in the hall like I asked you to.

Fuck you, Rick said, but the end of the word was clipped off by the strike of Mike's fist in his side. The blow had come without apparent physical precedent and with such speed that Rick seemed merely to stagger backward of his accord, slipping toward the doorway. In the next moment Mike's hand came forward and pressed him, almost gently, through that aperture and out onto the concrete platform that topped the stairs, swinging the door closed with his foot and locking the deadbolt.

Please don't hit me again, Nat said. I'll get it. I've almost got it.

Rick's fists were banging on the door now, his voice calling Nat's name over and over, the sound of it muffled through the wood.

My god that guy's irritating, Mike said. Look, you're gonna have to give me something.

Like what?

I'm not leaving empty-handed, Mike said.

I'm tapped out, Nat said.

Didn't you get paid last week?

Yeah, but it wasn't a good week.

Ah shit, Mike said, exhaling. What did I tell you last time?

Not to miss a payment, Nat said, but I'm not going to miss it. I'm just a little late. That's all. The hammering had stopped now and in the silence Nat could hear his own heart beating as if the distant echo of Rick's fists on the wooden door. I'm trying, Mike, Nat said. I really really am. I promise.

You promise? I'm pretty sure you promised last time. Johnny doesn't like excuses.

I know, I know, Nat said. He had straightened up now. His stomach felt loose and flabby, as if the muscles there had given up and were now hanging loose from his ribs. Look, you can take the Atari? OK? Will that work for right now?

What am I gonna do with that?

I don't know, he said. Pawn it. Or take it home.

Mike stood looking at him. What kind of games you got?

It came with Space Invaders. We got Pitfall and Frogger.

Pitfall's the one where you're jumping over those ponds and snakes and shit?

Yeah.

That's pretty fun, right?

I like it.

He seemed to consider for a moment. Both joysticks?

Yeah.

All right. Unplug it and put it in a paper bag, he said. But this is just a delay. I'm telling you, Nathaniel, if you knew the shit I had to do, you wouldn't be late with a payment. Not ever.

I know, Nat said.

No you don't, Mike said. He stood there for a moment in the doorway and then reached into his pocket and extracted a pack of Parliaments. You want a smoke? he said.

Yes please, Nat said.

He held up the pack and Nat took a cigarette and then was handed a silver Zippo upon which was engraved a skull surrounded by roses. The instrument weighed heavy in his hand and the flame it produced seemed to dance everywhere before him but he managed to get the cigarette lit and drew upon its smoke as if it were cool clean air.

You get that thing unhooked for me, OK? Mike said.

Nat turned and slid the television away from the wall and jerked the little tabs from their screws and then pulled the small game box forward, its four toggle switches shining in the grim slanting light. He wrapped the cables around its body and then went to the kitchen and hunted for a paper sack and was relieved to find one pressed between the refrigerator and the cabinets and he loaded that bag with the Atari and the two joysticks and then the game cartridges. His hands had stopped shaking now and his breath curled in white smoke before him.

What's this place cost? Mike asked.

Two hundred.

That seems like a lot for such a shitty little apartment, Mike said, and then added: No offense.

It's what they cost now, Nat said. The one we had before was three fifty.

Jesus, Mike said. That's just robbery.

Nat handed him the paper bag and he took it.

Why don't you make sure your friend isn't going to coldcock anyone when I come through the door, Mike said.

Nat unlocked the door and opened it, the cigarette held in his hand. Rick stood on the landing under the darkening sky. Somewhere he had found a small length of metal pipe and he stood there brandishing it like a stubby baseball bat. What the fuck? he said.

You gotta put that down, Nat said.

What the fuck is going on, man?

Just put it down. You're gonna make this a lot worse. His voice cracked at these words and he realized that he was on the verge of bursting into an agony of tears.

Jesus Christ, man, Rick said. He did not drop the pipe but he stepped back a few feet and stood there at the edge of the stairs. Down the walkway, a man leaned forward against the rail in a white sleeveless T-shirt smoking a cigarette, watching them impassively.

Nat tried to say something more but no words would come and he clenched his teeth tight against his own shuddering breath.

Mike stood behind him in the doorway, his presence all but filling it. Why don't you two head on down the stairs, he said.

What the fuck? Rick said again.

He did not move until Nat arrived at his side and then both of them, together, began to descend, Rick holding the short black pipe erect in the glowing air.

Toss me the keys so I can lock up, Mike said from the top of the stairs.

Nat paused, Rick looking at him. Then he fished the keys out of his pocket and threw them, underhanded, to where Mike stood in the doorway. The man exited the apartment and closed the door and locked it and then turned and tossed the keys back to Nat, midway down the stairs. You gentlemen have a nice evening, Mike said.

Neither of them made a sound in response. Instead, they continued their descent, Rick still holding the length of pipe even as they reached the parking lot and Nat unlocked the battered Datsun and they both slid inside, Nat puffing on the cigarette as he started the car and pulled them out onto Fourth Street at last.

What the fuck was that, man?

I owe some money.

To who?

Johnny Aguirre.

Johnny Aguirre? Are you fucking serious?

He did not answer. The road before them was cast under a sky the color of burnished metal.

Jesus Christ, Rick said. Jesus fucking Christ. Johnny Aguirre? Fuck me. What kind of money are we talking about?

A grand.

Jesus Christ, Rick said. He lifted the pipe as if to smash it against the dashboard but instead swung it back and forth in the air and finally set it on the floorboards at his feet. Then he leaned forward and depressed the car's cigarette lighter with a faint click. What happened?

They were already thick in the casinos, their lit facades towering over the car, all in flashing lights and colored signs. Harold's on one side and the Silver Dollar on the other, between which hung the arched sign proclaiming Reno the Biggest Little City in the World. They had driven under that sign when they first came out from Battle Mountain for the concert, and it had seemed a magic archway into some other world. Now he had driven under it a thousand times on his way to and from work, driven this way even though there were certainly other paths he could have taken, paths with less traffic, but the sign and that strip of casinos along Virginia Street still seemed to hold some power over him, over them both, the rotating metal star above the four yellow octagons that held the letters R-E-N-O shining its way into some universe that he had not known or was even possible, their dreams always a kind of abstraction: a way out of Battle Mountain, a way out of the cupped sagebrush desert of their lives.

And it had actually worked out that way for a while. Even though they never had any money and struggled each month just to pay the rent, it still felt like some kind of grand adventure. And yet he also knew, had known almost from the start, that it could not be the actual destination. It was like visiting a theme park or being on some kind of semipermanent vacation where reality could be forgotten but only for a moment. Even encased in that small brightly lit world that was forgetting, he knew somehow that another life reverberated in the darkness beyond the blazing casino lights, a darkness brought flat black and featureless by the glare.

I don't know, Nat said. His heart was still racing from Mike's visit but his voice was steady now. At least he had that much. I was playing blackjack. And I was up, I mean way up. And then I just started losing.

He stopped talking then and in the gap of silence the cigarette lighter popped and Rick took it and lit the bent cigarette in his mouth and drew upon it, the tip glowing bright and fierce for a brief moment like an orange star. Then what?

Well, I saw Johnny Aguirre there and I thought, you know, that maybe I could get a few hundred to try to win back what I lost.

You dumb fuck.

Thanks a lot, Nat said.

What the fuck were you thinking?

I was thinking that I had to pay the rent and that I'd need to eat. That's what I was thinking.

Christ.

Yeah, no shit.

So he gave you a thousand dollars?

No, he gave me three hundred. And I lost that but I made a couple of payments and so he loaned me three hundred more and then another five about a month later.

What the fuck, man? If I knew that I would've taken it easy last night. We probably blew through a hundred bucks.

It was your first night back.

You can't spend money you don't got, Rick said.

Seemed important.

It wasn't.

Nat shrugged.

What are you gonna do?

I don't know, Nat said. Hopefully I can get something together. I got two weeks. Maybe my boss will give me an advance on my paycheck or something.

His pulse continued to throb, a wild, galloping rhythm, and what flooded into him now was the abrupt and rushing desire to pull into a vacant parking spot and enter one of the big casinos that slid everywhere across the Datsun's windows, a desire that was surprising only because it made him realize, in the same moment, that he had somehow stopped circling that desire for several days, that it had simply evaporated from him as the date for Rick's release approached and finally arrived. But for nearly every day of Rick's absence from his life—most of those thirteen months—he had found himself focusing all day upon the moment his shift at the dealership would end and he could enter one of those vast carpeted rooms with their jangling slot machine bells, the pervasive odor of sweat and ammonia overlaying everything like a freshly cleaned locker room, time slipping out from under him so that the only thing that mattered was the possibility of the next card or the next pull on the slot machine's handle and the weird feeling that he was somehow in control flowing through him from everywhere at once. He knew that it was absurd to want to gamble right after Mike's visit but he could not shake that desire, optimism and despair riding upon him in equal measure like some dark skeleton the bones of which overlapped his own.

LANDRUM'S WAS not much bigger than the living room of the apartment they now shared, a prefabricated rectangle like a curved art deco boxcar, with room for eight stools along its counter. The cook and server was an older woman with orange hair whose face was perpetually caked with makeup, a ring of bright red smearing her sour wrinkled lips. She peered at them owlishly as they entered. It was rare to find any open stools but there were two open at the counter now and they slid onto them and ordered and the orange-haired woman turned away from them to resume cooking. Around them a few bleary-eyed locals sat eating and smoking and drinking sodas. Nat and Rick had sometimes come to the tiny restaurant at two or three in the morning to find it packed, a small crowd of nighthawks lingering outside with their winking cigarettes, high on cocaine and pot and beer, their eyes alternately blazing and sunken in, depending on which side of the evening they were riding. Once, when Rick was in prison, Nat had driven by during a break from work and had seen Susan standing out front, her arm around some man Nat did not recognize, the man's hand on her ass. He had thought about that for a long time, had even thought of asking her about it but never had.

Rick hardly stopped talking as they waited for the food. He asked Nat what movies he had seen and then told him a story from prison, the story of an inmate named Tiny who had seen a movie where Paul Newman had eaten fifty hard-boiled eggs. It had become the talk of the prison—although Rick could not recall the name of the actual film—and eventually someone had convinced the warden to allow a hard-boiled-egg-eating competition in the cafeteria. Tiny had boasted that he could beat Newman's record, if it even was a record, but only reached three dozen eggs before entering into a bout of vomiting so severe that he had to be admitted to the prison hospital.

He didn't come out of that for like a week, Rick said, clapping his hands and rocking back on his stool with laughter.

Man, that's awful, Nat said. They had received their omelets midway through the story and Nat sat chewing a forkful, smiling.

His belly looked like an egg, Rick said, holding his arms out in front of him to demonstrate. I thought he was gonna blow up. Like that guy in that Monty Python movie.

Nat was laughing hard now and it was into this laughter than the man's voice came: a sharp, gruff sound.

You just get out?

They did not at first register that the voice was directed at them, or rather at Rick, but after a moment Nat looked down the counter to where a thin figure sat with a hamburger clenched in one fist, a man distinguished by the tattoos that swung in a tangle of black lines and blurred colors around his wiry arms.

Their laughter died out.

You mean me? Rick said.

Yep.

Yeah, I got out yesterday.

Congratulations.

Thanks, Rick said. He was still smiling.

What level?

Medium.

Lucky you.

Yeah I guess so, Rick said.

You guess so? the man said. He had not looked in their direction. Word of advice. Don't tell prison stories while people are trying to eat.

Rick chuckled a moment and then sat staring at him. Why's that? he said at last.

Medium was a walk in the fucking park, I guess?

Come on, buddy. I didn't mean nothin'. Just telling my friend a story.

A cage is a cage, he said. Nothing to laugh about.

It's just a story.

Just a story? What do you weigh? One fifty?

Something like that.

Something like that. Yeah. You know what that says to me? Says you were someone's bitch in there. Medium or not. That's what it says. Bitch in a cage.

Hey, look . . . , Nat said, but Rick was already off his stool.

You calling me a bitch? Is that what I heard?

The orange-haired woman was saying something from behind the counter now, calling to Rick first and then to the thin man, who still did not look up from his plate. Nat did not move from his seat, did not even set down his fork, instead seemed frozen there, watching them, the man's burger descending so slowly that it seemed to float at the nether end of an arm that appeared to be constructed entirely of coiled brown rope and smeared tattoos. On his forearm, Nat could read the word *Woods*. Just don't be making it seem like it's fun and games, he said.

Don't call me a fucking bitch, Rick said.

It's a cage, the man said.

And again: Don't call me a bitch.

A beat of silence. The man still did not turn, although the hamburger rested upon his plate now.

Then Rick said, Fuck you.

And now, at last, the man turned to look at him, to look at them both, his eyes drooping in his tight skull like the eyes of a hound, the skin around them like gray leather. You know what I think? the man said. I think you go eat your omelet and shut the fuck up before you get hurt. That's what I think.

Let's go, Nat said quietly.

Rick stood with his hands clenched at his sides. The room around them seemed frozen, the other few diners waiting for whatever was to come.

Let's go, Nat said again.

Rick shifted his weight slightly and took a first tentative step backward. Then another. Asshole, he said.

Watch out, little boy, the thin man said. He had returned to his hamburger now and sat chewing.

Rick stood for a moment longer and then turned and disappeared out the door. The entire exchange had not even taken a minute. Nat fumbled with his wallet and laid a few bills on the counter.

Your boy needs to be more careful, the man said, and when Nat did not respond he said, You hear me?

I hear you, Nat said then.

Your boy needs to be more careful.

No one was talking to you, Nat said, his voice quiet, as if even in saying it he hoped it would not be heard.

Do I need to teach you a goddamn lesson too? the man said.

Nat looked up at him but the man only stared down at his dinner plate, the hamburger held in his hand above a plate ringed by fries and spattered condiments.

We're leaving, Nat said.

I thought so, the man said.

Outside it had gone full dark, the sky a black slate without depth or dimension, the streetlight in front of Landrum's pooling a brief lit circle upon the sidewalk. Rick was already a few dozen yards away, moving up South Virginia Street toward the car and the long hopscotch of bars they had run too many times to count. Grady's. The 715 Club. Del Mar Station. The Zephyr. And Rick's favorite: the Grand Ballroom.

He jogged up the sidewalk to Rick, saying nothing, only walking next to him along the street in silence.

That guy was bullshit, Rick said at last.

For sure, Nat said.

I should go back there and kick his ass.

Well, maybe, Nat said. Don't forget you're on parole.

Fuck.

Plus, you probably wouldn't be able to eat there anymore if you started a fight.

I didn't start a fight, Rick said. That motherfucker started a fight. His pace was furious up the slow rise, moving past a dark yard beyond which a house sat with a faint yellow light burning in the window. A small dog yapped at them from somewhere within.

For no reason he could think of, Nat remembered the nature documentary he had seen on Channel 5 that afternoon. Even now there was a place where lions and water buffalo and white birds circled a muddy watering hole in the center of a vast undifferentiated plain. The animals eyed each other warily, the birds fluttering between the backs of the buffalo and the branches of a scraggly olive green tree that provided a few bars of shade under which the lions sat, watching the water, watching the buffalos, watching the birds.

I've got that pipe in the car, Rick said. You got anything in the trunk?

Like what?

I don't know. A fucking tire iron or something?

Really?

Yeah really. We already let some guy steal our fucking Atari, Rick said. I'm not gonna pussy out again. Not twice in one day. He was silent for a moment. They had reached the car and stood now beside it on the dark sidewalk. You got anything in the trunk or what? Rick said.

I think I got that old baseball bat in there still.

Well? Rick said.

Well what?

Unlock the car.

Nat did so and leaned through and unlocked the passenger door and Rick pulled the short length of steel pipe from the floorboards.

You're really gonna do this? Nat said.

Yeah, goddammit. He held the pipe in his fist and swung it from side to side. You in or not?

Nat stood looking at Rick and then looking down at the mote of light below. OK, he said at last.

That's what I'm talking about, Rick said. Just to put some scare into him. No one fucking talks to me like that. Not anymore.

Nat unlocked the trunk and indeed the baseball bat was there. Part of him had hoped the trunk would be empty, but the bat had been there since long before they even came to Reno, an innocent implement now made sinister, as if he had somehow stepped into someone else's story.

They leaned against the car then, smoking, silently watching the front of Landrum's where a bright wash of light flooded across the sidewalk. A couple of men stood and smoked in the glow, their shadows casting out toward the street. Beyond that small oasis there was nothing, as if everything south of the restaurant had dissolved, as if everything outside this tiny pocket of light had faded away and was gone.

There he is, Rick said.

The man had come out of the restaurant now, turning away from them, downhill along the sidewalk. At the sight of him, Rick flicked his cigarette and broke immediately into a run, Nat behind him, soundless but for their feet striking the concrete, their bodies crossing through that light and into the darkness beyond.

The man had not yet reached the next intersection when Rick caught up with him and did not seem to understand they were there even as Rick's pipe struck him across the back of his legs and he fell to the sidewalk like some cut-string marionette.

Motherfucker, Rick said. You don't fucking talk to me like that.

Rick moved forward as the man rolled away from him and staggered to his feet again, his legs bent weakly but his hands already up, open-palmed, Rick swinging the pipe back and forth. From where Nat stood the two bodies were backlit by the traffic light at the intersection, their halos red and then green again. Someone in a passing car howled, the sound of it echoing up the street.

You just fucked yourself, the man said.

I doubt that, Rick said. He lunged forward with the pipe, feinted, and then lunged again, and this time the man's fist whipped out and struck him full in the face. Rick stood there a moment, the pipe still clenched in his fist, and Nat thought that it might already be over. You stupid fuck, Rick said, and in the next instant he was advancing down the street again, walking towards the man and slashing with the pipe, the man dancing backwards and sideways, his body all ropy sinew and muscle, like an older, harder, more tattooed version of Rick himself, and when he stopped and changed direction, flashing forward all at once, Rick's motion was caught short and their silhouettes became entangled, the light turning red again as their twinned breath steamed the air like a pale cloud.

Nat had been following behind, holding the bat over his shoulder as if a baseball might come shuttling out of the dark toward him. It felt like a scene unfolding in a movie or a television show. And yet it was he who held the baseball bat and it was Rick before him who was caught now in some kind of choke hold. The man leaned back, Rick's feet nearly off the ground, and in the next moment the pipe tumbled free of Rick's grip and went ringing off the curb.

When he swung the bat it was without clear direction or thought. He brought it down at an angle and the man saw it at the final instant, turning away from the blow as the bat struck him in the long muscle of his lower back, the impact vibrating into Nat's clenched hands.

There was a long yowl of pain and Rick stumbled forward out of his grasp. Fuck fuck fuck, the man yelled.

Nat lifted the bat again, the man stumbling in a tight circle but always facing him, his teeth drawn tight in a hissing grimace. He might have swung but then Rick was at his side. Give it to me, he said, and Nat did so, and Rick came forward, holding it above his shoulder.

Yeah go ahead, faggot, the man said. Hit me with the fucking bat again. That's a fair fight. Come on tough guy.

When Rick swung, the man did not seem to understand at first what was happening, as if he believed that his words would end the fight, that Rick would simply turn and walk away. The bat struck him in the shoulder and this time he went down, sprawling onto the concrete of the sidewalk, his shadow a sharp arrow pointing up toward Nat as the light changed to green once again. And Rick swung and kept on swinging, the man arching, twisting in upon himself, his legs spinning in place as if he was pedaling a bicycle, and the sound he made was a long terrible moan.

Fuck you, Rick shouted, repeating it with each blow. Nat's own voice had become a long chain of syllables pulling out of him in the adrenaline rush—Whoa whoa whoa—his hands on Rick's shoulders, pressing him, trying to push him away, but Rick continuing to swing and kick and rage.

Stop, Nat said. The man was coughing and his exhaled breath contained within it a gurgling moan. Stop stop, Nat said. And then: Look at me.

And now Rick looked, looked from the man on the sidewalk to Nat. That's enough, Nat said.

Rick nodded and then looked back at the man one last time. The man did not move at all now, his shape curled into a tight ball, the tattoos that encircled his left arm seeming to dance up and down that path of flesh.

Don't let us see you again, motherfucker, Rick said.

The street seemed to have flooded somehow, seemed to be underwater, as if he was pressed up against a curved glass wall. An aquarium. A bubble. And yet everything clear and bright and clean and you are a fish the color of silver night, moving through it, moving up through the stones, through a current you cannot even feel.

After a few steps they were both jogging up the hill and when they reached the car again they were panting and Rick's grin was a bright white arc floating in the black air.

Christ almighty, Rick said, did you see how he fell?

The adrenaline that coursed through Nat's body was like electricity. Like fire. He could not feel if he was smiling or not.

Don't let anyone fuck with you, Rick said. That's one thing I learned inside. That goes for you too. Fucking Atari thieves can go fuck themselves.

Yeah, Nat said. He thought of Mike. Of the Atari they no longer owned. Then he thought of the muddy watering hole. The water buffalo. The little birds that rode upon their shoulders.

Goddamn, Rick said, there's nothing like a good fight to make you feel better about the world.

That's the truth, Nat said, although he had no idea what either of them were saying at all.

5

NOT A SINGLE TREE IN ALL THOSE ENDLESS MILES, NOT EVEN on the flanks of the mountains that rise above the desert floor in all directions, the road coming down from the west, descending Golconda Summit in a slow curve before slipping into a straight black line that shoots across the shadscale without deviation like the trace of a gunshot. It seems impossible that anyone would live in a place like this, a place without trees, but along the ruler line of the highway stand occasional homes that crouch in the dry and colorless dust as if hunching against the desert wind that blasts down the slope of that summit and into the flats. Whether those homes are abandoned or occupied it is impossible to tell.

When the town appears it is as if someone has taken a collection of such homes and gathered them into a grid a few miles wide. Humboldt and Broad and Main and Reese and Scott, across them the graph of numbered streets at the far edge of which rests a line of trailers and the blocky turquoise-painted Laundromat. The school is nearby, as are the three ponds, an area familiar to every child in the town as it becomes, with the start of Little League baseball season each year, a congregating point for bicycles and motorbikes, children and teens swooping and yelling and reeling everywhere. To the north, a short few blocks, is Front Street and along its length run Lemaire's, the Quick, the Pak-Out, the Happy Ox, known to all as the Queer Steer, and two weather-beaten casinos, their flat fronts situated side by side: the Owl Club and the Nevada Club. A few blocks east of the casinos sits the Shell station, its sign suspended atop two white poles high in the air, the lightbulbs illuminating the S perpetually burned out so that the message it sends in bright yellow letters across miles and miles of desert is an invitation to hell.

For a long time there is only the anonymity of quiet movement: paint-stripped cars adrift on dusty streets, a few sweating figures on the sidewalks in front of the casinos. But then there you are: a boy come racing through the afternoon light in an undulating swoop between lines of boxlike homes, the fences of which guard patches of yellow grass. It is the dead center of the hot summer of 1974 and you sit on the handlebars of a bicycle piloted by your brother and you are smiling.

Your father has been in the ground four years and your brother—seventeen now—has become your entire world. On the hottest days he takes you down to the river near the iron shape of the Black Bridge and you build forts from the willow branches and swim and catch frogs and fish. A few weeks ago the two of you rode inner tubes from that bridge to the next, a journey of only a few miles stretched into a day so long and glorious that you will remember it ever after as the one perfect day of all your life. Today he has ridden you on the handlebars of his bicycle to the corner store, Lemaire's. He bought you a candy bar as he picked up two packs of cigarettes, one for your mother and one for himself, and now you are riding back across town, again on the handlebars, your brother taking a long, looping route, up and down streets lined with the worn and beaten homes of kids you know from school and the empty shell of what was once the town's only movie theater. You miss being in that giant dark room with your brother beside you. It did not even matter what film was playing. *Escape from the Planet of the Apes. Bedknobs and Broomsticks. Robin Hood.* One time he took you to see a movie called *Magnum Force*, telling you it had to be a secret. He was excited to see it

and his excitement made you excited as well but in the warm dark space
of the theater you grew bored and closed your eyes and drifted off to
sleep. When you woke, it was to your brother shaking you softly and calling you by the nickname he had used since before you could remember:
Hey, Champaign. Wake up, buddy. Movie's over. You will remember
that feeling for the rest of your life: that you are in exactly the place you
are meant to be. You wonder now if you will ever feel that way again.

When the bicycle chain breaks you nearly come off the front of the
handlebars. Bill shouts, Whoa! as you coast to a stop.

You jump down. What happened?

Chain slipped, he says. He looks down and then steps off the bike.

You hold the handlebars and he kneels. Dang, he says. Chain *broke*.
He emphasizes this second word, so sharp is his sense of surprise.

Can you fix it? you say.

I don't know. I hope so. He stands, looks up and down the street as
if a bicycle repairman might be within his field of vision.

You are only four dusty blocks from the trailers and so Bill lets you
ride on the seat as he pushes the bicycle, sometimes hurling the machine
forward so that you can pilot it in its long coast to a standstill.

The trailers are arrayed in two short rows in the dry and colorless
dust, each ringed with a variety of household goods like debris washed
up from some ancient inland ocean: abandoned sofas and broken cars,
discarded air conditioning units, bent and unusable folding chairs.
Some hold to stretches of brief and haggard fencing wrapping an idea
of yard filled with the broken stubble of dead grass. Many have ramshackle stairs leading up to their front doors, and all of them, each
and every one, peel and rust and bake under the summer sun and the
seemingly endless hot wind blowing down from Golconda Summit to
the west.

You are walking beside the bike now, Bill pushing it forward across
the dirt beside the road. It is then that you see him: a boy of about your
age who looks up at you as Bill upends the bike in the dust, its wheels
hanging in the air like twin zeros. Sweet bike, he says.

It was, Bill says, turning toward the trailer.

Chain broke, you say.

Bummer. The boy wears a bright blue T-shirt with a rubbery soccer ball iron-on that looks hot and damp in the summer heat. A red bandanna is wrapped around his forehead, most of it covered by dark shaggy hair that falls in wild curls nearly to his eyes.

Your brother has disappeared inside the trailer now and you and the boy say nothing while you stand waiting for him, both of you staring at the bike. When Bill reappears a few moments later, he is lugging the heavy red toolbox that had been your father's.

That's a cool bike, Rick says to him again.

Yeah, thanks, Bill says. He is already kneeling in the dust and has clicked open the toolbox but he looks up at Rick now. You new around here?

Yeah, we just got here.

Moving into Mrs. Brown's?

Who's Mrs. Brown?

That one, Bill says, pointing to the trailer.

Oh, yeah, Rick says. Me and my mom and dad.

I'm Bill, he says and he puts his hand out and the boy shakes it briefly. This is Nat.

You nod, wondering if you and the boy should shake hands as well but the boy only nods and says, Cool, and then turns his attention back to the bike.

Bill has pulled the chain loose and squats there upon the dry earth, staring at where the links have broken free.

Hey, uh, Bill, Rick says, can I bum a smoke?

Bill looks up at him, squinting at the new kid through a tousle of thick brown hair bleached almost blond by the summer sun. Heck, no, you cannot bum a smoke, he says.

Come on, man, Rick says. I'm out.

How old are you?

Thirteen.

Bill looks at him. No way.

Am too.

What year were you born?

Nineteen . . .

Bill waits, smiling, and then says, Yeah that's what I thought. How old are you?

Twelve.

Twelve?

Almost twelve.

How old are you now, Champaign? Bill says.

Same, Nat says. Almost twelve.

Bill chuckles.

Oh come on, the new boy says. When'd you start smoking?

Maybe I never started smoking, Bill says. That shit'll kill you.

Life'll kill you.

Where'd you hear that?

Just made it up.

Sure you did. Bill makes a sound, an exhalation that is like a tire losing air. No sale, kid, he says.

Shoot. I had to try.

And you did. Bill swivels around to look at you. This is gonna take a while. You might as well go find something to do.

The disappointment shows on your face. We were gonna go to the gravel ponds, you say.

Yeah, I don't think that's gonna happen, he says. Maybe tomorrow. I gotta figure out how to fix this thing.

Dang, you say.

Maybe you can show this guy the sights. Take him on back to Lemaire's and get a Coke or something.

Can I have a dollar? you say.

Jesus, it's like the mob, Bill says, but he reaches into his pocket and hands over a dollar.

OK. You turn to Rick now: You wanna come?

Heck yeah I wanna come, Rick says. Then, to Bill, Nice to meet you. He extends his hand again.

Yeah sure, nice to meet you too, kid, Bill says. He wipes his hand on his jeans and they shake. Bill is smiling as if the whole thing is completely absurd. Stay out of trouble, he says as you turn to walk away, the new boy, Rick, at your side.

All right, you call back.

I wasn't talking to you, Bill says.

You half turn and wave the dollar. Rick continues to walk, as if he already knows the way, stumping through the weeds and thistle that gap the asphalt and concrete as if it represents some forgotten and unused path. Occasionally he kicks a can or a bottle into the air, an action that seems somehow miraculous. Metal shining in the sun. The sparkle of green glass. Things made free.

IT HAD been, for four years, just you and Bill, fatherless, sharing the bedroom at the back of the trailer, sleeping next to each other in the twin beds, a scant aisle of floor space between you, your mother sleeping most often in the old green recliner in the equally tiny living room where, on Sunday nights, you and her and Bill would watch Marlin Perkins wrestle with wildlife on *Mutual of Omaha's Wild Kingdom*.

But now there is Rick and it is different somehow: not an older brother or a father figure but a friend, a real friend. The two of you are inseparable from that first moment in the dust by the broken bicycle, crisscrossing town every day, exploring its edges, its interstices, sometimes walking far out into the sagebrush wilderness that lines the settlement on all sides, Rick taking you farther than you ever would have gone on your own. Out there in the flats, you see coyotes, rabbits, kangaroo rats. Sometimes you bring along the book you were given by your uncle, *Wildlife of the Intermountain West*, and use it to give names to the thistle and scrub, all the while Rick in motion, his engine miraculous, so full of energy it can hardly be believed. Even during that first year you wonder how he keeps going and you wonder why. He is every-where at once. Later you will realize that his motion had been that of an animal probing a fence for weakness.

At night you will sometimes hear Rick's father's voice through the walls of their trailer, your window cracked open, your child's ear listening to the roar. Close the window, Champaign, your brother will call from his thin mattress across the room. That's Rick's dad? you will ask. Yeah, Bill will say, but you don't need to listen to that. Trust me. It's better to not have a dad at all if that's what he's going to do. And you will wonder if such a statement can be true. Your own father was a truck driver and was gone more often than he was home. It has only been four years but you sometimes have difficulty remembering much about him at all.

Sometimes the noise from Rick's trailer will end with the door crashing open and the sound of a car starting and then that car blasting off the gravel and onto the asphalt and screeching away. The following day Rick will not tell you what happened, not ever, but you know that Rick's father hits him sometimes, hits him and hits his mother as well, a fact you will learn only by accident when you playfully slap Rick on the back and his response is to howl in pain, his back covered in a patch-work of purple bruises.

But all of that—the yelling and the beatings and the screeching away of the car in the dark of the night—all of it ends soon after you learn of Rick's bruises, for Rick's father simply drives away in the family car one night not long after dinnertime and does not return, not to the trailer and not, Bill tells you later, to his job at the Duval mine. He is simply gone. You try once to ask Rick about it but in response Rick only tells you that his father had to go do some work stuff out of town, that he will return, that his absence is only tem-porary. So that becomes both the story and the waiting game, Rick believing—or at least telling you that he believes—that his father will return at any moment. You have no reason to argue with him even though Bill has told you Rick's father is not likely to return to Battle Mountain at all, not after what he has done. What did he do? you ask him but Bill only says, Maybe when you're older, Champaign, and will tell you no more.

DURING THE bicentennial summer your brother takes you and Rick shooting for the first time. You are thirteen now. Your brother has a rifle, an old Savage 99 lever action, and Rick is able to borrow his absentee father's .38 Special from his mother so there are two weapons between the three of you. Your brother takes you out into the sagebrush country, much farther than you have ever been able to explore on foot, and you set up some cans on a rock and Bill teaches you and Rick how to hold the guns, how to check to see if they are loaded, how to sight, how to squeeze the trigger. You will never get accustomed to the sound—each time you wince—but you love the way a can jumps when hit, the sound like a baseball bat striking a metal plate.

Hoo man, Rick says. You nailed that one.

Bill smiles. You're up, Nat, he says.

You stand and take the rifle and aim and squint and squeeze the trigger.

It'll be easier to hit if you keep your eyes open, Bill says.

They just kinda close automatically, you say. You squeeze the trigger and again your eyes squint closed but not all the way this time, the light there a sliver as the firearm barks in your grip.

My turn, Rick says.

Hang on a minute, your brother says. He'll get it.

Shoot, Rick says.

And you aim again and hold your eyes open and miss but this time you know that you were close to hitting your mark and with the next shot the can twangs off the rocks, the sound of it loud and metallic.

Hey! Rick says, clapping his hands together.

There you go, Champaign, Bill says. He has been drinking beer all afternoon and you can see the gloss of it in his eyes and in the roughness of his hand as he claps you on the shoulder.

I can't believe I finally hit the dumb thing.

Just gotta keep your eye on the ball, he says.

It is when you are returning from that trip that you come upon the hawk. It hops in the dust just beside the roadbed. You think at first that it must be capturing some prey—a kangaroo rat or a grasshopper mouse—and you expect it to fly away at the approach of the truck but it does not, only struggling there in the dirt.

Check it out, Rick says, pointing.

Red-tailed hawk, you say.

Bill has already slowed the pickup and draws it to a stop and the three of you step out of the truck again. The hawk still does not fly, instead hopping beside the road in a manic fury at your approach. A great brown bird, its chest lightening to pale cream, tail dark and red in the sun, its hooked black beak open and tiny red tongue testing the air. One wing is angled down as the bird moves, its long thick primaries dragging in the dirt.

Something's wrong with it, you say.

Broken wing, looks like, Bill says.

You stand there in silence, watching next to your brother, and then a small stone strikes the bird in the side, the hawk jumping at the contact and emitting a brief sharp squawk.

Jesus Christ, don't do that, Bill says.

I just wanted to see if it would take off, Rick says.

It's got a broken wing, Bill says. I just said that.

Sorry, Rick says. Jeez. It's just a dumb bird.

It's a red-tailed hawk, Bill says.

Whatever, Rick says, his voice low and sullen now that he has been chastised.

What do we do? you say.

You are afraid of what your brother will say in response but you have to ask the question, you have to know. And to your relief, Bill says, I think we'd better get her into the truck.

Really? you say. How?

CHRISTIAN KIEFER

Bill returns to the cab and emerges holding his denim jacket out before him. Let's get around her, he says.

The three of you form a triangle beside the road, the raptor hopping in a tight circle at its centerpoint, its eyes hard and wide, trying to watch all of you at once, one wing held out and the other limp at its side. It seems miraculous to you: something you have seen fly above the trailer, the town, the desert, now there before you in the stirred dust beside the road.

Let's just move toward it really slow and I'll try to drop my jacket over its head so it can't see, Bill says.

And then Rick: Goddamn.

You move forward then, all of you, so slowly, and when Bill is four or five feet away, he heaves the jacket toward the bird. The hawk is facing you now so that the jacket comes from behind and drops all at once over its head and back. Immediately the hawk is in motion and it is you who grab hold of it, Bill's coat jerking everywhere beneath your hands.

Holy shit, holy shit, you got it, Rick calls out, smiling and laughing.

Bill is beside you now, kneeling next to the hawk, the raptor calming and then becoming quiet and still. The jacket's denim has made its shape rough and imprecise but you can feel the heat of it rising up into your hands.

Awesome, Bill says. Let's get her into the truck.

Do you want to do it?

Naw, you're doing fine, your brother says. He stumbles a little in the dust, the effect of the six-pack he drank down to empty cans during the target practice.

When you rise, the great raptor is held between your hands. Bill holds the jacket in place over the bird but the hawk's huge feet are still visible, splayed out before you, talons sharp and terrible but also beautiful and so perfect that the sight of them empties your breath. When you set the hawk on the tailgate, those claws scrape and rattle against the metal like knives.

You climb into the bed as Bill holds the jacketed hawk in place. What are we gonna do with him? you ask.

We can call Uncle David and ask him, Bill says. Maybe he knows a zoo or someone who can take care of her.

Can't we?

I don't think so, Nat. She's wild.

We could try.

Let's just get her to town. Then we'll figure it out. And be super careful of those claws. They can probably cut you up pretty bad.

Damn right, Rick says, his voice high and excited.

Then you are settled in the bed of the truck near the cab, Rick beside you, Bill behind the wheel and pulling forward onto the road. The hawk is quiet but you can feel its life even through the jacket, a kind of fierce and fragile whirring that seems to run up through your arms and into your chest. What thoughts you have are about the impossibility of this moment, that some great and mighty creature of the air might find itself broken beside a roadway just at the moment that you and your friend and your brother happen to pass. And yet here it is between your hands, a wild thing as if from some storybook.

You keep that great creature close for the rest of the day, releasing it from the jacket and watching as it leaps around in the dust between the mobile homes. You wish you had a mouse or a rat to feed it but you can think of no way to get one and so you simply wait with it there, its one wing folded into its body, the other dragging, until, in the early evening, a truck from the Nevada Department of Wildlife arrives and two men load the hawk into a plastic box.

What are you gonna do with her? you ask.

There's a raptor lady out near Reno, one of the men says. She'll take good care of her.

All right, you say, but you are shaking your head no all the while.

When they drive away, Bill remains with you between the trailers for a long time, sipping at a can of Budweiser and puffing now and then on his cigarette. Neither of you speak. The sun is low in the sky to the west and the trailers cast long stripes of shadow across the road.

You did a good job with that bird, your brother says at last.

You nod and for reasons you cannot begin to understand, your eyes fill with unwarranted and irreconcilable tears. You turn away from your brother now because you do not want him to see, because he does not cry and so you will not either, and after a moment he says, Well, I'm going in, and you manage a quick, clear OK, and then you are alone and the sun is casting down beyond the edge of the mountains to the west and soon the whole of the desert is plunged into darkness.

*   *   *

TWO YEARS later, in the fall of 1978, you are perched on the edge of the tattered lime green sofa in your trailer's tiny living room, Rick beside you, your mother in her recliner, while on the static-snowed screen of the television Marlin Perkins wrestles an anaconda in a muddy pool. Coils and coils of slick tan and black scales and muddy water. A moment of black hair. Hands frothing the surface. And when Stan Brock's head once again appears, the coils are wrapped around his face, across his mouth, his jaw, and he struggles to pull them away. Marlin pulls at the beast's head, his teeth clenched, gripping the great snake's jaws between his fists, the rippling body wrapping around his legs even as it drags Stan yet again under the surface.

You are frozen, watching the screen. All three of you are. Your mother has offered a constant flow of words during the program, but even she is silent now, prone in the recliner. There is, for the moment, not even the sound of their breathing. As if the air itself has been sucked clean of the trailer and is gone. You are sixteen years old but *Wild Kingdom* is still a show that you do not miss, no matter what, and although Rick sometimes complains about your devotion to it, he manages to be there every Sunday night, arriving just when the opening credits begin and remaining until well after the show has ended.

On the screen, Marlin looks tired and perhaps even a little afraid. His characteristic khaki safari outfit is soaked through and his white hair is swept back from his face by the flow of the churning water around him, the beast's head gripped in his hands, its mouth snapping the air. Then he is on his back, his face just above water, one leg out of the water and completely wrapped in the snake's thick, crushing coils. Perhaps he will drown. Perhaps he will drown right now on national television and the snake will pull him down its endless throat.

And it is just in that moment when there is a knock at the door.

It's open, your mother calls.

The door swings open and when there is no further sound, you look up briefly from the television. The man there hesitates before stepping inside. Betty, he says. Then he looks at you and at Rick and nods.

You nod briefly in response, not knowing what else to say or do. The man is the sheriff, not a deputy but the sheriff himself, in his full uniform, khaki and stripes and badge shining in the light from the television.

Oh, she says. I didn't know it was you, Jimmy. I look terrible. She throws herself forward once, twice, and finally the giant chair swings itself into an upright position, the footrest tucking back into its base with a springy clang.

I'll need to talk with you for a minute, the sheriff says.

In your memory of this night, the door will be open and a strange white light will run through it, into the trailer from the street. The sheriff will be in silhouette: a dark shape cut into that flood. A halo. A wash. A river.

Your mother is standing now and the sheriff looks across to where you and Rick sit on the sofa. Maybe you'd better send the boys to their room for a minute, the sheriff says.

What's the matter, Jimmy?

The sheriff does not answer and after a moment your mother says, You and Ricky go on back to your room.

You complain briefly, since the show has not yet ended, although you see now that Marlin Perkins is free of the snake and they are bagging it in a huge burlap sack, but there is something in the sheriff's presence that is unnerving and so you rise and tell Rick to come on and the two of you wander back to the bedroom you share with your brother.

What's that all about? Rick says.

I have no idea. You flop onto the mattress for a moment and then reach down to slide your box of comic books out from the gap under the bed.

That was awesome with the snake, Rick says.

Yeah it was.

Hoo man, that guy's a lot stronger than he looks.

I thought it was gonna get him, you say. For a minute.

He looked pretty wore out.

You pull a comic from the box and as you do so a sound comes from the front of the trailer. A weird high keening. You look up at Rick and he at you. A chill passes through you, starting in your center and radiating out in all directions at once, like a ripple in a pool of still water.

You call out into the front of the trailer: Mom? The comic next to you on the bed is called *Chamber of Darkness*. An old man caught up under the arm of some creature. Maybe a werewolf. Something else. The sound again. For the briefest instant, it feels as if it has come from the comic book. That keening. A sob.

When you enter the kitchen you find your mother in the arms of the sheriff. You'll be OK, he is saying softly. Then you see that your mother is weeping.

Mom? you say again.

Oh god, she says. Then, between sobs: You have to tell him, Jimmy. I can't do it. You have to tell him. Her voice is high-pitched, strained, frightening, and she does not lift her head from the sheriff's shoulder.

OK, the sheriff says. I can do that. Let's sit you down.

He steers her away from you, toward the sofa, and tilts her into it as if she would have been unable to sit on her own. You have no memory of your mother ever sitting on the sofa so the image of her there is incongruous. The recliner is empty. You almost tell the sheriff that the sofa is not her place but he has turned to you, and to Rick, and stands there for a long moment, looking at you both before he reaches out and lays a broad, heavy hand on your shoulder.

Listen, Nathaniel, he says. Sometimes bad things happen to good people. Do you know that?

What happened? The sheriff's face is liquid. Already you know that whatever it is, it will be terrible.

The sheriff clears his throat. So something really bad happened tonight, and you're gonna have to be strong for your mom. You hear me?

You nod. Tears streak your face.

Your brother, Bill . . . well, look, he was in a bad accident. And he didn't make it.

Didn't make what?

He died, Nathaniel. Bill's dead.

The sheriff's eyes are wet too and his face warps and wobbles through your own tears. Everything flowing. Everything coming to pieces.

You're gonna have to be strong for your mom, the sheriff says.

Bill's . . . ? you begin, but of course you cannot finish the statement.

I'm sorry, the sheriff says.

There is no ground beneath you. Everything is water sucking into dry sand. You are in a muddy pond and there is a snake around your body and it is pulling you under. You are in a muddy pond and there is no television crew to help pull you from its depths.

THEY WILL tell you later that he was drunk, coming back from a bon-fire party out in the mountains by the gravel pits, and simply slid off the road, the truck's velocity well over seventy miles per hour. When the sheriff leaves your trailer, your mother disappears into her bedroom. You think she will return but she does not and you sit on the sofa in the silent trailer and think about the new knowledge that you have no brother, that you will never see your brother again.

Three days later you stand on the cut lawn at the funeral in the shiny black shoes you have borrowed from a neighbor, the toes of which, even in your memory, are covered in thin bright blades of wet grass. You cannot imagine that your brother is in that box, is going under the ground, even though at fifteen you are certainly old enough to understand. Your mother weeps with drunken abandon. You look at her momentarily, then back to the casket. You try to speak but no words will come and the tears that fall are frantic and endless. The feeling of liquidity has not ceased, as if all that dead sea has risen around you and you stand on the rough sand of its lowest depths.

Afterward you and Rick crouch in the dirt, huddling in the shadow of the trailer.

Shit, Rick says.

You look up at him and are surprised to see your friend's eyes similarly wrapped in tears. He's my brother, you say. What are you crying about?

I can miss him too, Rick says. He was your brother but he was still a friend of mine.

Get out of here, you say.

What?

Just get the hell out of here.

Rick looks at you, his eyes still wet with tears. Man, he says, but he turns and walks away, crossing into the sunlight between the trailers and disappearing from sight.

You sit in the shade of the steps, the wood worn and gray and splintering everywhere as if in the process of unraveling filament by filament. In the murmur of voices between the trailers, you think you can hear your brother's voice. They are barbequing some ribs out there, drinking beer, your brother's friends gathered in small clumps, occasionally laughing softly at some story that you cannot hear. Your mother is inside the trailer somewhere, perhaps with a friend, Rick's mother or someone else. You have hardly seen her in the days since the sheriff came. She has appeared only briefly to turn from her bedroom door into the bathroom, saying nothing, the door closing and then opening again as she returns to her room and the door once again closes. All the while you stand mute and baffled in the living room, trying to say something but finding no words.

That is the winter when you first begin breaking into houses. It begins when you knock on the door of Mark Matthews's house, a tiny boxlike structure covered in peeling light-blue paint, and there is no answer and somehow you decide to go around to the back door and knock there and when there is still no answer you open it and enter. Hello? Hello? Rick calls. You walk through the house quickly, moving through each room, not really sure what you are looking for once you are inside and not really intending to look for anything either, because you have not yet decided why you went inside the house at all.

You both know Mark Matthews so you do not feel like you are somewhere you should not be even though you both know that what you are doing is forbidden, perhaps even a crime, whether you know the occupant or not. And yet being there without Mark Matthews makes the whole home seem foreign somehow. A bowl of fake plastic grapes on the kitchen table. A console television. A small bronze cannon by the fireplace. A few magazines stacked on the floor next to the sofa. You make two peanut butter and jelly sandwiches on white bread and you and Rick sit at the kitchen table and eat them, listening all the while for the sound of a car from the front of the house. From the street outside comes the sound of a passing pickup truck and for a moment you are sure it is your brother's, but of course there is no possibility of such an occurrence and in the seconds afterward you are nearly crushed by an inexpressible wave of grief.

You take a small necklace from Mark's mother's chest of drawers and Rick takes a shining green ring. They are souvenirs of a sort, a reminder of what was, for you, a strange electricity that seemed to temporarily fill the huge vacancy that still rides in your chest.

Then there are other houses, no longer people you know but the houses, the homes, of strangers. When the back door of the first house you try is locked, Rick breaks the knob off with a brick and presses the door open. Neither of you take anything this time, although you will begin taking small items from each home you enter, mostly jewelry and cash, but that first time you only move through the small dingy rooms before passing once more through the rear door and into the fenced square of the backyard. From a few yards over—each a square of dead grass mottled with frozen dirt—a neighbor's dog barks at you lethargically. Beyond it, the flat plain of the desert floor is slowly erased by a faint pale drift of new snow.

What you learn over the course of that winter is that the worlds people draw for themselves are different. Sometimes the details of those lives are told in cheap scratched frames that stand upon countertops or hang from bent nails upon the walls, photographs that are sometimes of people you recognize—a teacher at the high school or the man who makes hamburgers at the Pak-Out or the woman who works at the bank—and the collection of those memories seems to transpire in the air all around you. The teacher on a beach somewhere with a woman so beautiful that the two of you have trouble pulling yourselves away. The man who owns the Pak-Out as a boy no older than you are, fishing pole in hand, the familiar stretch of the river you know as Catfish Bend curling behind him. In such moments it feels as if the structure of each home is made entirely of gauze and you have entered those enclosures as if entering into a dream. The thin and spectral webs of spiders. Of root and fungus. Intersecting bubbles on the still surface of a pond. You know now that what world you occupy is in the process of dissolving. As if you are dreaming and are dreaming within that dream so that it matters not whether you sleep or wake, for there is no world in which your brother is not dead.

6

HE TALKED TO HIMSELF AS HE DROVE, HIS VOICE A SLOW, NEARLY silent murmur, big trees sliding by at the edges of the highway and then the first ramshackle buildings of the town beginning to appear. He had been thinking about that day when they first met and that memory had sparked another and another. He could not have imagined ever being apart in those days, in the hot desert of his childhood. He could not have imagined a bridge from there to here, and yet here he was, driving toward the one person he had hoped—in the agonized guilt of what had happened, of what he had done—that he would never have to lay eyes upon again, even though he knew all the while that he would return, his voice in the car riding the same accusation: Why else would you have kept the safe for all those years? You might have rid yourself of it at any time but you never did and now here you are.

He parked the truck at the edge of the Safeway parking lot and sat there with the motor idling, still talking softly to himself and staring around at the various cars—dirty Subarus and pickups—for any sign of the man who had once been his best friend in all the world, willing himself to stay there only because he thought the cargo he held in the bed of the truck would be the end of it, would close that one part of his past that he had left flapping open. The last thing tethering him to the world he had fled.

When he saw Rick at last his first thought was that he had come to look like his father, the man who, when they were children, would beat him and his mother until their screaming at last brought the sheriff into the trailer park. The resemblance filled him with a sadness impossible to articulate. He did not know what he had expected after so many years, but not this tiny broken car, not this filthy yellow Honda, its fenders rusted into holes and the door squealing on its metal hinges. And yet here he was in the parking lot of the grocery store, his body the same lanky frame protected only by a loose denim jacket insufficient for the cold and jeans that rolled down over the tops of scuffed cowboy boots.

Bill stepped out onto the asphalt. Hey, he said.

Rick stood there by the car's open door, staring back at him, his face inscrutable. The years had streaked his black hair with gray.

I bet you're glad to be out.

So there you are, Rick said at last. The voice the same. The eyes sparking blue in the freezing air.

Here I am.

Across the expanse of the parking lot, the Safeway sign glowed dim under a sky rolling with dark clouds. Pickup trucks in rows. A maroon sedan passing slowly, the driver nodding as they made eye contact.

That a cop?

Just someone from here in town.

Rick's eyes followed the car and then turned back to where Bill stood beside the pickup.

You're gonna have to follow me, Bill said.

No way.

There're too many people here. Follow me.

I'm not following you anywhere.

You're gonna have to, Bill said, and before Rick could react he slid back into the cab of the pickup and gunned out of the parking lot, his heart pounding, hands gripping the wheel so tightly that he had to will them to uncurl when he turned onto the street. He looked into the rearview mirror and saw nothing but the anonymous vehicles of his neighbors. Come on, he said. Come on. His breath stilled, stopped. And then at last the tiny yellow car appeared from the receding parking lot and swung onto the road behind him.

The figure in the mirror: a ghost from his memory. Even at this distance Rick looked like his father. The angular shape of his face had hardened and weathered like the desert itself, implacable, lines running under his eyes and the eyes themselves drooping at their most distant and downward edges, wet and clear and wide. There he was. There he really was.

He followed the highway south out of town, through the Kootenai's broad, flat floodplain to where that valley pinched closed into a folded landscape of ridges and pines, scraps of cloud drifting between them like foam on some inland sea. He checked the mirror again and again, as if the yellow car might, at any moment, evaporate in a cloud of steam like his own exhaled breath. Because he wanted to be shut of it. He needed to be shut of it. And so he needed the yellow car to be there, to be following him as the forest hemmed in the road once more and their route was reduced to shadow.

Half a mile before the rescue he took a dirt turnout that expanded onto a brief patch of gravel partially hidden by trees and brambles and beyond which lay a small clearing surrounded by forest. Near the center of that circle, he drew the truck to a stop and waited for Rick's car to appear. Then he opened the door and stepped out. Even now, so close to the end of it, he could feel his gut turning as if run through with an iron rod. The earth covered with dry tamarack needles the color of toast.

Then Rick was out of the car, standing there in his thin coat. What the fuck is this? he said.

Just someplace out of the way.

Don't try anything, Rick said. This is bullshit. As if to underscore the statement, he pulled his jacket open to reveal a pistol handle extending from the front of his jeans.

Look, Bill said, you want to do it in town, with everyone watching? 'Cause we can go back to the parking lot if you'd rather do it there.

You're stalling, Rick said. You'd better have what I came up here for.

I have it. He dropped the tailgate and hopped up onto the bed of the truck and pulled the plastic tarp free. The safe looked smaller than it had in the closet, a squat iron box not more than two feet on a side, its thick black paint shining.

What is this? Rick said. The rancor in his voice was replaced by something like bewilderment now.

What's it look like? Bill knelt next to the box, pulling it forward a few feet clear of the cab and then stepping in behind to shove it the length of the bed.

I told you not to fuck around, Rick said at last.

I'm not. Bill was panting now but he had managed to get the safe to the tailgate and he stepped down onto the forest floor again. I never opened it, he said.

What the fuck you mean you never opened it?

He shrugged, his fingertips momentarily slipping into the tops of his jean pockets and then returning to hang loose at his sides.

Seriously? Rick said. He looked from the safe to Bill and then repeated that simple motion.

Seriously.

There was a pause and then Rick said, I don't get it.

There's nothing to get. Just put it in your car and go. You can have the whole thing. Whatever's in there.

Rick stared at the safe. No, man, I don't get it, he said. You never opened it?

I never did. I'm just trying to do what's right.

What's right? I should fucking shoot you. That's what's right. Why didn't you open it, you fucking idiot?

I don't know. I just didn't.

My mom fucking died, man. God-fucking-dammit. You stupid asshole.

How different he looked and yet how much the same.

It's like you just turned your back on everyone who gave a shit about you, Rick said.

I had to start over.

Rick looked at the safe again and shook his head. Put it in the trunk, he said.

Grab the other side.

Fucking asshole. You don't know what I had to do to survive in there. Some of those guys would kill you for a pack of smokes. So you've got to kill them first. Do you understand what I'm telling you?

Come and help me.

I already tried that and look how it worked out, Rick said but a moment later he came to the safe and they lifted it together. Rick was so close to him now, separated only by the two feet of that heavy iron box. How old he looked. His skin gray.

When they reached the car, Rick pulled open the hatchback with one hand and they lowered the safe, the little Honda's suspension heaving with the added weight. Then they both stepped back from the car. Bill was panting from the exertion, his hands on his knees. You got fat and out of shape, Rick said.

I guess so.

You know, I came up here thinking that if I saw you it might make sense to me. What you did. Who you are. All the fucking lies you told me. My mom. All the shit I did in prison. Everything.

Bill straightened and looked up at him, this broken man with his cane who returned his gaze with an unwavering stare, and Bill felt a shiver run through him as if that gaze were physical contact, a silver wire sparking against his flesh. He shook his head.

Yeah, you don't know shit. You just ran away and never looked back.

I made a life for myself.

Is that what you did? Because it seems more like you ran away and hid in the forest like a pussy.

It was silent for a long time. Bill looked at the dead needles that littered the ground at his feet. How'd you even find me? he said.

Shit, man, Rick said and there was actual mirth in his voice now, it's not like you moved to Paris, France. You weren't in Reno. You weren't in Battle Mountain. So where else would you go?

If you knew where I was, then why didn't you turn me in?

Because I don't fucking do that. Take care of your people. You think that was a fucking joke to me? That was the only thing that mattered. But you fucked it up. And you fucking killed my mom.

Bill had begun to quake inside, as if a faint flutter of panic had entered him and now flapped against his ribs. I didn't kill your mom, he said. That's ridiculous.

Same as, Rick said.

The quiet settled over them, two men in a clearing beside a road periodically sounding with the long hiss of a passing car.

I don't know what else to say, Bill said at last. He hoped his voice was steady. Now that the safe was out of his life, he wanted more than anything to simply drive away and be done with it, but he lingered. I'm sorry, man, he said. I don't know what else to say about it. You're right. I left all of it behind and never looked back.

Goddamn right you did. So what am I supposed to do now?

Exactly the same thing.

Oh, is that right?

Yeah, Bill said. You've got the safe. That's what you came here for, isn't it?

Fuck you. I know what you're doing. I've seen that weird little zoo. That's what you care about now? Those fucking zoo animals?

Yeah, he said, that's what I care about. There was a tremble in his voice now. He did not expect Rick to have seen the rescue and perhaps he was bluffing but the thought of it filled him with a thread of cold sharp air. What do you want from me, Rick? he said.

You're living a goddamn lie up here. Bill Reed. That's the icing on the cake right there. Bill fucking Reed.

I've changed, Bill said.

Now that's the first thing you've said all day that made any sense.

Go home, Rick, Bill said. Or go find yourself a new place to make into a home. You're free. Go do something with it. I did.

Yeah, Rick said. Easy for you to say. He looked out into the trees for a moment as if in thought and then, without another word, he stepped into his car and pulled the door closed behind him. A moment later the engine chugged and the little Honda turned out onto the asphalt of the highway and was gone.

He did not know how long he stood there in the clearing, watching the empty space the car had vacated, watching the trees and the white cloud of his breath. His heart seemed wrong somehow, beating much too fast, his breath coming in hollow rasps that he could neither slow nor stop. The metallic taste of adrenaline on his tongue.

HE RETURNED to the damp, dilapidated travel trailer he had inherited from his uncle and made himself a sandwich and then sat eating it at the tiny table, his eyes staring in the direction of the window but seeing nothing there, not the glass nor the trees beyond. Instead, he could see only Rick, his face so much older than he had expected. How time curls back on you, returns so completely that it is as if geography itself is the loop, all your choices rendered only moments in a chain of possibility that leads one to the next, the lit fuses pulling forward over the years and each tinderbox drawn by your own sense that you have chosen them and by so choosing are adhered. This no different. For twelve years he had wondered what would happen when Rick came out of prison at last, what payment would be exacted, hoping without cause or reason that his friend would have come to terms with what happened, that he might have been forgiven, but then he knew that this was unlikely to be the case, for he did not even forgive himself and he knew that Rick did not forget such things; he had not when they had been children and he certainly would not now. His rage was the same, as was his movement, his carriage and his bearing, the look in his eyes, and the occasional flash of his smile. Grayer and more haggard but otherwise the same.

It felt as if the whole of his past was closing behind him. Closing at last. His mother had moved to Phoenix to live near his aunt Lucy. His brother's grave in the desert of Nevada as it always would be but there was no reason to visit such a marker. The cluster of trailers where he and Rick had grown up were someone else's now, if they were still there at all. Sunday nights he would sit on the stained, broken green sofa with his brother at his side and his mother in her recliner, each of them with an individual oven-warmed compartmentalized meal, watching Marlin Perkins drive his Jeep alongside a cheetah, pilot a road grader into a hippo pool, guide a hawk to land on his outstretched gloved fist. His brother. His mother. Often Rick as well. Nothing in his life ever felt as safe, not before and not since. Then the night Marlin wrestled the anaconda, and everything was changed. It sometimes felt in the weeks and years that followed as if that night had swept clean some illusion, revealing the geography for what it had been all the while, the boundaries of his life circumscribed upon a landscape he had not chosen. Not even the Truckee River managed to flow out of that dry basin, instead pouring ever and always into Pyramid Lake and evaporating slowly into the sky. Kangaroo rats skittering through the shadscale. The sagebrush stretching in all directions, the cold bare peaks of the mountains like islands floating above, and you a faint dim speck between them, indistinguishable from the scrubby spike-covered plants that everywhere held fast to the dry, hard sand.

Now, at long last, the whole of that landscape was fading into a flat darkness and in its place a faint spattering of slushy rain against the window of the trailer. The wet forest beyond. And there he was:

reflected upon those trees, reflected on the glass, beard and mustache a bedraggled mess under dark-ringed eyes but the encasing of his world tight and shining once again, a glass orb containing the forest and the mountains and the animals, and the few people he cared about: Grace and her son Jude. His mother, although only via telephone. Bess and the volunteers. No one else. The world around him a forest of high-banked ridges filled with animals of tooth and hoof and claw and you among them, staring out the window of your pale white enclosure into the spitting slushy rain.

He looked at his watch and then stood and put on his coat and the cowboy hat Grace had given him and stepped through the door. The path through the birch trunks shadowless in the gloom: a dim reckoning of faint cloudlight against peeling white bark beneath which pockets of thick frost dotted the black earth as if some child had dropped a series of snow cones along the path.

When he came down through the gate, the two boys were at the new raptor enclosure, working despite the weather, the walls up and Bobby running the saw through a two-by-four as Bill approached.

Looks good, guys, he said.

They both looked across at him, Bobby setting the saw down and Chuck tapping a stubby pencil against the plywood floor. Thanks, boss, Bobby said.

The boys sat on their haunches watching him, their shaggy hair falling in scraggly cascades over their eyes. When they had first come on as volunteers six months before, he had asked them what they wanted to do with their lives and they had looked at him with a kind of wild confusion. No idea, Bobby had said at last.

He knew he might have answered the question the same way at their age and probably had, but the response still surprised him. What do you want to volunteer here for then? he had asked.

We like animals, Bobby had said in response.

And this place is cool, Chuck added.

Yeah that too, Bobby said. It's cool.

Bill had been taken aback by the response and for a long moment he did not even know what to say. In the end he signed them on. They were applying to do something for no reason other than to do it and while part of him did not trust the impulse—part of him ultimately did not trust anyone but himself—he thought that he should at least give them a chance.

As it turned out, the boys' work ethic was surprising. Within the first week he apparently mentioned that the roof of the Twins' holding pen was leaking and the next morning woke to find that the boys had torn much of the roof away and were repairing it with lumber they had scavenged—or so they had told him—from some abandoned building site, the two martens watching from a nearby tree stump with apparent interest. He had asked them how it was going and they had looked down at him from the rafters of the marten enclosure. It's going great, Bobby had said. This is like the best day ever.

He thought at first that the statement must have been meant ironically, for the two of them had already been working on the roof for at least two hours for no pay, just to do something, and in response he said, That so? and Chuck, who he had already learned rarely spoke, said, Heck yeah, and Bobby added, Totally. We're building the hell out of this thing. And Bill stood there watching them, the two of them watching him in turn, until he finally said, Well, good job then, and Bobby had said, Thanks, boss, and Bill had turned back toward his office again.

He had had to speak with them only about the safety and care of the animals, letting them know that they would need to check in with him or with Bess before tearing into anything related to the enclosures, but otherwise he found them to be totally remarkable, two young men unafraid of doing virtually anything, building or shoveling lion or bear shit or anything else, working as if they had just discovered it, a trait so unlike him at that age that he still wondered from time to time if their presence was some kind of bizarre joke, certainly the two best volunteers he had ever had and perhaps the best he ever would have, so much so that he had pondered ways of paying them although he knew in actuality that his budget would never allow for such a thing.

Thanks for the help, you guys, he said now, hands in his pockets, shoulders hunched up under the spitting rain.

Sure thing, boss.

I think I'll see if I can start getting the roof up later.

Cool, Chuck said.

Listen, I think we'll have a quick meeting in about a half hour.

Everything good? Bobby asked.

Yeah, just winter coming. That's all.

Cool, Chuck said again.

Literally, Bobby said, and they both chuckled.

From the fox enclosure came a high cackling and the three of them looked over to where their red fox, Katy, stood at the front of her enclosure, eyeing them with apparent curiosity, her orange hair shining in the afternoon light.

JUDE'S HOMEWORK was a single page, handwritten, the title WOLF penciled across the top in swirling letters above an illustration in colored marker. Bill held it in his hands while the boy watched him, his eyes bright and wide and shining. Really excellent, buddy. Super cool.

That's Zeke, Jude said.

I thought it was.

The boy was next to him on the couch, sitting but not really sitting, squirming with energy, his limbs folding and unfolding.

You got the whole thing right, he said. His eyes too.

Yeah, I know it, Jude said. He's got spooky eyes.

Sometimes.

It's just a practice drawing, he said. It's for Mrs. Simmons. We're doing a unit on ecology.

Ah right, he said. You told me. And that reminds me that I have something for you.

What is it?

Bill stood and went to where his coat hung on a hook by the door and from its pocket brought forth a clear plastic ziplock baggie containing the tattered and worn paperback, its pages held together by a rubber band. I told you I thought I had a book on desert animals, he said, and I found it.

He returned to the couch and handed it to the boy. *Wildlife of the Intermountain West*. The pronghorn antelope stood looking back at him from the cover without expression.

Cool, Jude said. He pulled it from the ziplock and removed the rubber band and sat flipping through the pages. What are these marks?

The page was open to pen-and-ink drawings of two lizards—zebra-tailed and collared—both of which had large blue check marks next to them. That's stuff I saw with my own eyes, Bill said.

Everything with a check mark you saw?

Yep, he said.

So you went to the desert?

I grew up in the desert.

Really?

Really and truly.

Jude flipped back to the cover. What's that?

Pronghorn antelope, Bill said.

Have you ever seen one?

Oh yeah. In eastern Oregon.

You've been everywhere.

He smiled, faintly. Not really. Just kept my eyes open.

The boy stared at the book in his lap. A full page of bats, all line drawings. Free-tailed and big-eared and pipistrel. Kangaroo rat, mountain vole. Ducks and woodpeckers and warblers. So hopefully that'll help some, if you have to draw some other kinds of animals for school.

Yeah totally, the boy said.

Grace had come into the living room from the hall. Time for bed, kiddo, she said.

The response was a long, drawling whine but the boy rose nonetheless, snatching the wolf drawing off the couch next to him and then returning to give Bill their customary hug and high five. 'Night, Jude said.

Good night, buddy.

Thanks for the book.

It's a good book, he said. I've had it a long time.

How long?

Since I was just a little older than you.

No way.

Yes way, he said. I'll come say good night in a little bit.

They retreated farther into the house, down the hallway that led both to Jude's room and to Grace's. Bill remained where he was for a time and then went to the table and sat and flipped through a small pile of mail there. Bills and circulars. At the bottom of the stack was the new issue of *National Geographic* and a paperback, *The Tibetan Book of the Dead*, its black cover emblazoned with a circle cut by three arching red waves. He paged through it absently but the words made little sense to him. Light-paths of the wisdoms. Bardo of karmic illusions. Near the center was a blurry and poorly rendered image labeled The Great Mandala of the Peaceful Deities, and he stared at that for a time. A circle containing a series of smaller circles, each of which contained, or seemed to contain, a figure or figures, perhaps human, perhaps not.

When Grace entered the room, the book was still in his hand. You're not going to join a cult or something, are you? he said.

Maybe.

You're reading this thing?

Sort of. It's from that lady Fran who had to put her dog down. She said it helped her guide Chuckles into the afterlife.

Chuckles is trapped with a bunch of dead Tibetan guys now. He's probably pissed.

Probably. It's pretty hard to read. I don't know what I'm supposed to get from it.

Maybe she's trying to brainwash you.

Wouldn't that be nice? Grace leaned in behind and wrapped her arms around his chest and neck. Jude's waiting for you.

He closed the book and stood. Don't go anywhere, he said. Then he moved down the hall and into the boy's room. The bed was a mess of blankets and stuffed animals, and as he entered the boy sat up out of that quilted space and said, Boo, and then giggled.

Ah, Bill said, staggering backward into the hall, you scared me.

You're a scaredy-cat, Jude said.

It's true. I am. He came and settled on the edge of the bed. *Wildlife of the Intermountain West* rested on the small white nightstand, returned to its ziplock, the antelope staring through the plastic into the mild twilight of the room. The sight of it there produced a strange and involuntary shiver through his body.

Jude lay back on the pillow, his wet child's eyes staring up at him. Will you take me to school in the morning? the boy said.

Probably.

Probably as in yes?

Probably as in yes.

Good. In the truck.

Ah, he said, it's the truck, is it?

The truck's fun.

What's wrong with your mom's truck?

Nothing. Yours is just funner.

I guess so, Bill said. He waited, looking at the boy. Then he said, Ah, heck with it.

Heck with what?

I've been wanting to ask you something.

Ask me what? the boy said.

Well listen, champ, I was thinking of asking your mom something.

I thought you were gonna ask *me* something.

I am, I'm gonna ask you if I can ask her.

You're silly.

Bill smiled. You're probably right, he said. So I was thinking of asking your mom, maybe, if she'd want to get married. So we could be together all the time. But I wanted to make sure it's OK with you first.

Would we get to live with you at the animals?

I don't know. We'd all live together for sure. Maybe not at the animals though. My trailer's pretty small for everyone to live in.

So you'd live here?

We'd have to figure that out.

The boy lay there on the pillow, looking at him thoughtfully. What about my dad?

Your dad's still your dad and he'll always be your dad. I'd be what you'd call your stepdad.

OK, Jude said.

OK?

Yeah, that sounds great. Let's do that.

He smiled and Jude smiled.

Don't tell your mom, though. It's supposed to be a surprise.

When are you gonna ask her?

I don't know, he said. It needs to be special.

Are you coming to Fall Festival?

What's that?

At my school. Fall Festival. We're singing a song about Thanksgiving.

Oh yeah, your mom told me about that. Yeah, I'll be there.

You can ask her then. At Fall Festival. That'll be special.

He smiled. Good idea, he said. Maybe I'll ask her when we get home after.

Yeah, Jude said. He giggled, pulling the blanket up around his mouth. It's a secret, he said.

Yes, it is, Bill said. You in for a bear hug?

The boy nodded and Bill scooped him up in his arms and pulled him against his chest and the swell of his belly and squeezed him tight, roughing his beard against the child's cheek. Again, Jude said. And once more. Good night, buddy. He brushed Jude's hair from his forehead as the boy turned on his side, his eyes slipping closed for a brief moment and then opening again. Sleep well. Dream good dreams, Bill said.

The boy's head nodded against the pillow and Bill rose quietly and stepped into the hall and returned to the kitchen table once more.

The Tibetan book was still there but Grace had extracted the *National Geographic* from the mail pile and she sat at the table peering down at an open page, the brown curls of her hair turning over her wrinkled forehead. He leaned against the wall by the corkboard with its barrage of notes and notices and calendars and scraps of paper and watched her.

There's a bunch of wolves in here, she said. This guy here reminds me of our Zeke.

Yeah, he said. Poor guy.

We'll find him someone, she said.

I hope so.

Maybe we need to be looking in Minnesota.

Fish and Game's gonna make it a lot harder now than it would've been.

We need to figure that out too, she said.

Fast.

I'll make some calls tomorrow. Maybe to the zoo in Boise.

I don't know if it's gonna matter. That new DCO seems pretty hell bent on closing us down.

It's probably not as bad as you think.

I don't know about that.

Don't give up so easy, Grace said, smiling faintly.

I'm not.

You sure?

No.

He was standing behind her now and she reached up to stroke his beard. Before her on the table, the magazine was open to a series of small photographs boxed in gray, indeed some wolves among them. One chased a flock of ravens. Another looked askance at the photographer. Black spruce and jack pine. Heron and eagle and nuthatch. From a frostlike tuft of red and green lichen peered forth the empty socket of a deer skull. Sunset birds. Slick waterways snaking through black spindly branches. Places not unlike his own forest and yet so different. The foliage. The feel of it.

Grace's finger moved to point to an image of a wolf standing by the snow-covered carcass of a deer. Pictures like that make me wish we could get him out, she said.

Crippled wolf wouldn't live long out there, not with winter coming. He still needs a pack.

I keep hoping that he'll figure out we're his pack.

I don't think that'll ever happen if he hasn't figured it out by now.

Maybe we need to call in to Minnesota. But I don't know how we'd get a wolf across state lines.

We'll cross that bridge when we get to it, Grace said.

You're always so dang positive about everything.

That's my job, she said.

They had put the word out to the various agencies across the Rockies that they were looking for a female wolf, not for breeding but to give Zeke a partner so that he would not feel so alone. But Bill did not want to bring in another animal unless it could not be released into the wild and he knew a tame wolf, a pet, would likely be killed by the wild creature that Zeke continued to be. And so they waited for responses, hoping that some rescue they had never heard of would call them to say they had an animal too maimed to be released into the wild, an odd thing to wish for and yet there it was. But no rumor of injured wolves of any kind had come to them in the two years since they had first picked up Zeke from a rancher, the wolf's paw ruined by the claw trap that had ensnared him.

The rancher might have shot the wolf—that had certainly been the intent—but instead he had called the sheriff who had then called the rescue, and Bill had driven out to the ranch and had seen the wolf for the first time, a creature of such beauty and dignity even in the moment of its greatest fear that Bill's heart shattered to see it. The wolf had stood when he had approached, not growling or cowering but only standing there, the look in the wolf's eyes one of intelligence and even understanding as he stared at the man who would likely kill it in the next instant, the evidence of such an intent held in his hands. But of course Bill did not kill the wolf. The expected bang of the bullet had instead been the short pop of the dart and the wolf had spun around quickly and then lay panting, its crushed paw dragging an orbit of blood against the white crust of the snow, the trap leaping and rattling at the end of its stake-driven chain.

Now what? the rancher had asked him.

Now we wait a bit for him to sleep and then you pull that trap off him.

He's not gonna bite me, is he?

If he does it won't be any worse than what you did to him.

The rancher shuffled his feet against the frozen gravel of the road. I should have just shot the goddamned thing.

Yeah? So why didn't you?

I couldn't. Don't know why. They've been at the livestock. Scaring the shit out of my old lady too. But something about it . . . I just couldn't.

They stood there, watching as the wolf began to whine and then, at last, to lie down in the snow.

Bill returned to the truck and retrieved the snout noose, although he did not think he would need to use it now, holding the steel pole over his shoulder and then handing it across to the rancher.

What's this? the man said.

Tell you what, Bill said. You slip this over his nose and I'll get the trap off.

He showed the rancher how to use it, the way in which the slipknot could be tightened at the end of the pole. Then he slung the dart gun over his shoulder and pulled his gloves over hands already aching from the cold.

The snow outside the bed of the road was deep and uneven and they moved those last twenty or so yards across it in slow, careful steps, the rancher's breath puffing white clouds into the air. When he reached the animal, they both stood looking down at it. A magnificent creature, sleek and thin, its fur light gray and tipped with black points, mouth open and tongue lolling pink against the snow. An animal so wholly suited to the forest that seeing it prostrate on the frozen earth seemed impossible. What was he to do with it once he had it back at the rescue? Killing it was inconceivable but holding it in a cage not much better.

Christ, the rancher said. Just that single word.

Bill's eyes had come to the paw, or what remained of it: a mess of purple tendons and raw red muscle and exposed bone. Had he come an hour later the wolf would have freed itself, the remains of the severed paw caught in the jaws of the trap while the animal disappeared into the dark forest, trailing blood from its stump. Bill knew such an animal would not survive long in the wild, not with the heavier snows of winter still coming. He would survive at the rescue but the paw was gone either way. There was no doubt about that fact at all.

He imagined the pack swinging south out of British Columbia and dipping across a border that held no meaning to its motion, flowing as one through the dark wet trees and taking its prey when it could, a group of animals perfectly evolved to survive and their understanding of that world distinctly drawn to render all other concerns invisible. They would be like ghosts fading into and out of the forest: sawtooth ridgetops, silver water, the scent of prey upon the air. And you some separate and recondite creature residing in an entirely different world. What you see are threats and disasters and horrors the likes of which those ghosts could not even imagine, time flattened out of its circle and running in a thin sharp band, straight and level, and that faint bubble of world in which all animals run and hunt and graze eviscerated everywhere by its razored edge. You are a man standing inside one such bubble above the unconscious body of a ghost from another, watching its breath steam and the purple-tendoned gap in its foreleg continue to bleed out slowly against the snow.

From where he stood, Bill could see the ranch house in the distance:

a wooden box with warm yellow light at the windows, the black stalk of a chimney from which rose a slow curl of pale smoke. The sheep were penned a few dozen yards away against the wall of an iron-gray barn that dwarfed the house itself, and in the several acres of cleared and snow-covered pastureland that stretched out before both structures a herd of six or eight horses stood in a tight knot against the cold. He could see how it all could look like a meal, the prey ready and waiting and out in the open as if arranged on a serving tray.

He knew then that it had been the last image of freedom the wolf would ever see, for when it opened its eyes it would be at the rescue, where all sense of free will would be lined and limited by the extent of the wire fence that demarcated its enclosure. A geography of endlessly moving mountains and rivers that flowed at last to a small ring of biting iron.

IN THE MORNING he dropped Jude off at school, the boy giggling and talking nonstop about the secret they shared and Bill smiling into the bright clear light as it streamed in upon them from every direction. The boy held the ragged field guide in his hand the whole while.

He was still smiling as he returned to the trailer in the woods, parking his truck and descending the birch path to the rescue once again. Bess was already there, the coffeepot in the office full and hot. He poured himself a mug and went about the morning feedings. Cinder purred at him when he approached, the sound of her like an engine, her big front paws pressing the moist earth. Hungry, little girl? he said.

The mountain lion looked at him, one-eyed.

He pressed the feed bowl through the hatch and closed it and she came down through the gate and then he could hear the sounds of her great sharp teeth gnashing the food. Breakfast is served, he said.

When he returned to the office it was after ten and a handful of visitors wandered the paths, Bobby, Chuck, and Bess acting as tour guides, Ashley manning the tiny, closet-like gift shop. He finished off the coffee and took the pot outside to refill it with water from the hose and returned to the office. It was then that he saw the red light blinking on the answering machine. He pressed the button there and listened to the tape whiz back and then the click as he poured the water into the coffeemaker's reservoir. *Mr. Reed*, the voice came, *Steve Colman at Idaho Fish and Game*. And he froze there next to the desk, listening, the now empty pot clutched in his fist. *I called over to my people at Interior and I'm sorry to say that the wolf and the bear are both gonna have to be removed from the site. Ditto with all the carnivores that fall under Fish and Game jurisdiction. So that's the bad news. Good news is that I think we can get you permitted for the smaller omnivores like, say, the raccoons and such, but—*

The message was cut off, the machine clicking and whirring again and then falling silent.

He set the empty pot on the desk and leaned forward and pressed play once more and listened again to the message and then a third time.

Removed from the site, Colman had said. So that's the bad news.

On the far wall, illuminated now by the slant of morning light and faded with age, hung the framed drawing he had made soon after that single visit to Idaho with his mother and brother: the drawing a mess of color and texture and line not unlike the drawing Jude had shown him the night before. There were few specifics from that first trip to Idaho in his memory, but he could remember the bear: how the animal would look at him with eyes that seemed both intelligent and interested. His uncle taught him how to feed the grizzly and he remembered, still remembered, the feeling, perhaps for the first time in his life, that he was doing something important, that he was needed and wanted. The bear seemed to respond to him in ways that he did not even respond to Uncle David, approaching the front of the cage whenever the boy appeared and the boy standing for hours there, talking to him and scratching his neck with a stick through the woven and welded metal.

He made the drawing when they returned to the dry basin of Battle Mountain and he asked his mother to mail it to his uncle. A month later he had been surprised to receive a package from Idaho containing the field guide, the book he had just given Jude, a volume filled with line drawings and terse descriptions of the plants and animals of his childhood landscape.

The second effect of the drawing he did not know about until he returned. He had been eight years old when he mailed his uncle the drawing. When he returned, thirteen years later, afraid and churning with guilt, he had seen that drawing again, that image from his long distant past, the same crayon and marker illustration of a smiling bear, now enclosed in a little frame upon the wall in his uncle's office, and the wooden sign at the bear enclosure had been made to match his childhood spelling, not Major but Majer. They had moved it when the bear had been moved and it was worn by years of weather but its carved inscription remained legible enough:

MAJER
Grizzly Bear (*Ursus arctos horribilis*)
Born 1958

Behind it Majer sniffed the air, scenting Bill's approach as he walked up the path from the office, the animal's great head tilting slowly from side to side in a kind of dance.

Hey old buddy, Bill said. The bear looked at him expectantly. How are we doing?

The bear nodded its head slowly.

No treats just now, but it's checkup day so Gracey's coming to see you. You know what that means.

The bear looked at him as if he might manifest a treat by sheer force of will or of longing.

You're just gonna have to wait, Bill said.

Can he understand you? a girl's voice said.

He turned. Beside him, just a few feet from the front of the enclosure, stood a young girl not much older than Jude, her parents flanking her on either side, both smiling expectantly. In some ways it made him sad to see her there. He wanted to sit alone with his friend. That was all. But here she was. He sure can, he said.

How do you know?

He lets me know what he's thinking.

But how?

He looked from the girl to the bear. Hey buddy, he said, you want a marshmallow?

The bear nodded, his mouth curling into a broad, almost crazed smile.

He turned back to the girl. What do you think he said?

I think he said yes, the girl said, smiling and wide-eyed.

Well, I'd better give him a marshmallow then. Don't you think?

She nodded.

He returned to the zookeeper door and removed a marshmallow from his pocket and slipped it through the opening. Majer took it carefully, pushing his lips out as if preparing to suck upon a straw.

The parents asked him some questions as he stood there next to the cage, questions about the bear's strength and life span, its eating habits, how long it had lived there at the rescue, how long the rescue had been in operation, and Bill answered them all, patiently and carefully, all the while the girl staring at the bear and the bear's sightless eyes seeming to return her gaze. He had been eight years old when he had first looked into those eyes and even though the bear was now blind, he knew the animal's gaze had not changed. In it, he thought he could feel time itself. Time pulling the ends together. Time and the bear.

The family moved on down the path and he watched as they disappeared into the little gift shop that ran up against the side of the parking lot where Ashley worked the cash register, selling T-shirts and patches and a few field guides and coloring books.

Well, old man, he said to the bear. Got some bad news today, but we're gonna fight it like crazy.

The bear did not make a sound, only continuing to sit on the big rock above the pool, his sightless eyes pouring out through the wire and into the forest all around.

A moment later came the sound of Grace's truck pulling across the gravel below. He slid off the stump. Don't you go hiding on me, he said as he walked away, and then, an afterthought, More marshmallows are coming.

He met Grace coming through the visitor gate. Chuck was nearby, telling a family with three young children about how they had found Cinder and had brought her, one-eyed, to the rescue to live out her days. The lion watched the group with yawning boredom.

Why so quiet? Grace asked him as they walked up the path past the Twins. In the next enclosure Katy stood at the edge of the wire, watching them, her orange fur aglow.

Got a call from Colman, he said. Now they were passing Napoleon and Foster and the raptor enclosures.

Oh yeah?

Yep.

What'd he say?

I'll play you the message.

The late morning was colder than it had been all week, certainly a few degrees below freezing now. Winter on the way and with the turning of the season came the need to tie things down and gather provisions: food for the animals, supplies for his own trailer up the birch path, a tune-up for the tractor so that he would be able to keep the road and paths clear during the heavy snows to come. But perhaps it was all pointless now.

In the office, the coffeepot was full and hot and the heater ticked away in the corner. He pressed the button on the answering machine and she listened to the message.

We'll just have to fight it, she said in the silence that followed.

He shook his head. I've got a bad feeling about all this.

I'll make some calls today. Maybe someone at the zoo in Boise can give us some advice or something.

You know anyone there?

I don't think so, but that doesn't mean they won't talk to me. She looked at him. You OK?

No, I'm not OK. I'm not OK at all. This is fucked up. They're acting like I'm a damn criminal.

Maybe we should call the newspaper or something. Get them involved as a public interest story.

I don't know, he said. He exhaled long and hard. Then he said, I guess let's get you started.

You sure? We can do this some other day.

Let's just do it, he said. Otherwise, I'll just sit in here and stew.

All right, so I'm planning on taking a look at Majer and Zeke today. If we have time left we can try Cinder.

I have you all day?

Only until noon, she said. I have patients at the office starting at one. Unless you really need me. I could cancel those appointments.

Don't do that, he said.

I would.

I know you would.

She sipped at her coffee and then turned to open a file cabinet, flipping through until she found what she sought. You need to get that kerosene heater fixed, she said.

I already have a heater. He gestured to the gently glowing silver dish in the corner of the room.

That's not a heater, she said. That's a toaster.

That's why I come over to your house so often.

Oh, is that why?

Yep.

A car horn honked from below and he opened the door and stepped out into the path so he could see the parking lot. He expected, or half expected, to see the forest-green Fish and Game vehicle, Steven Colman coming in person to bring more bad news, but instead it was the sheriff's SUV parked below, the man himself stepping out onto the frozen gravel. When he looked up and saw Bill there he waved and Bill returned the gesture. His thoughts went immediately to Rick and a feeling of sharp and immediate unease twisted inside him like a curl of wire. Shit, he said under his breath.

He looked to the closed door of the office for a moment and then turned back toward the parking lot once more. Shit, he said again. Then he cracked open the office door. Be right back, he said.

What's up?

He hesitated. Earl's here.

How come?

No idea. It's shaping up to be quite a morning.

She was seated at the desk, the contents of the file spread out before her—the charts of Majer's health during her tenure as the facility's veterinarian—but she rose now.

You get to work, he said. I'll see what he wants.

OK, she said, but don't call me if you get arrested.

That would actually solve a lot of my problems, he answered, half smiling. He closed the door and descended the path to the parking lot where the sheriff stood, watching him approach with hands on his belt like a character from a movie. Bill could think only of that black iron safe with its silver dial. The forest trees lay down in rows and sank one after another into the sand of a burning desert covered over with sage and thistle and stone.

He unlocked the gate and came through it, trying to unclench his hands.

Morning, the sheriff said.

Morning, Earl, Bill said.

How goes the wildlife?

He shifted his weight against the gravel. Good, he said. The sheriff did not speak further and so he added, Grace's up here getting ready for some vet stuff.

Doctor time, the sheriff said.

Every six months or so.

It was quiet between them once more. His gut knotted into a fist. You wanna come up for some coffee?

Yeah, I might do that, the sheriff said, but I think I need to show you something first.

Behind the sheriff, Bess's station wagon came up the road and turned into the parking lot. No dust rising in the cold. The air's sharpness all around them.

The sheriff waved him toward the back of the SUV. Uh, I don't know how you're gonna feel about this or if you want it or whatever, but look, that moose a couple weeks back . . .

The sheriff had his hand on the swinging rear door of the SUV but had not yet opened it. Bill stood in silence, waiting for the sheriff to reveal what he already knew would be inside. Black iron and the silver dial. He thought of serial numbers. Of what he had done.

You all right? the sheriff said.

What? He coughed. Bess had climbed out of the station wagon and was walking toward them now, her body a near-formless mass of down jacket, round face peering out from under the black hood. Yeah, I'm all right, he said. What were you saying?

The moose that got run into down near Ponderay?

What about it?

Well, first of all, I guess Steve Colman came to talk to you about it.

Yeah, that and some other stuff.

Well, heck, Bill, I'm real sorry about that.

I didn't exactly ask for permission.

Still more my fault than yours, the sheriff said. I got an earful from Fish and Game about it. I can tell you that.

They're really flexing their muscles, I guess.

That's not the way I'd put it but yeah, the sheriff said. He looked over at Cinder. The lion had come up to the front of the enclosure and stood looking at them, one eye permanently closed, the other a yellow disc.

Well, so look, the real reason I'm here is that the Connor boys were the ones who butchered that moose and they thought maybe you might want the bones and stuff. For the animals, I mean.

He pulled the door open at last to reveal a series of plastic bags packed with ice and the red of moose meat, long bent legs and bits of bone and ribs. The frozen carcass after the steaks had been cut away.

Jack Connor? Bill said.

Yeah, Jack and his brother. Frank or whatever his name is.

They've been here a couple of times with their kids, Bess said. She stood next to Bill now, looking down into the open trunk. The red meat. Some wet and partially frozen tufts of brown fur.

That's what they said. They knew it was you who dispatched her.

Him, Bill said.

OK then, the sheriff said. Him. Anyway, they wanted you to have it.

We can use it, Bess said.

Yeah, he said. He stood there in a kind of exhausted silence, breathing out a long slow hiss of steam. Dang right we can, he said.

I wasn't really sure you'd want it, the sheriff said. I mean, you didn't look too happy about what happened with that. How it turned out, I mean.

Who would be? he said.

True. Anyway, I told them I might better bring it up myself, in case there were any hard feelings or anything.

I'm always glad to get meat, Bill said. A smile spread across his face despite himself because he realized at last what was in the trunk and what was not. From one tragedy to another.

I'll go get the cart, Bess said, turning to walk back up the path.

Thank them for me, would you? he said.

The sheriff nodded.

How's the guy that ran into him? Bill asked.

He'll be fine. Broke some ribs and banged up his face some against the steering wheel.

Well, that's good I guess. That he'll heal up, I mean.

You said Grace's up there?

In the office, Bill said. She'll get mad if I let you leave without saying hello.

Let's not let that happen, then.

The hum of the golf cart now, coming down the path through the enclosures, all of which he could see from the parking lot: boxes of wire fronted by wooden platforms for viewing, wooden buildings, the portable rectangle of his office trailer and the equipment shed where he stored food and medical supplies and fuel. Midway up the hill, he could see Majer's dark shape moving slowly across his own loop of wire. From where he stood he could not help but feel that it looked more like a concentration camp than a rescue.

THEY TRANSFERRED the remains of the carcass from the sheriff's SUV to a box on the cart and then to the freezers at the top of the trail loop. The sheriff had disappeared inside the office to visit with Grace, an event Majer watched with apparent anticipation, nose pressed to the fencing and milky eyes staring out at the closed office door. When at last the two of them emerged from the office, Grace spoke to the bear and he waggled his head in apparent joy and followed the sound of her voice down the fence line.

He's looking like an old man, the sheriff said.

He's only thirty-eight but that's pretty old for a griz, Grace said.

The sheriff nodded and they talked a bit more about bears and then about his horses until the radio at the sheriff's belt crackled and he turned and answered it and then told them that he had to go.

Come bring the grandkids some time, Bill said.

We're due for that, the sheriff said. So look, Bill, Grace told me a little about what you're up against with the IFG. I know a couple of people. Maybe we can work out a way to help you out some.

Really? he said.

No guarantees but Judge Holcomb is my duck-hunting buddy. Maybe he can slow this process down. At least give you time.

I'd appreciate that, Bill said. Anything you can do.

They shook hands and then the sheriff walked down the trail toward the parking lot, talking into his radio all the while.

I told you we'd figure out a way, Grace said.

You're amazing.

Yes, she said. Yes, I am.

The bear huffed twice, a loud exhalation.

All right, you, Grace said, turning to him. I'm going to get your medicine and then I'll meet you in the den.

Majer's mouth curled in a grin.

He's got a crush on you, Bill said to her.

Well, I've got a crush on him too, Grace said.

The words of the sheriff had confused him. He had been anxious for the man to leave, only because part of him still believed that the past would flood back over him like the river's current and that the sheriff would suddenly reveal the true purpose of his visit. But maybe that was all over now. Maybe his past had been over all the while and he had worked himself up for no reason at all, the forest its own separate world broken off from everywhere he had come from and from everything he had done.

They mixed up a slurry of ice cream and fruit with a blender in the barn and she returned to the access door in Majer's enclosure, holding the glass pitcher in her gloved hand.

A way to a man's heart is through his stomach.

True, Bill said.

Then Bess's voice from down the path: Hey, Bill, telephone.

Who is it?

He didn't say.

He was going to call after her, tell her to take a message or at least find out who was on the phone, but she had already ambled away from the office door, toward the enclosures nearer the parking lot. Cinder and Baker. Elsie and Tommy. Mountain lion and badger. Owl and eagle. Well, crap, he said.

Get my folder, Grace said as he stepped forward out of the barn.

He crossed down the path and to the office, the room not much warmer than it had been outside despite running the heater all morning. Grace was right that he needed to get the kerosene heater working and brought in from the equipment shed. If he failed to fix it he would need to buy a replacement. Another expense. Coffeepot nearly empty. He picked up the phone. This is Bill, he said.

You son of a bitch, Rick said. And there came the sinking again. The fucking thing is empty.

He stood with the phone in his hand, staring to where the heater glowed orange in front of its silver dish, staring at the cold empty air between himself and the burning wire filaments. Empty? he said.

You fucking knew it was. You fucker.

I didn't open it. I told you I didn't open it.

You fucking liar. You sent me to fucking prison and you killed my mom and now you fucking steal from me too?

Listen, he said.

No, you listen, you son of a bitch. Twelve years. I'm going to fuck you up for this.

I'm not a fucking locksmith. I swear to god I never opened that safe. It's just been sitting on the floor in the closet all this time. I swear to god.

But the line had already clicked to silence. The conversation so fast that it hardly seemed real. A blur of words and then the click and he stood staring at the heater with the phone clutched in one hand and a file folder he did not remember picking up in the other. Jesus Christ. Jesus fucking Christ. What have you done? What the hell have you done now?

He stood there until the phone began its rhythmic alarm and then he laid it back in its cradle and moved outside again. The day bright and clear. Frost in the shadows. The faint drip of moisture inside the angle of winter sun. He turned up the path to where Grace stood talking to Majer. You're my boyfriend, she said. You're my new boyfriend.

He stood next to her without speaking.

Anything important? she said.

Nope, he said. Not important. Not important at all.

7

MILTON WELLS'S DOOR WAS OPEN BUT NAT STOPPED SHORT OF walking through it, instead lingering just out of sight. His eyes were in line with the brass plaque that spelled out Wells's name in block letters, under which ran his title: Owner, Milt's Reliable Ford-Lincoln-Mercury. Behind Nat, an occasional salesman passed down the carpeted hall, silent but for the swish of a pant leg.

Then Wells's voice came: Someone out there waiting for me? and Nat blinked and cleared his throat. Um . . . I wasn't sure if you were busy, he said, turning into the doorway.

Come on in. The door's open for a reason.

Nat had stood in the office only once before, on the day he was hired, but it looked just the same: black filing cabinets, stacks of papers, a calendar featuring an image of a car blurring around a turn—this month a new-model Country Squire station wagon with faux-wood paneling—and an oak desk behind which sat Milton Wells himself, a man of perhaps sixty, although his swoop of white hair made him appear much older than he actually was, bespectacled and wearing a Western-style button shirt with looping roses at the shoulders. Around his neck hung a bolo tie.

Nat, Wells said as he entered the room, peering at him over the top of his reading glasses. What can I do you for?

Hello, Mr. Wells, he said. The fact that the man had remembered his name was so surprising that for a moment he could not remember why he had come. He cleared his throat again and then said, I...uh... had a quick question.

Call me Milt. Everybody does.

All right, Nat said. And then added: Milt.

Come in, come in.

He stepped fully through the door and stood awkwardly before the desk until his boss asked him to sit and he perched at the edge of the chair opposite and began, at last, to mumble his question, the sentence punctuated by ums and ahs and long vowel sounds. He had not yet gotten to the verb when a salesman's voice came from behind him: Hey, Milt, looks like we got that EXP sold, he said.

No kidding? Hot damn, Milt said. Who did it?

Vince.

Man alive. That guy could sell you the shirt off your back.

Nat was looking at his boss and then he was looking away from him and into the room. A safe stood on the carpet in the corner, its black surface about two feet square and fronted with a silver dial and handle, books and binders and paperwork packing the shelves all around it. Then he looked away. The poster on the wall was of a Mustang with a dark-haired woman in a thin evening gown draped across its hood.

He's a beast, the salesman said. Tom's putting the paperwork together right now.

I hope you watched how he did it, Milt said.

Float like a butterfly.

Sting like a bee, Milt concluded. Good man.

The salesman apologized briefly to Nat for interrupting and Nat mumbled something in response and then the salesman was gone.

That's how it's done, Nat, Milt said, smiling. I challenged them to come up with a way to sell it and someone rose to the challenge. That car might have sat there all year, but someone took it up and got it done. You see what that does?

Yes, sir, Nat said.

It's like a calling.

What is?

Anything, Milt said. Anything you take seriously. Do you understand what I'm saying?

I think so, Nat said.

You're the brake guy in the shop, right?

Lube guy.

Yeah, OK, so the point is: even a lube-oil-filter can change a man's life.

All right, Nat said, although he did not understand this statement at all.

It was silent then, silent once again, Nat looking from Milt to the posters on the wall, to the calendar, and back to Milt. All right then, his boss said at last. What'd you want to talk to me about?

Oh, I wondered if I could maybe get a small advance on my paycheck, he said, his voice faltering, the syllables coming in pieces.

The expression on Milt's face was immediately one of concern. Jeez, he said, we don't usually do that. You all right?

Yeah, he said. Yeah, I'm all right. He looked at the bend of his own leg, his knee. There was an oil stain on the fabric there and a smudge of grease on the cuff of his pants. He had been surprised that Milt knew his name, but now he realized that it was emblazoned on the front of his pale blue work shirt: a white oval patch containing dark blue script. It's my mom, he said. She's pretty sick.

I'm sorry to hear that, Milt said. He leaned forward and took his glasses off. How much are we talking here?

I don't know, Nat said. A hundred, maybe. Just to get by.

A hundred? Milt said. I don't think we can do that. Maybe fifty.

I could use fifty, Nat said.

You sending her money?

Every month, he said.

Shoot, Milt said, that's gotta be hard.

Usually it's all right but, I don't know, I just ended up short this month.

How long you been working here now?

Almost two years.

That right?

Two years next month.

Well, that kind of makes you family. We take care of our family here, Nat. Milt sat watching him as if Nat might, at any moment, get up and sing or dance or do somersaults. Then he said, I'll call Joanne and you can swing by and pick it up.

Oh man, Nat said, relief flooding through him. I really appreciate it.

Don't make it a habit, Nat.

I won't.

Your mom here in town?

She's back home.

Where's that?

Battle Mountain, Nat said.

Battle Mountain, Milt repeated. He smiled faintly. I went out there for a rodeo when I was younger. Bull roping.

Rodeo's big around there.

Yeah, I had a good show there, if I remember correctly. In the fairgrounds.

Nat nodded.

Anything else? Milt said.

No, just that, Nat said, rising now to his feet. Thanks a lot. It really helps.

It's your money, Milt said. I'm just giving you a little of it early. I'll call Joanne right now.

He nodded, stepping backward through the door and thanking him once again before turning into the hall. When he reached Joanne in payroll, she was already on the phone and he stood before her, hands in his pockets, until she was done. Then she produced a huge bound book out of which she wrote him a check for fifty dollars. He returned to the shop, the final door opening into a long gray room lined with tires and toolboxes and chattering air wrenches, the air suffused with the smell of deep and penetrating grease and oil and gasoline.

There you are, the shop manager called. That red Fiesta's in for an oil change. Customer's waiting.

He looked up at the clock high up on the wall: 4:45. Almost done. He stepped out through the open bay and into the low slanting light. The owner of the Fiesta stood with his arms crossed next to the tiny car, scowling. Behind him, the highway, and yet farther away, an airplane lifted off the runway and rose slowly into the pale blue sky.

HE TOLD himself that he would sit in the car and would wait for Rick there but by the time he actually arrived at the Peppermill parking lot he had convinced himself that he should immediately cash the check from the dealership and that the casino cashier would be the easiest way to do so, even though he also knew that he really should not enter the casino at all, that finding himself within might drain him of all the money he had, a thought that remained with him even as he pushed through the glass doors and stepped inside. The entrance to the café lay ahead of him, the long line of poker slots stretching off to his left, their sounds bursting all at once into clarity and flooding out behind him into the scattered rows of dark cars.

The cashier handed him the bills and he folded them into his wallet and drifted down a carpeted hall through a vaguely luminous darkness until he reached the Fish Bar with its huge round aquarium, slot machines spaced around it at intervals. The room was mostly deserted and he stood there for a long while, staring at the brightly glowing fish in the tank, following their flitting motions across coral and rocks, telling himself that he should leave and then telling himself that he should not. The machines around him periodically bleeped and warbled querulously. Go now, he said to himself. You need to leave right now. And yet he did not move, continuing to stare at the circling fish and thinking that were his fortune to hold for only a few minutes, he might double the meager fifty dollars he had been given, that the cash might thicken in his wallet, that when Mike came again to make the collection, he just might have the whole amount and could pay off his debt to Johnny Aguirre and be done with it forever, everything outside of the tight encasement of the room fading slowly into fiction, replaced with a sense of possibility. Under the acidic mixture of adrenaline and sweat and joy and despair, he was sure he could smell the felt of the gaming tables, and with that scent the machines in his vision seemed to pulse with lucency.

He told himself ten dollars. Ten dollars only. No more than that, moving back down that dark hall to the table games, and although he had fantasized that he might free himself of Johnny Aguirre, he was not even thinking that he would win now, not really, but only that it might pass some of the time between this moment and the next. And then, without any reason he could determine, he was thinking of the lion, not the lions he had seen on television but instead the only lion he had ever seen in person, a thin but still massive male on display at the MGM Grand across town, the first casino he and Rick had visited when they acquired their fake IDs from the men at the warehouse where Rick had worked and the only casino Nat had entered while Rick was in prison for those thirteen months. When they had first entered, Nat had not known there was a lion inside the casino and had happened upon the animal only because he was lost within the lower level, a cavernous video arcade filled with games and an ice cream shop and on one side of which stood a long line of families waiting to have their photograph taken with the lion. The animal was out of place, out of context, thin and lethargic and chained by the neck to a platform, and yet retaining some sense of its former power and grace, and Nat stood before it amazed.

That was the first time either of them had ever gambled, but Rick plowed ahead with abandon and Nat followed. For the rest of that summer they would spend many nights at the slot machines, high and chain-smoking and filling the machines over and over again with nickels and dimes. And sometimes Nat would fade away from the slots, would return to the arcade to stand before the lion, to gaze at it. Sometimes the animal would look at him, its eyes the color of African grasslands stretching out for miles, the pupils dark water holes draining back through the sand. As he watched, the attendant would lift a hunk of raw meat to wave in the air, the lion's head rising for a moment, its eyes wide. And then someone would call, Smile! and there would be a flashbulb and the people and the lion would be frozen together, the raw meat already returned to the ice chest beside the stage and the great beast's head dropping back to the platform, its eyes dimming out, and Nat standing there all the while, mute in that huge carpeted space, beyond belief, beyond understanding.

When he returned to the MGM after Rick was arrested in front of Grady's the night they robbed the Quik-Stop, it was because he did not know how else to fill the vacant hours of the early evening and so he went to look upon the lion once more. Perhaps his return was only to assuage his own loneliness, to return to a place that reminded him of his absent friend. But when he entered the casino, he happened to see a calendar through the glass of the cashier's booth, and realized with a start that it was October 23, the anniversary of his brother's death. He knew he should call his mother back in Battle Mountain, knew too that she had probably tried to call him several times during the day, but he did not want to make a call in the clanging depths of the casino, not when its purpose was to acknowledge what and who they had lost, so he descended to the arcade, and he wondered, not for the first time, how his life might have been different had his brother still been alive.

There was no lion this time, only an empty stage in the corner, and Nat wandered back to the gaming floor because he did not want to be alone in the silent apartment and he could not think of anything else to do. Had he simply lost his money that night he might never have returned. But he did not lose. He had played only slots with Rick but that night he sat at the blackjack table, having already played the nickels for over an hour, and listened to the dealer explain how he could split a hand, what insurance was and when to use it, how to bet and hit and stand. And of course he lost the first hands but then he started to win and he left that first night with more money than he came in with, not quite doubling his thirty dollars but returning to the apartment with nearly a full day's extra wages. He made minimum wage at the shop, lubing and doing oil changes all day for $2.75 an hour. Returning home with twenty extra dollars amounted to over seven hours of work. He could not believe it. He could not believe just how easy it had been.

And so he returned, returned to the MGM—the old lion was once again on its platform—and returned too to the blackjack table. This time he did not win, but even in losing he felt a kind of electricity running through him. What he thought then was that he had tapped into the life force of the place in which he now resided in some miraculous way, that he had become, for a moment, finally part of it, part of the world in which he lived. The truth of it went beyond anything he had ever felt in Battle Mountain, at least since Bill's death, and certainly beyond anything he had ever felt in Reno, because it was not the playing and it was not even the winning that drew him in, but the chance of something happening. Anything. And over the course of that week and the next, he saw the manifestation of that chance two times. The first occurred when an Asian man in a tan suit stood before a slot machine, alarms howling all around him and the number $100,000 flashing above. Nat read later in the newspaper that the man had flown into town from Japan and played only a single dollar before winning the jackpot. The second had been an old woman with a white poodle in her arms. The jackpot that time had been a quarter of a million dollars. She leaped in place over and over again and the little dog yapped in rhythm with her motion. He saw people drop a hundred-dollar chip on a single hand of blackjack. Sometimes they won. Sometimes they did not. There was a lion in the arcade, but this felt like that lion wide awake and free, stalking a herd of gazelles through the carpeted expanse of the casino.

In his memory, the man and later the woman who had won those two jackpots stood as if in the imagined world beyond this one, their bodies adrift in the thin clarity of empty air, the ringing and clanging of the casino's bells fading into a slow reverberant silence and their bodies shining. He sat up late, thinking about how their lives must have changed after such an event, the golden moment that rotated them out of wherever they had been and into a world so unexpected they could never have imagined its geography at all. Lives made incandescent in an instant. The world around him was filled with separation, each object different from himself: unknowable, unknowing. And yet forces were at work that could pluck one individual name from the faceless luckless masses. The entire town an advertisement that made the possibility into a kind of promise: every casino, slot machine, poker game, barroom wager, like throwing coins into the same dark impossible sea in hopes some leviathan might, of its own free will, loft itself upon the shore.

But all of that had been before. Now he sat at the green felt of a blackjack table, and he actually won for a time. Within twenty minutes he had doubled the paycheck advance Milt Wells had approved, but then his luck turned as it always did. The remainder of the hands had been busts and he had doubled down repeatedly, losing his winnings at twice the rate he might have otherwise. And yet even in this, his despair was lined with a faint ripple of electricity, each new card spelling out a destiny he felt he could almost see into, the hole card facedown in front of the dealer, the players—two others beside him—staring down at their two cards as if they might, at any moment, change value. The fat man next to him laughed every time he lost, as if there was some joke that Nat did not understand.

The dealer's up card: an ace of hearts. Insurance or even money? she asked him. She was pretty, blond-haired and thick-lipped. He wondered where Rick was. Then Susan.

His cards totaled eighteen. Yeah, let's do that, he said.

One dollar, she said.

He slid the chip over and she moved it into the insurance line, where it sat just above his cards. She flipped her card over, showing a ten of diamonds.

Blackjack, the dealer said. Two to one on the insurance. She took the two chips he had bet on his hand from the ring before him and then slid two chips back toward him from the insurance line.

Damn, the fat man said. I shoulda done that too.

Nat shrugged. Sometimes it works, he said.

The dealer cleared the table and dealt the cards again. Nat was dealt a ten of spades, which he could hardly look at, so complete was his excitement and terror. He laid two one-dollar chips before him, the last of the ten he had decided to bet, although his pocket still held the remaining forty in cash. When the dealer flipped the next card faceup in front of him, it was an ace of clubs.

Hot damn, the fat man said.

Backdoor Kenny, the dealer said, smiling. Blackjack.

Nat was smiling now too, face slick with sweat, mouth dry. It felt so close sometimes, so close to the bone that he could hardly stand it, as if some essential or elemental or animal part of him was on the verge of shaking out of his skin. As if he had been circling something he could not even recognize but knew was perfect. And somehow he felt like he was in control of what was happening—even though he also knew that the idea of it was absurd and impossible—and yet he could not remember any other moment in his life where he had felt such a thing. Not ever. Here, at least, there was a sense of possibility. Outside the glass doors of the casino was only a narrow path that he already knew led nowhere at all.

She slid the chips in front of him. Six dollars. He had bet two and had he bet fifty he now would have a hundred and fifty. But he had only bet two dollars, the table's minimum, and so now he had six and was still down four. How quickly fortune could change.

On the next deal he bet ten. The fat man next to him said, Now you're talking.

Nat glanced at the woman on the other side of him but she did not return the look, instead staring down at the table, her eyes like glass pressed into the bruised gray meat of her face. Below them ran that

perfect plain of green felt, like a grassy field spread out to float above
the floor on a layer of thin cool air.

BY THE time Rick's shift was over at the café, all the money was gone
and Nat sat in the corner booth drinking a cup of coffee with the spare
change that remained, the feeling of despair and shame that washed
over him so acute that he nearly burst into tears, not only from the
despair and shame but also from fear and rage and the realization that
he wanted, in the sharp clarity of that moment, to be back in Battle
Mountain, a state of mind that entered him fully like demonic pos-
session. But when he had been given the loans, Johnny Aguirre had
told him that there was no backing out of them, that if he left or ran
or tried to disappear he would ultimately be found and it would be
much worse for him than if he remained in Reno to face what was coming, whatever that turned out to be. He had been told this soon after
he had missed the first payment and had been told it again when he
had missed the second. And yet the feeling of homesickness had come
upon him again and again while Rick was in prison, each time like an
endless well. Sometimes, during those months, he would stare at the
telephone where it hung above the stovetop and the impossible urge to
call his dead brother would come upon him with a sudden violence that
would nearly bring him to his knees. He had never told Rick about such
thoughts and he knew he never would. It felt, sometimes, as if a silver
wire fled back from the present and into the dark backdraft of the past,
not growing thinner with the years but only longer, some great measure
of absence that began at his heart and reached not to that night of the
anaconda but rather to all the golden days and nights before it, a time
that he knew was lost to him and would never be regained.

And now that feeling had returned. Even though Rick was back,
there was the undeniable sense that something had changed from when
they first arrived in Reno two years before. Then, it felt as if they had
stepped across a threshold into some unimaginable world, even though

they had no money and could barely afford a loaf of white bread and a package of bologna once they rented that first apartment on Fourth Street. But even that had held a kind of magic, not only because it was the first place Nat had ever lived outside of the trailer but because, in comparison, the apartment felt so tangible and solid that he found himself wondering how something as flimsy and insubstantial as a trailer could survive—had ever survived—the Battle Mountain winters that swept down from Golconda Summit each season and dragged away anything that was not in some way shackled to the earth. And yet he and his mother and his brother, for a time, had lived there together, and someone had lived in the trailer before them and would likely live there after them as well.

They had no furniture in those first months and talked often of driving back to Battle Mountain to collect their beds and another load of personal effects, but they could think of no practical way to transport their mattresses back to Reno. And in any case, Nat did not mind sleeping on the floor enough to care. Not then. He had come to Reno at Rick's urging but he also knew that it was the start of his life, of his adult life, and that Reno held possibilities for him that Battle Mountain never would. Back home, he might one day have gone to work for one of the mining companies on the flanks of the mountains. Rick's own father had moved their family to Battle Mountain because he landed just such a job. It was possible that, without Rick, Nat would have found himself at fifty or sixty having never gone beyond the town in which he had been born, that he might have spent all his life at the dry bottom of the same sand-filled bowl. Even had his brother lived, that might have been true.

But he had gone beyond the limitations of that dry plain and at first it had seemed like he was fulfilling some kind of destiny that he could barely imagine was real. Even landing jobs had proven easy. The day after they arrived, Nat was hired by a tire shop, and later that same week Rick found a job in a warehouse from which he would return, over the course of that month, with stories of the various scams and games and hustles of Reno's nightlife. He learned where to buy pot and where to find black beauties and cross tops and, finally, where to score cocaine, a near-mythical substance that neither of them had even seen outside of a movie screen. That spring they discovered the slot machines at the MGM Grand and they also discovered Grady's and the 715 Club, beginning there and eventually bar-hopping from the upper end of South Virginia Street all the way down to the Peppermill and Spats and the Met, Rick leading the way and Nat following, both of them drunk on Mad Dog and sometimes stoned and later still high on diet pills and occasionally on cocaine, all of it moving around them and they a part of that flow because they were in the city now, the Biggest Little City in the World, and it was, in comparison to everything they had known, like stepping into the center of a lightbulb and grasping the hot glowing electric filament.

HEY.

Nat looked up from the coffee as Rick slid into the booth across from him.

How long you been here?

Hour and a half, Nat said. How's the new job?

Eight hours of dishes. What do you think?

The sound of the casino floor was muffled but there was still the chattering and banging, the ringing of bells, the bleeping.

You hungry? Rick said. I get a discount.

Naw, Nat said. I'm pretty dang tired, actually.

Long day in the mines?

Something like that.

Rick's apron hung limp over his shoulder. His eyes darkly ringed.

You don't look much better, Nat said.

Shit, man, Rick said, that's what bennies are for. You want? He tapped his shirt pocket and Nat nodded and Rick handed across a roll of pills wrapped in cellophane like a thin roll of candy Life Savers. Nat pushed two into his palm with his thumbnail and handed the roll back. Susan's on her way over, Rick said.

Cool, Nat said, but even at the sound of her name he felt a jolt of guilt and longing run through him in equal measure.

So out-of-pocket on my mom's surgery is gonna be eleven hundred dollars, Rick said.

What the fuck?

Yeah, I called her on my lunch break. That's what she said. There's some fuckup with Medicaid so they're not covering all of it.

Shit, Nat said. Eleven hundred dollars. Jesus Christ.

Hopefully they'll just do it and I can pay off the bill for like twenty years or something. He looked out toward where the café opened onto the casino itself. They might not do it because there's still a big bill from the last time.

It's Medicaid. They'll do it, Nat said. I think they have to. It's the Hippocratic oath or something.

We'll see, Rick said. He returned his gaze to Nat. You all right? he said.

Yeah, yeah. Just wiped.

Shit man, don't pussy out on me. It's only like six or something.

I'm all right. Need to wake up is all.

He looked up but Rick was looking past him now. There's my girl, he said.

How he wanted to turn to see her walking toward them, toward him, but he did not, focusing instead on his coffee cup, that black circle surrounded by the white porcelain of the mug.

Hey baby, she said, slipping into the booth next to Rick, their lips meeting just for an instant and then her eyes turning toward him. What's up with you? she said. You look like hell.

Totally, Rick said.

You need a pick-me-up?

I just took one.

Dr. Susan is in the house and she's got just what you need.

Nat looked up at her now. Her smile. Her eyes sparkling in the café's yellow lights. She unzipped her tiny purse and extracted a small ziplock. No way, he said.

Yes way, she said.

This is why I love you so much, Rick said.

Very funny, she said, slapping him playfully on the chest. Shall we?

Oh yes, Rick said. We certainly shall.

* * *

THEY PILED into one of the stalls in the men's bathroom and Rick cut the cocaine into three thin lines on the surface of Susan's makeup mirror with a long-expired credit card he kept in his wallet for this reason alone. Nat stood against the metal partition. She was so close to him in that tiny space, her body bumping against his, her hands resting on his shoulders. Her hips. Her breasts brushing against his back. How he wanted her. How he remembered those breasts, those hips. God how he wanted her again, a thought followed immediately by the rushing current of his guilt.

You're up, Natty, Rick said.

He leaned over the mirror, taking the rolled dollar bill from Rick's hand and inhaling the only remaining line and then standing upright again, sniffing. That familiar stinging numbness. Susan clapped and giggled next to him and wrapped her arms around Rick and kissed him deeply, Nat pinned against the partition until they were through.

At the sink he laved water over his hair and across his face and nose and when he looked at himself in the mirror the visage that stared back at him was a wrecked shell, hair stringing down across his forehead and eyes sunken back into his skull. It would take ten minutes before the cocaine would fully enter his system and he wondered if he could even wait that long before passing out. Susan stood next to him smiling into the mirror and sniffing water up her nose from her wet fingertips. Ugh, she said. That's better. Rick at another sink farther down doing the same. A man entered the bathroom and looked briefly at Susan and then disappeared into a stall. A moment later came the sound of him urinating.

Christ almighty, buddy, Rick said. You really look terrible.

I feel terrible, he said.

Maybe you're getting the flu or something.

Could be, Nat said.

Susan put her hand on his forehead. It felt cool and smooth and he wanted her to hold it there for the rest of time. He could see himself leaning into her, her arms coming around him. He could see her naked, riding him on that stained mattress in his bedroom in the apartment midway through Rick's prison sentence.

You feel hot, she said.

He had closed his eyes at some point but he opened them now. I'm gonna go outside and get some air, he said.

You want us to come? Rick said.

Naw, I'll just be a minute or two.

Don't go too far, Susan said. Party's going to start soon.

He nodded but did not look at her. Could not. He pushed out through the lobby. From the receding hall that led past the Fireside Lounge and on to the Fish Bar and the room where he had just ground himself back to zero again came the harsh and tinny sounds of the poker slots, even now a siren calling him. Then the glass doors that led outside.

The night had gone cold in the hour and a half since he had first arrived at the casino and the air seemed to blow through his skin and into the dark red center of his body. He extracted a cigarette and asked a passing man in a blue suit for a light but the man continued to walk and Nat stood there with the unlit Marlboro in his hand. Susan was somewhere behind him, inside among the bright clanging machines. And Rick. The thought of them together almost too much to bear. And yet he had waited and waited and waited for Rick to return and what had happened between him and Susan would never have happened were it not for his friend's absence. He believed it and would keep on believing it as long as it took to become true. How desperate and lonely he had been. How desperate and lonely he still was.

But the cocaine was coming on now, the first hot thrill of it coursing up through him, and with it whatever he had been feeling—self-pity or guilt or the beginnings of some illness, he knew not what—was blown back from him as if upon the long foaming line of a receding wave. He had been leaning back against the cold smooth surface of the casino's outer wall and he stepped forward from it now, feeling his legs shake off their fatigue. He was not even cold anymore.

But then he looked up toward the parking lot and the cold chill of the night returned all at once. Idling before him was a rust-colored El Camino, its paint dull and its door dented in. Behind the wheel, peering at him through the open window, was the thin tattooed man he and Rick had beaten at Landrum's, one black-ringed eye staring out at him, the other clear and bright. His lips curled into a grin. From between the fingers that gripped the wheel, a cigarette's smoke twisted from the open window in concert with his steaming breath.

Nat turned toward the door, nearly breaking into a run, but he had hardly moved a step when a hand grasped his arm.

Hey, hey, where you going in such a hurry? the voice said.

The hand turned him, spun him in place with an effort that seemed marginal to its effect. Standing before him was Mike, his hand still gripping Nat's arm just above the elbow. Behind him stood Johnny Aguirre himself: short, black hair slicked back, white sports coat pulled over a turquoise T-shirt as if he stood not in the cold night of Reno but in the warm afternoon of Miami.

You got someplace to go? Johnny said.

No, I just . . . His voice trailed off. He glanced to where the El Camino had been but in its place was a long gold Lincoln Town Car.

You're on my list to track down.

I was gonna come see you, Johnny.

Is that right?

Nat placed his unlit cigarette between his lips, an action of habit, and a moment later Mike's free hand came up before him, clicking the wheel of a silver lighter, the flame like a hot orange teardrop. He leaned into its light and the cigarette burned before him.

So you have something for Johnny, right? Mike said, clicking the lighter shut and returning it to his pocket.

Nat looked at him. The cocaine was surging through him now, the cigarette burning down in his mouth as if he was breathing in the fire.

Johnny Aguirre's mouth traced a faint smile. He wore a gold chain around his neck and the colors of the casino lights chased up and down its length. Nat, Nat, Nat, he said slowly, shaking his head from side to side. What am I gonna do with you?

Nat looked at the men who stood before him, their faces models of seriousness. The effect made him giggle despite his attempt not to, the cigarette bouncing upon his lips.

This funny to you? Johnny Aguirre said.

And now Nat could not stop. It all seemed too ridiculous to be real. Nothing could happen to him now. He was invincible.

Let's take a walk, Johnny Aguirre said.

Mike's thick hand came around Nat's forearm and then they were moving, drifting out of the haze of light that fled from the interior of the casino and into the darkness of the parking lot beyond.

PART II

THE KILLERS

8

YOU ARRIVE IN IDAHO BEFORE THE FIRST SNOW BUT IT IS well below freezing and the ragged houses that peer out at you from the forest along the road each send a pillar of smoke into a crystalline blue sky. It is late November 1984, and you stand at a pay phone, your breath steaming, the cigarette you hold between your fingers trembling as the other clenches the receiver to your ear. The Datsun is parked just a few feet away, one of its headlights crushed and the bumper askew.

When your uncle answers, you expect to have to explain but he does not seem surprised to hear from you.

Just keep driving north until you see the sign for Naples, he tells you. There's a pay phone at the bar there. Call me and I'll come get you.

All right, you say.

What are you driving?

An old blue Datsun 510.

I'll find you, your uncle says.

Uncle David arrives ten minutes later, rumbling out of the trees in a rusty pickup, swinging in beside you and then waving you forward to follow. And you do follow: up off the highway through a forest so choked with foliage that it seems impenetrable. Scraps of cloud drifting through pine and cedar and spruce. Like paradise. And like a place where you will never be found.

When you reach the trailer, your uncle smiles and embraces you, his expression one of mingled joy and concern. This is quite a surprise, he says.

Did my mom call you?

Nope. He taps a pack of Camels against the palm of his hand. Smoke?

You nod. At forty-seven, your uncle appears much older than you remember, a mustached man with dirty blond hair streaked with gray who looks not unlike Bill. You have thought all your life that Bill looked like your father but now you realize that you were probably wrong.

You are handed a cigarette and then a lighter. There is a wooden picnic table next to the trailer and your uncle sits on its edge and when you return the lighter he lights his own cigarette and the two of you are silent for a time, blowing smoke into the pine-scented air.

I'm guessing you're not on some kind of vacation, your uncle says at last.

No.

You're in trouble?

Yes, you say. You have told yourself that you will not cry but now your eyes fill with tears.

Hang on now, your uncle says. That's not gonna help.

I'm sorry, you say.

How much trouble are you in?

A lot.

Police trouble?

You nod.

Your uncle stands and looks at you. The sun is behind him and his body cuts a black shape against it. Let me get a Pepsi, he says. And then you'd better tell me what's going on.

The two of you sit outside at the picnic table, both drinking the Diet Pepsi your uncle has retrieved from inside the trailer, and you tell him the whole story, every part of it, Rick and Susan and the job at the car dealership and Johnny Aguirre and Mike, pausing momentarily when your eyes fill again. It feels like it is someone else's story at times, as if you are narrating something out of a movie, but it is your own and it pours out of you like a torrent.

Christ you've had a run, your uncle says into the silence that follows.

I've done some pretty bad things.

Well shit, that's why people come up here. To start over. That's what the whole place is about.

I don't know what to do.

Well, your uncle says, you're gonna need a new name for one.

A new name?

Am I whispering or something?

No.

Good. There is no Nathaniel Reed. I don't know anyone by that name and neither do you. So what do you want to go by? Jack or Tom or something?

You sit there saying nothing for a long time. It somehow feels as if the two of you are merely camping up in the mountains. The sounds of birds everywhere. And then you say it: Bill.

Bill? He nods. That's actually a real good idea. We can get a birth certificate with that name.

I guess so.

I'm gonna need to talk to your mom some.

Are you gonna call the police?

Why would I do that?

I don't know. Because you're harboring a criminal.

Your uncle laughs then. Bill, you're a regular comedian, he says. Yes, you are.

The feeling of being called by that name is like a fire inside your chest. Each time it burns. You realize that your brother is the best person you have ever known and that had he been alive, had he survived Battle Mountain, you would never be in this situation at all. And because of this fact, you know you have failed him. He gave you a red-tailed hawk to hold in your hands and in the memory of it you can sometimes feel the heat of that great bird arcing up through your fingers.

You do not see the animals that first day, the few animals that your uncle is keeping in small, cramped cages. Instead he takes you to Spokane, a round trip of four hours, where you sell the Datsun to a used car lot for two hundred dollars because your uncle reasons that the car is the only concrete way anyone might be able to track you down.

That first night you sleep on the tiny couch in the trailer and in the morning your uncle takes you down through the birches and shows you the animals. Coyote and bobcat and one lumbering and slow-witted porcupine. You watch them all but when you reach the bear's cage something changes for you. It is a jolt. Like a wire of electricity that burns in the air between. You will remember, all your life, looking into those eyes, that conduit connecting you to the boy you were so many years ago when your father died and you came to visit your uncle for the first and only time.

Majer likes you, your uncle says.

How do you know?

He doesn't usually just stare like that. Maybe you smell funny to him.

Maybe, you say.

Majer, your uncle says. Meet Bill. He'll be staying with us for a while, so best get used to him.

I remember him from when I was a kid.

I expect he remembers you too.

Can he remember that long?

Oh sure, your uncle says. Time's different for these critters. Sometimes I think he can remember stuff that hasn't even happened yet.

You smile at the absurdity of the statement and yet in those eyes you can see snow and forests and your own eyes mirrored back at you, afraid, confused, and just stumbling forward into the life that would be yours. Your uncle calls you Bill and that is the life you will claim.

YOUR UNCLE receives disability checks for reasons he never clearly explains and that seems enough to pay whatever bills there are, or at least it was enough before you arrived. There is a little sign on the highway indicating North Idaho's Only Zoo, and occasionally tourists stop to look at the animals and your uncle acts the tour guide, talking about each animal in great detail, telling their stories, where they came from and in what situation he found them. Except for the great bear, all of them have been injured in some way and only the raccoons are allowed outside their cages. David tells you that he once entered the bear's cage regularly and they played catch with a Wiffle ball but then he was thrown against the back wall in a moment of excitement, breaking his arm and his collarbone, and he has not entered the cage since.

Most days you simply do not know what to do with your time. You consider applying for a job, either in Bonners Ferry to the north or in Sandpoint to the south, but your uncle tells you that you will need to wait a year or more just to make sure there are no agencies actively looking for you.

And so you are patient. Or try to be. You sit out in the sunlight and read whatever books your uncle has lying around—spy novels mostly—and then head down to the library in Sandpoint. At first you look at books on animals, mostly because you do not know what else to do and at least this is information applicable to the world in which you have found yourself, information physical and imperative. Later you spend those same hours reading through magazines and newspapers, taking notes: *Indy Car Racing* and *Wrestling* and *Sports Illustrated* and, always a day late, the sports pages of the *New York Times*.

When winter comes, it is like nothing you have ever experienced. It snowed in Battle Mountain, of course, and it snowed in Reno, but in North Idaho the snow is fierce and deep and covers everything. The roads become flumes, the sides of which are lined with huge berms like white walls, fences and gates and mailboxes hidden somewhere within. You find that you love the contrast: the wet black trees, the snow sparkling in the sunlight, everything so alive, and you standing there in that old forest breathing in the frozen bite of the air.

IT IS barely May when the bottom falls out beneath you. You bet on the Super Bowl and win but then lose on the next two Indy car races. You are in the library often, studying the sports pages, still circling the same dank mudwalled hole that drew you to Idaho to begin with, knowing what you are doing but somehow unable to stop yourself, the action as automatic and thoughtless as reflex or instinct, but it is not instinct, you know that much too, and yet you cannot explain what it is and so you cannot explain why. At least in the casinos there was some feeling of belonging and, however illusory, a sense of control, of possibility, but now there is only a crushing and endless loneliness and what sense of control, of possibility, you might have felt is wholly entangled with the guilt of what you have already done and the shame of knowing that you are doing it all over again. And yet still you call the bookie. It is automatic. Without thought. And when you say the words into the telephone you feel the faintest electric spark, a wire running through the center of your chest. It is not excitement so much as it is the feeling that you are grabbing hold of your life, that you are making some kind of decision, even though, of course, you also know that it is no real decision at all.

That final time, you switch your bet to another car but when the results come in you realize that had you simply kept your bet the same—Bobby Allison in the top three—you would have won, for Allison has finished third. This time you have wagered a thousand, the bookie's credit extending out with the goodwill of your regular payment upon loss. But there is no money left now, none at all, and you sit out in the forest on a downed log, sweating in the spring sunlight, your body filling with defeat and failure and shame. Next to you, separated from your uncle's trailer by a few dozen yards, is the even smaller oval travel trailer your uncle has procured through a trade with a neighbor. You told him you would pay him back but of course you know now that you will do no such thing. Your blood feels hot and your stomach churns with nausea.

That night, at the picnic table in front of his trailer, your uncle asks you why you are so quiet and the whole of it spills out. When you have finished, your uncle says: I figured there was something going on. You've been walking around talkin' to yourself like a crazy person.

Yeah, I do that, you say.

No shit. So is that all of it or are there more surprises coming?

That's it, you say. You wipe your runny nose with the back of your sleeve. There's something wrong with me. I can't stop.

You're goddamn right there's something wrong with you, your uncle says, but you'll sure as shit stop.

I can't.

Yes, you can, your uncle says. You know how long it's been since I've had a drink? He waits for a moment, looking at you sideways. Then he says, Twenty years. That's why I came up here to begin with. To get away from all those drunks down in Winnemucca. Shit, your dad. Your brother. That would've been me too. So I got the hell out of there.

But I'm up here and I'm still fucking up.

You're not listening. I haven't had a drink since I was twenty-seven years old. You make a decision and fight hard to keep it that way.

It's not a decision.

Everything's a decision, your uncle tells you. Every goddamned thing. But in that moment you do not think your uncle knows what he is talking about at all.

HE TAKES the pickup keys and will not let you use them but he tells you a few days later that he has paid off your gambling debts and that if you accrue any more he will turn you out onto the road, blood or no.

You agree, although you pack your meager belongings in advance of that day to come.

A week later, when the snows have mostly thawed and tiny flowers have begun to appear everywhere out of the black earth, he tells you that a call has come in about a fawn stuck in a fence near Crossport.

What do we do? you ask him.

We go get it, unless you're busy doing something else.

A half hour later your uncle pulls off the road near an olive green pickup beside which stands a couple who frame, between them, a stretch of square-knit fencing entangled within which is the shape of a fawn, a creature hanging upside down from a rear hoof, impossibly small and crying out in a voice that sounds not unlike that of a infant child, and your memory returns for a moment to the broken-winged red-tailed hawk you found with Rick and your brother. You wonder what became of it, if it lived, if it continued to have a life.

Dang, it's tiny, you say.

It is that, your uncle replies. You want it?

Do I want it? you say. I don't even know what that means.

It'd be some work.

What kind of work?

Well, the first part of the work would be figuring that out, he says.

What's the other option?

I can call Fish and Game. They'd probably just let it go. It'll starve without its mom. Or something'll eat it. He stops talking and fixes his eyes on you.

What? you say and when he does not speak you say it again: What?

You know, he says.

Do I?

You'd better.

You look back at the tiny deer and as you do it emits a loud piercing shriek. Let's get it out of there, you say.

I was hoping you'd say that.

The fawn's forelegs wheel in the air over the roadside ditch. All the while it continues to wail.

Your uncle has brought a plastic pet carrier box and you retrieve it from the truck and open it to extract a wool blanket and the two of you come to stand next to the couple.

You from the vet? the man asks.

Wildlife rescue, your uncle says.

Ah, the man says. How old you think this one is?

I'd guess a week. Maybe week and a half.

Get her out of there, the woman says. Her eyes do not move from the fawn. Limp now, limp and suddenly silent in the fence line.

That's what we're here for, your uncle says. You ready?

You nod.

Let's get her foot out.

You set the pet carrier in the gravel beside the road and then you and your uncle approach the animal, so slowly, and the fawn does not move until you are upon it, your uncle tossing the blanket over its body. Then it is in motion again and its cry starts up, loud, its shape writhing under the blanket as David wraps his arms around it. Get its foot now, he says.

You manage to pry its tiny hooves out of the V of fencing and then your uncle steps back with the fawn still kicking in his grasp, like a blanket come alive, kneeling before the pet carrier and pushing it through the opening. It slams immediately into the gated door but it is inside now and will not escape. The plastic box skitters and jumps beside the road and for the first time you can remember, your voice falls between faint shush and whisper: It'll be all right. We're here to help you. You'll be all right now. And the animal actually relaxes for a moment as if to listen to you, wide-eyed and panting in the shadowed interior of the box.

Wow, the woman says behind you. Wow.

You say nothing in response, only staring at the animal's terrified eyes.

Your uncle talks with the couple for a time as you lift the carrier and secure it in the back of the truck. When you drive away at last, the couple is still standing alongside the fence. Through the windshield you can see the back window of their truck: a round, red-bordered sticker proclaiming membership in the National Rifle Association and a series of deer and elk images outlined in white. And for the first time you understand that everyone is a killer: here in the forest, in the desert from which you have come, indeed perhaps the world itself nothing more than a vast field for the dealing out of death, some odds so slight as to be impossible to gauge.

YOU CALL her Ginny, after a girlfriend of Bill's you had a crush on when you were ten or eleven, and you pour yourself into that animal. Perhaps that was your uncle's plan all along, his way of keeping you on the straight and narrow. When other animals come in you do the same. The year pulls to a close and then another. There are three and a half years of that, days and nights of working and building up the enclosures, and figuring out ways to entice people to pay to see what they had gathered. A few fund-raisers in town. A family discount week. Ginny grows into a beautiful doe and when you release her a year after her rescue, when you watch her disappear into the forest, you cannot deny your tears. She returns briefly for a few seasons and then disappears forever among the others of her kind. You and your uncle rescue a one-winged bald eagle from near the highway where the Long Bridge crosses out of Lake Pend Oreille in Sandpoint, and the following year you bring that giant raptor to the local elementary school and the children treat you as if you are a god, the eagle perched beside you on the great wooden T you have erected for that purpose. The eyes of the children are wide and filled with wonder, and you can see your own childhood self reflected in their gaze.

And then your uncle is gone. The event is not unlike your brother's death a full decade earlier. One day he is there and the next the sheriff is telling you the news, that David has suffered a massive heart attack in Bonners Ferry while visiting his girlfriend and that he is dead. You can think of nothing to say so you say nothing.

You cannot fathom running the rescue without your uncle and you do not even know if that is indeed what you are supposed to do. Part of you simply wants to release them all, to open the doors of the enclosures and step back and watch them flee into the forest. In such fantasies their mangled bodies are made whole again, their minds clean and pure and made up of wilderness. Or wildness. They dream of fields of golden grass and meadows filled with elk and moose and stands of dark pines and white birch and cool clear rivers flowing from melting snow. And perhaps such an idea is true. Perhaps even now. But you know that were you to open the cages, the animals would simply stumble to their deaths. One-winged birds. Three-legged animals. A bear who would walk up to the nearest human, seeking a marshmallow, only to find fear and death.

There is no funeral, no service of any kind, and when it is revealed that there is a will, you learn that your uncle owned the property outright and that it has been—all fifty acres—willed to you and you alone. Your uncle's girlfriend receives nothing at all. Her only words to you are to tell you to fuck off. You never see her again.

You have thought less of Rick than you did years before but now in your loneliness and despair his face swims up out of the muddy darkness of your dreams. It has only been four years since you left Reno. Before your uncle's death, you might have claimed that the whole of that geography felt cut off from you, like a severed limb, but now it feels too close, as if just beyond the trees. Thinking of Rick and then thinking of Susan. You know in your heart that you will never see her again and your relief at such an understanding is mixed with a slow and painful longing.

Soon after the reading of the will you stop at a low, dark drinking hall in the strip of small battered buildings that comprise Naples, the town you ostensibly live in and which is in some ways no town at all but a dot on the map between Bonners Ferry to the north and Sandpoint to the south. The sign reads Northwoods Tavern. Wagon wheels line the entrance. Old chain saws in the rafters. Perhaps you somehow think you will be welcomed here in the way you had once been welcomed at Grady's. What you know is that you have never felt more alone in all your life. You take a stool at the bar and ask for a vodka on the rocks and then turn and look at the room. There are only two others present besides yourself and the bartender, two older men who sit at a back table, drunk and mumbling to each other. Beyond them are mounted all manner of animal heads: a big-horned buck, a moose of enormous size with a rack that extends like two huge fins, a feral pig of some kind, its mouth permanently molded into a snarl. Smaller animals as well. A badger and, mounted upright in a running pose, a mink or marten.

All mine, the bartender says.

What's that? you say.

Those kills. All mine.

Oh.

You turn back to the bar, sip at the vodka. The bartender is a thickset man, barrel-chested and possessed of an enormous round belly and a downward-curving mustache not unlike the mustache that Grady wore those few years ago back in Reno. Perhaps the fashion choice of discerning bartenders everywhere.

I don't really hunt, you say.

It's not for everyone, the bartender says.

Your eyes have fallen upon a ten-by-ten grid marked on a big sheet of butcher paper and decorated with felt-pen drawings of football helmets. Various names have been scribbled into a good many of the squares. What's that? you ask.

Football pool. Super Bowl. You want in?

How much?

Dollar.

Sure, you say, and even in that single word you feel the hard twist of metal in your gut. I pick the numbers?

The bartender looks up briefly and then returns his attention to a small, soundless television mounted up above the bar. Numbers will all be random, he says. Shirley'll pick 'em out of a hat or something, day of the game. I don't think I've seen you around. You new around here?

You look across the bar at him. I've been here four years.

Yeah?

Yeah, I live just up the hill.

Doing what?

My uncle has—*had*—a little wildlife thing. A grizzly and a couple of coyotes and that kind of thing.

You mean that weird little zoo up there?

You cringe at the description but not enough that the bartender notices. Yeah, that's the place.

What's the deal with that anyway? It's like wild animals, right?

Yeah, it's animals that can't survive without help.

That's what I mean. Those animals are wild. You don't put a wild animal in a cage.

My uncle'd probably argue you don't shoot one either.

That's not the same thing, the bartender says, glancing at you and then looking up and down the bar. At least out there it's understood. They're part of the food chain. Caging them up ain't right.

They'd die in the wild, though, you say. I mean they're mostly permanently injured in one way or another.

That's what they're supposed to do. They're supposed to die in the wild. Not in a cage.

You tip the contents of the glass into your mouth and swallow. Well, you say, thanks for the drink anyway.

Shit, don't be sore about it, the bartender says. We're just having a discussion.

What do I owe you?

The bartender tells you and you pay and slide off the stool.

Where you from anyway? the bartender says.

And you almost say, Battle Mountain, because you are angry but you catch yourself and in the end you simply say, I'm not from anywhere.

None of us are, the bartender says. You turn to leave and the bartender calls to you again, Hey, kid, and you turn back, standing in the doorway now. No hard feelings. Really.

Whatever you say, you mumble.

You are nearly back to the rescue before you realize that you did not give him a dollar for the football pool.

. . .

YOU SPEND the next three days feeding and watering the animals as always, but the bartender's words continue to burn inside you, a twist of hot anger that you cannot release. You find yourself thinking of calling the bookie again, although it has been many years since you have done any such thing. You fantasize briefly that you might place some insubstantial wager but for some reason you do not make that call and because there is no one to talk to—not about this urge nor about your uncle's death nor about the bartender's words—you find yourself talking to the animals, a kind of ongoing monologue that continues as you make your rounds.

Then comes the day when you happen upon the wreck. It is dusk and you see the smoking car first and then the animal and you pull to the side and before you can think you are running up the center of the road. What lies before you is a deer, a white-tailed doe well into adulthood who drags her paralyzed hindquarters across the asphalt, her voice coming in crazed high bleats like a child's screams cut short over and over again.

The man there calls to you: What do we do? He is dressed, incongruously, in a jacket and tie, eyes wide and breath coming in shallow gulps. Behind him his car steams, the gold hood crushed into a V.

There's not a lot we can do, you tell him.

Ah jeez, the man says when the animal's cry starts up again. Don't you have a gun or something?

Why?

So you can put it out of its misery, the man says. We have to do that at least. His voice is high and keening and when the doe cries it is so loud that it obliterates his words.

Hang on, you say.

You do not know it yet but you will see this scene many times: deer, elk, raptors, squirrels, and of course the moose. The long black slaughterhouse of the road. Now, you stand on the asphalt before the animal, the yellow line stretching out into the misting forest beyond its struggling shape. It lurches forward again, tries to, its backside already dead, rear legs dragging, draining urine and a wet discharge of fecal matter and blood. You think she is at least two years old. Maybe three or four. Perhaps older than that. You try to study the color of her fur, the long line of her head, her dark and rolling eyes. But you cannot answer your own question, cannot tell if she is the same doe you raised, the same that you bottle-fed, the same that saved you, four years ago, from who you were. Could it be? Could it be her, returned to you in this last moment?

Ah jeez, the man says. Look at my car. Holy shit. My wife's gonna kill me.

You do not know how long you stand there. The animal continues to struggle, to bleed and to cry, a long line of mucus hanging in a thin rope from her jaw.

When you turn to the truck, it is a motion nearly automatic. The old Savage 99 rests in the gun rack across the rear window, placed there by your uncle without comment at least a year before. As if he knew. As if he could have seen that it would be needed. And perhaps this was true.

You pull the rifle from the rack and lever the chamber open and see that indeed there are cartridges within. The sight of them fills you with dread.

The man has wandered over to his crushed car and now stands before it in silence. Another vehicle has stopped, a pickup, and its driver rolls down the window and calls to you: Hey, you need some help?

That guy might, you say.

You can hear the door open and close again and the man's voice calling to the driver of the smashed car: Hey, hey, you all right?

But you are not listening now. You have come to the doe. She has stopped moving and lies sprawled on the asphalt in exhaustion. You pray that she is already gone but then she starts her crying again, that explosion, that shriek of sound, so close now. Could this be her? Could this really be Ginny, who you pulled from the fence wire? Who you cared for? Who you named?

She is looking at you now. Her eyes roll.

You raise the rifle to your shoulder and aim. You wish you could say her name one time but your voice does not come and when you sight down the barrel at the hard cap of her skull you can say nothing at all.

YOU DO not sleep that night, so completely is the image of that blown skull burned into your mind. You bottle-fed her and learned that to help her excrete her waste you needed to wipe her anus with a baby wipe and so you did, many times a day, and she came to you and you held her and fed her and when she was a year old your uncle told you what you already knew, that you needed to release her back into the forest, and so you did. So much effort and care, and then there she was—if not the very same animal then one so much like her—and all your work has been for naught. You saved her and then you were her executioner. You wonder, in such moments, what Bill would tell you about living and dying, about what is right and what is wrong, but there is only you, alone. In your mind, pickup trucks blow past with gun racks, and mustached men brandish firearms that spark and kick white smoke into the trees. And you see the animals. How they leap into the air, twisting upon a fulcrum of blood, their bodies blowing apart over the snow. Marmot and muskrat. Black bear and grizzly. Beaver and raccoon and snowshoe hare. The great cats whining and hissing as they go down. Mountain lion, lynx, bobcat. See how their claws cut the empty air, how their teeth snap on the ice. And the deer and the moose and elk. And from the sky the first few faint red daubs of blood marking the paperwhite cold of the earth, each a meltwater crater lined with red like a bullet hole. Then heavier droplets, the torrent constant and unceasing once it has begun and all of it smelling of death. The first of the birds is a small dark shadow that ricochets through the tree branches and falls at last to the snow almost without sound. A faint puff like a quick exhale of breath. A tiny green hummingbird barely as long as your finger. You hold it in your hand but already it is too late. For this bird. For them all. Now come the woodpecker and the kingfisher and the warbler. And then at last the falcon and the hawk and the owl and the eagle. How their wings flutter backward over their curved bodies, as if trying to pull that last scrap of sky from the blood rain that surrounds them. Everyone a killer and so everything killing. Death coming into snow, into the fallen needles, into the frozen earth under our feet. Everyone a killer.

Even you.

IN THE late evening a few nights later, you find yourself at the Northwoods Tavern again. You can think of nothing else to do, of nowhere else to go, and you realize that your brief conversation with the bartender the week previous is the only real conversation you have had with anyone since your uncle's heart attack. Or perhaps you return because what the bartender said and what you have now done cannot be reconciled in your mind. So you return, and this time the bar is full, nearly to capacity, with a live band in the corner of the room busily wrecking the Eagles' "Take It Easy" and a few couples gamely attempting to swing dance to the faltering rhythm.

The big bartender you spoke with earlier in the week is talking to a group of flannel-shirted, bearded men farther down the small bar, but he comes down and says, Welcome back, and you nod and order a Budweiser and then try to find a place where you can stand in the crowded room. The band has shifted into a slow country ballad now, a song you do not recognize, and the dancing couples collapse together in various states of embrace. Behind the bar, the poster for the football pool hangs, a few more of its squares marked in with names.

Hours later you still have not added your own. It seems somehow less important now. You are in the full drunk of the evening and you find yourself amidst the animal heads, staring up at them, one after another, with a mixture of awe, horror, and confusion. A few feet away a group of men and women talk in loud voices about a planned hunting trip. They laugh and debate what they will bring and how big the animals are and what constitutes the Canadian wolf-hunting season and what kinds of weapons they have and do not have. They are young men, perhaps younger than you, but not by much. You think of Rick, of those nights at Grady's and all the other clubs up and down the strip, at first with the fake ID and later with the real one, of those last five months after you turned twenty-one and before everything totally turned to shit. The winter of 1984. They look like boys to you, although they must have been at least twenty-one, and you are only twenty-five. And yet it feels, somehow, as if you have aged in animal years, that you are somehow older than you are, a sensation that you cannot quite pin down and yet which is there nonetheless.

You're gonna need a gun with more power than that, one of the boys says.

Thirty-aught, another says.

Shit, man, that'll punch a hole the size of a baseball.

Seven millimeter, maybe.

I'm thinking that Browning my dad has.

The one you bring for elk?

Yeah, it shoots two-seventy.

I like that rifle. You should sell me that rifle.

Shit, I ain't selling you nothing.

You stand outside that circle, wondering what truth lies sprawled beneath the severed heads of the animals that stare down from every wall. In your drunken reverie, you wonder if the bartender was right, and if he was right then maybe what your uncle David was doing up there in the forest was wrong because the animals he was keeping in cages had lived at least some of their lives in freedom. Maybe that freedom still burned deep inside their muscle and sinew and in their veins and especially in their hearts. Maybe they still and forever could recall a time when the forest was endless and they ran through it like gods, their worlds holding that fire, tending it. Can you imagine such a thing to be true? Even were you to raise a grizzly in a cage all its life, even were it born in captivity, did it not still understand that its nature was wild? And then you are struck with everything at once—everything that has happened to you and because of you—the whole of your life come swinging into your heart and with it a sense of frustration and despair and fury that sends you staggering forward.

You think you intend to push out into the cold night but when you turn toward the door your leg catches the edge of something—a chair, the carpet, a table edge—and you stumble forward into the circle of flanneled men and denim-clad women, your beer tipping out of your hand so that when you try to right it you instead send it exploding everywhere like a tiny geyser. The men and women all step back and one of them lays a hand on your shoulder. Whoa whoa whoa, he says.

Some part of you knows you should simply walk on but the eyes of the animals are upon you and the alcohol is running in your blood and what comes from your mouth instead of an apology is: Get your fucking hand off me.

What's that? The young man leans in to look at you now, looks at you carefully. He wears a long blond mustache that comes down over his upper lip. On his head is a green cap with a yellow scrawl of words that you cannot focus on long enough to read.

And you say: You heard me.

Man, you need to take a break. Go get some air.

You go get some air.

Then the young man smiles. You watch his face carefully, his eyes on your eyes. You're trying to pick a fight, he says.

And you say, Fuck you.

Then, from one of the women: You gonna let him talk like that, Jack?

Well, shit, he says. I guess not. There is something like joy in his features. Something like excitement. So let's go, he says. He takes a step forward and you take a step back and in the next instant the young man's friends are around you, pulling you off your feet and dragging you backward through the bar. You can hear the bartender—the woman now—yelling, Hey hey hey, and the group around you stops dragging for a moment and one of them says, We're taking him outside, and she says, No fighting in the bar, Jack, and he says, I know, Laurie. That's why we're taking him outside. Then another voice, this from the bartender you spoke to those days earlier: Make it a fair goddamned fight. Don't you boys just trounce him out there.

You can hear movement now and you are smiling, thinking of Rick at the clubs and bars the two of you frequented in Reno, and more than ever you wish your friend was by your side. But Rick is gone now and your uncle is gone and even your brother is gone and so you are alone.

They take you down the stairs backward, your boots bouncing off each step, and when they let go of you on the asphalt of the parking lot you surprise yourself by regaining your feet.

You fucked with the wrong guy, my friend, someone says.

It appears as if the entire crowd from inside the bar has filtered outside now. They stand in their flannels and T-shirts and beards, leaning on the rail, making side bets, watching as you sway in the reflected light of the sign and the single lamppost that lights a faint patch of the road.

You think only that you are going to be pretty badly beaten and that tomorrow you will still have to rise and feed the animals, that no matter what happens to you tonight, tomorrow all the animals you care for will look to you to provide, realize this suddenly and completely, not only that you are responsible for them and that they need you, but that you need them just as much. Everything else, everything beyond these simple and irrefutable facts, is wholly and completely irrelevant: their world and your own overlapping so tightly that they have become, at least in this one area, indistinguishable from one another.

I'm sorry, you say.

It's a little late for that. The man in the green cap steps forward out of the circle of his friends and stands loose limbed before you, leaning into the dim light.

You open your mouth to speak and in that moment the man punches you full and hard in the stomach, doubling you over, and your breath rushes out of you all at once. Your hand is already raised. Wait, wait, you say, gasping for breath. Hang on. You think you are going to vomit, a sensation that comes and disappears and then returns again.

Hang on for what?

I got your point, you say between breaths. Don't hit me again.

Don't be a pussy about it, the man says. People are watching.

I get it. I was an asshole.

You're goddamn right you were an asshole, the man says.

I know. I fucked it up. I'm sorry.

The man stands looking at you as if contemplating what to do next. Well, shit, he says, don't be such an asshole next time.

There won't be a next time, you say. I'm going home now.

Good, the man says. Jerk.

Yep, you say.

They all stand there waiting for you to throw a counterpunch but when you remain doubled over someone says, Let's go back inside. The crowd assembled on the tiny front deck mumbles and murmurs and then the whole group begins to disappear through the door.

You got some problems. The words come from the same young man, the man in the green cap, who continues to stand there watching you.

I know, you say.

You need to get your shit together.

I know that too.

All right then, the man says.

He turns then and walks back up the stairs, his friends still watching you and then following the green hat back into the bar. The band stopped at some point during the fracas but now, from somewhere that seems very far away, it starts up again, the bass shaking through the walls without tune or rhythm.

You remain crouched on the asphalt in the darkness. At some point you vomit. Later still you stand and try to find your dead uncle's pickup truck.

* * *

IN THE months that follow, it feels at times as if you have given up everything, and you come to understand that gambling kept you believing, against all reality, that there was a possibility of change, that you might one day be levered up and out of yourself, but now that sense of weird and groundless optimism is gone. You do not know if you can live without it. And then winter is upon you and with it comes profound isolation. You cannot get to town except by a freezing trip atop the snowmobile and sometimes the electricity is out for weeks at a time. You have never been so alone. For days on end you find yourself talking not to yourself or to the ghost of your uncle or even to the memory of Rick, but to the bear, and sometimes you think you can hear him answer. You have moved into your uncle's trailer now, have sold the smaller trailer to someone who drove up from Sandpoint to retrieve it, and you sit at the little foldout table for many hours watching the vacant space that trailer once occupied. In your exhaustion, it feels at times as if your brother is somehow occupying that vacancy, as if he is out there, even now, in the snow.

And yet somehow, in that snow-quiet isolation, you find a sense of purpose. You keep the rescue running all that first winter, alone, and in the night in the trailer in the snowed-over forest you wonder at where you are, at where you have come to in your life, twenty-five years old and utterly alone in a world of animals. It is not unlike what you fantasized about as a boy when you watched Marlin Perkins on Sunday evenings. And yet it is not like that at all. Marlin would wrestle an animal into submission, would bag it and cage it and send it off for study, whatever that really meant. These animals are mostly accustomed to your presence, ignoring you so completely that you can enter most of the enclosures for cleaning and feeding and repairs. Occasionally you will look up to see one of them watching you: the raccoons staring at you in silence with their black-masked eyes. Or the eagle from its perch. Sometimes you stare at the telephone well into the night, thinking of calling the bookie back in Reno, but you never make that call. There are more important things now, things of life and death. You cannot yet know it but there will come a time, not so very far away, when the person you once were will seem someone else entire, some false doppelgänger set to roost in your memories.

9

EACH TIME THE PHONE RANG IN THE OFFICE, BILL JUMPED AS if a shot had been fired. Sometimes there were messages but Rick was smart enough not to leave anything that might incriminate him, only stating that he was waiting to hear from him, nothing more, not even a phone number. In his voice was a thinly disguised fury, a hiss that seemed to breathe through every word. Bill answered the phone only twice, both times listening as Rick berated him, accusing him of stealing from the safe an amount of money that slid between ten and twenty thousand dollars. Whatever the amount, Bill could not convince him otherwise, could not tell him that there had been no money, that the safe had been empty in the trailer's closet for all those years, that he had never once opened it.

This is gonna get ugly, Rick told him.

Just let it go, Bill said.

Fucking thief.

Just let it go.

He hung up on that second phone call and within a minute the phone began to ring anew. He let the machine answer but Rick left no message and after another minute the phone resumed its ringing until the tape recorder clicked on once again—*Hello and thank you for calling North Idaho Wildlife Rescue*—then the long buzz of the dial tone and the click and whirr of the machine rewinding to its starting point and the long silence as Bill waited, shoulders tight around his neck, for the phone to burst into sound once more.

Then a day passed where there were no calls and he wondered once again if the ordeal was over, imagining Rick returning to Nevada, resigned to the empty safe, to the years he had served in Carson City, to all of it. But the reprieve was short-lived, not because the calls resumed but rather because a few days later, on his way back home from Sandpoint, Bill happened upon the dented and rusted yellow Honda parked in front of the Northwoods Tavern.

It was early evening when he passed the bar, the sun dipping into the shadows of the tree line and the whole town darkening quickly into the forested night. He had driven up to Bonners to pick up an antibiotic for Perry, one of the three raccoons, who had a small wound that was proving very slow to heal, stopping in at Grace's veterinary clinic while he was in town just to visit for a moment, to see her, to touch her face, and then had turned around and gone all the way back through Naples and on to Sandpoint, where he had made the final payment on the engagement ring. Four months to pay off the three hundred dollars but he had it at last and he opened and snapped closed the black velvet box with one hand as he drove. It was Friday. Jude's event at the school was scheduled for Monday night, and because Bill had told him about his plans, he knew there would be no backing out of them. Perhaps that was, in fact, why he had told the child about it at all: to hold his own feet to the fire.

He thought she would say yes. Was sure of it. Then almost sure. Then had no idea. He flipped the box open again, glancing down at the gold ring with its small diamond, turning the truck left into Naples, instead of right and up the mountain to the trailer, thinking of stopping in at the general store to pick up a chicken potpie and a pack of cigarettes, although he had also promised Grace that he would try to quit.

That was when he saw the little yellow Honda, the ring box still held open on the palm of his hand, his eyes casting over the car just for a moment as he followed the curve of the road toward the store. Then he looked again and his foot came off the gas pedal, the truck slowing in the road.

He slid into a gap in the line of Subaru station wagons and pickup trucks and that one yellow Honda, but he knew he would not go inside the bar. Even if he did, what would he say? Why are you still here? What are you doing? Get the fuck out of my town? Get the fuck out of my life? He had already said such things and he knew that repeating them would serve no purpose. He did not know why Rick had remained but the possibilities flashed through his mind in quick succession and left him shivering and shaking behind the wheel.

After a few minutes he drove on to the store for his chicken potpie, and when he passed the Northwoods Tavern again, the yellow Honda was gone.

. . . .

THE FALL Festival at the elementary school was comprised of a parade of children dressed as pilgrims and Indians, all of them singing off-key songs that seemed to have neither melody nor lyrics. It was difficult to focus on what was happening onstage. Bill's ass was numb from the metal folding chair and he was nervous about the approach of his planned marriage proposal, a plan made yet more urgent by Jude's barely contained excitement. And yet seeing Rick's yellow Honda had shaken him inside, so hard and heavy that he wondered what he was doing here at all. Then he saw himself in the forest somewhere, just briefly, out of breath and struggling through thick wet snow, all the trees black and featureless, and then he was falling through that surface and into some dark twilight, the sense of which made him jerk awake in panic. But he was not in the snow. The children were still singing their monotonous, nearly tuneless songs, all lined up on the stage on a set of bleachers, and the room was still hot and overpacked with parents and grandparents.

He looked over at Grace briefly and was relieved that she had not seen him nod off, or did not acknowledge it if she had. She glanced back at him and then leaned in close and whispered in his ear: I'm dying.

Me too. My ass is dead.

I don't even have an ass anymore.

They smiled at each other and tried to suppress their laughter.

Jude's class came onstage at last, their construction-paper pilgrim hats lopsided and falling over their eyes as they tried to find their places on the bleachers.

There he is, Grace said. She waved. Jude's eyes were clearly looking for them in the audience but the boy did not see his mother and so Bill stood and briefly waved both hands above his head as if signaling an airplane and Jude found them at last and waved and smiled.

I think he sees you now, Bill, a parent behind him said, and a few people laughed.

The students on the stage began to sing again and Bill felt himself warm to the sound of it and to the sight of Jude, the boy's voice indistinguishable from the mass of fourth-graders around him and yet clearly singing strong and loud. Each time the boy's eyes found them in the audience, Bill could see them light up, the curl of a smile on his face, and Bill himself was smiling so broadly that he knew he probably looked utterly demented. And yet he could do nothing to rein it in.

Afterward he and Grace stood outside in the dark with the other parents, each waiting for their children to be released. Her arm was wrapped through his, her fingers interlaced with his own in his coat pocket. The weekend's snow, the first of the year, was piled up along the path in tall berms and the concrete sidewalk upon which they stood was crusted with salt and sand. It had been a brief heavy snow, early in the season but enough to remind Bill that he was running out of time to prepare the rescue for the true winter to come, the thought of which reminded him, once again, of the impending issue with Fish and Game. In some ways he knew he had been dragging his feet, that Grace was right about him already feeling defeated, but he also knew he would not let them lead his animals to slaughter. He could not. They had saved him and he would do the same for them.

He shivered.

Cold? Grace said beside him.

A little. You wanna stop and get a hot chocolate or something?

I don't know, she said. Jude's already half crazy today.

Is he?

You didn't notice?

Excited about the show, maybe.

She looked at him and for a moment he thought she must have found him out somehow but then she only said, Maybe, and looked toward the room where, at any moment, Jude himself would emerge. Around them, other parents and grandparents were talking among themselves, laughing, telling stories about their children.

That was fun, he said. Thanks for inviting me to come.

I always want you to come.

Do you?

Of course.

I'd come to all of these. I mean, everything.

Would you?

Well, I guess, he said. If I don't have anything else to do.

Oh shut up, she said, laughing and pinching his belly through his coat.

OK, OK, he said, smiling. Dang, that hurt.

Sissy, Grace said.

So?

Jude appeared a few seconds later, bounding out of the classroom and then telling them both that he was ready to go.

You want to stop for some hot chocolate? Grace asked him.

What? No, the boy said.

No?

No, let's go home.

You don't want hot chocolate? What kind of kid doesn't want hot chocolate?

This kind, Jude said. I just have something important. He glanced up at Bill when he said this and his mother looked from him to the boy.

Bill shrugged. All right, then, let's go home.

Jude practically pulled them to Grace's truck and then leaped inside and sat waiting for them. What's all this? she said.

No idea, he said.

Really?

He did not answer now and when Jude entered the truck she looked over at him and said, You sure no hot chocolate?

Positive, the boy said, his eyes fixed on the windshield as if something of intense interest were just outside the glass.

Weird, his mother said. Very weird.

Soon they were moving up Main toward the North Hill, where Grace's house sat on its small acreage of cleared land at the edge of the forest, their voices momentarily falling quiet as houses and businesses and trees and heaps of plowed snow flashed across the turning glare before disappearing behind them.

And then Jude spoke. Bill did not hear the words at first, or perhaps did not understand that Jude was speaking to him and not Grace, or perhaps he knew somehow, already, that he did not want to hear what Jude was about to tell him.

What did you say? Bill said.

I said I met one of your friends. At the hamburger place.

Who's that?

And now it came, that single syllable: Rick, Jude said.

What did you say?

Rick, the boy said again. Your friend Rick.

You met my friend Rick? His mind was blank. Outside the windshield, dark and angular trees rotated in the headlights. Where?

In town with Jimmy.

Today?

No, yesterday when we went for hamburgers with Jimmy's mom.

In Bonners?

At the hamburger place.

Who's Rick? Grace said. Do I know him?

Uh, Bill said, hunting for words, for any words at all. You don't know him.

Someone you know from the rescue?

Yeah, uh . . . not even really a friend.

He said he was your friend, Jude said.

We've talked about this before, Grace said to the boy. Remember? Stranger danger?

But he's Bill's friend, Jude said. So he's not a stranger.

He's a stranger to you. Maybe he just said he was Bill's friend.

Right, Jude said, although his tone implied that he did not feel this particular maxim applied to the situation at hand.

Bill said nothing now, could think of nothing to say. He could feel Grace looking at him but his eyes were outside in the forest where it rolled toward them out of the night, the headlights rendering everything before them flat and colorless.

He seemed really nice, Jude said. And he knew about the animals and he said he knew your mom from a way long time ago.

He said he knew Bill's mom?

Yeah, aren't you guys listening?

The car bumped onto the bridge that spanned the Kootenai. All beyond its walls rode blank empty space.

What else did he say? Bill said, not turning his gaze from the black window.

He didn't say anything, really, Jude said. Just to tell you hi.

Jimmy's mom let you talk to this man? Grace said. There was an edge in her voice.

She talked to him a little too. Why are you mad?

I'm not mad, honey, she said. Just no more talking to strangers, OK? OK.

I mean really. I'm serious. No talking to strangers.

The boy was silent now, watching out the window between them on the bench seat. He reached his hand into Bill's and squeezed it, something Bill could not recall him doing ever before, and Bill looked down at him there, this boy, and smiled at him, all the while his heart twisting in his chest. He wanted the truck to stop so that he could flee somehow into the empty space outside the glass.

Somewhere out there was the river with its loops and turns. The boy's hand warm in his own. That black snowy river: he did not know if it ever reached the sea.

WHEN THEY reached Grace's house, the boy would hardly leave his side, hovering next to him in the kitchen and then sitting so close to him on the sofa that he was nearly in Bill's lap. *The Jeff Foxworthy Show* was on television and Bill laughed when Grace and Jude laughed.

When the program was over, Grace stood and disappeared into the bathroom and Bill turned toward the boy. Listen, pal, he said. We're gonna have to do that thing later.

No, Jude said, his head shaking from side to side. You said after Fall Festival. You promised.

Shhh. It's still a surprise. I don't want her to find out.

Why can't we do it tonight?

I have to talk to your mom about something first.

What?

Something important, that's all.

Something else?

Yeah, something else.

When will we do it then?

I don't know. I'll have to figure that out after I talk to her.

But you're not gonna do it without me, right? Don't do it without me, OK?

I won't.

Grace had returned, sitting on the other side of her son on the sofa, her arm draped around behind the boy so that her fingertips rested on Bill's shoulder. On the television, the actor Brian Dennehy stood in front of a dark house telling the viewer to take a pill called Zantac 75. What are you boys talking about? she said.

Nothing, Jude said quickly.

Sounds fishy, Grace said.

Just talking about homework and stuff, Jude said.

Homework and stuff, huh? She leaned over and kissed his head. Time for shower and bed, little man.

He was staring at her now. At her and at Jude. How beautiful they both were. How lucky he had been to have them in his life at all.

Can't I stay up just a little while longer?

Show's over and it's already past your bedtime, she said.

OK, Jude said, his voice falling.

The boy disappeared into the hall with his mother and after a time Bill clicked off the television and wandered out into the kitchen. The black-covered paperback of *The Tibetan Book of the Dead* rested on the counter and he lifted it and stood flipping through its pages until he found the image he had looked at before. The Great Mandala of the Peaceful Deities. It made no more sense to him this time than it had the first.

Catching up on your research? Grace said, coming into the room from the hall.

The book was still in his hand. He closed it and returned it to the counter now. It doesn't make any sense.

Just ways to get through.

Through what?

Through to the other side.

The other side of what?

Of anything. I don't know. I've only read like fifty pages. It's pretty far out. Lamas and rituals and stuff like that.

Just don't start making altars or burning incense or anything, all right?

I'm just trying to get far enough into it so that I can tell Fran I read it.

Fran's that important?

She shrugged. Isn't everyone?

No, he said.

She looked up at him. I was the one who put down her dog. It just seemed like her whole soul kind of leaked out of her when that animal died. She doesn't need me to read the book. She just needs to be able to talk to someone.

You're the best person I know, Bill said.

She smiled at him. That's the nicest thing anyone's ever said to me. She went to the kitchen counter and lifted a manila envelope from its surface. He had dropped it off at the veterinary office a few days earlier: a sheaf of forms from Idaho Fish and Game, some of which seemed impossible to complete. You wanna talk about this tonight?

Not tonight, he said.

It's not just gonna go away.

He looked at her, saying nothing, only staring into her wide, beautiful eyes. He felt as if his body had filled with snow, as if dry and frozen powder shifted and blew and swirled everywhere through him. I just can't do it tonight, he said.

OK, she said. I know it's hard.

He nodded. That's one word for it.

Maybe I can come up this week and you and me and Bess can all talk it out.

He nodded again. Think Jude's still awake in there?

If you hurry.

He entered the boy's room and sat on the edge of the bed, looking at him in the softly lit darkness.

What? the boy said.

Look, pal, about that guy. He's not really a friend of mine, all right?

What do you mean?

He's someone you should keep away from.

But he knows about the animals. And he knows your mom.

I know.

How does he?

I knew him a long time ago.

How long?

We can talk about that some other time, Bill said. Point is, if you see him again, I need to know about it.

OK.

I'm serious.

I know. The boy looked for a moment like he might cry.

You don't have to be scared. Just don't talk to him again. And if you see him and he tries to talk to you, just walk away. And tell me. Tell me if you see him somewhere, OK?

OK, Jude said. His eyes were tearing up.

Bill leaned in close and kissed his forehead. You don't have to be afraid, he said. I'll take care of it. I just wanted you to know because you're a big boy and you should know what's happening.

OK, Jude said.

I love you, pal, Bill said.

I love you too, pal, Jude said.

Bear hug?

The boy threw his arms around him and Bill squeezed him hard against his chest.

He swung the door partially closed, said good night one last time, and then clicked off the hall light and returned to the front of the house. Grace was seated on the sofa, a blanket pulled around her, watching television.

I need to talk to you about something, he said.

She did not turn toward him at first, instead laughing quietly at something on the screen. *Murphy Brown.* Candice Bergen turning to look at her co-anchor before deadpanning a joke about his toupee.

Grace, he said.

His hands went into his pockets and he could feel the velvet box that contained the engagement ring there and the thought of it made him crumble as if everything inside him had become a tower of ash.

Baby, what's wrong? she said.

She was up now and he did not even know that his eyes had filled with tears until her arms came around him and he stood there watching the television warp and wobble, the laugh track rising in volume now, a scattering of applause mixed in with that curved wave of laughter.

What's wrong? she said again.

I need to talk to you about something.

She pulled back and looked at him. You didn't cheat on me, did you?

What? he said. No. And despite of everything he smiled. Why would I do that?

Well, then it can't be that bad, she said.

He stood there looking at her and again the tears came.

What is it, baby? she said. What's wrong?

Ah god, Grace, he said. It was all he could think of to say. Ah god.

10

THE PAIN WAS A WHITE LINE. HIS EYES WERE CLENCHED against it but still it came, running up the length of his arm and radiating into the cold flat light of the apartment bathroom. Susan was kneeling over him, her face throbbing with his pulse, and for a moment he could not remember where he was. Then it came back. Behind her, Rick stood in the open doorway. At Susan's feet and knees: a pile of unspooled toilet paper. Try to keep still or I'm gonna mess it up, she said.

I'm trying, he said, and with it that white line seemed to burn through the center of him. Fuck, he said through his teeth.

That motherfucker, Rick said from the doorway. I'll kick his fucking ass.

That's not helping, Susan said.

You can't just break a man's finger, he said. You can't do that.

Rick, Nat said weakly.

What, buddy? What do you need?

A drink.

Sure, man, he said. Anything you want.

Something strong.

You got it, Rick said, already disappearing from the doorway.

It was silent then, Susan wrapping his broken finger in toilet paper, leaning over him so that the neck of her T-shirt hung low before his eyes.

You're staring down my shirt, she said.

He might have been embarrassed, would have been under normal circumstances, but there was too much pain and all he could do was grit his teeth as she brought the toilet paper up around the break again. He just reached out and broke it, he said.

I know.

There was nothing I could do. It was so fast. And he could see it all again in his mind. He had expected to be beaten, expected the cocaine rush to hold him steady while they punched at his body, at his face, but then Johnny had said simply, Hold up your hand, and Nat had looked at his own hand for a moment, as if expecting to see something there, and Mike had reached out and grasped his index finger and, in one quick movement, broke it sideways. For a brief instant he had stood with his hand out before him, that single finger askew, the tiny bone broken just after the knuckle. Even in his memory it seemed impossible.

Next time you miss a payment and I'll break your arm or your leg, Mike told him. After that I bust in your skull.

Are we clear? Johnny had said.

And Nat had only been able to say one word: Fuck. Mike had been holding his arm but he released it now and Nat fell to his knees on the cold hard asphalt.

Good, Johnny had said. So we're all clear. Let's give it a week and we'll try this again.

He had come stumbling into the casino after that and had been lucky only in that Rick and Susan were just turning out of the coffee shop and saw him there near the door. He told them only that he could not go to the hospital, that there was no money for it, that there was no money for anything.

Now he knelt beside the toilet, leaning back against its curved shape, sweat dripping down into his face.

You have to stop moving, Susan said.

I'm sorry. He stared at her, her face so close to him, inches away now as she worked on the hand he clutched to his chest. He wanted nothing more than to lean forward and kiss her. He would have given anything to do it.

And then Rick was in the doorway again, holding a plastic tumbler that rattled with ice. Here you go, buddy, he said.

He handed down the cup and Nat took it in his free hand and might have drained it all in one ongoing gulp but his throat seized at the vodka and he gave himself up to paroxysms of choking and coughing.

Susan had her arm around him, her hand patting his back. Shhh, shhh, she whispered to him. Slow down. Slow down. You'll be all right.

What happened out there? Rick said.

I don't know, he said, his breath a wheeze. They didn't even give me a chance to talk. They just took me out to the parking lot and broke it. Saying the words made his eyes tear up, not at the pain but at the sense of helplessness he had felt in that moment, and in the knowledge that he had had the money to make the payment, had held it in his hands only an hour and a half before. What a fool you are. What a goddamn fool.

Fucking assholes, Rick said.

Nat brought the tumbler to his mouth again and gulped at it. This time it went down easy, the liquid so cold that it seemed to burst all through his chest, and when he lowered the tumbler, panting, there was nothing left in it but ice.

I still think you have the flu or something, Susan said.

I feel terrible, he said.

We're gonna have to go get him some medicine, she said. She was talking to Rick in the doorway now.

Yeah, he said. OK.

His eyes had fallen closed. He could hear the jingling of keys and then they were talking about what Rick should buy. Dimetapp or Robitussin or something else.

What do you feel like? she said.

I hurt everywhere, he said.

OK, she said. Rick's gonna go get some medicine.

He tried to speak but now a shiver ran through him as if he had stepped into a freezer and his teeth clamped together and began chattering like a windup toy.

You should lie down, she said.

He nodded but said nothing.

You're gonna have to help me. I can't pick you up on my own.

Where's Rick?

He went to get medicine, baby.

He vaguely recalled her saying something about that but it seemed like that had been hours ago. Why isn't he back yet? he said.

He just left.

All right.

He managed to get to his feet and stumbled, with her arms around him, out of the bathroom and into the hall and then into his bedroom. He had never purchased a bed frame and so the mattress lay on the stained carpet in the corner of the room, the bedding strewn amidst piles of dirty clothes above which was tacked a velvet blacklight poster of a panther in fluorescent orange and yellow and, beside it, a poster of Van Halen, the band's flying VH logo centered in gold around which the four band members were caught in motion as if onstage, their instruments glowing, their singer, David Lee Roth, shirtless and leaning forward as if ready to leap out of the image and into the apartment. It looked to Nat, in that moment, the pathetic squalid room it was.

He managed to slide into a sitting position, Susan holding him all the while, and then lay back upon the mattress. She sat next to him there, her hand sliding his sweat-soaked hair off his forehead. You don't feel warm, she said, but you're sweating like crazy.

He closed his eyes.

Rick'll be here soon, she said. You'll feel a lot better once you get some medicine in you.

Thanks.

Taking care of my guys, she said. That's my job.

Come here, he said. He raised his left arm, eyes open now, the broken hand still clutched to his chest. She leaned in and when he leaned up to kiss her it was as if an instinct had taken over. The pain. The crashing of his fear and anguish and anger. He could feel her lips for that brief moment and was sure she was kissing him in return.

Then it was over.

You should try to get some sleep, she said.

I love you, he said.

Shhh. You're just tired.

There's something wrong with me.

Get some rest. Rick'll be here soon with the medicine.

What am I gonna do?

Sleep, she said. That's what you're gonna do.

He was looking at her, so close, her face watching him with an expression that was pure concern and care and worry. And then he felt himself drifting outside. He hovered over an endless icteric plain: sagebrush and horsebrush, Mormon tea and shadscale. There were animals in the shadows. He could feel them there, could see their eyes reflecting back at him from the darkness. From somewhere, a murmur of voices: Rick's voice and Susan's, the sound a spectral echo drifting against a sky awash in the thin high feathers of alto cirrus clouds.

It's not your problem.

Yes, it is.

How, Rick? You weren't even here when he got himself in this shit.

That doesn't matter.

Yeah? Why not?

Because it doesn't, Susan. You take care of your people. That's what you do.

Blah blah blah.

Don't do that.

I don't know what else to say. He got himself into this, not you. And what about your mom, Rick? What about that? Don't you think you've got your own problems to worry about?

He seemed to be asleep then, although he could still hear the faint hum of their voices from somewhere farther away, and then he could see her at the door that night when Rick was still in prison, three or four months into his sentence, the day of the rainstorm. A knock and there she was, drenched, her breasts showing through the wet T-shirt, hair dragging in her face like something out of one of his secret fantasies. I need your help, she had said. It all seemed to spin out before him now. Even the feeling he had in that moment, the trembling rise of heat in his chest. It was all he had ever wanted to hear her say, not that she needed help but that she needed him, even though he hardly would have admitted such a thing, even to himself. How he had looked at her in those moments when neither she nor Rick would notice him looking. How he had imagined what her body might feel like in his hands. And then there she was, standing in the doorway, asking him for his help. He would have done anything, told himself as much and ascribed that telling to her status as his best friend's girlfriend. Was he not supposed to help her? Is that not what Rick would expect him to do?

She asked him to take her to the clinic because she was pregnant and did not want to have a baby, told him that the baby was Rick's, of course it was. He did not think about his response. Instead, he only said yes yes over and over again, his whole heart and soul shivering inside his skeleton as if a great string had been plucked and stood vibrating along the length of his spine. Now he thought this betrayal, the betrayal of his heart, the betrayal of being party to the secret abortion of Rick's child, was worse, much much worse, than the sexual betrayal that would come later.

He took her to the clinic and paid the full bill, much of which came from a recent loan from Johnny Aguirre, and then waited for her in the lobby, flipping through the various magazines there with a kind of manic fury, as if waiting for the birth of a child. He wondered how she would feel when it was done, hoping that she would need him to take care of her, already planning his call into work in the morning to tell them he was too sick to come in.

When she returned to the lobby she told him he could take her home now and thanked him and then fell quiet as he drove, the wet streets reversing casino towers as grainy and specular ghost images, their colored neon shapes pushing under a surface that rolled forever under his wheels. Occasionally she would murmur a direction until at last he pulled over next to an apartment building on the east side of the Virginia Street casinos, a two-story slab of cracked stucco and concrete not unlike the building he lived in.

This is where you live? The rain had stopped now but the clouds continued to roil atop the mountains to the west. The desert everywhere had already sucked its water down under the sand.

No, this is just a friend's place. I'm staying here for a while.

Oh, he said. Is your friend home?

I don't know.

Do you want me to come up?

What? She looked at him, her eyes a mixture of confusion and sudden mounting anger. No.

I just meant— I just wanted to make sure there's someone here to take care of you.

I don't need anyone to take care of me, Nat, she said. Her sense of anger seemed to have faded just as quickly as it had come. She leaned over and kissed him on the cheek and then opened the door and stepped out into the drizzling rain. He thought she might say something to him, some last thing, but the door swung closed and he watched her walk up the stairs to the apartment and disappear inside.

He did not see her the next day nor the day after that and although he knew that he had no reason to expect her to knock on his door again he still caught himself harboring that expectation, as if what he had done had cemented some bond that he knew they did not actually share. And then the guilt, because he also knew he was pining over his best friend's girlfriend, a condition that became acute only after he heard, from the car's tinny radio, Rick Springfield singing plaintively and publically about everything he held secret in his heart. He punched the buttons on the car stereo to find anything else but all the stations had turned to static and he drove on past the nightclubs and casinos with the hiss of dead air streaming into the car from all directions at once.

He did not hear from her for two weeks but then she appeared again, knocking on the apartment door on a bright warm day and asking him, of all things, if he would like to go see a movie with her, a question that seemed so surprising that all he could do was stammer out a brief, Sure, sure, that sounds great, all the while standing in the doorway in a kind of frozen bewilderment until she said, Well, OK, let's go then, and he turned and grabbed his coat and keys and came out the door so quickly that he nearly collided with her. Easy tiger, she said and laughed.

She put her arm through his as they came down the stairs and he smiled. When they entered the car she told him that she was grateful he was her friend. Her hand came into his own for a moment and squeezed it.

I'm glad I could help, he said.

He drove them across town to the movie theater by the Peppermill using the same route he used nearly every evening when driving to work, a route he did not have to think about but which turned them through the casinos and down Virginia Street past all the bars and clubs he and Rick had spent their nights in, the storefronts of which looked grim and silent in the white light of the late afternoon.

He bought them popcorn and sodas from the concession stand and they sat next to each other in the back row like lovers and midway through the film she laid her head upon his shoulder and then whispered up at him, Put your arm around me, Nat. I'm cold, and he did, stroking her hair slowly in the darkness while people danced on the glowing flat plane of the screen. That feels nice, she said. The heart in his chest seemed a machine blown clear of all measure, not beating anymore but ringing out like the hammer and bell of an alarm clock. He did not know what was happening on the screen and did not care. For years afterward, any time he would hear the film's title song on the radio he would be transported back to that theater, to the smell of popcorn and the warmth of her nestled there beside him in the darkness like a secret. As if they were innocent. As if anything was.

Later, they sat on the sofa in his apartment and she sat so close to him that her knee pressed against his own, the feeling of it a faint heat running into him. She told him that both her parents were dead, that her father had worked for the telephone company, that her mother had been an office clerk of some kind, and that both were alcoholics. She told him that when she was fifteen her father had tried to drive the three of them into the grave at the wheel of a funeral-black Oldsmobile. Both mother and father had been killed in the accident. She had survived. Her only living relative was an uncle but he was in prison in Carson City and for this reason they put her in foster care and she walked away from that house in the middle of the night and came to Reno.

The strawberry wine seemed to slosh back and forth inside his chest. He wanted to ask her more about those blank years but he also did not want to know what she had done to survive. As it turned out he could not have asked her anyway because in the next moment she had pushed him back onto the sofa and had slid her tongue into his mouth.

He thought that he should stop but his body was moving of its own accord now, moving with a ferocious and unstoppable need. He might have been saying something too but if so he could not stop that either. The words were like a colored ribbon pulling out of him.

What're you sorry about? she said into his ear.

What?

You keep saying "I'm sorry, I'm sorry." What are you sorry about?

Shouldn't we—, he began but there were no words beyond those two and when she pulled his hands to her breasts he could not even think of what question he was trying to ask.

HE AWOKE to the pain of his throbbing finger, opening his crusted eyes into his dingy bedroom, the contents illuminated by an angle of light that seemed incongruous with the morning. He did not know what time it was and at first could not remember what had happened but then it all came flooding back to him and when he pulled his hand up in front of his face he could see the tattered white tissues wrapping his broken finger. He pulled the clock from where it lay on the dirty carpet below him and set it upon his chest: 12:05. Then the lit window high up on the wall and then back to the clock again. It was past noon.

He managed to stand and to stumble forward out of the bedroom and into the hall and then into the bathroom, his head throbbing in concert with his hand. He was able to unzip his pants and to urinate one-handed but then could not further operate the zipper and finally gave up and came into the living room holding his pants up with his only functional hand, the other held tight to his chest.

There he is, Rick said from the couch as he entered the room.

I can't zip up my pants.

Shit. Rick stood and grabbed Nat's pants and snapped them closed and then pulled the zipper up. The things I do for you, he said.

No kidding.

How you feeling?

Pretty miserable, he said. And I missed work.

Susan called us both in sick.

Oh thank god, Nat said. I thought I was screwed.

You still might be. You look awful.

He was still sweating and had begun shivering now. She went home? he said.

To work, Rick said. Jesus, man, I can hear your teeth chattering. I think I should take you to see a doctor.

I can't afford that.

So don't pay the bill when it comes. What's your finger feel like?

A little better. Hurts but it's also kinda numb.

I think I'd better unwrap it.

No way, Nat said.

Yes way, Rick said.

He stood there for what seemed a long time, his balance seeming to shift in all directions at once. Then he slid down next to Rick on the sofa. A rerun of *M*A*S*H* on Channel 2. Hawkeye speaking in a dim quiet slur. Canned laughter following the punch lines.

Rick unwrapped the toilet paper slowly and while Nat had been sure it would drive him into an agony of pain there was almost no sensation at all. When the last piece came off, the broken pencil stub that Susan had used as a brace fell into his lap and they both sat looking at the finger: a pale, bent, swollen thing that looked more like a ruined sausage than any part of his hand. Through its center, where the break was, a dark bruise mottled his tight swollen skin.

That doesn't look good, Rick said.

Dang, Nat said. It made him sick to look at it.

We're definitely going to the doctor, Rick said. Maybe you'll get lucky and they'll give you some Percocet or something.

He nodded but did not move. Neither of them did. I don't know what I'm gonna to do, he said after a time. He was still looking at his swollen and discolored finger. What am I gonna do?

We'll figure something out, Rick said. We always do.

It's serious, Nat said.

I know it is, buddy. I've got some weed to sell. That oughta help some.

What about your mom?

Well, like I said, we'll figure something out.

From the television came Milt Wells's voice and they both looked toward it in unison. Milt stood in his characteristic Western shirt and bolo tie before a row of gleaming cars and trucks. That's right, he called out to them. Five hundred dollars cash back on any new car or truck. Five hundred dollars cash back. The man on the screen fanned a stack of bills in his hands as if they were playing cards.

And there's all the money we need, Nat said wistfully.

Yeah maybe we should start a car dealership, Rick said.

Nat did not respond now, only sitting there, staring as the commercial ended and the next began.

I tell you one thing, Rick said. If I see that motherfucker Mike or Johnny fucking Aguirre I'll knock his fucking head in.

Don't do that, Nat said. That'll make it really bad.

We'll see, Rick said.

Nat could feel a sharp twisting inside him, like a short thin blade was rotating through his intestines. The geography of the continent seemed to stretch out under his feet, the desert elongating so that the arrowed points between where he was and everywhere he was not fled from each other across that vast and unending plain of sage and cheatgrass and dry dead earth.

11

HE TOLD HER EVERYTHING, BEGINNING WITH THE NIGHT AT the car dealership and then trying to explain the gambling and Johnny Aguirre and fumbling through what had happened when Rick had been in prison for those thirteen months and he had been left alone in Reno, knowing that none of it really made any sense, not to him and certainly not to Grace, listening to his own story and knowing it was true but feeling, all the while, as if it were the story of a stranger, something he had overheard somewhere and was repeating, like the plot of a movie. When she told him to start over he began in Battle Mountain, his brother with the disassembled bicycle, and the new kid who rented the trailer next to the one he shared with his brother and mother, the sagebrush rolling out in all directions and the flat top of the Sheep Creek Range looming above the bridge under which he would find frogs in the summer and where the teenagers would swim and smoke stolen cigarettes, the two of them—he and Rick—wandering everywhere across that landscape, and, when they were teenagers, stealing into silent empty homes in the midafternoon, taking souvenirs and sometimes selling them at the pawnshop in Winnemucca. How they would talk about taking care of your people. How that had been a kind of credo, something to live by.

Then his brother's death. That terrible moment and the funeral that followed. He told her that it felt like there was a hole inside his chest that would never be filled, and when she asked him his brother's name, he could only tell her that he needed to give her the whole story first and she looked confused but mumbled, OK, and he continued, from Battle Mountain to Reno to the moment they both occupied, he and Grace, in her bedroom, the only illumination the pools of yellow light from the nightstands and a faint blur of snow falling beyond the window.

My god, she said when he was silent at last. That's all true?

It's all true.

You did that stuff? The robbery and the gambling and . . . all of it?

Yep.

My god, she said again.

I didn't want to tell you.

Apparently not, she said.

They were quiet then. The snow was coming heavy outside the window. He thought for a moment of the animals. They would be awake and moving in their enclosures, the snow a source of excitement, sending signals, sending messages of the winter to come.

Is that everything?

No, he said. There's one more thing.

God, Bill, she said, this is a lot to take in.

I know it is. There's just one more thing.

OK, let's hear it. Her voice was devoid of emotion: flat, lifeless.

You know I love you, right?

I love you too.

He exhaled. When I came up here I told my uncle David the whole thing. All of it. Just like I am now. We were pretty sure the police would be looking for me. So he decided I needed a new name.

She was silent then, staring at him.

Bill was my brother's name, he said softly.

Her mouth trembled and her eyes were glassy with tears. I don't understand what you're telling me, she said at last.

It's not the name I was born with. My name before was Nat. Nathaniel.

Nathaniel? she said.

Nathaniel Timothy Reed. My brother was Bill. William Chester Reed.

She sat there in the long silence that followed, no longer looking at him, instead staring off into the room somewhere, at the falling snow beyond the window glass. The forest was back there, rising up the ridge behind the house. Sometimes they would lie in bed and watch bats swirling through the thick stands of tamarack and bull pine and red cedar. Maybe that would never happen again now. Maybe everything he ever let into his heart would turn to smoke. Most of it already had.

So what am I supposed to call you then?

Bill, he said. That's who I am. That person I was before is just gone.

What the hell is that supposed to mean? she said.

He did not respond. He thought her next words would be to ask him to leave. She would not look at him, instead only stared into the far side of the room. Then her voice came at last: I'm gonna need a beer.

Me too.

Maybe a whiskey.

Me too.

I don't really know what I'm supposed to do with all of this, she said.

I just want you to know what happened. I don't need to you to do anything.

So this guy Rick . . . he's here. In Bonners.

Yes.

And that safe is the safe on the floor of your closet in the trailer?

Was, he said. I gave it to him.

He told her then that he had kept the safe all those years despite knowing that its serial number could, at any moment, tie him back to Reno, back to that winter of 1984, how he kept it even though his uncle told him that he should be rid of it, that it was evidence of the crime in which he had been involved, but he had kept the safe anyway, that perhaps it had been a kind of penance to do so, to be reminded of where he had come from, the black box holding a sense of gravity that rippled from where he had been to where he was and he knew, had always known, that he might have turned away from all of it were it not for the need to hold this final talisman, an iron to the knowledge that one day Rick would return and everything he had made of his life would be called into question. And of course that was exactly what had come to pass.

So if you gave him the safe and that's what he came up here for, then why is he still here? And why is he talking to Jude? She looked at him now, her eyes filled with rage and sadness all at once.

I don't know, he said.

That's not good enough.

I don't have a better answer, he said, his lie twisting inside his chest like a blade. I wish I did but I just don't. He won't leave. I don't know why.

Jesus. She was silent for a long moment. Then she said, You didn't tell anyone about this, did you? I mean you didn't tell the sheriff or anything?

I haven't told anyone at all in twelve years.

Goddammit, Bill. Or Nat. Or whatever I'm supposed to call you now.

Bill, he said.

Whatever, she said. You should have called Earl as soon as Rick called you the first time.

I was hoping he'd just give up and go away.

Christ, Bill. What if he does something? What if he does something to Jude to get to you? Isn't that what he's saying? That he can get to Jude?

That's why I'm telling you, he said. His eyes had brimmed over with tears and they flew hot and fast down his face but his voice was steady. There was that small victory over himself at least.

You should have told me before.

I know.

I mean all of it.

I didn't want you to know.

She fell silent again. Then she said, I need a drink.

All right.

Come on. She rose from the couch and he followed. The clock in the kitchen read two in the morning. It's late, she said.

He said nothing in response.

She removed a bottle from the upper cabinet and he pulled out two glasses and cracked a dozen cubes onto the counter and then filled the tray at the sink and returned it to the freezer. She poured both their glasses and then splashed hers with some water from the tap and took a long drink. He did the same.

I'm sorry, Grace.

You lied to me.

I didn't want you to know.

Why not?

Because it doesn't matter anymore. I left all of that behind.

Not all of it, she said.

No, I guess not.

Why'd you do all of that?

Honestly, it feels like someone else did all that stuff. I know a lot of it was just flailing around trying to find some way out.

Out of what?

Out of myself, he said. I guess that sounds pretty stupid.

No, she said, I know how that feels. Everybody knows how that feels. She sipped at the whiskey.

I'm just trying to be a good person, Grace. He stopped, faltered, then said, Or a better one.

Good people don't lie to their girlfriends.

I know that too.

I was already married to a guy who lied to me.

This isn't the same thing.

She looked at him, her mouth open.

It's not, he said. I promise. It's not the same thing.

He promised too.

He was fucking around on you, he said. This isn't that.

Goddammit, she said then. Is that everything now, or is there more?

Yeah, that's everything.

She paused a long moment and then blurted out: Christ, gambling?

Yep.

You won't even put money in the grammar school raffle.

And now you know why.

A silence fell over them. Outside the kitchen window, snow fluttered like moths against the glass.

You want me to go? he said.

No, I need you to stay here.

He looked at her without comprehension.

She set her glass on the counter and wrapped her arms around him and when her head fell to his shoulder she began to weep, huge, racking sobs that shook her against him, his own arms already around her. He whispered in her ear: It's all right, baby. It's all right. Everything's gonna be fine.

What if he does something?

He wanted to tell her that such thinking was absurd but he had the same fear and the best words he could find were to tell her that he would not let that happen.

She was quiet against him now, her breathing slowing into a more natural rhythm. Their bodies rocked together in the center of the room.

I love you so much, he said. I swear I didn't think I'd ever see him again.

But he's here, she said.

Yeah, he said. He's here.

BY MORNING, the snow covered everything, not with the dry shifting flakes of a cold-weather storm but in heavy wet clumps that fell like packed snowballs from a gray sky. The trucks in the driveway had been already rendered into nearly shapeless masses and he knew it would take a good long while to dig out the short driveway enough to make it onto the road where the snowplow would clear a path.

She had said almost nothing to him that morning and neither of them had slept more than a few quick hours. He felt broken and exhausted and the sight of the snow filled him with dread. So much to do at the rescue and now each task would be so much more difficult to complete.

Snow day! Jude yelled from the hall.

Maybe, Bill said. Why don't you turn on the TV.

The television lit up for about a minute and then the power went off.

I'll get the radio, Grace said from the kitchen, perhaps the first words she had spoken since the darkness of the night before.

She dialed in the local weather station and they sat listening to it. A foot of snow had fallen in the night and the storm would continue the rest of the week.

Dang, Bill said, not even Thanksgiving yet.

Was this in the forecast? she said.

I don't think so.

So it's a snow day? Jude said from the living room.

Guess so, little man, Bill said.

Awesome! Yes!

Bill stood there for a moment longer, sipping at his coffee, watching as Jude disappeared into the hallway toward his room. The house was suffused with a dim glowing light, a gauziness that seemed to come from everywhere at once, as if they had entered some liminal space that was both this world and the next. Well, he said, I guess I'd better get up there and see what's going on.

Are you ready for winter yet?

Barely started.

Are the kids coming up there today?

I don't know now, he said. Hope so. There's a lot to do if it's gonna snow all week. He stood there for a moment. Then he said, You want me to get your snow tires put on before I go?

No, I'll do it later. You'd better get up to the rescue. She rose from the chair she had settled into. Be careful today, she said.

I will.

He turned and then she said, I just need a little time to figure all this out.

I know. I mean, I get it.

She nodded briefly.

I'm gonna take care of this, he said. Everything's gonna be all right. He did not really believe this was true but it was the only thing that came into his mind and he knew that even though he had told her the truth at last he had started the day with a lie.

* * *

THE ROADS were slick with snow and already there were cars and trucks scattered into the ditches that lined the highway. He drove up the slow rise south out of Bonners. The flat plain that held the town and the farm fields had become an endlessness of white that disappeared into low clouds and it was into those low clouds that the road took him, a wash of gray that seemed to run at the windshield and through black trees in tatters amidst the blowing snow. The road had been plowed but he was worried about getting up to the rescue itself and of course to the trailer, a separate driveway that snowed over long before the rescue road would have. He knew he could make it had he already changed out the truck's tires for the studded tires he used in the winter months, but he had not done that yet. None of them had. It was only November, a full month or more before the winter snows generally began.

Nonetheless, he made it to the rescue's parking lot and was relieved to find Bess's car there and a moment later the pickup containing Chuck and Bobby. Snowing, Chuck said when they walked up toward where Bill stood looking in on the mountain lion enclosure.

We've got our work cut out for us.

You know it, Bobby said.

The lion moved in swirls through the thick flakes, its body ever in motion.

Cinder's having a good time, Chuck said.

Sure is, Bill said.

Snow day for everyone, Bobby said.

The lion swept past the outer wall of the enclosure, its body sleek and swift, like a current, like a tan river moving over the snow.

You guys wanna start the check-ins?

Will do, boss, Bobby said. You want us to blow the paths out?

If it'll work, Bill said. This is some thick glop coming down.

The two boys walked up between the enclosures through the snow, pushing each other from side to side as they moved, laughing. He had once had a friend like that, had tried for more than a decade to forget, but how can one forget such a thing. All his past resident forever in his heart.

Hey Cinder, he said to the enclosure. His voice quiet. You like the snow?

The animal kept moving, her body rippling between the dark trunks of the big trees.

*   *   *

THE SNOW continued all morning. The four of them worked at configuring the enclosures for the winter, checking and rechecking the heating systems, covering the areas that that been previously uncovered for the summer season, ensuring, the best they could, that the animals would have some shelter from the winter to come. They locked each animal in its smaller holding cell as they worked, dropping the heavy steel guillotine doors Bill had installed years earlier, the animals watching them from their snowed-over landscapes, the fences seeming to disappear in the swirl so that it seemed, at a glance, as if they were, each of them, free of the wire, of the need to be fed and watered, free indeed of their dependence. But of course it was only an illusion.

The four of them talked to the animals as they worked: Bess in her high singsong as if speaking with a very small child; the boys—Chuck and Bobby—each as if talking to a peer. Hey there, girl. Looking good in the snow, Chuck would say. And Bobby: For sure. Total owl babe. And they would both laugh, the owl watching them without expression.

He stood under the dark boughs of the pines and firs in the muffled silence of the snowstorm, Bess in the shelter of the wolf enclosure, switching out the feeding trays and making sure the heater was working, the two boys clambering across the tilted roof of the mountain lion's enclosure, tacking down a piece of corrugated steel that had come loose in the wind. After a time he went on to Majer's enclosure and stood watching the great bear where he sat on the rock above the pool, sniffing at the air. The animal's head pulled down briefly to stare at him with those sightless, milky eyes and then rose once more.

Hey old man, Bill said. What's out there? Moose?

The bear scratched its claws against the stone briefly and yawned.

Long night? he said. Me too. I can tell you one thing: you're lucky to be in there. Life's a lot more complicated out here in the wilderness.

The bear looked at him again and then turned his great bulk slowly and headed into the shadowed inner reaches of his den.

Hey, don't mind me, Bill said to that retreating shape. I'm not talking or anything.

But the bear was gone from view now. All at once Bill was gripped with the sudden and impossibly strong desire to call out to him, to pull him back to the fence wire, but instead he simply stood there watching the rock-strewn space that was the grizzly's home, his voice talking into the emptiness that remained.

THE SNOW kept on and the power finally failed just before noon, an event heralded only by the electric drill going silent and Bobby calling, There goes the power. He again listened for the ring of the phone but the sound did not come and did not come. At one point he checked for a dial tone and was relieved to hear that familiar buzzing and he hung up the receiver and waited, his mind wandering over the possibilities with a rapacity that made it hard to focus on any of the myriad tasks at hand.

It was Tuesday and he was scheduled to take the truck back out to Bonners Ferry to collect the expired produce from the two grocery stores there, both the Safeway downtown and the new grocery on the South Hill. He knew that he should send one of the boys as soon as possible, but when he saw the parking lot he wondered instead if he should tell the boys and Bess to leave for their own homes. At least six inches of snow covered the gravel road down to the highway. He would need to get the studded tires onto the truck if anyone was going to get all the way to Bonners and back up the mountain again and there was still so much work to do clearing and cleaning and getting all the enclosures ready for the winter months. He had taken to salting the fence lines to keep them clear of snow and had dug drains to channel the runoff but every year they needed to be cleaned and redug and he had not even done that yet. And then there was supposed to be a run to Sandpoint later in the week to pick up expired meat. Each trip would take a half-day to complete and all while the snow continued to fall.

Nonetheless, he dismissed Bess and the two boys shortly after one and stood at the end of the path by the mountain lion enclosure watching them spin and slide out of the parking lot and into a haze of snow so thick that it had become like watching a television station fade into and out of range. Then he turned and walked back up the path, first to the office, where the phone was still silent, and then up through the birches to the trailer, no path now but a scattering of black and white trunks jutting up everywhere from the snow, no other vegetation visible at all. Everything white, blank, and empty.

When he reached the trailer he was shivering with cold. He turned the gas heater on full blast and stood before it shaking and holding his hands out before its feeble blowing heat. His pants were soaked through and after a few moments he sat on the edge of the bed and peeled them off and then stood again before the heater, turning slowly, his hands cold and the flesh of his legs pink and blotchy like chicken flesh, his entire body trembling. At some point he reached into a drawer and removed his long underwear and a dry pair of jeans and pulled them both on.

The shivering slowed and finally stopped and in the stillness he turned on the radio and broke two eggs into a pan and scrambled them and then sat at the foldout table and ate, listening to the news broadcast and flipping through a day-old paper. The weather report in the paper said nothing of an impending storm but on the radio it was the only news, a dark and endless swirl of clouds spinning down from Alaska and over Washington and on across the North Idaho panhandle. *Get ready folks*, the radioman said. *It's a big one.* From the tiny window the open field behind the trailer was a haze of white through which he could occasionally see a glimpse of the granite boulders a few dozen yards away and from which, on a clear day, he could have seen the ridgelines extending out through the trees to the north and east.

There had been moments during the day when he convinced himself that everything would be fine, that Rick would simply dissolve back into his memory, that the Fish and Game would change their minds about the rescue, that he and Grace and Jude would form a family in the forest with Majer and the animals all around them and that they would be happy in their lives. But this was not such a moment. In the snow he saw only terror: his own and that of the people and the animals he loved.

He told Majer all of this when he returned to the rescue after lunch, talking to him softly and asking him to present various body parts to the gap they had welded into the cage door. A paw. An ear. His grizzled mouth. Each time Bill told him, Good job, buddy, and passed a marshmallow through the bars to his waiting lips. He told the bear about Grace, about how she had found him, how she had been the one to ask him out on that first date and how he had been so surprised that he had coughed out a fine spray of coffee against the snow.

That's an interesting response, she had said.

Dang, he said. That really took me off guard.

Apparently.

Um, yeah, he said. I'd love to.

Good. I'll pick you up.

Really?

Yeah. Is that a problem?

Not at all. Are you going to pay for it too?

I draw the line there.

Sounds good, he said.

They had both been smiling, standing not far from where he now sat next to Majer. Do you remember that? he asked the bear. Right about where that jack pine's coming up through the snow.

She had come out to replace the previous mobile veterinarian, a dour old man Bill had little relationship with outside of the animals, had visited the facility four or five times in that first month. After the first visit Bill found himself already looking forward to her return.

Within a few months they were dating regularly and she introduced him to Jude, four years old at the time. Grace told Bill that the boy's father was essentially gone from their lives, living in Spokane, a man who had had repeated affairs and essentially abandoned all interest in Jude once she divorced him and moved to Idaho.

I don't know what to say about that, Bill told her.

Just don't ever cheat on me and we'll be fine.

Deal, he said.

He had felt lucky. That was the word for it. As if something had changed for him, and indeed something had. He had awakened one day into the life he was supposed to lead all along, a life to which every bad decision he ever made had led him without his realizing it, an idea that he did not even believe in, that he would have thought ludicrous had it been spoken by someone else. And then Rick had returned and with it everything had scattered into unknowable and unanswerable questions. He did not even know if Grace would want to see him again. Maybe she would call later to tell him that it was over. Maybe that was how it would end.

Seems like I just figured out what I was supposed to do. You know? And here I am. The bear looked at him with longing. He slid another marshmallow through the gate and the bear took it with gentle distended lips. Well, buddy, Bill said, I don't know what's gonna happen now but I gotta tell you, you've been a good friend all these years.

The bear looked at him and to Bill's surprise a wave of sadness and concern seemed to pass over the animal's face.

Oh don't give me that look. You've gotten all the marshmallows I'm gonna give you today, he said. The bear put his ear up to the window and Bill scratched it through the gap in the bars. Good bear, he said. Good good bear.

When the muffled sound of the phone came, he leaped off the stump and went careening through the snow and into the dark office, crashing into the desk and lifting the receiver. Hello? Hello? he said.

Well, it's done, Grace said.

What's done?

Let's just say it's good to be friends with the sheriff.

Jesus, Grace, tell me.

Earl ran him out of the county.

What?

I called him and told him he was hassling Jude and he ran him out of the county. Simple as that.

Holy shit, he said. What did he say?

He had his guys check a few hotels and found him here in Bonners right away. So they told him to get out of Boundary County.

And Rick went?

Yeah, he went. Earl waited for him to check out of the hotel and then followed him out to the county line.

And Rick didn't say anything? About what we talked about?

Earl didn't mention anything else. Said to call him if he shows up again. I'm probably gonna have to do free work on the sheriff's horse for the rest of my life now.

Bill laughed with relief and breathed out into the cool air of the room. Ah man, he said. That's good news. That's really good news.

I guess he's maybe done with this and headed back to Nevada.

I hope so.

So that's it, right? she said. That's the whole thing? No more surprises?

No more surprises. That's all of it.

I'll make you a deal, she said. Don't lie to me again. I mean ever.

Oh I won't, he said. I never meant to.

I don't care what you meant to do. I really don't. I only care about what you actually do. That's important. The rest of it is just a bunch of bullshit.

You're right, he said.

Can you come over tonight?

God I want to, he said. But it's supposed to snow for the whole week and I gotta get the enclosures ready for it.

I got the snow tires on. Maybe I can come up.

Maybe in the daytime tomorrow. Not at night. That would just scare the crap out of me, thinking of you and Jude on the road.

I want to see you.

You do?

Of course I do.

I wasn't sure you did, he said.

You freaked me out but I love you, Bill Reed.

I love you too, he said, relief pouring through him like an avalanche.

They talked for a few more minutes about the days to come. There was the Fish and Game paperwork to complete. Grace would call Zoo Boise in hopes they might offer some advice. And Bill told her he would try to get out to Bonners the following day to pick up the expired meat and if so he would stop by the house to see her and Jude, saving them the trouble of coming out to the rescue in the storm.

His eyes had adjusted to the darkness of the room now. In the dim light bleeding through the curtained windows he could see the desk, the cold silent heater, his breath in a cloud. I better go switch out my tires before I'm out of daylight, he said.

OK, she said. Be careful out there.

Always am.

They said their good-byes and he hung up the phone, smiling.

The light outside was pale blue as if the sky was frozen into a single enormous plane. The snow had fallen unabated and his booted feet sank until they were buried. He would need to clear the paths out first or he would be struggling all day to get to and from the equipment shed. And he would need to fire the generator to get the heaters functioning. But first he would change out the tires on the truck. After that he would attend to the rest of the list. He would have tomorrow too, and the next day, and the next. If Fish and Game wanted to close down the rescue, they would need to come up here and do it, and with the snow dumping down the way it was, he did not think they would do any such thing. At least not this week.

12

IT'S FIVE HUNDRED CASH BACK, RICK SAID. THAT'S WHAT HE keeps saying on the commercials.

So what?

So that's a lot of cash to have around. He was sighting down the length of the 99, sighting and then dropping the barrel to look at the cans and the water jug and then raising the rifle and sighting down its length once more.

You gonna shoot at some point? Nat said.

OK, OK, Rick said. He steadied the rifle again and squinted and at last squeezed off a round. A can jumped and rattled away off the rocks.

There it is, Rick said. I was starting to think the damn thing wasn't shooting right.

I think we're not shooting right, Nat said.

Too drunk.

Too retarded, Nat said.

Water jug, Rick said.

We'll see about that.

Rick ejected the spent shell and then stood and aimed and repositioned and aimed and repositioned and finally pulled the trigger. The weapon's report made Nat wince each time and with it the thin muscles in his forearms jumped as if from a short, faint electric shock. The shot did not hit anything this time and so the water jug remained where they had set it upon a smooth yellow boulder a few dozen yards away, flanked by a series of rusted cans already filled with bullet holes from previous shooters, men and perhaps women with better aim than they. Shit, Rick said. I don't get it. The fucking jug is the biggest thing down there. I've been popping cans for an hour.

They changed positions, Nat with the rifle and Rick sliding to a seat on a stone beside a scraggly and ill-defined bush bristling with spikes and tiny gray-green leaves. The field guide lay next to him on the rock where Nat had left it and now Rick lifted the slim book and paged through it. What's this thing called?

Saltbush.

Saltbush, Rick said. Christ, how do you find anything in here? Everything looks the same.

It's just like reading a map, he said.

A map to where?

To here.

It was almost Thanksgiving and the cold of winter had already descended from the mountains, their breath outspiraling under a sky so pale it was very nearly white. The shallow draw they occupied was sunken between two low hills into which the sun shone lengthwise so that the whole of its short span was aglow.

Rick laid the book beside him on the rock and lifted the bottle at his feet. You said he had a safe in his office, right?

Yeah, so what?

So if Milt is giving people five hundred dollars cash back on every car sold, how much does he have on hand?

Nat stared down at the cans and the water jug. His broken index finger pointed down the length of the barrel. Depends on how many cars he sells in a day, he said.

Yeah, so let's say it's only like three or five cars. Something like that.

What's your point, Rick?

My point is it's open seven days a week so that would be ... what ... six days would be forty-five hundred and another fifteen so that's six grand. Probably all in that safe in his office. And that doesn't even include cash down payments and stuff like that.

Nat turned and looked at him now but Rick only lifted the bottle of Mad Dog from the dirt and took a long drink. You gonna shoot? he said.

Nat returned to the cans and took aim and fired, pulling the trigger with his middle finger. This time the bark of the weapon made his index finger jolt with pain. Nothing moved. Not even a puff of dust.

How big is that safe you saw?

I don't know.

Small enough to carry?

I don't know, Rick. Maybe. Probably ... This is crazy talk. That's what this is. Where's all this coming from?

Just talkin', Rick said.

No you're not, Nat said. He had turned toward Rick but now he faced the targets again. This is a bad stupid idea. Seriously. A bad bad idea.

Jesus, I'm just talking, Rick said. Don't get excited.

Can we just shoot? You're freaking me out.

It was Saturday. All week he had lain in the apartment, shaking with fever. The clinic had reset his broken finger with an aluminum splint lined with bright blue foam and had given him a prescription for painkillers and antibiotics, neither of which he could afford to fill, and so he had ridden out the subsequent four days in a fever dream awash with throbbing agony, his body temperature seeming to burst into heat and then drop into a freezing chill like an ever rising and falling wave.

With each missed day of work his paycheck dwindled. After taxes his full-time every-two-weeks pay hovered around two hundred and twenty dollars, but he had taken the advance and now had missed four days and what remained for him to pick up at the office would be closer to eighty. Rent was due on Monday. That would be two hundred. And of course he feared the inevitable knock on the door that would be

Mike coming to collect for his debt to Johnny Aguirre. He listened for that sound all day long and well into the night.

On Friday afternoon the fever broke and for the first time since the night in the casino parking lot he felt like he might survive whatever illness had descended upon him. Rick and Susan arrived after their shifts—Rick's at the Peppermill coffee shop washing dishes and Susan at a video rental store across town—and that night they remained in the apartment with him, watching Rick Hunter and Dee Dee McCall track down bad guys in Los Angeles at nine and then watching Sonny Crockett and Rico Tubbs track down bad guys in Miami at ten. He tried not to look at her and he mostly succeeded. When she left just after midnight she embraced him gently, leaning down to where he lay prostrate on the sofa. I'm glad you're feeling better, she said.

Thanks for taking care of me.

She glanced over at Rick briefly, giving him a look that might have held some meaning he could not trace, and then she was gone.

In the morning he came out of the bedroom to find Rick seated at the little kitchen table with the guns spread out on a ratty dish towel: the Savage 99 he had inherited from his dead brother and the .38 Special Rick had inherited from his absent father.

You're not going on a killing spree now, are you? Nat said.

Feeling better?

Finally.

Just thought we might get outside and do some shooting.

Really? he said. It's been a while.

No shit, Rick said. Might make you feel better to get outside. We can go out toward Pyramid Lake. Pick up a bottle of Mad Dog. It'll be like old times.

What about your parole?

What about it?

Isn't it against your parole to have guns around?

Only if they find out, Rick said.

And so a few hours later they stepped out onto the pale burned earth of the desert with the rifle and the pistol, a six-pack of beer, a bottle of Banana Red MD 20/20, and a couple of sandwiches they'd picked up from a deli on the way. Rick had received his first paycheck from the café the day before and so he paid for all of it and the ammunition as well.

Nat had hoped he would feel better out in the desert but he could not stop thinking about what would happen when Mike returned to find his pockets empty once again. As he aimed, he imagined Mike as a tin can down there, the sights swinging around that silver shape, but each time he pulled the trigger the can remained and he was left with a sharp arc of pain shooting across the broken finger bone.

So I went over to Bishop's this week, Rick said from the boulder behind him.

Yeah? He aimed but did not fire this time. His whole hand had begun to throb.

That guy with the weird shirts was there. You know that guy?

Not from that.

He's got that mustache that curls up. You know. The guy who looks like the guy on the Monopoly box.

Oh yeah. That guy.

Yeah, so I'm just sitting at the bar and out of the blue he said to me, "So you're with Susan now?" and I was like, "What do you mean *now*?" and he just sort of laughed like it was a joke.

Yeah?

Yeah so . . . Rick's voice trailed off. Then he added, Just seemed like a weird thing to say.

Nat looked over at him but Rick was not looking in his direction now, holding the bright red bottle of 20/20 in one hand and peering out behind them to where the draw opened into the desert beyond, out into the abandoned and unused BLM landscape all around them. I didn't know what else to say to the guy, Rick said. It didn't make any sense, but then I was thinking about it, you know, later, and I was like what the fuck?

I don't get it.

You don't get what?

So the guy said you were with Susan now. You *are* with Susan. So what?

It was the way he said it. Like I'm with Susan now but I wasn't before or something. Shit, I don't know. It was weird, man. That's all. It was just weird.

Doesn't seem weird to me.

I don't know, Rick said. Maybe it's not. He had lit a cigarette now and sat puffing at it, the bottle in the dirt between his feet, the collar of his leather jacket held tight against his throat. Just seems like there's something going on that I don't know about.

Nat tried to aim again but the sights wobbled everywhere across the cans and the rocks and the water jug and he lowered the rifle again. There's nothing going on, he said.

Yeah. Shit, you're probably right, Rick said.

Nat lifted the rifle and squeezed the trigger, not even bothering to aim this time. When he opened his eyes against the shot, the water jug remained unchanged. Shit, he said. It's impossible to hit.

Rick was silent behind him for a long time. Then he said, quietly, It's just that she's my girlfriend, you know?

Yeah I know.

No, I mean like when I was locked up she's all I could think about. Seriously.

Yeah, she's your girlfriend.

Yeah, well, it's important. That's all I mean.

Nat turned back to the targets and sighted quickly and squeezed and closed his eyes and fired and squinted and again the water jug remained there, unmoving. Dang, he said. In his mind, he could see her naked on his stained mattress, the Van Halen poster above them. Her breasts were small and had felt soft and warm in his hands.

The shadow at the bottom of the shallow draw had shifted as they spoke, crawling sideways across them both. His stomach was a tight ball now, a tight hot ball. So you're in love, he said. Rick Harris is in love.

Yeah, I guess so, he said. I guess I am.

Didn't see that coming, Nat said.

Me neither, Rick said. He took another draw on the cigarette. God-damn, he said. Goddamn.

Nat tried to speak but his throat felt small and tight and the only sound he could make was a faint, dry rasp. He coughed and looked back down the draw at the water jug and the cans. They seemed in motion now, as if adrift on some ocean that was invisible all around them. He breathed in slowly but the motion did not stop.

Hey, let's blow this fucking thing to pieces, Rick said.

Nat had not heard him come but Rick stood next to him now, the pistol held up in the air before him.

Hang on, Nat said. He reached down and levered a shell into the chamber.

You ready now?

Ready.

Rick leveled the pistol, both hands gripping the handle. Then he counted to three.

Nat squinted against the sound. Rick squeezed off shot after the shot. The cans jumped and fell. The water jug remained. Nat stood with the rifle against his shoulder and aimed and aimed and kept his eyes open, his broken finger pointing down at the targets. Then he squeezed off a round and watched the water jug as it exploded at last.

13

ALL WEEK CAME THE SNOW AND WITH IT A SERIES OF BLEAK
dreams that he awoke from each morning in confusion and terror, a
night spent scrambling through a blizzarding forest gone black and
malevolent, his movement hindered by snow that lay everywhere in his
path, clinging to him even as it seemed liquid, fluid, like quicksand. He
did not know how many hours he labored in those frozen and claus-
trophobic landscapes but when he awoke at last it was, each time, to
the muffled and strangling darkness of a trailer nearly buried, as if the
waking world had come to mirror the dream he had fled, the details
of which blew away with each gust of the storm, leaving only the sense
of it—fear, panic, terror—his body shaking with cold even though the
trailer itself was warm, the propane heater at a low constant hum. And
yet he awoke trembling, as if somehow his skeleton had frozen in the
night and he woke with cold dry bones everywhere inside him.

Each morning and evening he dug the snow away from the door,
creating a burrow that led up to the surface, where all night and day
fresh snow fell. By Friday morning it had reached the base of the windows and a heavy drift had accumulated on the trailer's west side: a
clean slope broken only by his dug-out passage, a partial tunnel that

led, at a short diagonal, up to the surface. Each morning a new layer of snow had crept up past the bottom of the door so that he would pull the door open and find an icy wall, as if someone had built a second door to mirror the first. One morning he dug the area down nearly to the frozen dirt, the filtered cloudlight coming through the rim of the tunnel so that the whole tube glowed faintly, sky blue and luminous, the stairs he had cut into its side with the blade of the shovel leading into a storm that seemed as if it would never end.

The power had been cutting in and out since Tuesday and the phone service as well but midweek the snow turned to ice in the night and when he awoke in the morning its evidence sparkled on every surface—tree branch and gate rail and on the trailer itself—as if the world he knew had tipped into some other, a world where everything was coated in the transitory and liminal substance of a fairy tale. There had been no power since that night but through some miracle the phone continued to function, although he knew it was only a matter of time until he lost that as well.

He had spent each day working to clear paths, salting the edges of the enclosures in an attempt to clear the fence lines. The snow was too thick to use the blower, too thick and too heavy, and so most of the work had been by shovel and after two days he was so tired and weak that he could not fathom how he could keep up with it, so he had stopped doing all but the most necessary clearing: the doors, some walkways, nothing more than that. He had called a snowplow service earlier in the week and they had come and plowed from the trailer to the parking lot and all the way down to the turnoff to the main road, a span of just over a mile, and despite the plow scraping nearly to the gravel surface of the road, it was already close to impassible. Each winter he took the pickup down to Naples, parking it in a gravel lot near the railroad tracks and thereafter using the snowmobile to span the mile between the rescue and town. That shift usually came well into December, when the snows were heavy enough to close the road between the creek and the rescue, but this season it was already apparent that the days he would be able to drive the truck from town to his trailer were numbered.

He had called Grace on Wednesday and talked with her for nearly an hour, standing in the relative warmth of the office, the kerosene heater he had finally repaired sending an invisible stream of hot air blasting into the room. In confirmation of his concerns about the road, she had told him that she and Jude had driven up to see if they could get to the rescue but the big snowplows had just come through, revealing the snowpack on the rescue road to be nearly two feet deep. Had Jude not been with her, she said, she might have skied up the road, but the route was a full mile and she worried about the boy and so they turned back to Bonners, their progress slow and steady amongst cars spun everywhere into the drifts. She sounded happy to hear from him and he thought that maybe, just maybe, things could still move back to the way they had been before Rick had arrived.

A few minutes later, as if in confirmation of his desire, the phone rang as he was still seated at the desk.

Bill Reed, the voice on the other line said. Glad I caught you. This is Judge Harper up at the First District Court.

Yes? he said, his chest a flurry of electric lines.

I guess you've got a problem up there.

A problem?

With Fish and Game, the judge said.

Oh, Bill said, relief flooding through him all at once. Do I ever.

Yeah, Sheriff Baxter was telling me about it. Asked if there was anything the court could do.

Yeah, Bill said, Earl mentioned he might talk to you.

Well, no guarantees what this will do in the long run, but I got a lawyer friend to file an injunction on your behalf.

What's that mean?

Means Fish and Game can't do anything until we work it out in the court. It'll just be temporary but maybe it'll buy you a month or two. Hell, with this storm it might buy you a lot longer than that.

Dang, he said. Thank you so much.

Well, you should thank Earl, really. I owe him a bunch.

I'll certainly do that.

The judge told him the name of the lawyer who would call him. They spoke for a few more minutes about the severity of the storm and then Bill set the phone down slowly and stood there in the new silence. It had stopped snowing momentarily but the sky roiled with ash-gray clouds. Through the tiny window in the trailer, the snow seemed to glow with a faint luminescence that flowed backward into the trees. From that pale light came a stunned silence that descended everywhere around him, as if falling from the sky and rising from the earth all at once, and when he tried to dial Grace at last, the phone emitted no dial tone and so he came outside again, the generator chugging away at the base of the hill, powering heaters for Cinder and the raptors and Katy the fox and the trio of raccoons. For a long while he stood in front of the office, wondering what he should be doing, wondering if he should be doing anything at all, finally walking up the short rise to where Majer sat just inside the overhang on the concrete interior of the enclosure, as if waiting for him.

Hey buddy, Bill said to him. I got some good news.

The bear cocked his head, dipping his long snout twice, three times, as if nodding in response.

We've got a judge on our side, Bill said. He sat on the stump in the little vestibule and leaned forward to open the aperture in the zoo-keeper door, thinking of lighting a cigarette even though he never smoked inside the rescue and especially not near Majer, who had lived too long to have to breathe in the aftereffects of his keeper's bad habits.

The bear nosed at the opening, asking for a treat. Oh buddy, he said, and inexplicably his eyes filled with tears. His fingers had come through the opening in the door and the bear touched them with his nose, so gently. The bear's great grizzled head. Those milky eyes. We might be OK after all, he said.

He sat there for nearly an hour, talking slowly, quietly, watching the bear, his friend, in that moment his best friend in all the world, sitting in the cage he had built for him, the animal nodding slowly as if understanding every word he said and then pressing its great head up to the wire and emitting a long, low moan.

ON SATURDAY he returned to the office after several hours of heavy labor in the snow to the ringing of the telephone. Despite the previous day's good news, he had awakened that morning from a troubled sleep of blurred and terrifying dreams. During the night there had been a moment where he thought he had seen a figure in the darkness but he often saw such illusions in the winter after days and days of solitude and when he went out to investigate he could see nothing and even the trailer itself was only a thin and wobbling shape in a swirl of black snow. When the morning came, he could not even recall if he had actually stepped outside the trailer to investigate or if that too had been a dream. With the blowing wind it had felt, most of the night, as if the trailer had become unmoored and floated down some dark river, toward what destination he could not imagine, but in the morning all was as he had left it: the snow everywhere, the truck buried to the windshield, the trailer nearly gone altogether, and all the while the thick flakes continuing to fall.

He ate a hurried breakfast at the Formica table and dug out the front door again. Then he bundled his coat and scarf around his neck and clambered up through the burrow onto the high surface of the new snow, the snowshoes clutched in his gloved hands. Perhaps two feet of the edge of the trailer were still visible, the rest buried in the drift. He sat at the top of the ramp that led down to the trailer's door and strapped the snowshoes onto his boots and then stood, blowing steam before turning downhill into the birches, his head lowered, teeth clenched and eyes squinting into the wind. Already his mustache and beard were caked with ice and he knew that the office below would be dark and cold, that it would take a full hour or more just to get the temperature above fifty degrees. Everything so much more difficult without electricity. He had about fifty gallons of gasoline in the equipment shed and had been running the generator to get power to the heaters inside the enclosures but fifty gallons was not much and he would need to get to town soon to resupply.

The snow completely unbroken. No sign of animals anywhere. No birds nor deer nor elk. No track. Nothing. As if, in the face of the storm, the animals had simply fled out across the mountains somewhere. Or as if he had already shifted out into whatever world lay beyond.

He spent most of the day trying to get the snowmobile to run, pausing only briefly to heat up a frozen burrito for lunch. His uncle had purchased the machine new soon after Bill had arrived at the rescue twelve years ago and it had served him well in the intervening years, but now when he pulled at the cord it simply would not start. He removed the fuel lines and the filter and carburetor and then reassembled the machine and then pulled and pulled and pulled at the cord.

When he reentered the office, the snowmobile still did not run but his hands had gone numb from the cold and his patience was finished. The phone was already ringing as he came through the door.

North Idaho Wildlife Rescue, he said into the handset.

Don't hang up, man, Rick said. His voice was calm. Quiet. And Bill did not hang up. Did not even breathe. I just want to talk for a minute. That's all. Can we just do that?

I thought you were gone.

No, Rick said, I'm still here.

He could feel the handset in his grip. Cold plastic. I don't have what you want.

Can we just talk? Just for a little while?

Leave me alone, Bill said.

I just want to talk for a minute, goddammit, Rick said, an edge in his voice now, and when Bill did not respond he said, more calmly, Let's say you and me grab a beer.

Grab a beer? Are you serious?

Yeah, I'm serious. You owe me that much, Rick said.

Not after you went and talked to Jude. That's crossing the line and you know it.

What line is that? I'm just trying to get your goddamn attention. You make it pretty near impossible. What else was I supposed to do?

You're supposed to go back to Nevada.

I just want to talk. We've been friends for a long time. Don't you owe me that much?

The drawing Bill had made as a child hung on the wall in its cheap wooden frame, faded with age but still recognizable as a bear, the animal's head much larger than it was in life, its eyes blue, and underneath it, in red crayon or marker: MAJER. He could not imagine being the child who had made such a drawing, and yet there was the proof. He thought of Jude. Of the boy's drawing of the wolf.

Twelve years, Nat, Rick said. Twelve years I've been locked up.

Shit, Bill said. He looked across the room to where the heater hissed a constant stream of kerosene-heated air into the room. All right, he said at last. All right. He already regretted saying the words.

AN HOUR later he entered the Northwoods Tavern to find the bar well attended despite the storm, a dozen or more patrons laughing and drinking and carrying on under the illumination of the same neon lights that burned ceaselessly in apparent disregard of the blizzard. Across the room, Rick sat at a table near a dim frosted window, a bottle in front of him. He looked at Bill as he came through the door, the expression on his face indicating no emotion at all, not even recognition, as if glancing up at something inanimate: a stone, a tree, a stick.

Bill had spent the hour between Rick's phone call and their meeting working on the snowmobile and jerking repeatedly at the pull cord, all the while snowflakes filtering in through the open door of the equipment shed and his heart riding in his throat. He adjusted the choke and pumped the gas and then pulled and pulled and pulled and at last, to his relief and surprise, the machine caught and warmed up enough that it would idle without throttle.

He had loaded it into the back of the truck, driving the machine up the metal ramps and tying it to the bed so it would not slide while he drove. The rifle remained under the seat in the zippered case with the dart gun. He did not know what he would do with such a weapon but he had held it across his lap for a moment before returning it to the space under the seat and exiting the truck.

At the bar he ordered a beer and the bartender told him he was mixing up some hot toddies and then asked if he wanted one.

I'm not even sure I'll be here long enough to finish the beer, Bill said in response.

The bartender nodded and handed him a bottle and Bill crossed the room to where Rick sat, staring at him dolefully as Bill took the chair across from him at the table. Here I am, he said.

Here you are, Rick said. Fat Nat with a beard.

Rick's coat was unzipped and Bill could see the edge of a tattoo at his throat. You got tatted up in prison, he said.

Rick laughed, a short harsh scoff. Yeah, he said, as if it were obvious to all.

You been back to BM?

Why would I go back there?

I don't know, Bill said.

You?

Not for a long time.

Rick lifted his bottle but did not drink from it. Battle fucking Mountain. What a shithole, Rick said. You know, when I first showed up there, you told me your dad was in the CIA. Do you remember that?

I didn't say that.

Oh yeah you did, Rick said. Every fucking thing that came out of your mouth was a lie, right from go. Now your whole life is a lie.

What'd you want to talk to me about, Rick?

He shook his head. I've been up there to your little zoo, he said. I've seen all those animals in their cages. You've got yourself a little prison up there.

I'm gonna ask you this again and then I'm gonna leave. What do you want?

I want to know what you get out of that.

Out of what?

Out of turning your back on your people and coming up here to run a fucking zoo. Because I've been thinking about it for a long time and it doesn't make any sense. I just can't figure you out.

Rick's skin looked both pale and gray simultaneously, as if he had grown old too quickly, his features carved into a thin membrane of flesh embossed upon a network of sinew.

There's nothing to figure out, Bill said. They need someone to take care of them. So that's what I do.

You let me rot in prison and let my mom die and turned your back on everything because you decided to take care of some fucked-up animals out in the middle of nowhere?

I made a life for myself.

Yeah yeah, Rick said, you've said that before.

Then I guess we're done, Bill said.

He started to rise but then Rick leaned back in his chair, the beer in his hand. I think you'd better sit and listen to me so you know what's coming next, he said.

Bill stood for a moment, watching him, and then lowered himself to the chair again. His jacket remained zipped and buttoned. Look, I know I did some things I shouldn't have, he said, but it's not anything I can change. I've already said I'm sorry.

A man with a feathered dart in his hand passed the table and seemed to survey both of them in turn as if sizing them up for a brawl. Hey, the man said, you two guys up for a dart game?

Not this time, Rick said.

Your loss, the man said, striding to where the dartboards hung on the wall in a slim alcove at the back of the bar. Someone closer to the door, behind Bill, burst into laughter.

I don't know what else you want me to say here, Bill said. I'm sorry about what happened. I'm sorry you went to prison.

Yeah, everyone's sorry, Rick said. He looked beyond Bill now, farther into the bar. Then he said, You know Susan wrote me a few years ago.

At the sound of her name, even after all these years, he felt his heart stutter in his chest. Oh yeah? he said.

Yeah, maybe four or five years ago. She married some guy out in Lemmon Valley. Had a couple of kids and everything.

Good for her.

That's not the point. Point is, she told me about you and her when I was in prison the first time.

Me and her what?

Oh come on, man, Rick said. Now you're just acting stupid.

The bottle on the table. The wet ring it made.

She said she just wanted to come clean about everything and that she was sorry but she had to get on with her life. So that was like the final piece of the puzzle, you know? I mean, you guys all just left me behind and didn't even look back once. And here I am with shit-all to show for it. Everyone gets a fresh start and I'm left holding the bag? I don't think so.

Bill lifted his beer and drank. He could taste nothing. Nothing at all.

Why'd you leave me there, Nat? Rick said.

He looked away for a moment and then looked back. I couldn't have gotten to you in time, he said.

Bullshit.

I don't know what else to tell you. It all went to shit so fast. There wasn't any time to think.

You shouldn't have had to think.

He sat watching him, the gray ghost that had once been his friend. Then he said, It just doesn't matter anymore. You gotta move past it.

Doesn't matter? It was twelve years of my life. Because of you, man. The whole fucking thing. That's what I realized in prison. Everything that got fucked up in my life was all because of you.

I don't know what to tell you, man. I really don't.

Rick sat looking at him.

We done?

Fuck we are.

If you keep asking me the same thing I'm gonna keep giving you the same answer.

You fucked this up, Natty, Rick said. Just like you fucked up everything you ever touched. You really fucked this up.

You don't know me anymore, Bill said.

Oh, I know you. You haven't changed that much.

Yes, I have.

I don't think so, Rick said. He smiled again, that thin shining line.

Bill sat looking across the table at him, his mouth dry, heart thumping away in his chest, Rick staring into his eyes. I don't know what else to say, he said at last. I'm sorry for what happened. I'm sorry for how it worked out.

Not as sorry as I am.

Why'd you want to see me, Rick? Why are you even here?

I'll tell you why, Rick said. His voice was cold now. I came up here to see what happened to the money but also to find out what happened to you. He shook his head slowly, dolefully.

This is what happened to me, Bill said. Now go home.

Rick looked up at him now, his eyes wet and clear. Go home? he said. I'm not done talking. He smiled now, his gray teeth shining in the bar's neon signage. I gave you a chance. I want you know that.

A chance for what?

Redemption, he said.

What's that supposed to mean? Bill said. His voice was steady but he felt as if he was shaking inside, his skeleton trying to loose itself of his skin.

It means I've been waiting twelve years to pay you back, Rick said. Now I'm the one done talking. Pay for my fucking beer. He stood quickly.

Rick, Bill said.

And at that word Rick spun, suddenly and without warning, his hand clamped to the back of Bill's neck before he could even flinch, Rick's face so close that he could smell the burning scent of his breath. You think you've changed, Rick said. The shit I did in prison just to survive you couldn't even begin to imagine. And let me tell you this, my friend. I know where you live and where your girlfriend lives and where she works and where her kid goes to school. So you just think about that.

You're making a mistake.

I'm not the one making a mistake. Not this time.

Bill's voice was thin through his teeth. I'm sure we can figure this out, he hissed.

Let's find out, Rick said.

He released his grip then. Bill knocked his chair over in his haste to stand, the table lurching forward and both beer bottles tipping. Rick! he yelled, but the man was already halfway across the room and then was at the door and then was gone.

Bill glanced slowly around the room, fists clenched and trembling, beer splashing the floor at his feet. The jukebox played its song of cowboys and lost love. Then he ran headlong for the door.

In the blowing snow, the yellow Honda was turning out of its parking spot, its chained tires whacking the surface of the concrete like muffled machine gun fire, the taillights a faint red blur as the car braked and then slid forward. Bill called his name again as he came down into the parking lot, his feet slipping everywhere but somehow reaching the car as it slid toward the asphalt of the highway, his fists battering the yellow curve of the roof, screaming that name again and again as the car pulled out and away from him, its tire chains flopping in the snow, pulling out onto the highway and into the darkness of the storm.

*　　*　　*

THE DRIVE to Bonners Ferry would have taken fifteen minutes on a clear day, but the snow was blowing sideways across the road and the pickup seemed to shift across that landscape as if adrift. They had plowed, had probably plowed many times, but the blizzard was so thick that he could sometimes not find the roadbed at all. And yet he kept moving forward, the snow a tunnel that seemed to curl in upon his vision, not opening up but closing upon him like a fist and the road continuing forever toward a destination that seemed, in the storm, to move farther and farther from his rolling tires.

When he finally pulled into the Safeway parking lot in Bonners and saw Grace's pickup there he nearly wept with relief, the truck sliding in next to hers, his door already opening. She stepped out onto the snow and he embraced her and told her he loved her and that he was sorry and she looked at him and put her hands against his face. This guy's nuts, she said.

He nodded. I called the sheriff from the bar. He's out looking for him.

Good, she said. Where are we going?

He hesitated before answering. Then he said: Coeur d'Alene.

Bill, she said slowly, you're coming with us, right?

I can't, he said.

She looked away.

You know I can't.

Dammit, Bill, she said. There were tears in her eyes now. What am I supposed to do now?

Highway'll be clear down to Coeur d'Alene. Get a hotel room and I'll come down later tonight.

Later tonight? She would not look at him. You probably don't even have a phone up there right now.

I can't leave them, Grace. I haven't even had the chance to feed them tonight.

They'll be fine for one night.

You're probably right but I just can't do it.

The truck's window cranked down and Jude's face appeared. Come on, he said. Let's go.

Hey big guy, Bill said.

Hey back, Jude said. We're going on a snow adventure.

Crazy, Bill said.

Hey I have your book.

That's all right, you keep it. He glanced over toward the truck and as he did so the book tumbled from Jude's hand into the snow. He stepped over and picked it up. It was still in the plastic ziplock baggie, the rubber band holding the whole thing together.

You can keep the book, pal.

Mom says I need to work on returning what I borrow.

Oh, he said. All right. Good job, then. He unzipped his parka and slid the book into the inside pocket and then zipped it up again.

So let's go, Jude said.

He looked from the boy to the woman and back. Roll your window up, buddy, he said. I need to talk to your mom first.

Hurry up, the boy said.

I'm trying.

Jude looked irritated but he rolled the window up and then scooted into the dark warmth of the cab.

Look, it's gonna take me a couple hours, Bill said. I'll have to take the sled up.

She did not respond, looked away from him out over the parking lot.

I just need you and Jude to be out of here, he said.

Dammit, Bill.

I know. Believe me I know.

What's wrong with this guy?

This question he could not answer.

She embraced him. You're pissing me off, she whispered in his ear.

I'll see you tonight.

You'd better, she said. Her voice was thin and her eyes glossy with tears.

*   *   *

NAPLES HAD never been much more than a scant collection of battered buildings along the railroad tracks and the creek but now it was full dark and in the blizzard it seemed as if the entire town had simply blown away. Everything black. No power anywhere he could see. Even the bar had gone dark. He parked the truck at a gravel lot near the school, a place he parked each winter during the heaviest snowfall, and pulled the ramps down and started the snowmobile, jerking the cable repeatedly until the engine caught and started running, and then backed down the ramps onto the snow. It felt solid and substantial under him, a heavy machine set upon tracks and ready to scream out into the snow like a banshee. He lifted the ramps and returned them to the bed and closed the tailgate. Then he opened the cab once more to look in at the interior. The rifle and the dart gun were both in their single case under the bench seat, and he thought that he should probably bring the case with him but there were only three or four rounds in total for the rifle and he did not know what he would do with it were something to happen, the thought of which sent a long shiver through him. In the end he left the case behind.

A car fled past him on the plowed highway. Then another. He sat upon the snowmobile, straddling it, the machine humming under his body, the truck behind him already disappearing from view. Then he pulled out into the road at last. The vehicles that had passed before him dissolved now into the blur of snowfall and no headlights appeared behind. Ice crystals stung his face, his beard and mustache already frozen, the snow a fleeting field of sparks that seemed to run out before the faint glow of the machine.

He turned off the highway onto the spur and turned again into the mile-long road that led to the rescue, following the path of a dark flat creek for a quarter mile, its edge rimed with ice and its surface a perfect unmoving black plate bordered by white, and finally turned up the draw toward the top of the ridge, a curl into darkness, the sled below him whining and growling, the throttle held nearly wide open. The snow was smooth here, although he sometimes thought he could see the faint trough of old footprints illuminated in the headlights, but if so the image was too faint to be sure of and seemed to materialize and fade each time he looked at it, like an illusion visible only in the peripheries. He thought of Grace and of Jude, riding south on the highway toward Coeur d'Alene, hoped they were safe, wondered then why he had not climbed into the truck with them. But he could not leave the animals. He could not leave without checking on them, without ensuring that they were all safe. It was simply something he had to do, every night, without fail.

When he saw the footprints in the lit swath of the storm, he thought at first that the track must have indicated the path of an animal, but the path was like a trough, not like the careful prints of elk or deer or even coyote but the slogging boot prints of a man. He turned the sled to the side, slowing, peering down as they approached and then seeing the trail where it came down the mountain and then moved into the forested darkness beside the road.

His body seemed to burst all at once into gooseflesh, his hand off the throttle now so that the machine stood idling at the side of the road, and the feeling that ran through him was pure terror, his eyes peering into the black trees where the boot prints disappeared as if some huge beast might emerge, something out of story, out of myth. He knew he was being watched but in that moment it felt like he was being watched not by a man, not by Rick, but by something else entirely. The darkness. The forest. The black trees all around.

He looked up the road to where the footprints disappeared beyond the glow of his headlights. The disappearing path he had seen earlier was someone coming up the road in the heavy snow and this deep trough of dragging footprints was made by someone descending.

And then he knew what he should have known already. That Rick had not gone after Grace or Jude at all. He had not even left Naples. Instead, he had only waited for Bill to drive away and then had come up the path, on foot, to where the animals were all held captive in their cages in the snow.

14

HE WATCHED FOR MIKE EVERYWHERE, RETURNING HOME with Rick only past midnight to grab a few scant hours of shallow, fitful sleep, all the while expecting to hear Mike's thudding hammer-like fist on the door. He had brought his meager paycheck to the cashier window at the Peppermill and had managed, somehow, not to spend it that first night, returning to the café to wait for Rick to appear from the kitchen at the end of his shift, wondering if Susan would arrive as well and hoping, more than anything else, that Mike would not. Even with cash in his pocket he was terrified that it would not be enough or that Mike, at Johnny Aguirre's instructions, would break his arm or leg or more of his fingers. When he looked at the aluminum splint, its bright blue foam now stained with grease after eight hours of oil changes and lube jobs, the sight of it produced a thread of panic he could barely contain.

The next night he sat in front of a slot machine, once again waiting for Rick's shift to end, near enough to the café that he could see the booth where he had been sitting moments before, his empty coffee cup still resting on the tabletop. He reasoned he could play the slots for a good long while and not spend more than ten dollars and so he dropped quarter after quarter into the machine, watching bars and lemons and plums and bunched cherries on little stems spin through their reels, but the repetition of that single machine bored him and he worked his way down the row and then into the next. After a time he found himself playing Wild Wild Nights, a dollar slot with five reels that spun simultaneously, the win lines moving in all directions, and he pulled and pulled and pulled at that handle.

He stopped when he was down sixty dollars, not because he was done but because he knew Rick was probably already sitting in the café waiting for him, and so he stumbled away from the machine in a wide-eyed daze looking like a man who had been struck by lightning or as if he had been asleep for some period of years and had now suddenly awakened into a world of clanging bells and ringing alarms. What have you done? You goddamn idiot. What have you done now?

He still had more than fifty dollars and perhaps it would be enough to keep Johnny, to keep Mike, from breaking more of his bones, but he still feared that meeting, even though he knew it was inevitable. But that night passed and then it was the week of Thanksgiving and he reasoned that even a man like Johnny Aguirre must have family somewhere. Perhaps Mike as well. Maybe they were both simply out of town. Maybe it was as simple as that.

He returned to work at the start of that week with a note from the medical clinic and with his finger still splinted and aching. On his break he bought a candy bar from the vending machine in the carpeted hallway that led to the sales floor. From there, he could see the door to Milt Wells's office: a plain wooden slab, painted white to match the hallway, sometimes closed, sometimes wide open. The alarm keypad was mounted on the wall by the back door, the same door he used to get to and from the lube bay. The screen read simply DISARMED. A waferlike sensor on the door itself and on the doorframe.

All day completing oil changes and greasing ball joints for one car or another: a Mercury Monarch, its shape floating above him on the lift like some enormous slab of powder-blue stone, a Fiesta, a Mustang, an

LTD, a Granada, a Lincoln Continental. With each pull of the grease gun's flat trigger came the sound of pressurized air escaping the valve and the low *galumph* of the grease pushing forward through the zerk. The cars different but the cars also the same. This was what he did, a thought that filled him with a sense of unrest and unease of such intensity that it made his splinted finger throb. He thought again of the lion in the arcade at the MGM Grand. Lethargic. Chained to the platform upon which it rested. The photographer waving the steak. The great lion's head rising. Those sparkling eyes. The grim smiles of the family as the flash popped. All its days the same.

When five o'clock came on Wednesday, his constant watching for Johnny Aguirre and Mike had worn him down to a frayed mess. He stood by the bay doors and smoked three cigarettes in rapid succession, watching the huge white airliners as they rose from and descended to the airport past the highway. Most of the mechanics had already gone. Down on the road beyond the rows of new cars, he thought he saw a rust-colored vehicle moving slowly along the frontage road but although he stood on his tiptoes he could not be sure. As he watched he puffed his third cigarette down to a stub and lit another. A newspaper swirled away from him in the direction of the runway, riding a freezing wind down from the mountains to the west. He could not see the rust-colored car anymore and did not know if he had seen it at all.

Hey there, a voice came.

He turned from his view out over the cars to see Milt Wells stepping through the door that led from the service bays to the long carpeted interior hallway within, his swoop of white hair just as perfect as it always was, bolo tie swinging gently with his step.

Hello, Nat said. And then added, Milt.

Milt held a small zippered bag in his hand with a bank logo on it, packed thickly with what Nat could only imagine was some quantity of cash.

Off to the bank? Nat said.

My weekly errand. Usually Fridays but with the holiday I thought I'd better get it in early.

Good idea. He stood there for a moment in silence. Then he said, You...uh...want a cigarette?

No but thanks, Milt said. My wife made me quit. If she smells it on me I'll be in for it.

Nat grinned a little at the thought.

You break your finger?

He nodded.

That happen here?

Naw, I slammed it in my car door at home last week.

Ouch, Milt said.

Yeah, not my most brilliant moment.

I came out to the shop last week but they said you were out sick.

Yeah, I got the flu or something.

Broke your finger and got the flu?

Yeah it was quite a week.

Feeling better though, now?

More or less. He looked out toward the airport again, where another white plane was descending slowly from a gray sky.

How's your mom doing? If you don't mind me asking.

She's doing all right. Needs surgery. So that's coming up.

Jeez, I'm sorry to hear that, Milt said. What kind of cancer?

Lung, Nat said. He looked at the cigarette in his hand. I guess I shouldn't be smoking this either.

Probably not, Milt said. You could quit right now.

I could, Nat said. But I'd just start again when I got home.

That's the choice you make.

Is it?

Absolutely. Everything's a choice.

Nat looked at him then. He wanted to tell him that he was wrong, that just because he had choices did not mean that those same choices existed for Nat or for anyone, that the life and experiences of the proprietor and owner of Milt's Reliable Ford-Lincoln-Mercury were by no means transferrable. But instead he only nodded and said, I guess you're right.

I am right, Milt said. You work the lube station and then you move to, I don't know, brakes or something, and at some point you're running the whole service department.

Maybe so, Nat said.

Not maybe, son. You just have to keep your eyes on the ladder. Rung by rung. You understand what I'm saying?

Nat nodded. Down below, on the frontage road, the rust-colored vehicle he thought he had seen a few minutes before had returned, idling down there in plain view now. It was as he feared, the dull, dented El Camino he had seen at the Peppermill the night Mike had broken his finger, and although he could not see the driver he knew it had to be the tattooed man from Landrum's, idling there, plotting his revenge. He knew the driver could see him, could see him and could see Milton Wells standing next to him, and in the next moment it sped off with an ostentatious screeching of its tires, the sound of which seemed to run through Nat's body like some shivering wire.

Plans for the holiday? Milt said.

Going to visit my mom, he said, his voice faintly wobbling.

It was Battle Mountain, right?

Yep, Nat said. Battle Mountain.

Well, you give her my best.

I will.

Milt stepped forward across the parking lot. Behind them, the shop's service manager appeared and began to pull down one of the bay doors, the sound of it rattling out across the asphalt. Evening, Milt, the manager called.

Milt waved briefly, hardly looking up, and then stopped and turned back toward Nat, fumbling for a moment with his wallet and finally extracting a bill. Look, he said, you get your mom a nice turkey or something. On me. All right?

It was a twenty and Nat reached for it automatically. Thanks, he said. That's really really nice of you.

It appeared for a moment as if his boss might say something more, but then he simply nodded and walked away across the parking lot to where his long shining LTD was parked in a slot labeled with his name.

He's a nice guy, the service manager called from the next bay, his hand on the partially closed roller door.

Sure is, Nat said.

You wanna give me a hand with these doors?

He nodded, staring at the bill in his hand before stuffing it into his coat pocket and reentering the shop to pull down the remainder of the doors, kicking the latches into place and wrapping the chains around the metal pegs beside them, his splinted finger pointing everywhere as he worked.

When he walked outside again, the wind was gusting down hard. He looked toward the road but the El Camino was nowhere to be found.

His car was parked in the employee lot and when he rounded the edge of the building the wind struck him so hard that he had to tilt his body into it to keep walking, reaching the little Datsun and opening the door and sliding inside. The car shook under him with each gust and even when he had started it and was driving down to the road he could still feel its force, the car creaking and trembling all around him as if afraid.

The first thing he saw when he reached the road was a police cruiser pulled over to the side just a few yards away, a green sedan parked just ahead of it, red and blue lights flashing. The second was the El Camino, moving slowly toward him on the opposite side of the street.

Nat slowed and stopped, his car remaining there at the edge of the employee parking lot as if waiting for a break in traffic. But there was no traffic. Only that rust-colored El Camino sliding soundlessly toward him, the windshield reflecting at first only the flat gray pane of the sky and then, suddenly, clearing all at once so that he could see the tattooed man's smiling face through the glass. The man's hand came up slowly, his two fingers mimicking the act of firing a pistol through Nat's windshield. Then he had passed, the El Camino rolling away, so slowly, two red taillights adrift along the road before the car turned the corner at the edge of the dealership and was gone.

Nat looked at the police cruiser again and the officer glanced up at him and Nat raised a hand in greeting. Then he pulled out into the street.

When he reached the Peppermill he returned to Wild Wild Nights, and within the hour he had no money left in his wallet at all.

·   ·   ·

WHAT THE fuck? Rick said when he told him about the El Camino.

I don't know, Nat said. He's freaking me out.

I haven't seen him.

I'm telling you he's watching me. Probably watching both of us.

Fucker, Rick said. I guess he needs another lesson.

They sat at the Peppermill café once again, waiting for Susan to materialize, eating club sandwiches that Rick had brought out from the kitchen at the end of his shift. Nat waited for her with a kind of nervous tension that he ascribed to the El Camino, to Mike and to Johnny Aguirre, to the entire situation he had found himself in, but he knew it was actually because of her. She had come to feel like a thin barbed hook inside him, something that he continued to tug at despite its stinging, its pulling and tearing, all the while telling himself that he was either Rick's best friend or he was not. Not even a decision but rather a kind of creed to live by. When they were children there had been no one to take care of them but each other, especially after Bill died, Nat's mother drinking herself into oblivion day after day on the tattered recliner, the television waffling between game shows and soap operas, and Rick's mother a lifetime hypochondriac who was finally diagnosed with cancer the year after they moved to Reno. So they had taken care of each other. He knew that Rick was still taking care of him, or was trying to. As for himself, he had no idea what he was doing. No idea at all.

What he had come to understand, perhaps what he had always understood, was that Rick was a survivor, was like a wolf or a coyote, some canid that had come out of the desert fully prepared to survive, tooth and claw. He had been that way for as long as Nat had known him, since they were children, certainly since they were teenagers. It was his natural condition. But the metaphor fell apart when Nat tried to apply it to himself. He was no canid; that much was clear. But then what the hell was he? When he watched nature documentaries on Sunday afternoons in the apartment, he sometimes felt like he could almost see into some truth beyond any he had imagined: a kind of thread that was nearly visible to him. Each animal, each insect, built to serve a particular and specific function and each performing its function without question and seemingly without will or logic, even though the structures built by creatures he deemed the least intelligent—ants, wasps, bees, spiders—held within them a will and logic and beauty that he could hardly comprehend. What will and logic he possessed had led him to complete oil changes and lube jobs and gamble away all his money and fear for his safety everywhere he went. What use his will if this was where it would lead him? But then most of the time he did not feel like he had any manner of free will at all.

As if to punctuate this thought, from somewhere inside the casino one of the slot machines let out a shrill hard ringing and a loud excited voice called out, I won! I won! The sound of it turned in his chest, pulling at him, everything pulling at him, always.

Hey, so I talked to my mom earlier, Rick said. I told her we'd be there around two or three.

Yeah, that works, Nat said. How'd she sound?

Pretty shitty.

When do they want to do the surgery?

A couple weeks.

They can't turn her away for treatment, he said. Even if you don't have a way to pay them.

It's not just that. Last time she went through this my cousin

Charlene came out from Elko to help, but she's not gonna be able to do that this time.

Why not?

I don't know, Rick said. She's got a job or something I guess. It's not her responsibility anyway. It's mine.

So what does that mean?

Means I'll either have to move back there or hire someone to take care of her.

Dang, Nat said. Move back there?

I don't know what else to do at this point. I'm pretty much out of time.

It was silent for a long moment and then Nat said quietly, I can't move back.

I'm not asking you to.

No, I mean, Johnny Aguirre told me that I can't leave. He said if I leave he'd find me. And he knows I'm from BM.

How does he know that?

He asked me when he was giving me the first loan.

Rick looked out into the casino now. Christ, man, you really got yourself in it, didn't you.

I didn't mean to, he said. It just kind of happened.

I don't get it, Rick said. I don't get it at all.

I'm trying to pull it together.

Are you?

Yeah, Nat said. Totally.

Seems like you're just digging yourself deeper.

What do you want me to say?

Rick shook his head. I'm done talking about it, he said. He looked up past Nat and called out, Hey, babycakes.

Susan had arrived and she slid into the booth next to Rick. How are the boys? she said.

Boys are OK, Rick said. He glanced over at Nat briefly. How is the girl?

The girl is tired of stupid video store questions, she said. Do you have that one movie about that guy who did that thing? Um yeah, we have that. It's over there. She gestured vaguely around the room. I swear I'm going to shoot someone one of these days.

Did you get a video machine? Rick asked.

I tried, she said. Everyone wants one for the weekend.

Damn, Rick said. That's too bad.

Yeah, well, the store's pretty much picked through anyway.

Rick shrugged and then lifted his coffee cup and sipped at it.

I gotta hit the bathroom, Nat said.

He slid out of the booth and skirted the slot machines and then stood at the mirror in the bathroom, staring at his own reflection. There were no thoughts now, no guilt or fear, only his own face staring back, his eyes, his hair, his mouth. His hands on the edge of the sink. This is who you are. And no one can save you.

He turned on the tap and splashed water into his face and when he stood upright once more he thought the image of Johnny Aguirre staring back at him from the mirror was only his imagination. But then that reflected image spoke: You're a hard guy to track down.

Mike stood next to Johnny. On the other side stood a large, block-shaped man Nat did not recognize. He felt himself go cold. His finger throbbed.

Johnny, he said, his voice wobbling. I was just thinking about you.

Were you?

Totally.

Turn around.

He did.

Behind them the door opened and Mike's hand caught it. Bathroom's closed, he said.

Uh . . . my friend's in there, Rick's voice came.

Who's your friend?

Nat Reed.

He's busy, Mike said.

Uh . . . I think I can help, Rick said.

Mike looked up at Johnny. That's the dumbest thing I've heard all day, Johnny said. Mike smiled. The other man, the one Nat did not recognize, only stood there expressionless, his face mashed in like a gangster from some old black-and-white movie.

All right, Johnny said. It's a party. Open the door.

Mike pulled the door open and Rick stepped into the bathroom, Mike frisking him quickly, Rick finding Nat across the room, their eyes locking for one single moment.

So who are you?

Rick Harris.

All right, so here's the question, Rick Harris: Does your friend have money for me or does he not?

Rick had moved to stand next to Nat and now he looked back at the trio standing near the door: Johnny and his two bodyguards. Yeah he's got money, he said. He just got paid on Monday.

That true, Nat? Johnny said.

Nat was silent for a long moment, his eyes on the floor.

What the fuck? Rick said. You just picked up your check two days ago.

Still Nat did not respond. He could feel himself falling out of his body somehow and he could feel himself stuck inside it, not only his body but the town, the desert, the basin from which no river reached the sea.

This is starting to get pretty old, Johnny said.

Whoa whoa whoa, Rick said. Hang on.

Nat looked up now. Johnny held a black pistol in his hand, its angles square and sharp.

We'll get you the money, Rick said.

Yeah, I'm sure you will, Johnny said.

He stepped forward then and with one quick fluid motion struck Nat in the side of the face with the pistol. Nat went down all at once, the pain sharp and terrible, and in the red darkness he could hear Johnny's voice: Get the fuck back.

Jesus Christ, Rick said. I told you we'd get you the money.

Keep your hands where I can see them, Johnny said.

Let me give you what I have in my wallet. Can I do that?

He opened his eyes then. His face felt warm and he knew he was bleeding. His finger throbbed where he had jammed it when he fell and his face felt like it had simply exploded, the pain arcing into his jaw, his eyes, his skull. Above him, Mike had taken Rick's wallet.

Eight dollars, Mike said.

Eight dollars? Johnny was smiling now and when he said the number again his voice broke into a laugh. Eight dollars? You two are like peas in a pod. Un-fucking-believable. Eight dollars?

The door behind them cracked open and the other man said, Bathroom's closed for cleaning, and slammed the door with a loud crack.

What's your name again? Johnny said.

Rick Harris.

Do you think I'm fucking stupid, Rick Harris?

No, he said. But listen—

No, you listen, Johnny said. I've heard all the excuses I want to hear for today.

Nat looked up at them from the floor. Rick and Mike and Johnny Aguirre. The other man. Behind them the urinals covered the back wall. Rows of sinks. The toilet stalls lining up beyond them into the room.

Get him up, Johnny said, and then Mike was crouching over him, pulling him to his feet. I've given you plenty of time, Johnny said, his voice calm and clear.

Nat managed somehow to continue standing, even though his body felt limp.

Just give us a little more, Rick said.

Listen you little faggot, Johnny said, turning to him now, the gun barrel floating between them in the air. You can go fuck yourself.

We've got some stuff we can pawn, Rick said. We'll get the money together. I promise.

You promise? Johnny stepped forward toward Nat, his face only inches away now. The thing is, I don't hear you saying anything, Nat. Not a word.

His hands were shaking so hard now that they seemed separate from his body. Flapping like the wings of birds.

Tell him, Nat, Rick said.

Yeah, Johnny said, tell me. Tell me you're gonna pay me back. Because I haven't heard that before.

Please, Johnny, Nat said. He had begun crying, weeping, his body wracked with the force of it. Please.

Please please please, Johnny said. He stepped back now and nodded and Mike came forward.

I told you, kid, Mike said. Nat tried to speak but the words were a mumbled whisper and Mike leaned in to his face. You got something to say?

I gave you the Atari, Nat whispered. What about Pitfall?

Ah Nat, Mike said, his own voice quiet and soothing like a parent calmly sympathizing with an errant child, his hand coming up to lay for a brief instant against Nat's cheek. We're way way beyond that now.

And then the first blow came and Nat doubled over. There was no air. He could see Mike's legs, watched as the blue shape of his pants cocked back and the foot came blurring forward. He could not understand what was happening even though it was all clear and plain and obvious. He was on the ground and he was in pain and he deserved it all. Christ, he's pissing himself already, Mike said. I've barely even started.

Fucking leave him alone, Rick said, you fucking cockhole.

What'd you say? Johnny asked.

I said leave him alone. Rick's voice was clear and sharp and angry.

What did you call me? Johnny said. A fucking cockhole? That's not very nice.

Nat's eyes were cracked open now. In the tear-blurred bathroom before him he watched as Mike grabbed Rick by the shoulders and dragged him backward toward the stalls, Rick's hands flailing and his voice coming hard and fast: What the fuck? What the fuck are you doing?

He could see their feet under the stalls and then he could see Rick's knees and his hands, his friend steadying himself against the tile floor. He was facing the toilet, Johnny Aguirre's slick leather shoes and Mike's black loafers behind him. Then the sound of gurgling followed by the gasping of Rick's breath and then the gurgling once more, his feet kicking everywhere against the tiles as water splashed out all around him.

What's that, Rick? You want another drink? Sure, Rick, you can have another drink.

And then the gurgling resumed, his feet kicking out, the partition banging and banging.

When Rick's voice came again it was between a series of choking coughs. Why are you doing this? he said.

And then Johnny's voice: Because you have an attitude I don't like.

I'm sorry, Rick said.

I'm sure you are, Johnny said. There was a brief silence and then Johnny said, Hold him down.

No, wait, wait, Rick said, his voice both muffled and amplified.

Then the sound of someone urinating, not into the water-filled bowl, but against a surface.

Jesus fucking Christ, Rick's voice came, reverberating through the toilet bowl. Then the gurgling again and then the sound of Rick vomiting as Johnny pissed down on the back of his head. Nat's eyes screwed closed now and in the howling sound of his heart the name he cried for was not his friend's or his mother's or his father's but Bill's, and he could see, before him, on the floor of the bathroom, the hawk he had once held in his hands, the animal's wing dragging against the cool surface of the tiles, and then his brother's smiling face, his hand on Nat's shoulder, but when he opened his eyes there was only the man he did not know, standing by the bathroom door, staring down at him, his expression impassive.

Keep out of my fucking business next time, Johnny said from the stall.

In the next moment he stepped out to the sink and washed his hands in silence. Mike stood by the door now, his hands crossed before him. This is the end game, Nat, Johnny said from the paper towel dispenser, where he stood drying his hands. Goddammit, I think I got piss on my pants, he said woefully. Then, You got Thanksgiving plans?

Nat tried to speak but his voice was dry and silent and the sound he made was a long weird vowel.

Yeah, that's good, Johnny said. Hey, Mike, you got that piece of paper?

Mike nodded and extracted a small folded sheet from his jacket pocket and handed it to Johnny, who stood reading it for a moment by the sink. Then he turned and faced Nat. 503 East Fourth, number thirty, he said. That mean anything to you?

My mom, Nat said.

That's right. That an apartment?

Trailer.

Ah, of course it is, he said. Then he stepped forward and knelt beside him. I'm a businessman, he said. All I want is what you owe me. Do you understand that?

Yes, Nat said. He was shaking with fear now, trembling everywhere.

Let's get this taken care of. Maybe you can borrow something from your mom.

I'll try, he said.

Good boy, Johnny said. That's a good boy. His hand touched Nat's hair, slowly, almost tenderly, stroking it for a moment and patting Nat's shoulder. Then he stood. Let's get the fuck out of here, he said and in the next moment all three of them were out the door.

NAT'S MOTHER had gained some weight since he was a child, becoming heavy and pear-shaped, but otherwise she was just the same: an immovable woman, now living alone in the trailer on food stamps and doing occasional piecework for a mail-order company she had worked for as long as Nat could remember, stringing beads onto thin clear fishing line over and over again, her eyes on the television, hands moving without thought, rising for the bathroom or to make herself lunch or dinner or to refresh the Long Island iced teas she drank from a huge plastic tumbler, one after the other, until at last passing out in the chair again.

Happy Thanksgiving, Mom, he said, emerging from the filthy, cramped kitchen with a dinner plate. Fried ham, canned beans, and cranberry sauce.

Oh that looks good, his mother said.

He set the plate on the TV tray and then returned to the kitchen for his own and sat on the sofa, pulling the second tray nearer to him and setting the plate upon it.

I'm glad you're here, Nathaniel, his mother said. I miss you so much.

I know you do.

Are you still having fun in the city?

Sure, it's fun, he said. There's a lot to do.

Do you get to see any of those shows?

Too busy working, he said. Loretta Lynn was in town a few months ago.

Oh my gosh, she said. I just saw her on *Hee Haw*. Does she look like she does on TV?

He had not seen her but he said, Yeah, she looks just like on TV.

That's so exciting, she said.

Yeah, it's a fun place.

They watched *Simon & Simon* for a time without speaking and when he looked over at her again she was staring at him.

What? he said.

What's the matter, honey?

Nothing. I'm fine.

Something's wrong. I can tell.

He looked away from her now, back to the television, where the commercials had ended and the program was just starting up again, but when he glanced at his mother once more her gaze had not left him. I've just got a lot on my mind, he said. That's all.

You can tell your mom, you know.

I know. It's not anything important.

Sounds like it is.

Just trying to do the right thing.

That's all you can do, she said.

Yeah, well, it's hard to figure out what that is sometimes.

You know what your father used to say? Take care of your people. There's not much more to it than that, is there?

I don't know. He didn't take care of us.

Don't say that, honey, she said. He couldn't help what happened. Neither could Billy. Those are just accidents.

Accidents? They were both so drunk they drove off the road.

She sipped at her tea and then lifted her cigarette and puffed at it briefly before returning it to the TV tray unfolded at her side. You know, you look just like your father, she said after a time. You've got his sad eyes.

I'm fine, Mom, he said again. He looked to the television again but could feel her staring at him and at last he turned to face her once more.

You know you always have a place here at home.

The statement nearly brought him to tears. I know that, he said.

Well, just so you know. No matter what happens you've always got a home.

He nodded.

What's happening with A.J.?

Nat did not at first understand the question but then he glanced to the television to where the characters were embroiled in some kind of intrigue. Oh, he said, I'm not sure. I guess we should try to figure it out.

It's a mystery, she said.

Always is.

The next time he looked over at her, she was asleep in the chair. He watched the program for a few minutes and then rose and changed the channel. The next program was mostly static but he sat and watched it anyway, rising again to pour himself a glass of vodka from the bottles his mother had always kept up in the cabinet above the stove, sitting again as that program ended and the next began.

He and Rick had driven to Battle Mountain in near silence, listening to cassettes and smoking until the car seemed to contain within it a haze of fog, and when they reached the row of mobile homes and travel trailers at last the only thought that came to Nat's mind was to ask himself where he could go if not here. If not Battle Mountain then where?

Rick's mother had come to the door of her trailer looking ten or twenty years older than the last time Nat had seen her just a few months before, her skin a rough gray and her hair bleached to a crackling blond that spiked all around her head like an exploded bird's nest. She screamed when she saw Rick standing there and in that scream Nat could see her as already dead, a creature comprised entirely of bones, her mouth a dry hole filled with gray teeth. She threw her arms around her son, drawing him into the trailer, the door snapping shut behind them.

Nat's mother confirmed what he already knew. Mrs. Harris's cancer had metastasized everywhere through her body. Nat's mother did not know how much time she had left but she told him she would be surprised if the woman lasted more than a year.

I don't think Rick knows it's that bad, Nat had said in response.

I'm sure he knows now, his mother said. It's not like she can keep it a secret.

He had half expected that Rick would knock at the door at some point during that night, looking for a drink or a cigarette or just to get away from the sad sight of his dying mother but no such knock came and eventually Nat wandered to the back of the trailer, to the room he had shared, so many years ago, with his brother, first in a double bed where they lay side by side, and later in two single beds, and finally with only one.

The room was empty but for his old bed and a few boxes stacked in one corner. When Bill was alive, there had been a poster above his bed and sometimes when he could not sleep Nat would stare at it, its features faint in the dim light from the slatted window: the cover of

the Eagles album *Hotel California*, a dark image of some fancy Span-
ish-style building flanked by the silhouettes of palm trees, the title
emblazoned in blue neon in one corner, the memory of which spawned
another, a time when he had been sitting out in the desert at some bon-
fire party by the gravel pits, sixteen or seventeen years old, and the title
song from that album had come pouring out of someone's dark car in
the night. Nat had been stoned or drunk or both, and when those guitars began they seemed to move him, physically, to float him out across
the desert, and at the start of the vocal melody he was indeed on a dark
desert highway and the cool wind was in his hair. And his brother was
dead. That was what he remembered most of all. He was stoned and
drunk and listening to the Eagles and his brother was dead.

He had occupied that space, lived in it, right up until they had left for
Reno, but Bill's had been the left side of the room, and even after a year
had passed and then two, Nat sixteen and then seventeen, right up until
the day he moved out, nineteen then, he had never really expanded his
territory to that side. Someone came to take Bill's bed away and the gap
it left became a kind of receptacle for dirty clothes and cassette tapes and
the other detritus of a boy's life, not a space that he used but a space that
collected the overflow. Now that gap was bare carpet and he knew that
it had never really been his room but always shared with his brother and
he also knew, looking into that gap, that this would always be the case.

And then he understood that he would never see this room again,
for when he returned to Reno it would be to die.

When he returned to the front room it was to find his mother
still asleep, the final tumbler of Long Island iced tea still half full on
the foldout tray. He knelt before the television and flipped through
the three channels the coat-hanger antenna managed to collect from
Reno. A rerun sitcom on one. A commercial on the other. And then,
on Channel 5, a close-up image of a wasp dragging a paralyzed insect
to the entrance of its burrow in the dirt, its alien limbs pulling at its
immobile prey. It lingered there for a moment, its antennae moving,
and then disappeared into its burrow as if to ensure all was ready within

before reappearing once more to seize the insect and pull it into the darkness. The narrator's voice was calm and instructive, even soothing, explaining that the wasp would now lay its eggs on the body of the insect, providing a ready food source for the hatching of its young.

But then something changed. Another wasp or perhaps the same. The insect in place at the entrance and the wasp disappearing into the burrow but at the moment of that disappearance an instrument like a metal toothpick appeared at the edge of the frame, pushing the paralyzed insect a few inches from where the wasp had left it. The wasp appeared from the burrow for a moment, paused, its antennae waving, and then moved forward and grasped its prey and dragged it once again to the entrance and disappeared into the burrow again. In its absence, the instrument reappeared and pushed the insect a few inches away. The wasp emerged, once again found the insect, returned it to the entrance, and once again disappeared inside.

The sphex will repeat this behavior over and over again, the narrator said while the wasp checked and rechecked its burrow, the instrument shifting the insect each time it disappeared from the screen. *What we might initially see as a behavior rooted in decision-making is revealed to be programmed instinct. The simplest action—in this case moving its paralyzed prey—creates a loop from which the wasp cannot escape. In some cases, researchers have created conditions where the sphex will check its burrow up to fifty times, triggered each time by moving the paralyzed insect a few inches.*

He was shaking as he stood and clicked the television off and stepped past his sleeping mother to lift his coat from where he had draped it on the back of the sofa before opening the metal door and stepping outside. The night was frigid, his breath a tower of rising steam, and the trailers in their rows were dark. The whole town around him a blankness but for a distant streetlight swirling with frantic insects. A shush of cars on the interstate but otherwise no sound at all. The high desert endless around him. He extracted his cigarettes and lighter but his hands were shaking and he could not spin the tiny wheel to spark the flame. After a moment he rolled the wheel back and forth across the edge of the stairs, an old trick he had seen his brother do once in the rain, and at last a thin flame rose from the cylinder, its shape shaking and dancing as he lit the cigarette. Then he leaned against the peeling rail, puffing smoke into the black night, the cloud of bright insects throwing themselves against the hot burning globe, the Datsun floating amidst those circling frantic stars. Wasps everywhere caught up in their loop of activity.

He stood there for a half hour before he heard the door of Rick's mobile home open and click shut again and Nat came across the gravel, his breath a hot white cloud before him.

Hey, he said quietly.

Rick came down the stairs. You got a light?

He handed across the lighter and there was the brief bright moment of the flame.

My mom's dying, Rick said.

What do the doctors say?

That *is* what the doctors say.

What're you gonna do?

No idea.

He took a drag on the cigarette. That thing you talked about the other day, he said.

What thing?

About Milt's safe. You think we can pull that off?

Rick scoffed. If we can get in there, I don't see why not.

Nat puffed at the cigarette again. Across the desert floor came the distant roar of a truck barreling down I-80. I think I know a way, he said.

No shit?

He nodded faintly.

Goddamn.

The night felt sharp and clear around him. The distant streetlight seemed to falter for a moment and then shone steady once more, the insects swooping and curling all round it, their shapes striping the air.

PART III

THE BOOK

OF THE DEAD

15

AT THE END, THE BEAR FINDS HIMSELF LOOKING DOWN AT A vast sagebrush plain lit only by starlight and ringed by dry colorless mountains gone the color of black night. The two men stand at the edge of a collection of battered buildings and trailers that huddle in the middle of that darkness. Around them is a bleak town of some sort and the bear knows this even though he does not know what a town is, has never seen one, and yet knows more now than he ever has in his life, here at the end, although he does not know where he is or how he has come to such a place. There are questions but the bear does not ask them. The time for questions has long passed. One of the figures below him is the man he knows, the man the bear might call friend if he knew such a concept. Maybe he does. But what the bear wonders at now is the man's smell, for it seems to come to him across time and across the darkness. He can smell him across all his life and the sense of him there makes the bear call out in a long protracted moan. How much he misses the man in that moment. And how much he knows that he will never see him again.

The bear knows too that the other is the stranger who came up earlier from the bottom of the mountain, came up from the snow near where the river crosses the road, bearing with him that hard sharp scent that felt like a jagged cloud swirling all around him.

He tries to call down to the man he knows but now his voice will make no sound at all and what exhales out of him is only a long slow hiss that flows upward into black trees that hang above his body like porcupine quills punched through a snowed-over night sky. And then he knows that he is in the forest again, even though he can smell the desert, a scent he has never smelled before but which he recognizes because there is something of the man he knows in that place, in that dark plain. Now he is in some other night, in some other time, as if the blizzarding gray sky is only a thin membrane so insubstantial that it has become transparent, so that when he casts his sightless milky eyes upward the snow seems to part, does part, circling away to be replaced not with the sky but with the dark desert plain ringed with high bare mountains gone flat black in the moonless night.

Once again he can feel that deep shifting color inside him, the jagged scent that the stranger brought up from the bottom of the mountain, and with it comes the feeling, the desire, above all, that the man he knows will somehow sense his need, his encroaching panic, and will rise through the trees to talk him back from the darkness. But the bear cannot even feel the man now, cannot sense him at all except in his memory and in that spectral dark shape on the floor of the black desert below.

He can hear the wolf panting somewhere and all he can think is that something is wrong, and then thinking again that if he can somehow will the man to his side, can summon him back from wherever he has gone, that it will be all right somehow, that the man will fix everything. But he cannot even feel the man now, cannot smell him anywhere on the freezing wind, which continues to rise from below, passing beyond mountain lion and badger and turkey vulture and eagle and porcupine and through the wire boundaries of his own enclosure, and then on past the wolf and into the forest that breaks into peeling birch and rises yet to spin around the empty trailer where the man dens and up to the top of the ridge and into the high thin dark impossible desert air, its passage curling everywhere in endless spirals like fern frost spreading upon an endless sheet of clear dark glass.

The jagged black scent of the stranger is headed away now, into the blizzarding wind so that the bear can feel him, smell him, can sense him all the way back down the road through the stands of cedar and black spruce and through the shaggy hemlock trailing, down at the river, long pale swaths of old-man's beard that now hang heavy with ice. Through all of it moves that jagged scent, diminished now that the stranger has dropped the raw meat into the enclosures, has tossed it up and over the fences, has managed, even for those fenced in roof and all, to squeeze it through the gaps in the wire, so that every one of them has had the taste of it. He could sense that something was not right even then, could smell it through and under and above the blood, and he might have called out to them, to all the animals in all their enclosures, but he could no more do so than he could resist the raw flesh that had flopped onto the frozen and crystalline snow at his feet, and before he could even think about what it was, about the scent he had followed up from below, he had swallowed it down. They all had, and he knew it. Wolf and raccoon and porcupine and badger and eagle and turkey vulture. The jagged scent in every one of them, pulsing slowly, from one to another, into their blood.

He had known it was not right. No strangers came at night. And no strangers came when the snow fell. Only the man he knew, the man who was his friend and who sat with him day after day on the stump beyond the fence. Only he would come at night or in the storm, descending through birches the bear had never actually seen and yet could witness in his body when the wind came crosswise through their slim peeling trunks, could pick out their scent as it curved down through the others: the heart-leaved sticky twayblades sprung up through dark fragrant earth, fringed grass of Parnassus with its curled leaves and white lobed flowers, and the pale bouncing crowns of cow parsnip, those tiny blossoms held aloft on thick stalks filled with milky sap. He could sense all of it out there, even though most of what he sensed, smelled, felt, he had never seen. And yet it was there and he knew it was there and it came to live in his body, as palpable, when the wind was right, as if he walked down that path every day with the man. And in many ways, this was exactly what he had done.

But the man he knew was not coming and the wind would not blow his scent to the bear. Instead, what he could smell came to him from the base of the mountain, the thick white stream of it rising from the river where sometimes he could feel moose and deer and elk moving along the banks and the slick and diaphanous flashes of silver fish streaking the current. There had been times when he had longed for them, when he had lain in his den with his nose crushed under his paws, trying only to will their scent away, but the silver moved in his mind evermore and would not be stilled, and he could see, feel, smell, the slick lightning of them coming up the rapids, and in his heart he grasped for them, his claws flashing in the foaming wake of the current, his breath coming in gasps.

But all that is already past now, the stranger long departed and the bear alone by the frozen pond with the snow coming down all around him and the smell of the desert deep in his body. The wolf quiet. The bear thinks he hears a distressed squawking from the raptors but the wind seems to blow in all directions at once and he can form no image of them at all. He wonders if the wolf has gone to his warm place at the far side of his enclosure, a place the bear can sometimes sense with such detail that he can nearly lie down in it himself in his mind. That enclosure was his own for so long he ceased to understand that there could be anywhere else for him to place his scent, but it had become a vast and confusing geography to him as he grew old and weakened and then lost his sight. He might have continued to live there but the man had moved him to this smaller place and there was the pond and the man had come often with his marshmallows and such things were good enough. He knows the wolf does not like the old place, perhaps because it continues to smell of bear or perhaps because the wolf still remembers running through the big trees. The bear can feel that memory all around the wolf, coming up through its blood like sharp young jack pines bursting free of black earth. In his heart are snow-covered mountains and a pack that flows down from the high places like a river.

As for his own: he still held, as a vague scent somewhere deep inside his mind, that gray winter when he and his mother came up out of the den and wandered down through the forest. Even now, in his dreams, he sometimes feels her warmth against his face. He might once have remembered her eyes, the sound of her voice, but if so these have long since disappeared from memory. What he has been left with is that moment of being totally alone, when all the trees in the forest turned black and the big bears rumbled and roared from every mountain and ridge while he trembled: a tiny furred thing mewling in the shadows of the giant trees.

The men who found him tied a rope around his neck and pulled him into a cage that smelled so strongly of dogs that the little bear screamed and fought, so sure he was that if he entered that space he would be immediately torn apart. But there was no such attack. He remained in that cage until he could hardly smell its previous occupant, peering out at a rotating group of men and women who came to stare at him as if he were some kind of exotic creature. And perhaps, to them, he was. Their smells confused him, some so strong that he could not help but press his face to the cage wire and moan.

Then he was taken to the place where he would live all the rest of his days and he was fed berries and carrots and lettuce heads and sometimes elk or moose or beef and there were others too: raccoons and a coyote and an opossum but never, ever, another bear.

He had felt alone until the summer the boy first arrived. Even now he can remember his scent, not so different than it would be tonight were the wind to blow it to him through the trees. Were the bear not blind, he might have formed the image of the man's face as a boy, a cub, staring back at him through the wire that first time, but in the blurred and milky darkness there is only the face of the man as he is now and when he sees that face in his mind he does not see a man at all but rather a bear.

There comes a time when there is no cloud-choked sky above him; there is only desert and the flat sagebrush plain. There runs the long straight line of the highway. And there lies the town. For a long time, there is only the anonymity of quiet movement: paint-stripped cars adrift on dusty streets, a few sweating figures on the sidewalks in front of the casinos. And then he can see the boy, a thin hot shape come racing through the afternoon light, his path an undulating swoop between lines of boxlike homes, the fences of which guard patches of yellow grass. He sits on the handlebars of a bicycle piloted by someone the bear does not recognize but he recognizes the smile on the boy's face as the boy's life, the life of the man he knows, runs out before him like the oxbow curves of some thin cold river, the whole of it running backward and forward at once, the sky shivering with snow, the sky the floor of the desert, the road between the places: a boy riding on his brother's handlebars through a desert town, and everything to come after, the whole of it spread out across the sky, the bear staring up into the great depths of that dead ocean, no longer aware if his eyes are open or closed but knowing now that everything he has seen and will see has led to this moment and that no matter what happens next he cannot help the man, the thought of which brings a long warm bloom of raw desire shaking through him. Again he tries to call out to the man he knows but there is nothing but his breath and then there is not even that anymore. He can smell the snowed ridges pouring away from him in all directions. He can smell the slick silver shapes of fish pressing out across the sage, over mountains, across towns. He smells a city made of light and his friend moving through it and he smells the stranger too, the one who had brought that black jagged scent up the mountain, smells him laughing and talking and smoking cigarettes on the street, smells him screaming in pain and anger and frustration and then smells him as he is locked away. Then there is the long stretch of the desert back to Battle Mountain again, his eyes blurring with tears, and the hands that hold the wheel he knows are his own for he has become a man as surely as his friend has become a bear.

In the end, he finds himself upon a golden plain, the rise of yellow grasses in the late morning sunlight, the cold blowing in through a gap in the window glass. There is an animal atop a hill, a creature that reminds him of an elk but which, of course, is no elk and which stares down at him impassively, black-eyed. He knows he has dreamed of this animal, of this moment. He fishes a book from the backseat and on its cover is the same wheat-colored creature, the same grassy hill. Then he stands and steps out of the car. His hands are empty. He expects the animal to flee but the animal continues to watch him, without moving, without even seeming to be afraid. And then he knows that it is waiting for him. It has been waiting for them all. He steps forward, up the slope, through grasses the color of summer sunlight. The animal calls him Majer and when the man moves to correct her, his throat seizes and he sees that his pink hands have become furred claws and that in his mind there are no words at all. What he holds to in that final moment is the sense that the man he would call his friend has come to him at last and he pulls that feeling around him like a coat of fur as a scent as wild and free and clear as any he could have ever imagined wells up inside and pulls him away at last.

PART IV

THE ANIMALS

16

HE CAME TO THE GATE WITH THE THROTTLE FULL OPEN, THE
flat yellow of the headlights arcing across the blurred snowfield before
him and the tracks spinning a long rooster tail out behind. He could
already see the cut padlock, its bent shape hanging from the spotlit gate
latch, and the sound he made was a howl of panic and rage as he leaped
from the sled, flinging the goggles off his face and flailing up through
the snow.

The enclosures were dark and what details were held within were
rendered grainy and insubstantial, shapes without color or depth, an
occasional stone or tree trunk rising through the continuous fade of
the onrushing snow. He called to Cinder, his fingers lacing through
the fence wires, called her and called her and called her until at last a
low groan rose from the muffled silence. He could just make out the
snow-covered shape of her body fading up from the static, her body
on its side, panting, tongue out and single eye staring up into the con-
stantly descending snow. She growled now, low and deep, and when he
tried to speak to her again the only sound he could make was a high
keening whine. Still she did not rise.

He was running then, floundering uphill toward the top of the loop, the dark silent cages passing him on either side, his boots following the path that Rick had made, the line of which curved toward each enclosure and then moved on, uphill or down, the path mostly covered in snow now and the whole compound appearing as if it were some dark jail or prison: cages everywhere with hills of snow between them. The sight of it made him shudder. And that was when he saw Majer, the great hulk of the animal's back fading out of the granular and shifting darkness, unmoving in the center of his enclosure as if he had fallen asleep by the frozen pond, Bill flailing toward the gate through the high drifts between the fence lines in silence but for his heaving breath.

When he reached the front of the cage at last, he wrapped his fingers through the wire, sucking air and watching the silent unmoving shape within and then his hands had curled into fists and he was banging the fencing and scrambling sideways through the drifts, stripping off his gloves and fishing the keys from his pants pocket and unlocking the door, his heart gone wild, hands shaking, the door coming open now and the night clamping around him, everything hushed and muffled so that his rasping breath was the only possible sound.

His first steps postholed directly into the snow so that he fell forward into the drift, frantic now, scrambling up and through that rise until Majer's body lay there before him, the bear on its side, its great head covered with snow, mouth open, tongue lolling against the ice. He laid his hand on the bear's mouth, felt the flesh there, not yet frozen but cooling. Above the long snout, the eyes remained open, pale and faintly blue and holding, somewhere deep within, a darkness like black night covered with the translucent but impervious film of his blindness.

And he knew that Majer was dead.

He tried to speak but there were no words and after a time he leaned forward, his knees crunching the snow, one arm reaching up to lie upon that furred back, a back still carrying a hint of the animal's warmth. He lay upon that great carcass and wept, his face pressed to Majer's thick brown fur, one hand stroking, so slowly, the long snout. He tried again to speak but what came was only a long howl that rose up from the center of him and would not stop, his heart unspooling all around him, a red ribbon that turned and looped and fell everywhere, into the sky, into the snow, around the two of them, the man who lay upon the body of the bear in a cage at the center of a white and frozen forest, and in the falling snow it was unclear where the man ended and the bear began, for both had begun to shift into white, the man sinking into the body of the bear, the bear rising into the body of the man, both of them dissolving into a blowing whirl of snow that seemed, in that moment, to come from all directions at once, the rush of it upon their bodies like an avalanche.

THE ANIMALS had been killed in their cages. The bald eagles both dead on their sides on the floor and in the adjacent enclosure the turkey vulture was also dead. Tommy and Betty and Chester. The porcupines were quietly in motion but both the martens were dead, side by side, in a kind of tortured embrace, their mouths open and tiny teeth shining out in the darkness. The raccoons—Perry, Tony, and Barley—all huddled at the back of their enclosure, alive, although they would not come forward no matter how long Bill stood there. Baker the badger was dead and Goldie the bobcat and Katy the red fox, all of them frozen in attitudes of fear and agony. And then Zeke. The wolf lay in his customary location at the back of the fence line, panting and growling at him, not moving away even when Bill came right up the chain link, only staring back at him with eyes yellow and rolling and Bill's voice offering that same wordless keening in response.

Of the raptors, only Elsie, their great gray owl, was alive, her bright yellow eyes peering back at him from within her partially snow-buried cage. He came to the fence and looked back at her, his voice a kind of cooing like the sound of a dove. On the floor, not far from the edge of the wire where he stood, lay a strip of meat, cold and partially frozen, beef or venison or something else. He came around to the zookeeper door and unlocked it and entered the enclosure and knelt there before the frozen strip, the owl hopping on its perch and looking down at him with her huge pie-shaped face. Bill knelt and took the meat into his hand and remained there, looking at it, smelling it, staring at its color, at its shape, but such an examination revealed nothing and at last he slipped it into his coat pocket.

He stepped into the office briefly to confirm what he already knew—that the phone was out—and in the moment of holding that cold plastic to his ear, of listening to the silence it brought, he knew that the night would likely end with his death, and then he understood what he would do next, what he had to do. He returned to the bottom of the loop and opened the doors to Cinder's enclosure and stood watching for her in the falling snow, in the wind, the panic he had felt replaced now by a kind of rage. The place where he had first seen her was vacant now, the area covered over with fresh snow so that there was no evidence she had been there at all, as if everything about her had been a hallucination, a fantasy. But then her head came up out of the far side of the enclosure and a moment later her body seemed to fade into being, not quickly, not the sleek moving river he had watched for so many hours, but instead a slow laboring creature climbing up out of the rocks of her cage toward whatever freedom lay beyond. Go on, Bill said. The lion was panting but she moved past him and then through the open door, not even glancing at him with her one good eye as she did so, her walk unhurried as she moved on through the thick falling curls of winter snow and disappeared into the dark heavy trees all around them.

He opened all the enclosures, even for the animals that were dead, even for Majer, and when he turned back from the top of the loop, it was to watch the porcupines, already out in the path, walking downhill slowly through the blizzard as if they knew where they were headed. Of the animals that had been poisoned, he did not know if any of them would survive but he knew that he had to give them the chance, even though he had told himself, for all his years at the rescue, that they would die in the wild, that they were simply not capable of living without him. But perhaps even that had been a lie. Perhaps he was the one who needed them, keeping them in their cages, not a savior but a prison warden. That was what the Fish and Game officer had told him—that he did not get to decide who could be put in a cage and who could not—and maybe this much had been true all along. In the end, maybe his entire life as Bill Reed had been only an atonement for failing his best friend so many years before. And yet that life had led them all to slaughter. Majer and Tommy and Chester and Baker and Goldie and Katy and the Twins. Perhaps Zeke and Cinder as well. Because of what he had done. Because of what he had failed to reconcile. At least beyond the enclosures they had a chance. At least he could give them that much after so many years.

Zeke's was last, the door opening upon an enclosure that appeared completely empty. No print. No sign of fur. No sense of the animal hiding from him. Nothing. As if the creature had simply dissolved into the storm altogether.

Then he was scrambling back down the hill through the snow, his hands numb, the gloves somewhere behind him where he had pulled them off and dropped them, his face frozen but his body moving, returning through the cut-locked gate to where the snowmobile sat already partially covered with fresh snow, panting and coughing and gasping for air even as he grasped the pull cord and began to heave at it, three times before even remembering to turn the key, and then once more and the machine burst into sound, its engine rattling, clouds of dark exhaust pooling out behind it in the frozen air and its headlights illuminating the swirl of snow that seemed to descend upon him from everywhere at once.

He came down the road at full speed, following his own track with the storm blowing straight up in his face from the creek below, his eyes tight and squinting into the blast. When he came to the point where Rick's footsteps veered off into the trees he pulled into the same track marks he had made on his way up the mountain and turned the machine off, stowing the keys in his jacket pocket and stepping off into the thigh-deep drift beside the road. The roadway suddenly dark and silent. He could see Rick's tracks leading off into the black shadows of the forest and he followed them to the edge of the trees, each step jerking and stumbling against the surface, but there was no seeing past the first big pines. If Rick rose all at once, in that moment, from those dark trees, he did not know what he would do at all. Rick had a pistol—he had seen it—and Bill stood there in the snow at the edge of the forest holding the empty air in his hands. What a fool you are. Again and again. What a fool.

He climbed back onto the machine and returned the key to the ignition and pulled the cord again. The snowmobile rumbled to life and he clicked it into gear and continued down the mountain, the headlights blasting out before him like a flame, his eyes watching the side of the road where the unblemished surface of the snow descended, flat and clear and perfect. And then Rick's footprints returned from the forest, the path intersecting with the tracks the sled had made on its ascent, and Bill pulled off to the side, not stopping but slowing for a long moment, watching the tracks as they led downhill, then opening the throttle again, watching for the path to swing away into the forest again, but the track went on and he followed it to where the road bent along the creek, to where that dark surface stretched off beside the road and where, in warmer months, he would sometimes see moose standing in the cool slow water, their mouths dripping with wet sedge and pond weed.

It seemed impossible that Rick would have made it even this far on foot in the storm and yet the tracks continued and he followed them, a grim, dark trough cut in the lit snow before him, all the while the wind blowing into his face, the sound of it a constant hiss against his jacket, eyes screwed down to slits and his bare hands in frozen agony. The snow everywhere like a veil that had fallen over him, over everything, sticking to his face, to the goggles, the headlights dimming under the accumulated pack of particulate ice that seemed to rise from the road and fall from the sky in equal measure.

The tracks led to the highway and then disappeared. What he saw before him was a ghost town. Not another human being visible and no lights on the highway but his own. He turned off the machine and clicked the headlamp off and then sat listening in the muffled silence. The buildings before him had become white boxes in the night. Across from him ran the road that led into the center of town, to the Northwoods and the general store and the empty lot where he had parked the truck.

He was shaking now, trembling everywhere from the cold and from the increasing understanding that he had lost Rick's trail, that Rick was gone. His pants had soaked through where his flesh had warmed the ice enough to melt it, his face a solid mask of frozen mustache and beard and his breath hard and fast and steaming the black air.

Then a sound. The chugging of an engine's ignition somewhere out there in the darkness. And a reflection of faint yellow light glowing briefly between the buildings and then just as quickly extinguished.

He could not yet see the car but he knew already that it was Rick's, as if a scent on the air blew to him from everywhere at once. And then there it was: the tiny Honda, its tire chains flapping along in the snow, headlights dark. He watched where it turned out onto the highway, pulling south toward Sandpoint, the car seeming to linger for a moment before accelerating, slowly, into the blowing storm and then the headlights silhouetting the tiny box of the car against the cyclone of snow beyond it.

He pulled the snowmobile to life again and throttled out across the highway and when he reached his truck he leaped for it, digging his numb hands into his pants pockets, jerking the keys out and then dropping them and cursing and scrabbling in the frozen snow, his hands like claws, the keys seeming to jump everywhere of their own accord. But at last the door was unlocked and he started the truck and shifted and pulled out onto the road, the headlights illuminating a vast wall of swirling flakes that flew up at the windshield from a point ever above him and away, and when he reached the highway he extinguished those lights for a moment, spinning south down the invisible road in the direction Rick had gone, but he could see nothing without them and after few dozen yards he twisted them on once more, the blizzard tunneling down upon him and the truck seeming to rise into it forever.

He thought of the bear then, its great furred back covered with snow, and all the days and nights when Bill would sit on the stump by the zookeeper door, talking and feeding the animal marshmallows, one after the other. He thought of the wolf hiding in its shallow depression by the fence, growling in pain and confusion. And he thought of the dead birds. The frightened raccoons. His weakened and half-blind mountain lion. His dead bobcat and badger. And then he thought of Grace and of Jude, and of the engagement ring held, even now, in the drawer in his trailer. How the boy had giggled when Bill hugged him at bedtime. How Grace had forgiven him for everything he had done.

The snow a terrible blur around him. There were moments when he thought he had surely spun from the road and the truck was careening through some empty field in the darkness, but then the snowbanks would reappear on either side of him again and he knew that he was still in the roadway. Twice headlights approached and cars slid past him in the opposite direction. Both times his heart beat quickly for the moment of their passing and afterward his hand hunted under the seat for the gun case, finding its edge and drawing it up to the seat as the truck slid forward upon the frozen road, its motion akin to a sickness he could neither control nor predict. But neither pair of headlights were Rick's tiny car and they passed him and returned to the darkness from which they had come.

And then, at last, the rear of the Honda emerged from the silent swirl of the blizzard. The car had spun off to the side of the road, its nose embedded in the snowbank. He slowed the truck to a stop. His view through the windshield was of snow and the wrecked car and nothing else and in the quiet hum of his idling truck he leaned forward, unzipped the gun case, and set the rifle across his lap.

Then the Honda's door opened and Rick stepped out into the storm: a grim and haggard figure in a tattered flannel jacket. He held the pistol in his hand but did not raise his arm to fire, instead only stood by the car's open door, facing the headlights impassively.

Bill pulled the handle and the truck's door creaked as it swung open. Then he, too, slid outside, the rifle held in his grip.

What's it gonna be? Rick called to him. Behind him, the pickup's headlights illuminated a high berm of packed snow, an unbroken wall maybe eight feet in height and which ran the length of the highway as far as Bill could see.

You don't know what you've done, Bill said.

Rick stood there for a long moment in silence, the pistol still held loose at his side. Then his face curled into a smile. I warned you it was gonna get serious, he said.

You don't know what you've done, Bill said again.

They stood facing either then, neither moving, Nat holding the rifle across his body, one hand on the stock and the other on the barrel, Rick near the snowbank next to the wrecked Honda, the blizzard swirling down upon them as if they had become inanimate figures in some vast snow globe.

What you gonna do, Natty, Rick said. You gonna shoot me?

He could feel a hollowness inside his chest. And then a bloom of warmth flooding through that hollow space. For a moment he could see fish threading their way up a cold river comprised entirely of snow. Yeah, he said quietly, I'm gonna shoot you. Then, in one quick, fluid motion, he raised the rifle to his shoulder and fired.

Rick looked surprised for a brief moment, his face frozen in the flash of the shot, and then he was moving, the pistol raised and its bright flower exploding repeatedly and the sound of the fire whacking the side of the truck like hammer blows. Bill fell sideways into the cab, scrambling onto the seat and crashing his foot down upon the gas pedal as he levered the truck into gear. Around him came the roar of the engine and the seasick feeling of the tires spinning for a moment before the whole vehicle burst forward, his body rolling back, and then the low hard crunch of impact and his body slamming forward against the base of the steering wheel.

Then another shot. His heart was a wild creature running in his chest. Hands shaking and all the while his voice filling the cab, the passenger window exploding into glittering dust and his hand scrabbling in the pocket of the gun case. One cartridge fell to the floor of the truck but he managed to grasp another and to jerk the lever down and press the shell into the breech and then lever it into position to fire.

He breathed and breathed and breathed and then reached for the door handle and pulled it as his foot kicked and his body came out of the cab, the cold rushing into him like a river and his feet slipping everywhere on the frozen road. He pointed the rifle in the general direction of the snowbank and pulled the trigger, the rifle emitting its loud sharp crack in the muffled frozen air, the kick in his cold hands, the stock striking his shoulder hard enough to bring him staggering backward against the truck again. Frantic. His panting breath sharp and terrible. He looked everywhere around him but all he could see was the afterimage of the muzzle flash that rode against his eyes. He ejected the spent shell. Already his hand searched for another in the pocket of the case. What have you done now? What have you gotten yourself into now? And then thinking that he should have just let Rick drive away. But it was too late for that. It was too late for anything but what was.

And then Rick's voice from somewhere near the Honda. This what you want? he called.

Bill yelled in response but it seemed as if what words he called simply blew backward over his head and were gone. Snow blowing into his face like tiny needles, eyes squinting into the wind. He leaned into the cab, his hand fishing for another cartridge in the pocket of the case, but he could not find one now. The darts. The small black box that held the tranquilizer. And then at last a cartridge and then another.

That the old ninety-nine? Rick called to him from outside. Three shots came in quick succession then, each of which blasted a new hole through the shattered windshield, glass raining down upon his back as he lay facedown on the seat, his eyes closed tight at the sound. You hear that? Rick's voice came. I've got a nine-millimeter with a twelve-round clip. Who you think's gonna win this fight?

He had managed to open the breech of the rifle and to load the two shells with trembling hands and to pull the breech closed again, the pin sliding the shell into position to fire, the rifle seeming to jump everywhere in his hands.

Natty, Natty, Natty, Rick said. You're really in it now.

And then his own voice, a bellowing scream: I just wanted you to leave me the fuck alone. And then he came leaping out of the cab with the rifle held to his shoulder, firing and ejecting and firing again, each bright flash of light freezing Rick, halfway up the snowbank, and then at its lip, and then gone.

17

HE KNEW THAT IT WAS CLOSE TO EIGHT NOW BECAUSE HE
had been listening, for what seemed like a long while, to the various good-
byes and see-you-tomorrows of the salesmen as they exited the building,
the sounds of motion—footsteps and voices—decreasing until what
remained was his own breath and heart and what sounded like a single
remaining figure whistling tunelessly, the sound of it fading into and out
of range like a distant television station. He hoped to god it was the sales
manager and that his long wait in the darkness was coming to a close, the
whistling rising and falling and then rising again and finally passing just
beyond the door and down the hall toward the exit. The water heater next
to him rippled with flame again and the soft growl of its ignition nearly
made him gasp with surprise. From the floor came its faint orange glow.
Then a moment of silence followed by a muffled and rhythmic beeping,
after which the strip of light that had been illuminating the base of the
door for as long as he had been secreted in the supply closet blinked out
all at once. There was a loud metal bang . The alarm's beeping continued
for a few more seconds before it fell silent. Then nothing.

The phone panel opposite him had been flickering incessantly with
green and red dashes and in the long two hours he had been hidden in

that tiny space he had tried to find patterns amidst those constellations, imagining it a map, a game, a drawing of some kind, but failing to discover any meaning in the random blinking of the lights. Now the dashes had fallen to a single green row gapped by occasional empty spaces. He stood staring at it, listening for any movement beyond the closed door. Then he breathed once, twice, and finally reached for the handle, finding it in the new darkness, and slowly, so slowly, opening the door.

The hallway in shadow. At its nether end, the tight corridor opened into the broad glass-fronted showroom, the windows there reflecting a faint glow from the streetlamps that lit the main lot with its rows of sparkling new cars. He stood in that profound silence, watching, through the glass, as a great jumbo jet descended across the floor-to-ceiling windows, its engine roar muffled to a distant whispered hush. He stood listening for any sound from within but the showroom was empty and silent.

He knew they were on schedule and that Rick would arrive soon. The two of them had parked down the street for three consecutive nights, timing the final employee, the sales manager, as he drove out of the parking lot near eight o'clock each night. On the first night, a police cruiser had passed them slowly, its driver looking at them with care as it slid by, so when seven thirty came the second night, they were parked a quarter mile down the street, watching the black-and-white as it drifted by in the distance. They waited until nine o'clock but did not see another police car and apart from the few employee vehicles leaving the dealership between seven thirty and eight they did not see another car at all. What they had learned was that the movements ran like clockwork: police cruiser at seven thirty, sales manager at eight, and nothing but a ghost town after.

On that final night he had tried to speak to Rick about what he had done and had failed to do, but the words had become entangled. Out before them through the windshield, oval pools of light marked the road along the fence. I just want a clean slate, he had said. That's all.

And Rick had broken his silence then. There are no clean slates, he had said.

You know what I mean.

Man, Rick said, this thing we're gonna do . . . do you even get how dicey this whole thing is?

Yeah, of course I do.

Do you?

Yeah, Nat said.

Rick was silent for a moment. Then he said, I've known you about as long as I've known anyone ever.

Me too.

Thing is, I don't understand what's been happening with you anymore. It's like you're, I don't know, out of control or something.

Down the long length of the street, the police cruiser appeared, its taillights moving slowly away from them in the distance.

It's like you're not yourself anymore, Rick said. I don't know how else to put it. It's weird.

I'm still me, Nat said. He looked out the side window. An airplane, bright white and luminescent in the night sky, ascended off the runway. He could think of nothing more to say and so he said nothing. The sound of the airplane ran all through the car: a long hiss that seemed to grow louder and louder and louder and would not stop.

The sound of the descending plane was quieter through the floor-to-ceiling glass of the showroom floor but it felt much the same. He had been holding his breath and he exhaled now, long and hard, returning to the hallway and moving down its length to the alarmed exit door that opened outside. The panel there glowed faintly. Its screen read simply ARMED in blocky electronic letters. Next to that message was a green light. He knew that the alarm would be triggered when he pushed open the door, but whether that triggering would directly contact the police or would activate some blaring siren or would do something else entirely, he did not know. Rick would knock and he would push open the door and they would deal with whatever happened next.

Then Milt Wells's office at last: a dark space cluttered with furniture and files and binders that burst into shadows in the blaze of the flashlight. The safe in the corner looked more substantial than it had when he looked at it from across the desk: a thick, almost featureless black box perhaps two feet square and fronted by a silver dial and handle. At first he simply grasped that handle and pulled but the safe did not move and for a moment he wondered if it was somehow bolted through to the floor. The wall shelves had been built around it and he cleared one side of books and binders and then swung his foot up into the gap he had made and pressed it against the wall, levering out with his body, pushing with his foot as he pulled hard upon the handle, and this time the box slid out slowly across the carpet and into the room.

When he had pulled it as far as he could, he sat on the flat surface of the safe in the dark, panting, his arms tired from the effort of moving that thick box even a few feet, and then rose and entered the hall and stood near the back door, listening to the too-loud sound of his own breath and staring at the alarm's glowing keypad with its single word of menace. He waited there until he could hear the sound of a car outside, the gears shifting, the sound growing louder and then the car's engine sputtering to silence. The familiar squeak as the Datsun's door opened and closed. He waited. And then came the knock, shave and a haircut, the sound so loud in the quiet of the dealership that it startled him even though he had been expecting it all night.

The alarm panel again. The glowing numbers. The green light. ARMED.

Then he turned the handle and pushed open the door.

Rick stood there in the darkness, his father's .38 revolver clutched in his hand, the Datsun just behind, its trunk already open. There was no sound, nothing to indicate they had tripped the alarm, but when he looked back to the panel the light had gone from green to red. A moment later the phone began to ring.

What the fuck? Rick said.

I don't know.

Fuck, he said. Then he stepped over the threshold and Nat pulled the door closed behind him.

What took you so long?

That fucking El Camino, he hissed.

No way.

Yeah way.

I told you that guy's been on me.

I had to drive all over town to get rid of him. Kind of freaked me out.

You lost him?

Yeah, totally. Where's the safe?

Down here. What's with the gun?

I don't know, he said. I brought the rifle too. It's in the car.

Dang, Rick.

Let's just get this done and get the fuck out of here. I'm all spooked out now.

The phone had stopped ringing although it felt like some part of that bell-tone drifted in the black air all around them still.

He led Rick to the office and Nat closed the door behind them. Then the flashlight, everything bursting into shadows.

Christ, turn that off, Rick said.

Nat pointed to the safe. There it is, he said.

Yeah, I see it. Now turn the light off.

They both kneeled and then struggled to lift it, the two of them on either side, the box only two feet square but heavy, solid. The faint sense of something sliding within. Then it was up and in their grasp and they were moving through the door in tiny, mincing steps, Rick's face there before him, as if they had embraced, or tried to, only to find this heavy iron cube between them, their expressions the same, as if each faced a mirror and the other had become his dark reflection.

Careful careful, Rick whispered.

They moved down the hall, the box heavy but manageable now that they were moving, and when they reached the exit door, Nat fumbled backward, catching the handle and opening it and then they were outside, the night cold and open and miraculous, and they laid the safe into the trunk, grunting and groaning and cursing, the little

Datsun heaving down from its weight, and in the next moment the trunk was closed and they were both in the car.

Holy shit, Rick said. That was fucking intense.

We did it, Nat said. We fucking did it. He turned the key and the engine cranked and started and he levered the car into gear.

We sure as hell did, Rick said.

Nat was smiling. The sense of relief that flooded through him was like nothing he had ever experienced, a great slackening as if some over-inflated tire had burst through its own sidewall, hot and stagnant air rushing out all at once, and all he could think was that he had done it and that he was free. He turned the wheel downhill toward the opening that led out onto the street.

And that was when he saw the El Camino.

Its low slanting shape slid out before them like a huge door rolling shut across their path, the Datsun's headlights shining upon its front wheel, its long rust-colored side panel, and finally upon the tattooed man's face in the driver's-side window, a face that stared back at them without concern or expression.

No, Nat said. And then he said it again in a long frantic stream: No no no no. He did not stop the car, could not. Instead his foot came down hard on the gas, his hands pulling the wheel and the little Datsun's engine flooding up in a quick hard hum and then leaping forward at a diagonal as if possessed of some new purpose or function, the gap between the front of the El Camino and the metal pole that marked the edge of their escape route closing even as they sped toward it. Rick was yelling next to him but he could not hear the words, only the weak roar of the tiny engine and then the crunch of metal as the Datsun struck the El Camino at the wheel well and both cars ground immediately to a stop.

What the fuck? Rick said, his voice high and loud and his hands scrabbling the floorboards for the .38.

We gotta get out of here.

I fucking know that.

But the tattooed man was already out of his car, Nat slamming into reverse but the front of the Datsun clinging to the El Camino, the little car's tires squealing against the asphalt and then abruptly breaking free, that moment coming just as Rick's door flew open and Rick himself was pulled outside, the man grabbing Rick's jacket and the Datsun whipping him out of the car by the pure force of its sudden motion, Nat staring now at a scene unfolding in the diminishing distance below him, all of it caught flat and brutal and impossible in the yellow of his headlights: the tattooed man throwing Rick to the asphalt, the baseball bat coming down and coming down and coming down, Rick's body seeming to collapse in on itself and his voice rising into that lit nightscape in a flurry of curses and screams.

He stopped the Datsun at the top of the driveway almost in the same location Rick had parked, the car's single functioning headlight pointing down the long slope, a parking lot empty of cars, the whole of the night crushing down on him all at once. Then he reached into the backseat for the rifle before wrenching open the door and stepping outside.

Stop goddammit, he yelled. Stop stop! and when the man raised the bat again Nat pointed the rifle into the sky and pulled the trigger. The sound of it was bright and hot and the flash blinded him for a moment but the man had stopped now, looking up to where Nat stood, the rifle held in his grip.

Now you think you're gonna shoot me? the man said.

Get away from him, Nat said.

Rick slid backward across the asphalt on his elbows, his feet kicking out for purchase.

I told you, you fucked with the wrong guy. A man repays his debts. And I sure the fuck owe you two sons of bitches.

I said get away from him, Nat said again.

The man laughed then, the black smears of his tattoos snaking up and down his arms, his teeth shining in a wide grin. Let's have a look at what you got in your trunk, dipshits, the man said. Maybe we can make a deal.

We triggered the alarm, Rick said from the ground. The cops are already on their way.

Then I guess we don't got much time, the man said. Despite the cold, he wore an unbuttoned collared shirt with the sleeves torn off, and he pulled the shirt out of the way to reveal the grip of a pistol extending from the front of his pants. You think you can shoot me before I draw? he said.

Shoot him, Rick said from the ground.

The man laughed again. He's not a killer, the man said, and neither are you, Mr. Medium Security. He smiled. Then he said, But I am.

And that was when Rick came at him, his body nearly parallel to the earth as he dove, crashing into the man sideways and both of them coming down. Nat could not see anything in the headlight glow, there were only bodies, hands on the bat, a kind of furious dissolve of flesh as if they had become one man with four arms and four legs, one man gone wild, striking at himself, predator and prey all at once.

He thought he could hear distant sirens now and he called his friend's name again and again, the rifle still held in his hands, the car behind him, his own shadow cast as a long straight arrow pointing down to that crazed and multiarmed figure. And when the shot rang out he jolted backward, staring for a quick moment at the rifle before realizing that he had not accidentally pulled the trigger on his own, that the shot had come from below.

Ah shit, the tattooed man said, smiling gleefully. Look what I did. He moved the pistol from one hand to the other and then looked up at Nat and turned toward him, the weapon pointed uphill now but not firing. Instead, the man simply advanced, walking quickly and with purpose up the slope, his shadow weaving out behind him to where Rick lay sprawled on the asphalt beside the El Camino, his shinbone bent at an impossible angle and a bright red mushroom of flesh bulging up through a rent in his jeans from where he had been shot, this shadow strung out behind him in the glow of the dealership lights like the shadow of some huge desert tarantula. You fucking shot me, Rick said, his voice a howl of impotent and impossible rage.

Nat stepped backward toward the Datsun's open door and as he did so, perhaps in direct response to the sound of the gunshot, a siren chirped twice, not so very far away, and then came blazing into full volume. Nat felt his heart clutch in his throat and all he could think, the only word that would come to him, was no no no.

Ah shit, the man said. You fucking dipshits. He looked up at Nat, then at the Datsun, perhaps thinking in that moment that it might be easier to take Nat's tiny car, but instead he simply said, Next time you won't be so lucky, and turned and ran back down the slope, past Rick and into the driver's seat of the El Camino, Rick's voice calling up at Nat all the while: Help me. Jesus fucking Christ. He shot me. I'm fucking shot.

The lights were coming along the street now, blue and red and illuminating everything, and Nat could not tell if there was one car or a hundred. The sirens loud and screaming. The tattooed man sat behind the wheel of the El Camino and its engine was roaring and roaring but the car did not move and Nat could see that its wheel well was crushed into the front tire from where the Datsun had hit it.

Jesus Christ, Rick called out to him. What are you doing? Come on!

The lights and the sirens. The tattooed man leaping out of the El Camino now, the pistol in his hand, running out beyond the lights, out into the darkness of the town and the desert that held it, the first of the police cars passing the stranded El Camino, sirens blazing, lights flashing everywhere.

Nat had backed to the door and slid now behind the wheel. I'm sorry, he said, his voice quiet, calm, and when he pulled forward it was not into that blaze of rotating police lights but instead to the right, the Datsun following the long stretch of the building toward the far exit, Rick's voice following him as he drove: What are you doing? Don't leave me! Don't fucking leave me here. But he was already out amidst the rows of new cars glistening under the white glow of a quarter moon. He could hear Rick's voice calling to him long after he was on the road, long after the casinos disappeared in the mirrors and the desert blew out all around him, empty and endless and as black as an ocean, a voice that called and called and called his name and would not stop.

18

HE CAME DOWN THE ROAD AT A DEAD RUN, THE RIFLE IN HIS hands and the zippered case flapping over his shoulder, thirty or forty yards and already panting, his feet slipping every few steps against the icy surface of the plowed asphalt. When he turned and leaped for the embankment he was not sure if he would be able to get through it at all, his body a heavy, floundering shape against the slope, but somehow he managed to scramble through and up and over, snow-covered and heaving for breath, his heart a hammer in his chest. Beyond him, the road was dark and the forest darker still, but in the glow of an approaching pickup, he could see Rick a few dozen yards away where he stood just at the edge of the trees, his body silhouetted for a brief instant as the lights swung out through the forest and the swirling snow as if rotating on some vast dish, that slash of illumination reaching Bill just as Rick looked up in his direction, the pistol already raised before Bill had even managed to regain his feet, trying to stand now and fumbling with the rifle, pulling the trigger only to realize he had not yet levered a shell into the chamber and propelling himself, in a staggering crawl, into the downsloping branches of a black fir as the pistol barked and its bright sharp light bit the air, all the while his own voice like a crazed whine in the darkness.

The shots came quick and fast now, thwacking against the trunks all around him. His own finger pulled the trigger but he was not aiming anymore, had stopped aiming when he saw the flash of Rick's pistol. His own shot seemed to fly up into the air like some bright yellow flower and he stumbled backward toward the darker forest, pulling the bolt to bring another cartridge into the chamber and then knowing that the rifle was empty. Another shot came as he ran, low and dim through the snow, and then another, Bill's breath coming in gasps, his feet sinking everywhere into the frozen earth as he stumbled behind a tree. He thought he might break apart, or that he was breaking apart already. And yet he knew he could not simply stand there, that doing so would mean death, and so he breathed in two quick sharp lungfuls of the frozen air and looked around the black trunk, the rifle held tight in his grip. There was nothing there now. No dark figure. What he stared into was a stretch of dim and endless forestland swirling with snow and an angular patchwork of tenebrous shapes that fell into a Möbius strip of distance. No sign of movement anywhere.

He thought of Majer then, of Majer and the animals, and all he could muster for them was an apology for their collective deaths and for his own and a question he could not answer: What good had he been to them? The bear had stared out at him from his cage with eyes that clearly knew him, that recognized him, but what circled through the bear's mind he would never know. But did he even know what circled through his own? Everything he had done seemed utterly foolish, running out into the storm like a madman. He should have gone with Grace and Jude. He knew that now, and he also knew that he should have understood that from the start.

But it was too late and maybe it had been too late since the beginning. Everything beyond his sight mere abstraction—memory, history, perhaps even love—and the time for such things had ended. Instead there was only his motion as he turned around the trunk and stared into the storm. This time he could see Rick once again, his figure limping and struggling through the snow, not away from him but toward, some fetch or wraith or grim doppelgänger come to end him, and the fear that clutched at his heart held him there, watching in terror for a long, trembling moment until, at last, he turned and began an erratic, panicked stumble uphill, each step postholing up to his thighs, his feet numb but his body pressing forward in desperation. He could not remember how many shells remained in the case but knew that there were not many.

The trees around him had begun to shake and hiss and the snow blew sideways against his face. He stood with his back to a tree again, the rifle spattered with ice, his hands red and burning. The gun case was still hanging from his shoulder and he unslung it and pressed his crabbed hand into the pocket and came up with a single shell. Certainly the last. He loaded it into the rifle and closed the breech and stood panting.

Then the tree next to his head exploded, a burst of wood chips spattering his face. He jerked back, the rifle fumbling in his grip as the flat pop of the pistol repeated, the bullet whizzing past him and into the forest. He spun around the tree and the rifle cracked, the flash arresting each flake so that the storm held, for the briefest moment, in the air all around him. His breath came fast now and the shot still rang in his ears. Goddammit! he screamed. He crouched and ran forward, his breath a wheeze, his motion jerking, spastic, the rifle barrel warm against his freezing hands, stumbling from one tree to the next, the snow blasting, all the while, into his squinting eyes.

The slope upon which he moved rose to a bulbous ridge where only the tops of the trees protruded from the snow, short and twisted shapes that provided no shelter from wind or gunfire and beyond which the slope ran down at an angle precipitous and blind. He staggered out along its edge, his hands shaking, heart trembling in his chest. Across the line of the ridge, exposed rocks stood everywhere like black skulls in the blizzarding night. His breath ragged and his head light and dizzy. He had to stop once when a fit of coughing racked his body and he thought he might vomit but he did not vomit and he stood again and went on in his staggering slow-motion run, expecting at any moment that the killing shot would come to claim him. When he turned again, he could see Rick's ghost-shape: a bleak shadow lunging from behind a dark tree and then disappearing and reappearing again, moving up the slope toward him in stuttering cuts and edits like some strip of damaged film. And so he ran, his feet heavy, clambering and sliding until he had achieved the top of the ridge.

He could not see the surface beyond but there were trees rising from somewhere below and so he rolled himself forward and tumbled over the frozen lip. On the opposite side the wind was yet stronger. He lay in a scant forest of dwarf and twisted trees, the empty rifle still held between his numb hands. Already he was so exhausted he could barely get to his feet and yet he managed to do so and to move back along the edge of the ridge, back toward where he had seen Rick struggling up the mountain and then he knelt in the snow, listening and staring into the swirling darkness for so long that when the first close footstep crunched the snow he was momentarily confused as to what it could be. Then there was another. And another. So close.

What thoughts he had were simple and desperate and his body moved as if controlled by instinct alone. He lunged forward off the ridge without sight or plan or idea. For a moment he was nearly airborne, such was the curl of the cornice upon which he had launched himself, but then Rick flew to him from the grainy frozen night and their collision was with the full force of Nat's weight and then both of them were falling. He had wrapped one hand into Rick's coat but he released it now and the figure next to him flailed in the snow as he too flailed, their twin bodies rocketing all at once down the mountain, powder and frozen chunks of snow following them, and the inarticulate sirenlike wailing was his own scream as he fell. Everything the downward arrow. As if the entire forest had become liquid. Blurred ghosts of dwarf trees. White ribbons of crystalline snow in a night that had become so utterly dark as to achieve a kind of vacancy or emptiness. When he looked to the side he could no longer see Rick at all.

For the briefest instant he found himself suspended in a geography broken loose of the world: the dark boughs of pines and firs, the curvature of rocks and stones, the swirling cyclonic curl of blowing snow all around him, all adrift in that white blurred night sea, his hands paddling the frozen air before plunging at last, backward, into the freezing water of the swollen creek below.

For a moment he was blind. The cold was everything. Coming into his skin, into his blood. His brain. Like burning. His nerves exploding with it.

His hands came up. Then his head burst again into freezing air and he groped in desperation and delirium for anything solid in the world and his hand fell upon a black tree root jutting from the icy bank and he grabbed it and stopped himself, the current pressing against him so that his legs came out sideways in the flow. Already he was pulling himself from the water, his teeth chattering in his head and his voice coming in a staccato hum he could not control.

He did not know how he managed to climb the bank but he scrambled upward until he lay upon the steep broken surface above the rushing water. The cold was like nothing he had ever experienced: an agonized numbing that seemed to enter him directly through the heart and radiated outward into every part of his being. His clothes were wet through to bare skin and his beard already freezing into a solid block in the wind. The rifle was gone but the case remained slung across his back.

He clawed himself to hands and knees and then raised himself again to his feet, bent over and choking with cold. The creek poured out below him, a waterway only a dozen feet deep but blasting black against the white mountainside and disappearing under the snow and reappearing again before curling on through the trees. At its frozen edge, a few dozen yards away, lay a dark shape that, as he watched, seemed to uncoil itself, rising and staggering to its feet and then falling again to the snow and rising once more. Rick. He too from the river, freezing, a bleak shape against a plane of grainy fuzz like a static-smeared television screen. The figure seemed to peer at him from its position on the opposite bank and Bill raised a hand to him weakly. It was an odd gesture but he could think of no other to perform. If the figure made some gesture in response, Bill did not see it in the shadowed and swirling darkness of the storm.

He was shaking with a force so profound that it seemed to pull his skeleton from his body, the cold occupying his chest like some great bird come to roost there, in his bones, his limbs, in the frozen center of his being, so that it felt as if his blood had turned to slush and the snow drifted right through the insubstantial film of his skin, curling briefly inside him before swirling away through the trees. Three times he fell before reaching an area where the angle lessened enough for him to scale the ridge, turning only once to see if he was being pursued and finding no one. His footsteps were slow and labored and although he knew he was freezing to death he could not stop moving, what connection of body or of mind he did not know but his feet continued to move and his heart continued to beat in his chest. He felt as if he were drifting up through the cold shocked air.

Then there was a shape in his mind, a flowing gray and aquiline shape that appeared and disappeared and reappeared once more. A wolf, its body moving through the black in utter and complete silence, not moving toward him or away but simply moving. He did not know if his eyes were open or closed now. All around him the same dark trees and endless snow and he drifted toward some warm dry distance he could not identify. But then there was a voice, somewhere, faint, and it pulled him back into the snow again. He lifted his head, expecting to see the wolf, but there was no wolf. Perhaps there never had been.

He had assumed he would die. That was why he had released the animals. But now that the moment was upon him he wondered what else he could have done. He thought of himself as the boy who would go down to the black bridge in Battle Mountain with his older brother in days of heat and sunlight. And perhaps he still was that boy, even after everything that had happened. If there were any rules left to dictate his life, only one remained, and that was to take care of his own. But of course he had not even done that much: not for the animals, not for the bear, and certainly not for the friend he had left behind.

His eyes slipped closed for a moment and then flashed open again. He could feel a strange warmth entering his body. It came in through his fingers and toes first and hung there for what seemed an eternity before drifting slowly into his forearms, into his lower legs. He remembered that Rick's shape had been coming up the ridge toward him but it felt as if he had seen that shape many days ago and what sounds there were seemed to come to him now as if from that time, as if filtered out from some universe similar to this one but ultimately obeying different rules, where objects came untethered from earth and flowed of their own agency, each animate and distilled of a purpose and function as clear and sharp as a diamond.

The world felt soft and blue and warm and he knew what he felt was death itself. The voice he heard was calling his name, his true name, and he lifted his head to meet it.

And there stood the wolf at his feet, a gray shape in the night, its forepaw held up out of the snow.

Zeke, Bill said. His voice was a quiet whispering croak.

The wolf stood there before him as if in answer and then it came forward, passing him so closely that he might have reached out a hand to touch its fur and moving up the ridge in the darkness, its motion slow and silent and so ethereal that Bill was not sure if what he was seeing was real or was simply part of his death. Zeke, he croaked again. And the wolf stopped and looked back over its shoulder at him, as if waiting for him to rise.

And he did rise, coming to his feet and stumbling forward through the thick snow, his body racked with shaking, teeth chattering in his head, limbs jerking as if they had come loose of his brain, and yet still he came forward, up to the base of the short granite cliffs that rose from the darkness at the top of the ridge. In the storm they were lumbering shadows. Colorless. When he reached them he fell forward and crawled on his hands and knees through the snow and into a break in the cliff wall, crawled without thought, his body only wanting to get out of the storm, and when he collapsed at last his breath screamed in his ears and the rush of wind through the trees was distant and terrible. His face like a block of ice and when he touched his hair crusts of frost broke free and fell to the frozen rocks upon which he lay. His clothes freezing solid around him like an encasement of stone.

He had come into a dark place and he lay within it for a long time without even being conscious of whether his eyes were open or closed. His teeth had ceased their chattering now and were locked tight together, his limbs curled against themselves as if they could somehow be willed back into living. Then a few small details began to fade in from the black: stones, rock shadows, a pile of broken branches and leaves like flotsam from an incoming wave. Whether such materials had been collected by man or animal or by nature itself, he could not tell.

He was in a recess, a small space not quite a cave, formed by the apex of overhanging cliffs and huge blocks of talus. He dragged himself to the pile, his hands shaking so badly that the leaves he pulled from the debris were crushed in his grip. Still, he managed to amass a small pile of them in the center of the area and reached in his pocket for the lighter and could not at first recall what else was held there, could not imagine what it was until he had extracted it with his shaking and unmovable hands: *Wildlife of the Intermountain West*, still contained in its clear plastic bag. He pulled it free and began tearing the pages out, one after another, plants and animals into a crushed pile: raccoon and shrew and bat and black bear, weasel and skunk and fox and coyote. He found his lighter and beat it, upside down, against his leg, and then turned the thumbwheel against its tiny flint again and again, his entire body shaking in its seizure of freezing. When the flint would not spark he turned to the stone wall behind him and ran the wheel repeatedly against its surface, back and forth, back and forth, thirty, forty times, until finally he could see the bright star of the spark and then held down the lever to release the gas, continuing to roll the wheel against the stone. At last a slow, miraculous flame appeared, sputtering and choking against the damp and the cold. He held it to those torn pages and they blackened and twisted and finally began to burn, curling into bright flames.

He could not feel the heat even when he let the flames flow across the bottom of his palm but he knew it must be there and so he leaned over and pulled some of the loose and dry tree branches from the back of the tiny cave and found a few small twigs there and chips of wood and bark and he placed them carefully over the burning pages and leaves.

The fire was small and for a long while seemed on the verge of failing, but after a time a bright orange glow appeared and he pulled more branches over to it and placed them above those embers and waited for them to come into flame. His actions were automatic, and at times, staring at those flames, he did not even remember why he was building a fire or what he was doing out there in that cold world. He remembered a long collection of paired yellow eyes staring at him from the darkness but beyond that only a haze of strange and echoing voices and people he did not even remember or care about anymore. And if he had followed someone out into this wasteland he could not recall to what purpose he had pursued or had been pursued.

He piled all the wood he had over the fire and after a time the front of the tiny cave was filled with orange light and he lay with the granite wall against his back and his beard grew soft and slushy and at last began to dry. The false warmth that had entered his body fled from him now and the quaking reentered him completely, his skeleton seeming to gather its own intelligence and struggling to break from his flesh. It rattled inside that skin sack to the rhythm of his freezing.

After a time he lay on his side, the glowing coals inches from his face, and he felt there, in that single location, the first true warmth return to him and then realized that the burning pain he felt was the sensation of his skin coming back to life. He closed his eyes, breathed the warm and smoke-filled air, so slowly, into his body. For a long time he thought his clawed hand was curled around the black velvet box that held the engagement ring he had purchased for Grace, and as he lay there he thought of what might have been, sitting at the dining room table with Jude hopping up and down with excitement as Bill produced the ring and she opened it and Grace's smile lit up the room around them like a flame, but when he managed at last to uncurl those fingers, he saw that they held nothing but cold vacant air.

THE FIRE roared and he lay half awake, propped once more against the rock wall at the back of the alcove. He had remembered now that Rick was out there somewhere and that he could probably see the orange glow even through the falling snow and so he remained as alert as his body would allow. A semblance of warmth had returned to him even though his clothing was soaked through. His boots were frozen solid and he could not have taken them off even if he had wanted to. Instead they lay as dead weight at the edge of the coals, steaming slowly.

He had opened the canvas case and filled a dart with fluid from the only vial that remained in the zippered pocket and now he loaded the dart into the gun and sat with it held across his lap.

The night was still black and the snowfall had not lessened. When Rick's voice came, it was as if from a dream and he thought that he must have fallen asleep, if only for a moment. But then it came again and he lifted his head from his chest and peered out into the darkness. The world beyond the firelight seemed another universe entire. As if there was nothing out there but an endless void.

But then the voice again, closer this time and calling that name he hoped he could forget but knew now that he never would: Nat, the voice said. Nat.

He started to speak, stopped, tried to sit up, stopped that too. Fuck you, he said at last. His voice sounded weak and far away and when Rick called his name again he took a deep breath and shouted the words: Fuck you!

There was silence for a long time. Then Rick's voice came again, slowly, quietly, like a tiny bird out there in the snow. Like something already lost. Everything beyond the orange crackle of the fire, an empty hole. I'm freezing out here, he called, his voice stuttering with cold.

I don't care.

Nat, goddammit.

Fuck you.

I'm coming in.

I have a gun.

Nat, please.

You poisoned them, he said. You killed them. He was shaking, his grizzled face cradled in his hands. Just leave me alone. Leave me alone.

You left me there.

I didn't want to.

You should have helped me, man. You were my best friend. Why didn't you help me? His voice cracked over the words.

Nat said nothing in response but the tears came fully now and he sobbed into that firelight. His body shaking and wet in the snowmelt. Tears transpiring into invisible clouds that fled into the darkness beyond.

I went to prison for twelve fucking years, the voice said. I could've turned you in. I could've done that.

You should have.

I didn't.

I don't care.

You're my best friend, Nat, the voice said. I'm going to fucking die out here. I'm freezing.

Silence.

I'm fucking freezing to death.

Again. Silence.

Nat, goddammit. I'm sorry. OK? I'm fucking sorry.

He thought of Bill then, his dead brother, smiling at him as he held that broken-winged bird in his hands. And then he thought of the broken-backed deer he had shot soon after his uncle died, and when he spoke again, his voice was loud and clear: All right, he said. All right. Come in.

You're not gonna shoot me?

No, he said.

He waited then, the dart gun remaining in his lap. He could see almost nothing beyond the fire, only a blur of snow that ended in absolute darkness, and out of that darkness Rick materialized like a ghost, a wet snowman shaking with cold, his face a pale mask. If he still had the pistol, it could not be seen. Instead, there was only the figure of the man, tattered and freezing, his eyes sunken in his head.

Bill lifted the dart gun to his shoulder and fired.

Rick said a single word, No, and raised his hand. The dart hit him mid-thigh, the red feathers like a strange flower that had sprouted there. Rick looked down and tried to pull it away but his hands did not seem to work and the dart wobbled and finally fell loose.

What the fuck was that? Rick stuttered.

Just a warning, he said.

Fuck you, Rick said, but he kept moving forward, his steps stumbling. What the fuck was that, man? A fucking dart? His words seemed to slur through his frozen face.

That's exactly what it was.

What the fuck? Rick said. He staggered forward and then crumbled—half sitting, half falling—to the snow by the fire. His teeth were chattering so loud that they sounded like a child's wind-up toy. You said you weren't gonna shoot me.

I'm not anymore, he said. He set the dart gun beside him in the snow.

Fuck, Rick said.

Stop talking.

Snowflakes continued to fall beyond the light of the fire. He watched them come. His name was in the air, although he did not think Rick had said anything at all. It moved as if vaporized, as if it had become the snowflakes that fell above the flames, breaking back into water, then vapor, then disappearing entirely as if they had been pressed by heat alone to return to the ether from which they had come.

I'm so tired, Rick said.

Yeah?

Aren't you?

No.

What was in that dart?

Ketamine.

What did you do, man? Rick said. What the fuck did you do?

I'm taking care of my people.

And now Rick laughed, a long weird braying that seemed, midway through its run, to slow down, to shift lower, as if the world was spinning apart.

You need to know something, Bill said. My uncle took that safe to a guy he knew in Spokane the day after I got here. He figured out the combination.

Rick did not answer for a long time, only staring at him. Then he said, slowly, I fucking knew it. His voice slurred out like a drunkard. His eyes slipped closed and then opened again. How much?

About three grand is all.

Where is it?

The guy who cracked it took a cut and I paid off Johnny Aguirre and there just wasn't much left after that. Couple hundred.

You still should've sent it to my mom.

I wanted to.

So why didn't you?

He exhaled. Then he said, When I paid off Johnny, that guy Mike asked me if I wanted to make another bet for old time's sake.

Rick just looked at him, eyes sunken, face still coated in snow.

I thought about your mom all the time. I got a little money when my uncle died but by then she was already gone.

You should have just told me, Rick said, his voice a mess of slurring syllables.

Bill looked at him for a moment, at his glassy, unfocused eyes. I made something for myself here, he said. And you were gonna fuck it up. I just wanted you to go away. I thought you'd just give up and go home if I gave you the safe.

Ha, Rick said, deadpan. Bad bet.

Turned out that way.

Rick was silent, staring now into the flames, and when he spoke again his voice was like a long single word mashed to pieces: Man, he said, you've always been the survivor. Even when we were kids.

Bill sat forward now. That's not true at all, he said. His voice sounded loud in the little cave. You were. Not me. You.

Oh yeah? Well, look at us now, my friend. Look at us now. His voice trailed off and after a moment his body slumped to the side in the firelight.

Bill sat for a long time, staring at the thin, soggy shape before him, at the steam rising from the wet coat and pants. His hands were trembling, although they were no longer cold. Rick lay at his feet, eyes closed. Bill thought he was unconscious but when he leaned in and grabbed his coat collar and pulled, Rick's eyes rolled open. What are you doing? he whispered. Then the eyes closed again, slowly, like the eyes of a doll.

Bill stood and staggered backward out of the tiny cave, back into the blowing storm, Rick's body a low heavy weight that he dragged behind him like a sled dog pulling his load, and when he was done, when he had come out beyond the glow of the fire and into the dark curl of the snow, he stopped and released his grip and stumbled back to the cave again.

When he reached its warmth, he sat and closed his eyes and prayed sleep would come to claim him. After a time even the fire disappeared. The darkness complete. He could feel his body floating in that black emptiness. Desert all around. His mother. And the brother he had lost. Other things too. The blue Datsun. The trailer he had grown up in, its metal siding sheeting off to wobble in the empty air. Impossible shapes in the snow. And Grace. And Jude. And himself. And Majer. He could feel the animals as they unscrolled themselves in that single loop of endless time and he wondered if there had been any meaning or purpose in it at all but then he knew that such questions held no meaning or purpose. And Rick. Of course. And Rick.

The forest was only wind.

.   .   .

WHEN MORNING came at last, the fire was only a heap of smoldering coals. It was freezing and he was shaking again and could not stop. His feet and his fingers had gone completely numb but as he lay there the sun appeared from behind the clouds and shone into the mouth of the little alcove and for a few moments he could feel a faint warmth against his face. Beside him in the frozen slush lay the dart gun and what was left of the book, its pages gutted but the cover remaining, and from that the pronghorn antelope stared back at him with the same guileless and implacable expression it had held for all his life.

He tried three times to stand, each time careening back to earth again. His feet like stumps tied to unbending knees. Clothes still wet next to his skin. On the third attempt he rolled over onto his back and scooted forward on his elbows. The snow was deep and heavy and his body plowed into it but he was able to push his way from the cliffs and up over the slight rise.

The trees were scattered down the length of the slope. Beyond them, beginning at the base of the ridge and stretching out across a broad flat plain, lay a pale and thickly packed forest coated in a clotted layer of wet snow and through which ran a black river that coiled through those bleached and albescent conifers in loops and turns and which encircled, at its center, a vast field as empty and clear as a blank page. The wilderness seemingly without end, the ridges folding into an accordioned distance. Above them rode a series of towering clouds in blue sky, their shadows cutting the lit surface of the forest below into scraps and tatters and rags. The span between here and there as impenetrable as the forest all around him. Some impossible distance. And no sign of motion anywhere.

He slid forward on his back and elbows again and managed to get himself partially down the slope before he came to Rick. He lay encrusted with snow, his skin blue and white as if the blood had been drained from his body and what remained was only a shell curled into the position that is, for all our race, the first and last on earth. He leaned in close and peered for a long time at that frozen face. A gaunt visage of sharp angles topped with eyebrows now weighted with ice. Once upon a time: your best friend.

He rolled away from the frozen body and lay for a long time on his back, staring up at the motion of the clouds, his body trembling everywhere at once. There were things in the world he would never understand. The rules men created to guide them through their lives were little more than guesses meant to fill whatever purpose they could imagine for themselves. Sagebrush and poverty weed. Ground squirrel and pronghorn antelope. Grizzly and wolf and raccoon. All designed to perform a function. But the universe held its workings in secret and a man could claim nothing from that void and instead would need to design in that obscure and private place that is his heart the laws that would govern his life. The clouds a blur of unrecognizable shapes without meaning or purpose. Only function. His had been to survive in the world he had chosen for himself. And he had succeeded. There was no law simpler than that and when he wept it was for himself and himself alone.

The sun fell once more behind the clouds and the temperature dipped until he was shivering again. At some point he managed to rise into a sitting position, although he could not remember doing so, and he remained there for a long while, his eyes drifting closed.

When the first flash of light came he thought he had dreamed it but then came another. Far below him, pools of sunlight drifted across the valley floor and from somewhere amidst those snow-covered trees, that black river, came a flash of bright, dazzling light. He sat up and watched and waited and then it came again: a quick burst like a white star burning out of the trees. At first he took it for some sign or signal and then imagined that he could see movement in the empty field below, as if that blank space had been visited by the tiny shapes of distant animals: martens and raccoons and the flapping wings of raptors. A wolf and a mountain lion. And of course the bear. But he knew that such a vision was impossible and so he waited and when the flash came again he understood what it was: sunlight glinting off the windshields of passing cars. As if in confirmation, the sun broke wholly through the clouds for the briefest instant and the highway itself blazed as a long strip of bright white light, as if it suddenly had been drawn in glowing ink upon what had been, only moments before, the endless wilderness.

He did not know how long he remained there but the sky was covered in clouds when he finally began the process of struggling to his feet, his breath hard and his body feeling as if it were fading out all around him. And yet he managed to stand, his legs knee-deep in the snow, and then to take a single agonized step forward, and then, at last, to begin his descent. Below him lay the shining line of the highway and beside it the slow oxbow curves of the river, its surface reflecting the sky so that clouds seemed to float gray and swollen in its depths. Sometimes in his descent, he could see them as they ran free through the fresh snow, their muzzles blowing steam, their bodies long and muscled and whole. All of them. Even you. He could see them and then he could see only the vacancy of that snow-covered meadow beyond.

If he could just reach the highway, he could flag down a passing car to drive him the hour and a half to Coeur d'Alene, although in the profound depths of his fatigue he could not always recall what might be waiting for him there: people he loved, people who loved him in return, and between an endless geography of white earth and black trees. In his descent, what he held fast to was the bear. He took that shape with him through that forest of frozen pines. Sometimes he fell. Sometimes he rested. Sometimes he staggered on.

ACKNOWLEDGMENTS

TO MY FRIENDS AND FAMILY WHO STRUGGLED WITH ME THROUGH endless drafts and redrafts, pondered new ideas, concepts, and themes, wrestled with philosophical debates, and/or put up with late-night phone calls: Jason Sinclair Long, Andrew John Nicholls, Jason Roberts, Tim Rutili, Amanda Eyre Ward, Josh Weil, and Lance Weller. Of particular help were the detailed notes of Lois Ann Abraham, Lydia Netzer, Michael Spurgeon, and Karin Erickson. Thanks to Chip Conrad and to my father, Gary Kiefer, for joining me on research trips to Reno, Battle Mountain, and North Idaho, and to my uncle, Jeff Kiefer, for straightening out my use of plant biology terms. Especially helpful were the thoughts of my wife, Macie, who allowed me to fill her head with my characters so I could watch them walk around (and watched the children so that I could actually write the thing).

In and about Reno, Nevada, many thanks to L.C.; Tim Dees (Reno Police Department, retired); the particularly fine memory of Kathy Eastland and everyone at Reno's Wonder Bar; Linda Gardner; Tupelo Hassman, author of *Girlchild*; Steve Reed; Lynn Tower, LCSW; the fine novelist, musician, and Nevada native Willy Vlautin;

and Michael Wirtschafter. I would also like to acknowledge that participants in the Facebook group *You are probably from Reno if* . . . were consistently helpful.

In Battle Mountain, Nevada, many thanks to the patient information provided by Lori Price at the Battle Mountain Cookhouse Museum; Paula Tomera, executive director of the Battle Mountain Chamber of Commerce; Lander County sheriff Ron Unger; and Robin York. Josh Scovil was the first to introduce me to Battle Mountain. His stories and those of his father, Jonn Scovil, were invaluable.

In North Idaho, my aunt and uncle, Pam and Greg Mangum, and cousin, Dale Mangum, were excellent guides to the area; wolf handler Mario Marzio helped with information related to that beautiful animal; Dory McIsaac offered her expertise in rehabilitating ungulates at Mystic Farm Wildlife Rescue in Sagle; Kathleen St. Clair–McGee of American Heritage Wildlife Foundation helped me navigate through the paperwork associated with the care of injured Idaho wildlife. For news and geographical information, I am indebted to Mike Weland of *News Bonners Ferry*; to the research skills of Jessica Bowman, cataloging assistant and reference technician for the East Bonner County Library District, for providing me with copies of the *Bonner County Daily Bee*; and to the memories of the Facebook group *Bonners Ferry Back When*. The Northwoods Tavern is a real place, fictionalized for the purposes of this book. Apologies to its patrons and its current owners, the very kind Roger and Laurie Doering, for any liberties I have taken.

Special thanks to the very patient Jill Lute of the Folsom City Zoo Sanctuary for answering my questions on the practical side of zoo management, and to the San Francisco Zoo's Debbie Marin-Towey, assistant curator of carnivores, and Sandy Huang, carnivore animal keeper, for specific information about grizzly care. M. Paul Atwood, wildlife biologist, Upper Snake Region, Idaho Fish and Game, kindly shared his insight on grizzly behavior and cognition, and on the paperwork and legal ramifications of running a wildlife rescue in Idaho. (The IFG conservation officer in this novel bears no relation to him or any other real IFG CO whatsoever.) I should also mention here that the wildlife rescue in the book was inspired, in part, by Animal Ark, north of Reno, Nevada.

To the various patient answerers of questions, interviewees, expert witnesses, careful and measured listeners, researchers, and divulgers of secret lives—in person or via e-mail and/or telephone—know that you helped situate these characters in their world: Lottie Ashton; Robert M. Dale; Jennae Harwell; Michael Hinch; Katie McCleary; American River College librarian Debby Ondricka; Jeffry-Wynne Prince; Tristan Soderberg-Mull; Henry Twilling; Dennis Yudt; and many of my students at American River College in Sacramento. My gratitude to all.

I am indebted to four master writers who have offered friendship, care, and counsel when needed most. Richard Ford was kind enough to help me navigate the business side of things, offering expert advice and perfectly timed words of caution. Pam Houston's friendship and support have been invaluable, both on a personal and professional level. Denis Johnson kindly suffered a slew of stupid questions about Bonners and North Idaho and then pushed me to create better lies to answer them. Finally, I would like to acknowledge the lasting impact of my first writing teacher, now a friend of more than two decades, T. Coraghessan Boyle, fellow explorer of the collision of human and animal worlds. These people are the stars of my particular brand of heaven, and I am grateful for their friendship.

I did a great deal of reading during the drafting of this novel. In particular, I would like to acknowledge a few texts I returned to over and over again: Michael Allaby's *Temperate Forests*; Reed W. Fautin's *Biotic Communities and the Northern Desert Shrub Biome in Western Utah*; Dwayne Kling's *The Rise of the Biggest Little City: An Encyclopedic History of Reno Gaming, 1931–1981*; James A. MacMahon's *Deserts*; Roberta Parish, Ray Coupé, and Dennis Lloyd's *Plants of the Southern Interior, British Columbia, and the Inland Northwest*; Jakob von Uexküll's *A Foray into the Worlds of Animals and Humans*; William T. Vollmann's monumental *Rising Up and Rising Down: Some Thoughts on Violence, Freedom and Urgent Means*; and of course

Vinson Brown, Charles Yocum, and Aldine Starbuck's *Wildlife of the Intermountain West*, a book given to me by my grandparents when I was a child. The copy of *The Tibetan Book of the Dead* referenced is the 1960 Oxford University Press edition, as translated by W. Y. Evans-Wentz. I should also note that the work of John Brandon, Doug Peacock, Else Poulsen, Paul Shepard, Gary Snyder, and Clive D. L. Wynn were important in helping me find ways to approach the animals in this book.

Thank you to everyone at Liveright and W. W. Norton, especially my lovely editor Katie Adams, Cordelia Calvert, Peter Miller, and Philip Marino. Also many thanks for the lovely cover design by Jaya Miceli and copyediting expertise of Miranda Ottewell.

Finally, profound gratitude to my wonderful agent Eleanor Jackson, who was honest right when she needed to be. This novel would not exist without her.